6203

Y0-CBL-366

Celebrating the American Woman

THEODOSIA

Theodosia

MEREDITH BEAN MCMATH

Grace Chapel Library
Havertown. Penna

Servant Publications
Ann Arbor, Michigan

© 1995 Meredith Bean McMath, For Old Times' Sake, Inc.
All rights reserved.

Vine Books is an imprint of Servant Publications especially
designed to serve evangelical Christians.

Published by Servant Publications
P.O. Box 8617
Ann Arbor, Michigan 48107

95 96 97 98 99 10 9 8 7 6 5 4 3 2 1

Printed in the United States of America
ISBN 0-89283-890-6

Library of Congress Cataloging-in-Publication Data

McMath, Meredith Bean
   Theodosia / Meredith Bean McMath.
      p.   cm. —(Celebrating the American woman : bk. 1)
   ISBN 0-89283-890-6
   I. Title.   II. Series.
PS3563.C3863T44   1995
813'.54—dc20   95-7459
                                 CIP

Dedication

For my husband, Chuck, and my son, Palmer—
my two favorite characters.

Acknowledgments

My gratitude and thanks to Cathy Deddo and Susan Jinnett-Sack for their kind assistance in the editing process, to Wanda Munsey Juraschek and Joyce Carrier for being the two best friends and editors a writer could have, to Christ's College, Cambridge and the Cotswolds for a summer of stories, to David Hazard for putting in a kind word at a good time to nice people, to Gloria Chisholm for her expert editing and Beth Feia for making the process seem easy, to my sister, Rebecca, for her encouragement and guidance in writing, to my mother for her love of roses and afternoon tea, and most especially to my husband, the sourcebook for all my heroes.

Preface

"If I were asked to what the singular prosperity and growing strength of Americans ought to be attributed, I should reply: 'To the superiority of their women.'" Alexis de Tocqueville made this unique observation after visiting America in the early 1830s.

The books in this *Celebrating the American Woman* series were written because I wanted so much to tell someone why Tocqueville was right. I wanted to bring to life the Christian American woman's unique ability to blend a spirit of independence with a willingness to compromise, the love of justice with the love of mercy, an iron strength with a profound softness. But I also wanted to tell someone what Tocqueville couldn't have known back then: how sisters (and brothers) in Christ have had influences on one another that extend well past their lifetimes. I wanted to show how God uses a sometimes tenuous but very long line of persons to bring about life-giving change to us as individuals. And so the lives of the characters in my books intertwine to influence one another—sometimes years later and sometimes in an entirely new generation, now and then knowingly but more often unwittingly—just as they do in real life.

The verses and quotations at the beginnings of the chapters are pearls of thought and rhyme that set the tone for the words that follow. Like the nursery rhymes that take on new meaning when we read them again to our children, American women's history can be read a hundred times, but if reread in a new context it might be brought to shimmering life before our eyes.

Meredith Bean McMath

ONE

⁓

"Take some more tea,"
the March Hare said to Alice, very earnestly.
"I've had nothing yet," Alice replied in an offended
tone, "so I can't take any more."

Lewis Carroll
Alice's Adventures in Wonderland

⁓

Hastily she pulled the volume up from the floor to check for damage, but in a moment she fell to admiring the gilded roses which trimmed the soft red volume. With trembling fingers she traced their vines and petals and then rested her hand upon them. The well-worn leather seemed warm to the touch. Now she glanced at the title.

"Eglantine Roses," she said aloud. "Most certainly you are a book with a cover worthy of your subject."

Now, if Theodosia Brown hadn't noticed the sheaf of papers rising half an inch above the volume's upper edge, it would have satisfied her to merely look again at the pretty gilt-work and then return the book to the top shelf where it belonged, but now she looked with dismay at the papers and tried to push them down into the volume, thinking they'd come loose from the binding with the impact of the fall.

It was then she realized they were much too tall to be a portion of the book.

Now, as she opened the book quite carefully, her eyes fell on the document that lay there; "The Last Will and Testament of Alfred Lord Brooks" was laboriously penned in large script across the top.

She looked down the page a moment longer, then snapped the volume shut. "No, I shan't look at it! I shan't. Oh, this is horrid!" She looked about her rather desperately. "Whatever could cause someone to put a will in a book in a library—a library where the family sends strangers to wait by themselves, for Heaven's sake?! Lord Brooks ...this is Lord Brooks' will! Oh, my goodness."

She shook her head with dismay. If Aunt Selda had only allowed her to wear her spectacles, she would not have felt the need to climb the library stair to look at book titles. More importantly, she would not be here at all if Aunt Selda hadn't decided to dip Theodosia into the waters of polite society by having her attend an afternoon tea at Brooks House—to meet the Viscount and Viscountess Brooks, and their eldest son, Alfred. It was all Aunt Selda's fault, of course. Testing the waters was proving to be more of a dunking than a dip. Now the damage was done: indeed, she *had* climbed the stair and she *had* leaned too far to attempt the reading of a title and then tried to steady herself by holding on to this particular leather volume.

And then it had fallen all the way down—ten feet—to the floor.

Afraid that at any moment a servant would return to fetch her for tea, she retrieved the book from the floor and rushed back up the library stair. But Theodosia had a weakness with regards to curiosity and there lay the will. She glanced back once more to the library doors, then turned to look again at the red book in her hands.

She closed her eyes and breathed deeply. "Theodosia Brown, *you put it back,*" she soundly told herself, and Theodosia Brown grudgingly obeyed.

Plunging the volume in to its resting place, she muttered, "Wills should be kept properly locked up in safes. Papa has the Black Betty for his clients' wills. There should be a safe in Lord Brooks' study, wherever that may be! I understood this family to be a sensible lot. This is very odd." She descended the stair. "And why was I made to wait in their library in the first place, if I may ask?" Theodosia continued chattering to herself. "They invited me to tea a full two days before this. Why was the tea not ready at the moment I arrived? Oh, yes, but I forgot—this is England. A proper amount of waiting must precede any event considered worthy to be waited for."

She stared up at the red book. "Wills kept in books! Books marked *Eglantine Roses* with pretty covers—of all the inexcusable inanities." She shook her head and her dark brown curls bumped against her cheeks, expelling into her nostrils the scent of a ghastly pomade. Her cousin, Cecelia, had insisted she wear the hair oil for an elegant appearance, but the scent reminded Theodosia of nothing more elegant than rotting apples.

She found herself trying very hard to keep from going back up the stairs, and so her brown eyes fell to staring at the red volume above her, now quite hazy to her poor vision.

She mumbled, "'And how do you do, Lord Brooks?' I'll say. And then sweetly during tea I'll simply toss off, 'Sir, have you perchance thought of purchasing a Black Betty in which one could put... oh, say, wills and such? In the library, you say? How very unique. Oh, well, of course my papa *used* to keep his will in the encyclopedia, but when he insisted Mama make room for her jewels in Gibbons' *Rise and Fall*, she suggested a safe instead.'" Theodosia shook her head once more and wrinkled her nose at the pomade.

Tea at Brooks House was to be the beginning of Theodosia's "coming out," in her Aunt Selda Bannoch's sense of the words. Theodosia ("Tee" to her friends and family) came to England for the summer to visit with her aunt (who always called her "Theodosia") and her aunt's children (who called her by any name as little as they could). Her father wanted her to learn proper behavior from these, her very proper relations, a course of action she thought unnecessary since she had finished her studies at the Ladies' Seminary and, at eighteen years of age, felt certain she already knew everything needed to fulfill her duties in life. She assisted her father with his legal work now and then, helped run the household, and that was as much as she wished for. There were no beaus on her horizon that she should worry over dress or manners.

But her father had insisted, and since coming to Star Cottage one week ago, Theodosia had learned from her mother's sister that eighteen years in America had taught her virtually nothing of deportment, gentility, manners or dress, and that, furthermore, without these items one had simply not fulfilled one's duty to one's family "in any sense."

And now Theodosia was waiting in the library to be called to tea with the most important family in the entire area, and already she knew where Lord Brooks' will was kept. As she heard the library doors creak open behind her, she felt her face grow bright red, but she forced herself to turn about.

"Miss Brown? I am Austin." The proper-looking servant smiled and bowed.

She nodded but his eyes looked past her to the library stair behind her. He must have known she'd moved it. "I'm sorry, but... I... I moved the ladder to look, you see. I shouldn't have, I'm sure... and... but I do love books, and... ah ...um...," but here she closed her mouth for any further words had roundly knotted themselves into a lump within her throat.

"I am to bring you to tea." The servant bowed again, formally ending her need to continue. He was too far away for her to see his expression.

"Ah, well then...," and she colored once more. It would not go well for her at Star Cottage if rumor of this sort of behavior made its way back to her aunt, but his very formal manner reminded her that English servants pride themselves on confidentiality, and so she allowed herself to breathe once more.

"Tea awaits," he said patiently.

So very English. It was all so very, very English! She looked around the room once more, and half-thinking she might be forgetting something, she smiled despite the situation. She wished she could stay there longer, and she realized her desire had nothing whatsoever to do with the will.

Never in all her life had she seen so many books in one place. If she were to ever imagine a library, this would be the one. No, it was better than anything she could imagine, for how could her mind create for its own amusement a library room whose size was roughly the equal of her father's entire Virginia home?

Oh, how she wished she had her spectacles.

She wanted to properly say good-bye to all of it and so, slowly looked around her. Casting her eyes upward, she saw deeply carved arches gracing mahogany bookshelves, arch after arch arranging themselves cathedral-like along the walls. A veritable church to learning. She looked down once more and glanced about her. If only she could see! Two huge corner fireplaces warmed the room—one would not have been enough—and to either side of her windows hung from the ceiling to the floor. Each deep window's well allowed for a broad seat plumped with pillows that begged to be leaned against, with a view through the window's large panes that further begged to be seen from over the top edge of a good book. And if that was not enough to send her into raptures, at the very end of the room stood wide, tall doors of glass apparently leading to the out-of-doors, for the view through these was filled with a splashy blur of pink and red that she could only assume to be a rose garden.

This last view of a bright, intangible grandeur propelled her senses beyond awestruck and stole her away into the realm of enchantment. That she was likely never to see it again only made it all the more lovely.

But then there was the will to quickly sober her and keep her from reaching heights of pure delirium.

And so she turned and smiled at the servant.

"The room pleases you?" he asked.

"Oh, yes, it *pleases* me," she said wistfully. "I wish I could stay and read every one—" but then it occurred to her a servant might not be able to read at all.

He seemed to smile, although it was hard to tell at that distance. He nodded and turned to the door.

With bowed head and sluggish step, she came behind him and followed his march, hoping beyond hope she could learn between here and there to think before she spoke, to think before she acted.

The will. Finding the will had caused all sorts of strange and guilty thoughts. There was curiosity, yes, a deep curiosity to go back and read it all, a feeling that made her horribly uncomfortable, and then remorse over having done something so terribly incorrect on a day she was supposed to do everything with absolute correctness. Lastly there was a certain seediness to knowing such a thing about a family, and furthermore, to know it of strangers—strangers with reputations held far above her own. None of it felt good and all of it, by this time, had provided her with a sense of evil foreboding.

As for the will itself, she was growing weary with the wanting to know and the knowing she shouldn't and the wishing she didn't know at all.

The manservant's footsteps echoed on the gray marble as they passed room after room and double door after double door along the great entrance hall of Brooks House. Sensing she would soon be before the Brookses like a convict before the bench, Theodosia was forced from thinking about the will to thinking about the terrifying interview to come.

Today she would meet the Lady and Lord Brooks, Benefactors of the Cotswold village of Thistledown and owners of Brooks Tea, Teamen to Queen Victoria herself. Aunt Selda had tried to prepare her for this moment, but as Theodosia attempted to recall the list of social formalities she was to perform ("In hopes they can be shaken from their view of American young ladies," Aunt Selda had said repeatedly), she now realized with dismay she had barely listened to her aunt's advice. All the while she had thought (and naturally so) that Aunt Selda herself would accompany her when the time came and could, at crucial moments, give her signs and nods to help her through an afternoon tea.

But at the last minute, Aunt Selda was called away to assist her son in a business arrangement. "One must never cancel one's social engagements," her aunt had explained, "unless of course there comes a family matter of greater importance. They are gracious enough to accept you without an escort." Theodosia had politely argued that perhaps they could go to the Brookses at another time, but Aunt Selda had grandly shook her head. "No, my dear. Society does not recognize familial responsibility outside one's own in these cases. It would be considered a terrible effrontery." How Theodosia would ever learn one case of effrontery from another was quite beyond her. There were lists of cases, lists of duties, lists of proper dress. In her aunt's words, "A list for everything and everything in its list."

She sighed as they walked along. The only list she could remember at this nervous moment was dress. From the first moment Theodosia had come into the Bannochs' fashionable home, she could see that Aunt Selda was particular about dress. "A first impression well exceeds the term *important,* Theodosia. A first impression is *everything.*" Theodosia looked down now to see the toes of her shoes poking out from her skirt intermittently—right, left, right. She smoothed the pleated fabric of her cousin's pink lawn gown, tucked in her chin and pulled one shoulder forward—left then right—to be certain her lace collar was lying properly flat. Then she inspected the cream silk fringe around her trumpet sleeves to see that it hung straight around the edge and finished by pulling at the gathering of lace on each wrist. *"The lace lies lovely, the fringe falls freely, and pleats are properly patted,"* she thought in a spate of good humor and then held out her hands to briefly note her clean fingernails.

"Gloves!" she cried aloud and came to a full halt.

"Miss?"

For a moment she turned, thinking to retrieve them herself, but then she blushed; it was infinitely more appropriate to have a servant retrieve them for her, and so she stood still. "Oh, my... I've left my kid gloves in the library... on the center table."

Without a word he nodded and walked quickly back to the library.

While she waited in the huge hallway, she began to rock ever so slowly on her heels—a habit her father detested, referring to it as "a latent sign of instability in the girl"—and then looked back and forth at the full standing armor on either side of the hall. She stood still and laughed somewhat nervously at their bleak forms. Glancing down the hall to see the servant disappearing into the library, she walked softly to one specimen and leaned toward it to observe the fine coat of mail more closely. But it was as she wondered over the hammered scrollwork on the helmet that she leaned in too far and touched the raised arm holding the pike axe, causing it to move ever so slightly toward her head.

She jumped back with some force, threw her hand against her throat and stood there for a moment until finally giving up the tremor of a laugh at her own ridiculousness.

She stood in that exact spot until the servant returned with her gloves, and although she felt the sudden overwhelming need to explain why the pike axe to his right was now on the attack, she forced herself to keep silent.

The servant glanced at the pike axe and back to Miss Brown but said nothing.

I will never get through this meeting, she told herself fiercely as in a severe quietness she took the gloves from the servant. *I am certain to spill my tea and with my ungainly and gangly ways it is quite likely I will spill it on Lady Brooks herself!* She soon found that her shaking hands made pulling on those leather gloves quite difficult if not impossible. *It was my own stupid fault I stepped up that ladder. Whatever was I thinking? Of course I never should have climbed it! And why did I have to examine that armor so closely? I can just see the letter Aunt Selda would write home, "arrived for tea and died of a pike axe to the head." Papa would expect it of me!* She became so engrossed in her thoughts and so disgusted with herself while trying to button the impossible little pearl buttons at her wrists that she moaned aloud, "Oh, I will never, never do this," and stamped her foot before she realized anew that she was not alone.

Looking up with horror to the manservant she thought she saw the flicker of a smile. Realizing the humor in the situation, she giggled and then gulped, "You're not to tell anyone of this!"

"I am in a position to keep full confidence," he replied, clicking his heels efficiently.

"Well, after today, I will probably never need count on your confidence again," she said with half a laugh, "for the Brookses will surely throw me out on my ear."

"I hardly think so."

"Do you?" she asked, more earnestly than she had intended. She stopped buttoning for a moment. "Are...are they very terrible?"

"Pardon?"

She had no doubt he was being purposely obtuse, but she was determined to get an answer from him in hopes of easing her present state of mind. "The Brookses. The Viscount and Viscountess and their son. Lady and Lord... oh, I've muddled their titles. He is Right Honorable, isn't he? And the son is Honorable? Do I call the son a Lord? No, just . . ." but, deeply lost in thought now, she was speaking to herself.

A slight "ahem" caused her to look up to the servant and blush.

"I am so sorry ...I'm ...I'm afraid I'm very uncomfortable about this interview."

He bowed slightly. "Titles are seldom used in average conversation, so you needn't fear."

"But ...are they terrible?"

The fellow pressed his lips together. "They treat me well, miss. But they are as human as the rest of us, I suppose."

"Not according to my aunt. No." She shook her head and her curls bounced vigorously from side to side. "Not according to my aunt." She stopped to look over each shoulder and brushed a speck of fuzz from one before continuing to button her gloves. "She will tell you the Brookses are infallible, omnipotent, and above all else terribly correct! Well," she said, finally catching up the last button, "I fear I am about to give them a proper justification to place themselves high above American young ladies, in any case." And she took a deep breath as if it might give her strength.

"With all respect due your aunt, you should judge each of the family for yourself, miss." He blinked and with a little grin, nodded to the armor beside them. "I will tell you this—the Lord and Lady of Brooks House are not as empty-headed as these fellows that they would intentionally frighten a young lady ...though, to be certain, I can not vouch for the Brookses' sons."

She looked at him and laughed pleasantly. She thought of conversations with her aunt's butler, a brilliant man whose brilliance was wasted on the servile system into which he was born. Her smile faded as she thought on the plight of English servants; here was another bright fellow, and where would he be twenty years

Grace Chapel Library
Havertown. Penna.

from now? Still opening doors to guests and trying to quell their fears? In America, he could be whatever he put his mind to. Such a waste....

He must have sensed her concern. "Miss Brown, you would do well not to take afternoon tea so seriously."

She nodded, laughed, and trying to sound cheerful, she said, "Well, my gloves have fought a good fight, but they have lost their little war with me, and so..." She paused. "I suppose it is time to go."

"Yes, miss," He turned and led her to the doors at the end of the long hall.

Just before opening them, he stopped to whisper, "The family expresses regret that you had to wait such a long period of time in the library. The drawing room is presently being refurbished, and as it is deemed too cool to sit outdoors, the family have retired to the orangery for tea."

She stared at the paneled doors and, thinking it unlikely she would have another opportunity to speak to him, she said most earnestly, "In America, we have tea wherever we like, with whomever we like ...and whenever we like, as well."

She did not look up at him but heard him reply in a small voice, "I think I'd like America."

Indeed you would, she thought briskly, *and I would like to be there myself just now.*

And then he pulled open the doors.

As they entered, again she longed for her spectacles so as to enjoy the view, but nothing could be done for their loss. Her aunt had told her on her second day there that she would keep her spectacles for her. "Out of harm's way," she explained, "for if given half a chance you are certain to break them. Your face has little enough to recommend it to a gentleman's eye, Theodosia. Besides, I am certain the work you did for your father was what caused the weakened condition in your eyes, and wearing spectacles has only encouraged their laziness. I've no doubt by removing them, your vision shall improve greatly by summer's end! We will not coddle you here as your father has in the past." Theodosia could have argued on almost every point but knew it was useless. To make matters worse, her aunt had commanded her that under no circumstances was she to squint, nevertheless the shining brightness in her eyes as they walked onward forced her to do so now.

But it was well she did squint, for it was the only way she could see the group of people standing all the way across that broad, bright space.

Those are the Brookses, she told herself and swallowed in fearful anticipation. The servant held his arm out for her, and out of a twofold fear of her limbs giving way or finding something on which to trip as they crossed the vast unknown, she took his arm.

She could not help but tremble as they moved along the stone floor. Halfway across, as the dark silhouettes began to form faces, limbs and movement, the servant whispered, "Are you feeling well?"

She did not immediately reply, so intent was she on viewing those whom she approached. She sensed the faces were all intent on her as well, and she was troubled to see they were quite somber. An older woman who could only be Lady Brooks herself was seated stiffly at the tea table, and three gentleman stood in a row to the right and behind her, all of them in black. To the far left must be Lord Brooks, judging from the thick build and whitish hair, but to the right? Two sons? Yes, it must be. She hadn't expected to meet more than one. This was truly a nightmare.

Every step that took her closer caused her to believe she was already somehow displeasing them. Lady Brooks was frowning. Was it the pink lawn dress, Theodosia wondered? All was in order just a few moments before. She'd glanced at herself in a mirrored glass not two feet from this room, and, though the image was unclear, she had certainly seemed presentable.

Could it be her escort? Her aunt's words returned sharply: "*Never* familiarize yourself with servants; it is a humiliation to them as well as to yourself." Suddenly she knew she should not have taken the servant's arm. The words she'd heard her aunt use a dozen times a day on the servants of Star Cottage came readily to her lips, and she said quite loudly in her frightened state, "Austin, you may go now."

The servant took in a sharp breath, bowed slightly and drew away. She closed her eyes briefly and curtsied to the group as she stood alone before them not ten feet from the table.

When she looked up, Lady Brooks quietly greeted her.

Theodosia tried hard to concentrate on the formal address one gives a lady and, although she did it haltingly, she accomplished the feat and gave herself a small bit of congratulations for the same.

Lady Brooks nodded once more and proceeded with introductions. Theodosia was by now able to judge a little more of their looks. Though the overstuffed chair was evidently built for comfort, Lady Brooks sat squarely in the middle of the seat, her back perfectly straight. The only portion of her that seemed at rest was the hand that lay on the tea table. Her face was taut and firm lines were carved alongside each withered cheek. Quite possibly a frown was the most natural expression her face could form, and so perhaps she had not been displeased with Theodosia after all. The Lady's eyes were hooded with thickening lids, their color and meaning inscrutable, but there was an air about her Theodosia recognized; an uncertain quantity bound up tight in her thin frame. She was looking into deep orbs that knew much but said little—eyes very like her aunt's.

She turned from Lady Brooks' firm gaze and curtsied to Lord Alfred Brooks. Now the first smile from the group met her, but she surmised that it was not from appreciation but amusement. He had a lovely long moustache and twinkling gray eyes, but a drooping despondency to his lower lip, and he held an eyepiece to his face with an affectation of limpness Theodosia found most distasteful.

Now with Lord Brooks appearing slightly spineless and his wife looking as though she could take on his spine and several others besides, Theodosia knew that she would not like the Brookses—not at all. But then she blushed violet to think she knew exactly where this family's will was kept.

She curtsied again but with a tremble as Lady Brooks began to introduce her to her sons. To Lord Brooks' right stood Alfred, their eldest, a dour-looking fellow with a pale face and a distracted air. Theodosia took in his unkempt hair, the sparse beard shaved to the edge of his face (a fashion she abhorred) and the silver spectacles drawn almost off the tip of his nose. Perhaps, if he did not have such an unhealthy color and a silly trim, he might be well to look upon. Perhaps.

Once more she turned to the right and curtsied to the last son, and this time she met a smile that seemed genuine. Allan Brooks was arch and handsome and at ease, and immediately Theodosia was in awe. He held a lapel gracefully with one hand and everything about him seemed to say, "Welcome, Miss Brown. Nothing to fear here. It's only tea," much as the manservant, who now stood guard to Allan's right, had told her. He had dark green eyes, well-managed hair and a bright ascot at his neck. She took Allan's attentions with pleasure, smiling confidently at him. The Brookses were not so horrid after all, and when all was said and done this could be a most pleasant afternoon.

And though life had a way of bringing library ladders to Theodosia's feet, so much so that she had come to expect them now and then, nothing could have prepared her for the fall she was about to take. As Lady Brooks continued to make introductions, she suddenly made it clear to Theodosia Rose Brown of America that not all was said, and that quite possibly the worst of all possible things had been done.

"And it seems, my dear, that you've already made a *personal acquaintance* of our third son, Austin...." ❦

TWO

Pussycat, pussycat,
Where have you been?
I've been to London
To look at the queen.
Pussycat, pussycat,
What did you there?
I frightened a little mouse
Under her chair.

Nursery Rhyme

"I could almost wish to wash my hands of you, Theodosia Brown," said Aunt Selda, and she punctuated every other word by jabbing the fingernails of her right hand into the fleshy palm of her left. "This attempt to humiliate me will not succeed." Here she stopped to twine her hands together and pull them into her wide waist. "In fact," she paused dramatically, "I *refuse* to have it succeed. I will simply make it right. I have to. I have a duty to your papa. Lord *knows* if I had thought the younger sons were anywhere near the house, I would not have let you go today….*so* inappropriate to meet them *all* at tea." She shook her head violently, sending a wave of motion through her, such that every bit of fringe that wreathed her dress shook mightily as well. Her head then snapped to attention, and her gray eyes fell on her niece once more. "Cambridge! If only they'd been at Oxford, they should still be in a summer term. Not what I had in mind at all, not at all. No! Allow me to remind you this behavior will cause only *your* humiliation," she sputtered, soundly contradicting herself. "So by all means, Theodosia, stay in bed! Stay in bed for a week! It will take at least that long to make things right."

Aunt Selda's fury was based solely on Theodosia's coming

home from tea due to a sudden unknown illness. She didn't know Theodosia had suffered such overwhelming humiliation at mistaking Austin Brooks for a servant that she'd "taken ill" just to be relieved of having to stay in the Brooks' home one minute longer.

Nevertheless, Theodosia was quite sick now. She was lying in bed with a terribly upset stomach. When Theodosia first returned to Star Cottage, she was afraid her aunt would call a doctor to the room. She was grateful to hear that the woman had no intention of calling a doctor, but then she heard the reason.

"I know your trouble exactly, Theodosia, and for your sort of sickness no doctor has a cure." Aunt Selda folded her long fingers before her knowingly. "But *I* know the cure for *I* know the ailment. You do not stand testing. Yes, I know it. I've known it for some time. There is a certain lack of strength of personality within your family—the fact of which I will not go into at the moment— but I have willingly taken you in hand for the summer months to purge you of the family disorder, and purge it I will. You do not feel well?" she puffed. "Very well, then you certainly do not need supper. And to make certain you are quite comfortable in your despondency, you will not be served a breakfast either. I shall check on your health tomorrow at noon, child, and I am sure I will find you perfectly well."

Aunt Selda moved to the door but turned back to add a footnote. "Ah, and a Miss Mienzes is here to visit you in your *distress,* Theodosia. See that you keep your conversation limited to needlework and the weather, as I told you." Her eyes narrowed and her nostrils flared, an expression, Theodosia noted, that made her look ever so much like a finch. "I should hope you know that to repeat anything of your unfortunate visit to Brooks House is likely to be the beginning of *rumor.* And if word ever came back upon this house from Thistledown, I would know where to lay the blame, hmm?"

She watched her aunt leave and tried hard to hold back tears.

The loss of meals meant little to her; Aunt Selda's threats meant little. But her lips were parted in amazement and her heart had grown cold within her at her aunt's words, "a certain lack of strength of personality within your family..." Theodosia repeated the words to herself when the door was shut. She wondered at its possible meaning. Knowing Aunt Selda could be harsh at times, still Theodosia could not quite conceive that things said regarding her own family—her sister's family, no less—could be lies. She'd been angry with her father for sending her here and in her heart of hearts she wondered if they were keeping something from her by sending her away. This little doubt must have crept in and done its cruel work, for Aunt Selda's words would never have hit her so hard if Theodosia had felt assured of her family's devotion just then.

Now she thought of them one by one. Her father was a well-known lawyer and, a rarity in its own right, an honest one, highly respected in his field—a man asked to write books on his life's work, for Heaven's sake! And Theodosia's mother, Aunt Selda's sister, was a gentle woman whose only failing might be she loved books too well, a passion she had perhaps unintentionally imparted to her daughters. Theodosia's older sister, Martha, was settled and had started a family of her own not far from their home place in Virginia, and Martha's husband had come into great success these last two years. Theodosia's older brother, Parker, a born hunter, was to the best of his sister's knowledge happily trapping beaver somewhere north of their home state and was perhaps all the way to Canada by now. She herself had just finished Ladies' Seminary and looked forward to helping keep house with her mother and assisting her papa...until her papa requested...no, *demanded*...that she visit Aunt Selda. And last but by no means least, her younger sister, Kimberly, the little beauty of the family, was considered by anyone's account a star in the family crown, with the amazing gift of a great beauty within but with a lack of affectation concerning the beauty without.

Yet Aunt Selda implied there was something to be ashamed of in that group. Her father's words floated to mind: *"A rare opportunity, Tee. She's well schooled in manners, and the British wrote the book on etiquette. Ladies' Seminary seemed unable to train away your...awkwardness. Besides which, your Aunt Selda wants you, so we'll send you!"*

But why? Theodosia wondered. *If she dislikes my family so, why am I here?* A creeping sensation stirred within her then as from the back of her mind something evil whispered, *Aunt Selda knows something you do not, Theodosia Brown.*

She shivered.

A knock came at the door and then it opened to reveal the Scottish schoolmistress, Fiona Mienzes, whose sudden presence was like a gift of spring flowers to Theodosia. Spirited and comely, and with an affable, charming nature, Fiona was a bright young woman, a true Scottish "lass" who lived up to every pleasant expectation in that name. The two young women had met purely by accident in the market of the town square; Theodosia had watched as Fiona wheedled a hawker down to nothing for his chickens. They smiled at each other from two booths apart as Fiona finished with the merchant, and then and there they began a friendship. Theodosia found her shy at first, and yet they had called one another friend before they'd finished their first discussion.

With pale brown hair and a mild face, Fiona looked like many a pleasant-featured young lady, but then there were her eyes: bright green stars set about with thick black lashes. The contrast to her pale complexion was so strong that Theodosia had seen those eyes from twenty feet away, and it had made her look twice at the young girl haggling for goods. Then, after having spoken with her for a while, Theodosia had sensed a glowing spark of fire burning within that shy exterior—just as vivid a difference as those dark eyes in the pale, pretty face.

Theodosia sighed with relief to see her now and held out both arms even as she struggled to sit up further in bed. Fiona gave her new friend a great hug, then carefully sat down on the edge of the bed.

It wasn't long before Theodosia told her the true nature of her illness.

"Fiona, the boy actually smiled as his maman introduced him to me. Austin Brooks must have thought it was so terribly funny, and in that one horrific moment I looked away to see Lady Brooks frowning at me, Lord Brooks sniggering, and Allan smiling ever so sweetly at the joke of it. The backward little American girl mistaking their youngest for a servant. Hilarious. Horrible." She looked away and smiled ruefully. "If I were at home, I'd think my brother had had a hand in it. It'd be just like him...to introduce Austin Brooks as if he were a manservant and then stand back and watch me bumble through.... Always has been one to make jokes and hold pranks at my expense." Smiling sadly, she turned back to Fiona. "I'm afraid I've always been terribly gullible." Then suddenly she laughed. "Ha! The truth of it is, no one at home would have considered it such a major error as they did here. We would have called it an honest mistake. I would have asked for forgiveness and received it...at home." Her brow wrinkled as she wondered if her papa had grown tired of forgiving her such things.

Fiona replied in the rolling accent of her homeland, "I've a notion Master Austin Brooks has a similar turn of mind as yer sly brother, and I shouldn't wonder if he didn't help the ruse along."

Theodosia smiled and looked into the eyes of her friend. "Well...a servant had ushered me into the library, so I suppose I expected a servant to usher me out again. He came right over and introduced himself as Austin—you know, just one name—as a servant might, and it *could* have been a surname." She looked away again. "Of course, now I see he assumed *I knew* his last name, already. But then nothing seemed out of the ordinary in his speech and he never corrected me, and, another thing...his clothes were light. Well, pale colors with brown. His family was all in black, but he had on white trousers and a brown coat just *exactly* like the fellow who'd taken my bonnet and shawl at the door..." She nodded but then stopped. "Oh, no. I suppose he had on a red coat...and gold buttons...Oh, my." She blushed and looked back to Fiona. "Well, anyway, Austin doesn't look anything like his brothers." Her eyes grew wide. "So even when he stood to the right of Allan Brooks, I thought absolutely nothing of it."

"Well, then, it was an honest mistake, as ye say, and I think it's Master Austin Brooks who's owing you an apology."

"No. The Brookses expected a backwoods American girl, and that is exactly what they met." She laughed a little. "I don't mean to complain, but I am such a fish out of water here. I've always been clumsy, *always*—my papa used to say I tripped out of my mother's arms into the crib at night—but I have never been so socially ill at ease...ever since I've come. It's awful. I can never remember all the rules of etiquette that I'm told I absolutely *must* remember. 'Must remember or *what?*' I keep asking myself. One gets along very well in America on a list of etiquette one-twentieth the size of England's."

Fiona laughed. "Ah, ye needn't remind me. The English view Scots with as much favor as they view Americans, and maybe for the same reasons; we make up our own rules of behavior, especially when it cooms to fightin'."

"But they think Americans have no rules at all. Oh, yes. Don't I know it. The Brookses invited an ox to tea. Lady Brooks, I'm sure, will never forgive me, and I cannot imagine Aunt Selda could say anything that would smooth things over. Why would she even try?"

"To make it go better for you, Theodosia?"

"Please call me Tee. All my family and friends at home do." She smiled but lost it quickly. "I know Aunt Selda is not satisfied with me, Fiona...even before today. I really don't understand why she invited me here at all. Truly, I don't."

Fiona had no answer.

"Unless it was to insult me... unless it was to humiliate me. I never even knew she disliked my family so... until now, and now it's painfully obvious and much too late for me to do anything about. My papa is sending monies for my return, but he said I shouldn't expect ship's passage until August... three whole months..." She gulped, and wondered again if the monies ever would come.

Fiona smiled and shook her head. "Well, I for one am glad ye've come, and doobly glad ye'll be here a *whole three month*. I'm sure it's no comfort to ye, but ye'll be makin' my own stay tolerable."

"Thank you, Fiona. Thank you for that." She smiled and patted her hand, but then dropped it again. "There is something else I haven't told you... about today... about the Brookses, and if I don't tell someone I think I'll burst and there's no one in this house I can trust to tell." Fiona nodded and Theodosia looked about her, then whispered, "It was when I was waiting in the library... I came across something... odd. Lord Brooks' will."

"No!"

She nodded. "It was tucked away in a book on a top shelf, of all things. I knocked the book down by accident and there it was!"

"The Lord's very will?" Fiona's dark lashes batted with amazement.

"Yes. I'm certain of it."

"And why would they be puttin' their wills up on shelves?"

"They don't hold them on shelves in my father's offices, that's for certain."

"P'rhaps it's only a copy of an old one then," Fiona said sensibly, once more folding her hands into her lap.

"Perhaps." Theodosia blushed. "But I... I read a little bit of it...just at the beginning."

Fiona's eyes widened. "Did ye now?"

"I know it's awful of me. I don't know what you must think of me right now, but I tell you I did it from a simple force of habit. My papa has always liked my penmanship. I'm particularly good at a copperplate script—it may be the one thing Papa truly admires about me—and so in the last few years I've copied hundreds of wills and codicils and a host of other legal documents and grown so used to reading them, it was all...quite natural...truly. Kind of interesting to see the different language used here, and it was quite pretty. The script was of a...what was it?... it was... a Gordon... no, a... " Theodosia's eyes settled on a distant wall and her voice fell away in concentration. Fiona smiled as Theodosia remembered herself and added, "Well, I did put it back. I did. But, oh, how I wished I could have read the rest of it, but no. I wouldn't. And I won't. I won't," she repeated in the most honest tone she could muster.

"Ye're too honest for yer own good, Theodosia Brown."

"Call me Tee..."

"Tee, then. You Americans think aloud while the rest of us keep sich things to ourselves..." She patted Theodosia's hand. "But think them we do, nonetheless. Was it quite a task to keep yerself from looking into it again?"

Theodosia smiled ruefully. "You couldn't know how hard."

"Oh, I don't know as all that," Fiona said. "Many a child in my classroom has told me the family secret unawares, and I've bitten my lip a hundred times if a one as the townfolk take to gossiping near me, for I know all *and then some* of what they *think* they know."

The girls laughed, and Theodosia's heart felt lighter for the bright conversation, but sooner than either wished it grew time for Fiona to depart.

After Fiona left the patient's room, Theodosia tried to keep her spirits up, but alone with nothing but Star Cottage and its brood to look forward to for company, her thoughts soon grew doleful once more. She found herself thinking back on the first night she came to Star Cottage.

The roads were tracts of mud from heavy rains the week before and it was a miserable ride from the docks of London westward to Thistledown. Thistledown—that name had always sounded so lovely to her; it held such glorious promise. "My sister, your Aunt Selda, lives in a beautiful little village named Thistledown west of London, and Lord willing someday you'll visit her little home," her maman used to say often enough to create a lovely dream of it in her young daughter's mind.

If they walked through a garden with lavender borders, her maman was wont to say, "Thistledown is probably just filled with lavender, Tee. In England, lavender grows as tall and as stately as the ladies and gentlemen of London, and is just as abundant, so I've heard."

They would struggle with the roses in their garden and her maman would say, "Roses grow like dandelions in England, dear. My sister says her yard is filled with them, and they bloom all summer long. Just imagine." And Theodosia would readily imagine. Thistledown had sounded very much like a place in which the fairies might choose to live.

So, for the whole long journey across the sea, through the gritty docks and crowded streets of London, onward past the towns of dark industry at London's edge, she had let herself dream of Thistledown. She had comforted her mind with her imaginings and the gentle expectation of a cozy little home and the welcoming arms of her mother's sister and her children.

When London was far behind them and she could look out on the rolling hills of England dotted as they were with quaint-looking townships, she readied herself for the fulfillment of those dreams.

So when the driver stopped at the large mansion whose guest room she now occupied, she of course thought he had pulled the horses up for a feeding at a fine hotel and begged him to tell her how many more miles to Star Cottage.

"Beggin' yer pardon, Miss. No further than here."

Theodosia had then stared up at the house before her, and up and up, Georgian symmetry commanding a wall of stone before her eyes. Its facade was a wide three-story square with rows of long windows and a grand entrance set low in its center. No lavender. No roses. Stone. "Star Cottage? The *Bannoch's* residence?" she had asked meekly.

The driver nodded.

She had not seen her aunt since she had toddled to her to say goodbye fifteen years before, and she had not seen her cousins since playing in the yard with them that day. So it was to strangers she was introduced that evening.

And strangers they remained.

Her thin-lipped cousin, Cecelia, had looked her up and down with disapproval. Cecelia's brother, Frederick, had practically sneered when Theodosia removed her cloak—he had a gift for fashion, she soon learned—and Aunt Selda's plump arms had no more warmth in them than did the cold stares of her children. They were outstretched stiffly in greeting and were followed with a kiss that missed Theodosia's cheek entirely.

The Bannochs' respective roles were clear from the first moment of meeting. Aunt Selda made notes as to Theodosia's dress for Cecelia to later correct, Frederick cheered his mother on in her critical comments, and the overall course and flow of instruction was efficiently steered to a cold dock by Selda Bannoch herself.

Then Aunt Selda had rung a bell and a servant had appeared.

Now, Theodosia's house had a cook, but Anna May was considered an employee, not a servant. The fact that her widowed aunt was wealthy enough to actually have people serving her came as somewhat of a shock. She learned that her aunt had five members on the house staff: a cook, a butler, a domestic servant, a gardener, and a maid. Aunt Selda smiled to see Theodosia's surprised face when the servant entered and asked cat-like if anyone wished for tea. Everyone nodded to Selda. Theodosia, feeling immediately piqued at the treatment she was receiving, decided to test the waters. She did not want English tea.

"I'll have coffee, please," she said.

Aunt Selda nodded. The servant disappeared.

When the servant reentered, she carried a large silver tray, heavy and full. Upon it was a wide, squat silver teapot, a ceramic pot of warm milk, a silver pot of cold milk, a ceramic pot of warm water, a cone of sugar with snips, a bowl of crushed brown sugar, a dish of lemon halves wrapped in cheesecloth, a tea strainer, a small tea caddy with a measuring spoon to its side, three delicate china teacups and four hand-embroidered linen napkins.

And sitting in the corner, hiding between the napkins and the lemons like an unwanted child, there was found (but only by those with a keen eye) one tiny white porcelain cup full of a dark black brew.

After everyone was served tea, the cup of coffee was set before her. She waited for everyone to doctor their tea. Then she took a sip along with them, but she could not help but draw her lips together in a puckering of disgust. It tasted as though the grounds were boiled right in the cup and no less than an hour before; the liquid was as tepid as it was bitter.

Theodosia put it down quickly, and her aunt saw the movement. "Is there something wrong, dear?"

"Yes, Aunt," she confessed. "I'm afraid this coffee is... tepid."

"Ah, well. Sarah, take it away." Sarah whisked the cup away and hurried from the room.

While Theodosia sat with her hands in her lap waiting for another cup of coffee to appear, everyone continued to drink their tea as before. But the servant never returned. She expected to fill the waiting with conversation, news from home and the like, but the Bannochs made it clear they were tired, barely answering her eager questions about their adoptive country.

The Bannochs were on their second cup of tea when Theodosia decided her lips were absolutely parched from the long ride, and she very much wished to have something... anything... tea would be fine, and so she ventured, "Aunt, might I join you all in tea?"

The cousins exchanged knowing glances while Aunt Selda nodded discreetly to her children, and then she turned to Theodosia with a cold hard look. "There is no spare cup."

"But couldn't we send for one?"

"A servant comes only *once* with tea, Theodosia."

* * *

Despite her earnest resolve not to let Aunt Selda ruin her peace of mind, as she thought back on that first hard night, a tear found its way down her cheek. Weakly, she stood up next to her bed, then slowly crossed to the window and opened it, hoping the warm air of evening twilight would lift her spirits as Fiona's conversation had done before. She prayed, earnestly asking the Lord to make everything all right, to help her find her way through the maze this visit had become, and that she would survive until she could go home again. But just thinking the word "home" caused the tear that had waited patiently for its moment of glory to slide down the other cheek.

Pulling her face into the thick curtain by the window, she stared out to the gathering dusk, past the stone patio, past the bushes toward the green fog of lawn and forest beyond. And just as she was ready to let herself have a good, cleansing cry, she heard a noise in the bushes to her right. Wiping her eyes quickly with the back of each hand, she looked out to see what it could be. She wasn't afraid. Only curious. Oh, how she wished she had her spectacles. The pale light of the evening made it quite difficult to see much of anything.

She pushed her head all the way through the window, looked to the patio pillars to her right, then to her left. Nothing.

Ready again to slide into a world of tears, she very clearly heard the words, "Miss Brown?"

She clutched at the curtains for dear life when slowly from around the right hand pillar came Austin Brooks. Theodosia pulled her head away from the sight of him, her cheeks burning as if she'd been slapped.

But he came right up to the window, pulled off his hat and addressed her, "May I have a word?"

She swallowed the hollowness of tears in her throat. "*Mister* Brooks?!" she cried in a voice both incredulous and amazed.

"Yes." He smiled tentatively. "I know it's unusual..." He sighed. "... And in some circles unforgivable to come to a lady's window like this, but I'm afraid I'm determined to apologize to you this evening and I was unsure whether you would accept a note from me. You were utterly honest this afternoon, I realize, and I've come to believe you deserve... better... of me." He ran a hand through his blonde hair and began to finger the edge of his hat and look into her face attentively.

Was he sincere or only meaning to tease her further? She examined his gaze to try to sense his real meaning. "You've really no need to apologize. I mistook you. I mistook you... and, I am sorry for it, but still and yet, sir..." She looked right and left. "I... I'm quite certain you should not be standing at my window just now. My mistake was an honest one, but this..."

He began to smile—and just as pleasantly as his brother Allan could have allowed. Austin was fair-haired and blue-eyed and wore the same clothes she'd seen him in that afternoon. He had an open face, and with its rounded cheekbones and clefted chin, he looked every bit a cherub at that moment. When he smiled, as he was doing just then, his cheeks revealed two dimples, one slightly deeper than the other.

But the dimples, for the most part, disappeared and he cleared his throat. "Well, as I've said, I feared you would not have accepted a note from me, and the fact remains I need to apologize, and..."

"Oh, I would have, Mr. Brooks... accepted a billet from you, I mean to say." She stopped herself once more. She was about to tell him that Aunt Selda was the one who might have kept his note from her, but this last thought reminded her that Aunt Selda would be very upset to find her at the window with Master Austin Brooks. "You needn't apologize. Really. It's quite all right. Don't explain yourself. Truly." She glanced toward the door to her room and then quickly turned back to him. "Really, you must go." She reddened as she said it to think she was dismissing him once more.

She drew her hand to her mouth in embarrassment, but he laughed silently. "I will. Truly I will. I will make my apology short."

Why were the English so odd? It was proper to apologize and completely improper to come to her window. How is it that one took precedent over the other? And why did gentlemen have different rules than ladies? She drew her hand away from her mouth. "If...you feel you must, but, oh, please, sir, don't stay here longer than is absolutely necessary. I don't believe my aunt would understand this visit at all, and already she is not pleased with me today."

He humbly bowed his head. "I just wanted to tell you how very much the incident this afternoon was entirely my fault. You see, I wanted to meet the American visitor to ask her all about her country, and so while my family was in the tea room discussing when the visitor should be brought to table and by which servant, I suddenly decided to simply go and fetch her. The normal method in our household seemed to be a rude sort of behavior under the circumstances, and so I came for you.

"Then...when you treated me as if I were a servant, I thought you were chiding me for taking on a servant's duty. I had no idea you really thought I *was* a servant until... well... until you took on a rather sickly color at our introduction. Then I knew just what a terrible thing I'd done. I ask your forgiveness."

"Oh, my," she said, anticipating the troubles a lack of knowledge of manners might cause her that summer.

He continued, "I've laid it out to Mother that I was being rude to you by having gone to... to escort you in the first place, and so you had good cause to send me away."

"Oh. Oh, you needn't have done that. Why, it was all my fault."

"But because of my impudence, you didn't stay for tea."

"No, but I was ill... I really was quite ill."

He gave her a lazy smile. "Well, you were unsteady, it's true, but it was nothing that a little tea wouldn't have cured."

She looked straight into his eyes. "You English think everything is solved with tea, don't you?"

"Everything in my house, yes," he countered.

She remembered anew how the Brookses came to be the famous Brookses—Teamen to the Queen, and for the first time in the conversation she smiled.

He smiled back. "There now. I haven't seen your smile since this afternoon. But don't spoil me with it. Make me work for it. I'm used to work," he said happily. "Well... well, I've caused you to miss tea at Brooks House—and so do you think you could return sometime soon?"

"For tea?"

He nodded.

"Yes. And actually..." She felt herself blushing. "I would like very much to see the library once more."

"Tea in the library. Unusual but not impossible. It shall be done."

"Thank you, Mr. Brooks."

"Thank *you*, Miss Brown. I bid you good day." He bowed slightly and returned his hat to his head as he turned to leave.

"Mr. Brooks? Before you go I would like to say one thing more."

"Yes?" He slid the hat back off his head and smiled.

She watched the motion so attentively that for a moment she forgot what she was going to say. Lowering her chin, she gathered her thoughts. "Americans on the whole are well acquainted with honesty and frankness." Her head came up. "And so, while it's true I do appreciate your coming straightway to discuss this with me..." He beamed once more, but she added, "I might also tell you that you frightened me half to death coming to my window, and I would hope you would never choose to do so again."

His smile was lost. "I frightened you? I am sorry, but I did...I did pass by your window three times before I had the courage to come round." She gave a little smile as he brought his hand to the column, looked about him for a moment, and then leaned toward her again. "You know, your cousin, Cecelia, and I used to play hide and seek around these porticos when we were little. I believe she fell out this very window once." He picked at a flake of paint on the column.

"Cecelia?" she said while thinking, *Was Cecelia ever a child?*

"Yes, but I hope you can keep a confidence as well as I can." He looked back to her again. "I believe I told you that this afternoon... that I could keep a confidence? I meant that." She nodded shyly. She loved his voice even more as it grew low. "Then perhaps I can tell you what else happened to me today." She held on to the curtain and leaned ever so slightly out the window, her curiosity leading her to listen intently to his words. "I passed this house today thinking to have Cecelia give you a note when I came across your window. I passed it once when it was first coming open. I passed it again knowing someone was standing just inside. The third time the young lady approached the opening. It was the American visitor I had so rudely insulted earlier in the day. But the vibrant young lady I'd met this afternoon was gone and in her place stood the saddest visage I'd ever seen. She was looking out on to the gloaming, and tears were falling from her eyes. There she stood, hanging on to the drapery as if her life depended on it." He smiled and lowered his gaze. "With some arrogance I presumed I was the cause of her sorrow, and so I came to undo the damage if I could." He raised his eyes to hers.

Her lips trembling, she smiled. Were young men really capable of speaking so beautifully? Was he quite serious? His face and manner told her yes.

"Have I... undone the damage?" he repeated softly, gently, so that she was momentarily lost in the beauty of his words.

But a clear view of her aunt's face came to mind just then to break the spell. She blushed and pulled her head back from the window. His face did not reappear at the opening and then....

Then Theodosia's world went black.

The heavy drape she had tugged on for so long had finally given way and come down—rungs, rod, and tassels—all about her head.

This was the sort of thing Theodosia was used to, the very sort of situation that caused her mother to laugh and her father to stomp about the room in consternation. Her mother simply blamed it on Theodosia's curiosity, while her father usually gave vent to a string of unkind jokes at her expense, thinking to somehow humiliate her into proper behavior. But in his heart he blamed himself; he had experienced continual accidents as a child, and so, as with most parents whose children begin to display their own weaknesses, he was harder on Theodosia than he'd ever been on himself. All the while he justified his harshness by saying it was all well and good for a boy, but a girl ought not to be so clumsy, and if she didn't learn to curb her awkwardness, she would never gain a husband.

Theodosia only understood that her father was never quite pleased with her.

She didn't really have a name for this sort of clumsy incident, she just knew she had come to expect it as part and parcel of her daily life. If a table was going to be overturned, Theodosia was going to do it. If a precious piece of china was going to be fractured, leave Theodosia in the room with it for a while. Her father had said more than once, "If you take interest in a thing, for Heaven's sake learn to ask someone to show it to you!" He hadn't always been like this but seemed to have become impatient with Theodosia only in the last few years, coincidentally the exact number of years in which his business had begun to slacken.

The fact remained Theodosia liked to examine things for herself, and her inquisitiveness was such that she could no more keep her curiosity at bay than she could will herself to stop breathing.

Besides, it was only while she was in the grip of a certain passion for something, as she was when listening to Austin's pretty words, that she found these things happening to her.

Now, the falling of the heavy rod—more precisely, the clunking of its brass finials on the floor—soon brought Aunt Selda's maid-servant to Theodosia's door, and Theodosia could not refuse her entry. In trying to remove the curtain from over her head she realized the rod, laden as it was with thick, dark velvet, was too heavy for one person to set back in place.

So she and the servant, a kindly woman with an age and demeanor remarkably like her mother's, reset the curtain in a silence Theodosia was glad for.

"You needn't... you... I hope..." Theodosia whispered when they were done, wondering whether the woman would tell her aunt what had occurred.

"No 'arm done, miss," replied the servant.

Theodosia lowered her voice still further. "I suppose you should tell my aunt..."

"Noaw." She cheerfully brushed her hands toward the curtain. "I'll wait to tell her...'til a warm day in January, miss." She smiled.

Theodosia trembled a laugh.

Then the servant was even more forthright. "Never rile the mistress 'less'n I 'ave to.

In a fit of gratitude, Theodosia touched the woman's shoulder. "Thank you."

But the woman's shoulder jerked out from under Theodosia's hand with a swiftness that needed no discussion. Clearly Theodosia had humiliated her with the familiarity of her action, and now Theodosia looked away in mute embarrassment as the woman quit the room.

Her American upbringing caused Theodosia to wait until the servant closed the door behind her to begin crying. Later, when she began to dry her tears, she wondered if a well-bred English girl ever let herself cry at all. ᜒ

THREE

∽

Now Chin-Chin was a clever Man!
Which comes from drinking tea.
For books he was mad,
And he always had
Confucius on his knee
                    19th century advertisement for Tower Tea

∽

"Mr. Brooks," said Lady Brooks, "I told you we should expect a letter from Selda Bannoch, and here it is. Yes, with the young lady's billet as well... apologizing for her sudden illness, et cetera, et cetera...."

Lord Alfred Brooks was refilling his pipe and settling into a chair near the writing table and only half-listening to his wife. "A note is it?" came mumbling from his lips.

"Did you see the look the girl held on us as she entered the orangery? Derisive. Haughty, the way her eyes narrowed. And the way in which she dismissed Austin was not to be believed. Yet she has apologized. Or, at least, her aunt has caused her to apologize, which shows hope. What will we do with her?"

"Will we do..." He paused to draw deeply from his pipe.

"Mr. Brooks, you are not listening. If you were listening you would have heard me ask what we should do about the girl. Is she to be considered or not?"

"The girl. *Hrrum.* The American? A note, did you say?"

"Oh. Heavens, yes. Here it is." Lady Brooks handed Theodosia's little note to him.

He held his monocle to the card. "Fine writing."

"Most people are able to manage a proficiency in one thing."

"Well, I thought she had a bright look about her."

"Alfred, she had the bright look of an idiot in Bedlam! She's no match. No. Frightful. How could we even have considered an American?"

"You know very well how we could have considered her, Mrs. Brooks."

Lady Brooks thought for a while and finally, reluctantly, nodded. "If only we were allowed in better circles. It would be easy to find them each a suitable mate. You know the blame is yours, Mr. Brooks."

"And my father's, Mrs. Brooks. Let us not forget. Also his fault we're in this house with this blasted decision lying before us."

Lady Brooks sighed.

But just then their discussion was cut short by the entrance of their youngest son.

"Good evening, Mother, Father," said Austin.

"Son," Lord Brooks said efficiently while Eleanor Brooks chose to say nothing at all.

"I've come to tell you I've made things right with Miss Brown."

"You did *what?*" flashed his mother.

"I made my apologies to her. We shall have her for tea tomorrow, I think."

"For tea. For tea!" Lady Brooks sputtered. "My land, what are you thinking? Alfred, what is he thinking? You can't just... That's impossible. I won't have it!"

Alfred Brooks knew exactly what Austin was thinking, but he also knew enough to keep the answer to himself.

"Please calm yourself, Mother. I believe I am old enough to straighten my own messes, thank you. You've taught me well, don't you think? Miss Brown accepted my apologies and I'm sure she'll feel perfectly well if she could be formally invited to come tomorrow . . ."

"Mr. Brooks, do you hear this? *Do you hear this?* Are you going to stand for it?"

"My dear lady, do you wish him to rescind an invitation? Or, for that matter, remove his apologies?"

"Well. I... well." She stared at Austin and then back at her husband. "Hmph."

"The date for tea was not perfectly set," Austin admitted, trying to appease his mother in the only manner the circumstance might allow.

Her husband smiled into his pipe and then Austin began to smile but only briefly—until he caught his mother's most severe look.

She answered, "So you are having her for tea, then? Well and good." Her voice turned mocking. "Take her to the tea room over in What's It. Have a picnic on a lawn in Thistledown. But she will not have tea in *my* house tomorrow! I have taught you, Austin, yes, but not well. There should be a proper amount of time given for the young lady to recover herself. I've only just received the young lady's note of apology. I was not planning to ask them back for tea for at least seven days. Seven days would be proper."

"Contrary to your opinion, I think she behaved exactly as she should have... in every respect," the boy said cheerfully. "And by her accepting my apologies, you will see that everything has been patched up nicely."

Lady Brooks stared at Austin and then cautiously looked him up and down. Pulling her head up smartly, she said in a bit of a growl, "Austin, it occurs to me you did not have time to speak with her at church this morning. Tell me..." Her eyelids closed carefully. "Tell me you did not visit with her."

Here Austin grew entirely too silent.

Lady Brooks opened and then rolled her eyes and looked over to her husband who was suddenly very busy with his pipe.

"Surely you did not announce yourself to the Bannoch Cottage without our permission."

"No, ma'am. I simply... she... we happened upon a meeting." His mouth twitched with the hint of a smile as he remembered their conversation at the window.

Lady Brooks' eyes grew colder as she watched him. "Austin, please remember that on a matter of such grave importance as with whom you may socialize, it is not for you to decide. When the time comes for you to choose a wife, we will do the looking. *We* will find someone suitable. Meanwhile, these flirtations must remain simply that: flirtations. Do you understand?"

Austin did not reply.

She said more pointedly, "I hope to Heaven that that American girl, Miss Brown, understands. If a young lady were found to be suitable, we would naturally consider the older sons first. The need to establish a home goes to the firstborn if he so chooses..."

"Eleanor!" said her husband sharply.

"She's not telling me anything I don't already know, Father." Lord Brooks turned and looked out the window. Austin pressed his lips together and then added, "So if Alfred or Allan take a liking to her I'll be out of the running, eh?"

From Lady Brooks a sniff was heard and then another. "I am not even speaking of that... that *chit* of a girl. Did you see how she tripped in the aisle leaving services this morning? I have serious doubts as to her suitability for any... And treating *you* like a common... *well*, I am amazed that you would even consider her. You should never have found the need to apologize to that piece of *fluff*."

"But if the *fluff* is found rich enough, I suppose your opinion of her personal merits could be altered." Austin interrupted coldly.

"Austin, that's enough. Please remove yourself," said his father.

"Gladly, sir," and so he did.

The next day an invitation to tea was extended to Mrs. Bannoch, her daughter, and her niece by Lady and Lord Alfred Brooks, the date set seven days hence.

Seven days later, when the time came for the three ladies to attend tea at Brooks House, Theodosia was more nervous than ever. She had heard nothing from Austin during the week, and so she was not at all certain how things were between them. She had no idea whether he had left at the moment the curtain rod had fallen or right before, but giving herself some encouragement, she thought he seemed the sort of fellow who would have helped her if he'd seen the accident. Still, she was afraid he took her lack of response to his quiet question about undoing the damage as an estrangement. When Sunday arrived, the day they were to go for tea, she fell to wondering as soon as she awoke and quickly gave herself a headache.

But she found two things to be grateful for that morning: the Sunday sermon by the Reverend Pickett, and the fact that at tea time her aunt was not called away at the last minute. This time both Selda and Cecelia would be there for Theodosia to follow, mannerism by mannerism, through the maze of expectations that took the simple guise of afternoon tea in Thistledown.

The coach came up the round path to the Brooks' home. They were ushered into the library, but no tea was in evidence. With a smallish disappointment in her heart mingled with a larger aching in her head, she placed herself stock still by the center drum table and tried to keep her eyes from wandering to the books on the high walls, especially not up to *the* book. She tightened the hand holding her gloves into a fist.

Her aunt noticed Theodosia's strain. "Theodosia, do not squeeze your gloves so!"

"Oh, my," she said pitifully, looking at them for the first time. "Oh, my," she repeated.

Just then Alfred Brooks, the younger, entered the library and asked the ladies to accompany him to tea in the orangery.

Theodosia stared at him dumbly and slowly realized they'd sent a son to fetch the ladies as a means of showing they *might be* disposed to forgive her previous error. But then they'd made further comment by making sure it was not the *same* son. Such an obvious statement on their part, the clear recognition of her mistake, only caused her fresh humiliation, and she turned her throbbing head away to stare at an unfamiliar statue of Diana in the corner. She was sure it hadn't been there last week. Now Aunt Selda made an unsubtle remark to Theodosia about learning to admire Greek statuary without taking on the look of it, and Cecelia followed her mother's harsh comment by stepping up and pinching Theodosia's cheeks.

"There, now she'll have color enough," Cecelia quipped.

Theodosia bit her lip to keep from crying out and stared in amazement at her cousin. She put a hand to one cheek and wondered how quickly a bruise might show, and then her eyes narrowed slightly as she watched an unconcerned Cecelia turn and, with her mother, move toward the doors.

Why, they wanted her to fail. Why else had they allowed her to come to Brooks House alone the first time, knowing she wasn't ready? Certainly Aunt Selda never would have allowed it for her daughter. Say what they would, they wished to publicly diminish her. And right there Theodosia decided she would not allow it. With a sudden look of determination in her eyes, she followed them. *I will do exactly as they do and everything will be perfect, or they'll have only themselves to blame for it.*

But she had to tell herself this over and over as they stepped down the long hall, and when the group reached the doors of the orangery, she cried out in her heart, *Lord, help me! Help me! Amen!*

The Brookses were set around the tea table once more, and Theodosia noted the positions of all the chairs set about for the guests. She felt her way through the choice of chairs by watching the movements of her aunt and cousin, and soon she was seated. She was delighted to be introduced to the Reverend Pickett, a kindly, scholarly looking man of later mid-life whose round face, balding pate and bushiness about the hair above his ears gave him an owlish appearance. She had enjoyed his sermon immensely and gave him a tremendous smile that told him so. He was congenial, trying to make Theodosia feel comfortable in the setting, but those very attentions caused her to wonder if it were so obvious how uncomfortable she was.

Lady Brooks often looked at Theodosia during the conversation, and more than once the girl cast down her eyes to avoid the Lady's gaze. Austin, she noticed, did not join the conversation except when asked a question directly, and so she feared she had drawn a curtain on their relationship in more ways than one, a thought that made her choke on her buttered scone and cough once—only once—but then all conversation ceased.

"Are we feeling better today?" asked Lady Brooks demurely.

Theodosia nodded and blushed. "Yes. Yes. Quite, thank you," was all she could get out for fear of choking once more.

Alfred Lord Brooks said, "I've always said tea is medicinal to the body and mind," which drew a sharp glance from his wife.

"And thus for the spirit, I should think!" said Reverend Pickett happily.

But young Alfred Brooks, ignoring the Reverend, said, "What you say is true, Father, but I have always maintained that such can only be said of certain teas and certain ailments. The beneficial use of teas should be left to scientists to determine." He obviously took his father's remarks quite seriously.

"Well, Alfred, you're the scientist in the family and I leave it to you, while I may safely leave matters of the spirit to the Reverend Pickett here," he said politely.

Allan's handsome eyebrows rose up. "I'm sure the Reverend Pickett would agree that every *useful* thing does *not* evolve from science."

"Hear, hear," and the Reverend smiled at Allan.

But Allan added, "With all deference due things spiritual, I might also point out that the scientist would have no tools to work with if *business* hadn't provided the room and the time in which he might play."

The older brothers glared at one another, and the room took on an uncomfortable silence. Reverend Pickett cleared his throat loudly as if ready to add comment, and the ladies reached for their teacups and looked to the Reverend simultaneously. Theodosia's eyes grew wide with apprehension, but she was late in taking up her cup.

For reasons unknown, the Reverend's kind eyes fell upon her, and he did not speak to the group, after all. She observed his look and his eyes seemed to say, "Don't fret, child." She smiled shyly and drew the china cup to her lips.

Unfortunately, since all had looked to the Reverend as he cleared his throat, everyone saw the exchange between him and Theodosia. Everyone, that is, except Alfred, the scientist, who had apparently found something to pique his interest on the far wall—and so all but Alfred had taken to watching Theodosia as she sipped her tea.

So, with all of those pairs of eyes on her, she looked about and wondered in the heavy silence of the moment if she were expected to make some sort of comment. She gulped her brew and then, "Lord Brooks, I understand your tea house deals in the very best of teas."

He smiled and nodded once. "Brooks House have been purveyors to the Queen for many years, an honor wrested from others by hard work and a fine product." The words came out bland and flat, as if he'd said them a hundred times before and had never quite come to believe them.

Austin suddenly spoke up. "And sometimes a little change of order is necessary to keep up with the demands of the British Empire, eh, Father?" Austin looked away from his father to Theodosia and smiled graciously. "You see, a good tea was once a simple affair: the leaves came from Lord so-and-so's plantation in India, were brought over by the Duke's ships, mixed and packaged by Earl so-and-so's factory and there you had a good tea. Nowadays it's not so simple. Now a good tea is sometimes actually based on a good tea leaf, which comes as an advantage to everyone who drinks it but seems to miff those who never will allow for a change... even a change for the better."

"Good leaf, *my eye*," Allan said. "Has nothing to do with it! Proper connections make a proper tea. The average person can't tell one leaf from another."

Alfred jumped into the fray. "Well, if you're not willing to blend the leaves properly, you'll have nothing to sell. Any fool can tell the difference between Earl Grey and pure China Black." He shook his head, and his silver spectacles slid to the tip of his nose.

When the tempers of the young men began to flare, Lord Brooks spoke up. "Many ways to make a good tea... many ways. My sons will be the next generation of tea-makers, and may God enable them to carry on our fine tradition."

"Amen," said Reverend Pickett firmly. "Scripture says, *But every man hath his proper gift of God, one after this manner, and another after that.*" His voice deepened, "Now in the realm of glory, a gift for making tea may seem a trivial thing..." He paused for emphasis and Lady Brooks straightened her back, obviously wary of his message. "... and then again it mayn't be trivial to Him at all. It could well be the proceedings of tea in Thistledown are all-important to Him. We will not know how important until we are face-to-face with Him, but I for one was taught to take little for granted in this life." He looked about the group with a doting smile, and Theodosia, despite her discomfort, smiled in agreement. He then said in a hush, "Knowing that He loves each of us in turn, I choose to believe His grace abounds even within the confines of a Thistledown tea." He turned slightly and Theodosia felt her eyes must be deceiving her. She thought she saw him wink at her.

Theodosia blushed. "It is certain, sir, He has blessed Brooks House."

"Yes, and we are ever grateful." Lord Brooks cleared his throat and thrust his chin forward all at once.

"Your encouragement is ever appreciated, Reverend," Lady Brooks said rather tersely. "And as delighted as I am to hear a discussion of the many fine properties of tea, in this household the subject actually falls under the heading of business, and business, as we know, is not to be discussed at tea." She glanced at Theodosia, holding her lidded look on her just long enough for the girl's cheeks to grow pinker than even her cousin Cecelia had made them.

Reverend Pickett, seeming to ignore the harshness in the Lady's tone, piped up merrily, "Ah, madam, I beg pardon. Tea has such a way with it as to move hearts to speak honestly what they know they should not. Religion being my business, as it were, my conversation has failed on two points. Do forgive me." Lord Brooks smiled and Lady Brooks made an attempt at one, but the Reverend continued, "Seeing the bounty before me causes me to reflect on the bounty of God... but I shall drink my tea now and be satisfied." He bowed politely. Lord Brooks smiled again, and Theodosia blushed her appreciation for his taking on the burden of indictment. Spectacles or no spectacles, there was no imagining the kind wink he sent her way this time.

Soon the discussion moved to lighter topics—the weather and geography—those pillars of polite conversation around which so many useless conversations take their turn.

When tea was finished, it was suggested that everyone take a walk in the garden. Theodosia was thrilled at the chance to see up close the flowers she'd eyed so fuzzily through the glass of the library doors.

Lady Brooks led the group outside, dominating the main path in both movement and conversation, pointing out this particular floribunda and the other to her guests with as much pride in their blossoms, Theodosia noted wryly, as if she had planted and pruned them herself. The very latest in rose cultivation was evident in the wide sprays of abundant flowers, but when Theodosia chose to bring her little nose close to a clutch of petals to smell the scent of their blossoms she was amazed to find they had no scent at all.

At the next bush, she tried again. The flowers were glorious, full of rich color with petals so thickly set upon each flower it was hard to imagine how one stem could hold them all. The blushing petals looked as if they would pull the entire bush to the ground with their load, and yet these, too, had no smell.

As her cousin passed behind her Theodosia touched her arm and whispered, "Cecelia. Is it possible these roses have no scent?"

Cecelia rolled her eyes. "These hybrids have no scent, darling. It's bred out of them. Haven't you been listening?"

"Well, why ever would someone choose to breed out the scent?"

"You'd be so surprised to find, dearest cousin, that some people only want a thing for its appearance." The thin lips took on a cat-like smile. "Rather like the way a man will choose a fool for a wife... you know... all because she's taught herself to blush."

Theodosia watched Cecelia turn about to join the group, while she herself began to lag behind.

She didn't like being spoken to that way. At the beginning of the summer Theodosia had thought she knew everything about life, but she was becoming certain she knew nothing. And the new things she was learning were giving her no pleasure.

But now the dashing Allan Brooks took notice of Theodosia's solitude and came to her, offering his arm and directing her to a bench under a bower of wisteria. As soon as they were settled, he asked if she would tell him about America.

Flattered by his rapt attention, Theodosia quickly forgot her late unhappiness, and gladly began telling him everything she thought he might find interesting concerning her country of origin. She told him about the new railroads near her home and then about their seat of government. She had gone to the capital city right before leaving, and so she fell to describing the new capitol building as somewhat hatless, for the dome was not yet built.

With a quick smile he said, "Yes, we burned the city out rather badly a while ago, I understand."

Theodosia was not amused. "I had a great-uncle who died defending our state house." She momentarily turned her eyes from him.

"Oh. I am sorry," he muttered. "What an idiot I am. Completely overcount myself at times."

"Well..." She smiled wanly, repenting of her tone. "How could you have known? And it was a long time ago now. Forty some years, isn't it? Though I suppose... that wouldn't be considered so very much in England."

He smiled again. "How very kind you are to so readily forgive."

Blushing slightly she asked, "Was there anything *else* about America you wished to know? That I might know to tell you, that is."

"Yes." He drew his handsome brows together and lightheartedly asked, "Tell me how a young American girl chances to pull herself away from her admirers and venture to a stuffy little English town of stuffy little English people and attach herself therewith for an entire summer? However does she stand it?"

Theodosia could not answer without compromising herself or her companion so she remained pensively silent.

"Pardon me," he finally said, but she could not tell if it was spoken with condescension or sincerity.

Theodosia shook her head and sat quietly. She wished she could give him an honest answer: that she had received more attention from him and his younger brother in the last two days than she'd received in her entire life.

He sat back into his seat and sighed. "I just thought you might be willing to speak your mind. I'd heard that about Americans."

"Americans and their honesty..." She paused, then, "... seem to be a topic of great interest to everyone I meet here."

"Forgive us, Miss Brown, but when you've breathed the stale air of Thistledown for a number of years, you come to beg for a breath of freshness. You have all that open land in which to free yourself of troubles. Here, the young ladies are kept under lock and key until their coming out."

"I understand, but please don't romanticize America. We have streets and air as dirty as London's. I'm sure you have problems as difficult."

"Ah, but you have land for the asking."

"Land for the taking."

"Hm. True. But that's half the fun, isn't it? I've often thought I'd do well there—fighting Indians and bears and such, creating a plantation off the land I took up with my bare hands."

With surprise, Theodosia saw that Allan was half-believing himself. "You are a romantic, then."

"It can't be helped," he said, his lip curling.

"Well, perhaps I will see you pass through Alexandria County, Virginia, someday with a wagon of supplies behind you—a Kentucky rifle in one hand and the tether to your cow in the other."

"Do I note a touch of mockery in your voice, Miss Brown?" he said easily.

"I am trying to imagine you heading into the woods, Mr. Brooks, but for the life of me I cannot."

"And why ever not?"

"Well, I'd say my brother might have something to do with the image. He is himself a trapper."

"Really? A real trapper, eh? And what does he trap?" he asked with some amusement in his voice.

"Mostly beaver."

"Do you mean to tell me I might be holding before me the product of your brother's skill?" Here he held his top hat out before him and examined it as if quite suddenly he'd found it made of gold.

"I suppose so," she said with some agitation.

Slowly he lay the hat down on the seat between them and brought his arm up to the back of the bench, brushing her sleeve lightly. "I don't believe I've ever before met the sister of a trapper who traps *mostly beaver.*"

"I am proud of my brother's skill."

"Yes, I imagine it takes quite a bit of endurance to follow beavers wherever the little fellows choose to roam."

She glared at him and pulled forward in the seat, but he only gave her a most gracious smile in return.

He pulled his arm away. "I am being rather brutish, aren't I? I'm sorry. It's my competitive nature, I'm sure. Perhaps you'll forgive me if I read you a bit of poetry. Have you read Keats? No? Ah, then you're in for a treat. Now, mind you this is only English poetry—none of your lively frontier prose—so I pray you will not judge it too harshly." He snickered as he brought forth a little book from his breast pocket.

She pursed her lips together, determined to sit still through the conversation or die trying, for she was loathe to run from her troubles as she had the week before.

"Here it is," he said, "*Modern Love.*" He glanced at her to see if she cared for the title.

Her eyes took aim, but she did her best to look as though he'd said nothing unusual. Within herself, however, she was frightened to have found herself in such a compromising situation.

"'And what is love?'" he read and stopped to glance at her again.

Theodosia raised her brows. "I would be more suited to listen to English poetry, I am sure, if you could refrain from silent comment."

That brought a great, "Haw!" from him, but at least he kept his eyes to the text from then on. He read,

And what is love? It is a doll dress'd up
For idleness to cosset, nurse, and dandle;

A thing of soft misnomers, so divine
That silly youth doth think to make itself
Divine by loving, and so goes on
Yawning and doting a whole summer long,
Till Miss's comb is made a pearl tiara,
And common Wellingtons turn Romeo boots:
Then Cleopatra lives at number seven,
And Antony resides in Brunswick Square
Fools! make me whole again that weighty pearl
The Queen of Egypt melted, and I'll say
That ye may love in spite of beaver hats.

He snapped shut the thin volume and smiled into the air. But then in surprisingly reverent tones he asked, "Tell me what it's like for him, Miss Brown... truly. How *does* one hunt for beaver?"

She looked into his eyes to try and take measure of his meaning while the anger rolled within her.

"Really, I'm quite in earnest," he said with a sincere look. "Nothing to match your brother's prowess, I am sure, but I myself happen to hunt."

Staring him down, she was not too angry to forget how proud she was of her brother's skill, and so she was not likely to have minded answering him even if he were not in earnest. She raised her chin. "He learns the beaver's trails, sets traps and lives off the land. He'd find a way to live in any woods. The Indians respect him. He goes for months without seeing a white face, and after he gets the number of pelts to suit him, he sometimes has to fight other trappers to keep them. He comes home about one month out of the year, 'to get his fill of civilization,' he says. We worry for him constantly, but this is the life he's chosen, and I'm very proud of him. He's put aside a tremendous amount already that he says he'll one day invest in the business of his choice."

"Haw. That's raw. *Get his fill of civilization.*" He laughed. "And I suppose he's built like an oak tree, too," he said with an unbecoming snort.

"That would be a fair estimation," she replied, smiling. "I

would say American trappers, homesteaders and their ilk are the strongest, toughest people I have ever met—mind, body and soul."

"No doubt your rough terrain affects you all in terrible ways, although you seem personally to be spared from its effects."

She brushed aside his words with a wave of her hand. "Since you express such interest in knowing what Americans are made of, may I trouble you with an American story?"

"Only fair since I've forced our poetry upon you."

She gave him a sidelong glance. "Well, it is this: On a diplomatic journey to France, Mr. Jefferson and his American contingent were invited for supper to the home of a prominent French philosopher—it was in Paris, I believe—and during the meal they began a discussion of a similar nature to ours. The Frenchman had boldly theorized that due to the rough country and the hard life Americans suffered trying to tame its wildness, we, as a people, were destined to grow stunted and deformed over the years, much as you've said."

Allan smiled.

"Mr. Jefferson's reply was this: He first asked the Frenchmen at the table to rise. He then asked the Americans to rise. Every one of the Americans stood taller—by almost a head—and stood straighter than the Frenchman beside him, and after a dramatic pause Jefferson said something to the effect, 'I rest my case.'"

Allan laughed heartily. "Ha! Ah, that's good. Strong in body, perhaps, but compare their brains and now you've a different argument, I'll wager."

This brought her blood to a perfect boil, but she succeeded in staying calm. "Mr. Jefferson is a great scientist and inventor. The philosopher would not have had him at table if he could not equal him in a discourse. Yes, I would say our people are strong in both mind and body—they have had to be. And I would also say our people are willing to work and die for their chance in life, and I wonder...are you willing to die for your chance, Mr. Brooks?"

He smiled but his eyes narrowed slightly. "Probably not. Probably not." He looked out over the rose garden to the high hedge of the boxwood labyrinth beyond. "Then again, I might be willing to kill for it." He glanced back and smiled at her shocked expression.

"Sir, you cannot mean what you say."

He laughed. "Miss Brown, have no fear, the only implement of death I carry on me is a pocket pistol." He put his hand into the pocket of his frock coat, and she pulled to the edge of her seat with fright. He smiled and opened his hand to reveal a little silver flask. "I don't know the American name, but perhaps your brother would?"

Her face burned with indignation, and at that he quickly stood up, returned the flask to his pocket and bowed slightly. "Good day to you, Miss Brown."

As he walked leisurely away, she pressed her lips together in irritation. *Of all the impudent rudeness,* she thought, just as the Reverend Pickett and Austin Brooks came around the corner of the alcove.

"Miss Brown?" said the Reverend Pickett.

"Oh, yes?" she said and stood. For the first time she saw the Reverend's face quite clearly; his cheeks and forehead were deeply pockmarked. A childhood pox, no doubt. His grin deepened the shadows in his face but was genuine and kind.

"Young lady, is there a way we may make you feel more at home while you are visiting our fair surrounds?" he said gently.

She smiled, trying to avoid looking directly at Austin beside him. But Austin had turned his head and was looking out toward his older brother Allan with a grim expression.

It was then Theodosia realized they both had overheard the argument with Allan, and that the Reverend, at least, was trying to make amends for his rude behavior. "No, nothing. I so appreciate your concern, but I will manage... somehow."

Austin suddenly turned back. "I believe you had expressed an interest in seeing the library again?"

She blushed a deep shade of pink and yet she nodded.

"Good," said the Reverend heartily. "A lover of books! I, too, admit to the habit. You will have to come to tea at the vicarage soon and list for me your favorite works, eh?"

She smiled and gave another more ready nod.

"Well, then, I leave you to it!" said the Reverend, leaving her to wonder what he meant. "I must speak to Allan for a moment, if you'll excuse me. It was such a pleasure to meet you, Miss Brown. If ever you have a need, please don't hesitate to call on me at the vicarage. Tea is served at four and I enjoy nothing better than to have visitors—as Austin can tell you—especially youthful visitors that might open my eyes to books and other worlds."

She looked into his eyes; he certainly seemed sincere. "Thank you, sir. I am certain I will."

"Good day then! Good day," he said cheerfully and walked in the direction Allan had taken.

There was an awkward moment of silence before Austin said gently, "If you would follow me?" He did not offer his arm, and so she chose to walk behind him down the path.

On the walk down, she wondered what she might say to him, or he to her, but she'd had such a miserable conversation with his brother just then that she didn't feel at all sure of herself. Besides which, she didn't know of any way to properly end their last discussion. She could not very well blurt out, "You are forgiven!" without a context for the words, and so she simply followed him.

For his part, Austin Simpson Brooks had felt his mother's words and was keeping his distance from the girl as best he could, that is, until the Reverend Pickett had led him straight to the bench. And so they had overheard the last of his brother's rude conversation as they approached the garden seat, and if the Reverend Pickett were not beside him Austin's temper would have bested him then and there, he knew. The Reverend saw Austin's frame of mind exactly and whispered he would have words with Allan, and so Austin had held himself at bay.

As for forgiveness, he felt no need to hear the words. He'd seen it in her eyes that day at the window, and so he had turned and walked away without feeling the need to force her thoughts into words.

He opened the double doors to the library, and she passed him and entered. Austin bowed and smiled, but to her mild surprise he then said, "You will pardon me," turned, and left her alone in the great room.

Momentarily sorry he felt he had to leave her, in the next instant she was relieved he had. Ever since she'd first come to the library she'd wanted to come again, but she'd wanted to do so alone. She told herself it had nothing to do with the will, but she could not help looking up now at the red volume. Still there. And she was alone with it.

Austin made his way down the path, wanting at every step to turn back. He remembered how she said she'd climbed the library stair, and so he knew it was for books she'd wanted to return. She loved books. The thought pleased him.

He saw the Reverend Pickett walking away from his brother Allan who was now chatting smoothly with Cecelia Bannoch at the entrance to the labyrinth, and he smiled. Allan had clearly ruined his chances with Theodosia, besides which Allan didn't like her, he was sure. *And so there is only Alfred, and Alfred...well, if Theodosia were the shape and color of a test tube or had the polish of a laboratory instrument he might take notice of her,* Austin sniffed.

Austin stood still for a moment with his hands behind his back watching his brother bring a blush to Cecelia's cheek. "Bless my brothers' proclivities," he whispered to himself. "My turn with Theodosia Brown will come soon enough, I think."

Allan held his arm out for Cecelia, and they disappeared around the boxwood hedge.

Austin thought of the library. *What if she wants to reach a book too high for her? Better go and assist,* he decided, leaving logic by the wayside. He turned and walked briskly back to the library doors.

FOUR

❦

Miss One, Two and Three
Could never agree,
While they gossiped around
A tea-caddy.
Of a little take a little,
You're kindly welcome, too;
Of a little leave a little,
'Tis manners so to do.

Nursery Rhyme

❦

"*Very* well placed," said Selda Bannoch with a knowing smile. She was speaking to Lord and Lady Brooks and their eldest son in a corner of the rose garden, and in the last half hour Selda's every motion and every word were meant to impress the trio. Singing the praises of her niece's family, the Widow Bannoch had shown the Brookses all of her cards. All but one, that is; she had left up her sleeve the one card she might use when all else failed to impress the Brookses regarding the Browns of Alexandria County, Virginia.

Lady Brooks tilted her head in the direction of the speaker, while her eyes rested graciously on a yellow rose bush nearby. *If we must, we must*, she thought. *Without a doubt I could mold that silly girl any way I wished once she was in my house, and Alfred could choose to ignore her and go about his science. Ah, but she's fannings and dust. Still, it would be better to have a wealthy unknown American family for in-laws than to suffer the way we have in London. Yes, I suppose the American will have to do. The marriage, of course, will be a slap in the face of London society! And it will serve them!* She sighed without realizing the fact. The truth was that to serve them and be blessed for it by gaining status among them was all Lady Brooks had ever wanted in this life.

Selda Bannoch, however, took Lady Brooks' sigh for disinterest, and so she steeled herself to play the winning card and win the hand. "As you know, my brother-in-law is a *barrister*..."

Lord Brooks raised his brows. "I was not of the impression the term barrister was used there."

"Well..." She smiled in deprecation. "You are so very correct, of course. There they are in fact referred to as *trial lawyers*." She put as much pomp and circumstance in the announcement as was physically possible.

Lord Brooks, clearly unimpressed, looked toward his son and was not surprised to note Alfred's mind had wandered far away from the entire discussion. Lord Brooks wished he might do the same, but he politely turned back to Selda Bannoch and raised his brow in feigned interest.

Irritated with the drifting back and forth of Lord Brooks' attention, Selda Bannoch felt the familiar call within to load upon the conversation a little more than truth required (much as she could not seem to help herself from having her seamstress sew yet another set of tassels and furbelows upon her gowns). "My brother-in-law is an American, of course, and there the title of barrister, in fact the whole system of honorariums, is considered... *out-of-date*. Nevertheless, he presents his cases to the court, and he is a man of some property, and it is upon these I've no doubt he would be considered a barrister. And none but *you* shall *hear* of it..." Selda lowered her voice in a dramatic hush, "but he holds a *variety* of properties in his possession, not the largest of which is dear little *Star Cottage* itself!"

Despite the ridiculous spectacle she'd made of herself in the telling, this bit of news did in fact bring the group around just as she hoped it might.

Lady Brooks' brows drew together. "Star Cottage is not yours, my dear?"

"Indeed, not. It is my brother-in-law's gracious *gift* to me that I should reside there." She lowered her head in proper respect, quite willing to suffer the humiliation of the moment for a far greater good—that good which she felt greater than any other on the planet: her own.

The Brookses were notably impressed.

Lady Brooks raised her hand slightly. "Alfred, did you hear? That dear Star Cottage is owned by Theodosia's papa." She turned back to Selda Bannoch with a smile.

Alfred Brooks focused on his mother's face for a moment and grunted slightly. He knew exactly what his mother was about, and he did not like it. He never wanted a wife. As eldest son somehow he had expected to be above an arranged marriage, a tradition he found personally repugnant—as if he were a stallion being put to stud. No. He was a man of science and had every hope of leading his colleagues into new horizons of research. He had no time for wives and children and such. Ever since young Alfred had shown an interest in laboratory work, he'd been provided with anything he'd asked for. So, by the ripe age of twenty-four, he'd studied the effects of mercury on mice, the viscous property of various oils, the temperature effect on rubber and, only barely relating his research to his father's tea house, he had also observed various disease and blight on certain hardy bushes, some of which happened to be tea.

With such a variety of interests and such a commitment to research, what would he do with a wife? Woman being an unknown and unquantifiable substance to be counted on as certainly as mist, she was not even of interest to Alfred in the role of experimental subject. But it would not be his decision. The family wanted a marriage, an heir, and he by twist of fate was first in line. *Why can't they have Allan marry her?* Alfred thought suddenly, as he saw Allan round the corner with Cecelia Bannoch on his arm.

Now, if ever Alfred had shown interest in a woman, that woman was Cecelia Bannoch. She had, in his estimation, displayed a more manly and therefore higher sense of reason than many of her species. However, he'd never seen Cecelia blush as she did now under his younger brother's gaze, and the view unnerved him.

As he turned back to his mother's discussion, the entire group noted a sudden spark of interest in Alfred for the topic, and his mother bestowed on her eldest a small, thin smile which he promptly chose to ignore.

Eventually Alfred bothered himself to ask Selda Bannoch more specifics about Mr. Brown and his work and the discussion soon took a surprising turn.

In explaining how Mr. Brown's star had risen to the heaven in past years, the widow Bannoch mentioned offhandedly that her brother-in-law had fallen into the shipping industry, an aside which had soon consumed and increased his work to a great profit.

If the mention of Star Cottage had piqued Lady Brooks' interest with the possibility of a fine dower for her son, it was the word *shipping* which now drew Lord Brooks into the conversation with the power of a heavy magnet.

And so Lord Brooks was suddenly and completely fascinated, and it was all too obvious to Selda Bannoch that she had hit on the trump card without realizing she'd held it all along. Such was her luck in the world, she told herself with pleasure, and with the merest hint of condescension she smiled at the Brookses. So then it was the simplest of tasks to cover the truth with a bold lie, and so she told them her brother-in-law was in shipping still.

★★★

Theodosia had struggled with her conscience and then she'd struggled with her thoughts, but now she struggled to drag the ladder stair back over to where it had rested a week before.

She was determined to read that will.

She pulled and she pulled and finally the stair sat against the shelves once more. She stepped lightly up the stair, and clasped her hands together before she reached. This was the time, the very moment in time, that she had reserved to *really* consider her conscience.

"Here you stand, Theodosia Brown," said she, but that was as much consideration as she was presently willing to give to the question.

She cast her eyes behind her and around the room to make certain she was still alone. She reached for the red volume, but then— whoosh—the glass doors opened from the garden.

Snatching back her hand, she stepped back. What made her retreat was one of those mysteries about herself she would never understand, for of course, there was nowhere to retreat *to*. Down she went.

"Miss BROWN!" cried Austin, bounding toward her.

"Oh. Oh, why did I do it?" she cried pitifully. At the last moment she grasped at the carving on the bookshelf and kept herself from falling all the way to the bottom. With some effort, she pulled upward and succeeded in tearing her sleeve. She groaned once more. Austin was at the bottom of the stair by the time she steadied herself completely on the ladder.

"I suppose I'm too late," he said. "I came back thinking you might... need assistance."

She turned to look down at him, and her face was cherry pink.

He smiled.

She laughed a bit uncomfortably and carefully made her way back down the stair.

"May I?" Austin stepped up the stair before she could realize why. "Is this the one you had in mind?"

To her horror she saw that he was reaching for the red volume. "NO!" she said quickly. "No, thank you," she added. "No... no."

"I gather that it is not the book," he said still smiling.

Her embarrassment was excruciating. "An-another entirely."

"Ah. This one?" He pointed to a little green book.

She gave him half a nod.

"Foul Play?"

"Pardon?" she gulped.

"This one is... *Foul Play.*"

"Oh, oh no. That is not the one, after all.... It must be standing further to the right, I think."

He knew she wasn't telling him the truth, but he decided to make her chafe under the circumstance for as long as he could.

"This. This must be the one!" he said happily as he looked back down to her.

She smiled sweetly.

"Thrown Together. A Story."

Her face went pale. "No." How could she end this insufferable little game?

"Ah this, then, is the one," he said boldly. "*He Knew He Was Right.*"

She blanched once more and shook her head, but quickly rallied. "The one I truly wish for, sir, is *Why Did He Not Die?* Is it there?"

Theodosia had used the name of her sister's favorite novel to good effect. Austin Brooks was too stunned to speak for a moment and then found himself laughing too hard to speak for another. She tried not to laugh and kept up most of a somber appearance. "Is it not there? I thought I saw it. But perhaps I should be the one to look for it, after all. I promise to be more careful on the stair this time."

"Good show, Miss Brown. You win this round." Austin stepped back down the little stair, still chuckling. Then, with sincerity, "And I do hope you will find what you're looking for."

"I'm sure I shall, thank you," she snipped and daintily took herself back up the stair. But she turned to look at him even as he stood below watching her. She cocked her head and smiled with a glint in her eye.

He nodded. "Miss Brown, you are becoming altogether too proficient at dismissing me, I think." But he smiled as he spoke and then turned and walked back out the doors.

When she was once more alone, she looked back to the row of books and saw with some surprise the very titles he had read aloud. They were all there, and he had not had to make up a one! This could only be Lady Brooks' private collection. More than slightly surprised to think the Lady read anything of their ilk, she knew there could be no other answer.

This family was surprising her in strange ways, but—and here she looked back toward the rose garden—not all of them unpleasant.

Austin's sudden visit had jarred Theodosia's mind, however, to the extent she no longer burned to read the family will. On the contrary, she was all too certain now she would be caught trying, and so she perused the titles directly before her instead. *Wilde Flowers of the Virginia Colony* caught her eye. She pulled it from the shelf and stepped carefully back down.

She rolled a deep chair to the large round drum table in the center of the room, sat down, and opened the book to find hand-painted engravings of all her favorite flowers. Fiona Mienzes had asked Theodosia to speak to her students about America, and now Theodosia wondered if she could borrow the beautiful volume to show the children.

Her eyes rested on the picture of a starry little blue bachelor button, causing her to feel the familiar pull of homesickness, when Lady Brooks and Aunt Selda entered the room from the rose garden. Lady Brooks seemed a bit more pleased to see her than she had before. But Theodosia was only thankful that the Brooks will had not been found in her lap just then.

After a short discussion, Lady Brooks graciously agreed to allow Theodosia to borrow the book, and Theodosia was quite surprised at Lady Brooks' affability. In fact, she did not seem at all the same woman Theodosia had shared tea with an hour before.

The carriage was brought around then, and Theodosia and her relations headed "home" to Star Cottage. And while she was glad to hold the book, and she enjoyed the view of the pastoral hills, the thick stone walls, and the cool tunnels of trees grown over the deep and ancient roads as they bumped along them, she still wished more than anything she were really headed home that day and not to a cold Sunday supper with her equally cold relations.

***

Fiona Mienzes was brought to Thistledown the year before to school the local children—ten boys and five girls. The luxury of an education was, of course, provided to the town by the good people of Brooks House. Now, although the term was almost ended, Fiona would stay there that summer, she explained to her new friend, because she'd found a tutoring situation nearby. In the next breath, though, she spoke of her Scottish home and her wish to be there, sentiments the American girl readily shared, and then Theodosia knew why Fiona was staying in Thistledown—monies could not be overlooked for homesickness.

It came to light in their conversation that a certain number of families from Fiona's hometown—twin cousins, an aunt and uncle, the family of her best childhood friend and, most importantly, a sister—had emigrated to America. Her older sister had fallen in love with a visiting American a dozen years before and he'd taken her back to his home. When Fiona found that Theodosia was from Virginia, the friendship was sealed, for Virginia was the very place to which he'd stolen her sister away. Fiona wanted to know everything. Theodosia was charmed with Fiona and pleased to have made a friend so quickly, and so they fell together, leaning on each other when they thought of home, and laughing together when they weren't.

And so Theodosia very much looked forward to meeting the children Fiona had spoken of so often.

Of course, Aunt Selda thought it a waste of Theodosia's time to visit the school, but since Selda wished a little time to herself and Cecelia had already planned her afternoon, she let Theodosia go.

Theodosia began the ride to the school in the Bannochs' carriage but soon felt the call of a walk along the road. She asked the coachman to halt and requested he pick her up at the school. He argued as politely as he could, but to his surprise, even as he spoke, she jumped down out of the carriage, smiled and waved him to go on.

He stayed for a moment, and as he looked down at the young lady, he decided he was not in the business of bodily placing strong-headed young ladies back in carriages. He'd had quite enough of Cecelia Bannoch and her tantrums, thank you very much. And so he let her go.

When the sound of the carriage wheels had died away, Theodosia could hear the birds singing long, sweet notes as she stepped lightly along the road. She had half a wish to sing back to them. Looking around at the rolling hills, she sighed. This was like home—so like home, in fact, it hurt to look on it. Even without her spectacles, she could see the same stone walls, the whitewashed farms nestled along the creeks and streams, and a winding road not unlike her own drive which led to a house on the hill beside her.

But there were differences too.

First to be noted was the lush, deep green grass. She stopped to examine it more closely. She stood straight up, put her boot into the green and found to her surprise the grass a foot deep. Not like home at all!

She thought of how verdant England seemed compared to home, with fields such as these, lovely parks, and flowers in the windows of every farmhouse. No one seemed to have time for flowers back home. A back garden, perhaps, but nothing for your neighbors to enjoy when they strolled past. And she liked a thatch roof instead of shingles. She looked over at a field where sheep milled about. Even without her spectacles their wool appeared thicker than she could possibly imagine, but then when she looked back at the grass they fed on, she supposed it was not her imagination.

She cast her gaze far across the field and saw great pools of purple surrounding a wide tree in the middle of the grass. *That must be heather,* she thought. *Or lavender. Well, we don't have heather... no, we don't and it's a shame, but at least we have Queen Anne's lace.* She laughed as it occurred to her that her favorite field flower had an English name.

She looked back to the road that curved and led down to the town of Thistledown and she fell to wondering how many English had gone to America from Thistledown. *What must it take to give up your home that way? And what did it take for my grandparents? Well, when I get home, I will simply ask them, and I think they will tell me, too.*

Slowly she descended into Thistledown, a matter of a ten-minute walk—twenty if she'd begun from Star Cottage. All the buildings were of a gray-tan stone the color of tea with cream, and the little city had a cozy look that made her sigh with pleasure as she approached. The peaked roofs over every doorway, the high walls that held the homes together—it was as if one man had built a home and liked it so well he built another and another until he had made an entire city. The homes and shops were set one after the other, with no more form to the plan than ants on parade, and bright flowers tumbled from window pots and steps in a beautiful anarchy.

Two stone bridges led into the town, and she walked briskly across the west one that went into the heart of the village. As she began to pass the row of shops in the center of town she slowed her walk and looked at everything as carefully as she could. Past the shops, she turned left behind a large stone building and rested her eyes on the little pebble-dashed cottage—the public school. Fiona opened the door to greet her, and they gave each other a great hug.

Fiona then introduced Theodosia to the fifteen students who were lined up along two long benches in the small space inside. While the little girls' eyes widened, few of the boys seemed impressed by their visitor. But having an older brother herself, Theodosia was not at all surprised with their behavior.

After introductions, Theodosia produced the book of wild flowers and began to discuss the land of Virginia. She saw a world of questions in their eyes as she spoke, and finally she allowed time for them.

The questions came one after the other and Theodosia did not stop answering for at least an hour. "Have you seen Ind'ans, miss?" "Do ye know your President?" "How big are the mountains there?" They were shocked to hear that the whole of England was roughly the size of her own home state, probably one-twentieth the size of the entire continent, and they were shocked again to find she had indeed seen Indians. Momentarily disappointed to find they were peaceful Indians, Iroquois who passed through town to confer with statesmen in Washington, the students rallied by asking her to describe each one she'd seen in great detail, and then the boys began an imaginary war with tomahawks.

When the war was ended by the Great Chief Mienzes, the boys settled down and asked the bigger questions: "Is the land really free to anyone?" and "What would it cost to go there?" One timid little girl actually asked if there were men to marry in America. While amused at their intensity, Theodosia also saw that more than a few were in dire earnest. These were the ones most poorly dressed, she sadly noted. These were the ones who really listened and didn't laugh when she joked about her homeland. *My grand-parents,* she thought to herself somberly, *were likely as poor as these, and so perhaps I will not ask them why they came to America, after all.*

While she found herself exhausted by the children's persistent attentions, all told, she enjoyed her visit immensely. When Fiona finally dismissed the class for playtime out-of-doors, she took Theodosia aside to thank her.

"Ye almost make me wish to go wi' ye to America, Tee. I believe ye could talk milk to butter!"

Theodosia laughed. "Well, I don't see why you *shouldn't* go back with me. You should go to visit your sister."

"And my niece. They have a daughter, and I've never e'en laid eyes upon her." Fiona's eyes misted for a moment, then she laughed. "But I ken there's many a lonely soul in America who hasn't seen their relatives in quite a while."

"Speaking so long about my home... it makes me long for it and...by Heaven, it hurts."

"And here I am making ye speak of it all the livelong day."

Theodosia smiled a tired smile.

"I canna' help you get back home, Tee Brown, but if ye're looking for something to take yer mind away from here, you could help me. Are ye good at arts?"

"Fair to middling."

"Ah! Lord bless ye. What is it ye know how to do?"

Theodosia thought for a moment. "Would the children like their likeness cut from paper?"

"Ye mean a profile?"

"Yes." Theodosia rattled the chains pinned to her waist. "You see? I forgot to take off my chatelaine this morning, and so I even have my embroidery scissors with me!"

"Tee, that'd be wonderful, it would, but..." Her eyes swept

over her charges as they came in from playtime, and she took to whispering the rest of her words: "... but I have to tell ye, it may not be considered... it may not be..."

"Are you saying someone would disapprove?"

"Do yer common folk have their profiles made?"

"Of course they can, if they want," answered Theodosia, but as she thought on it she wasn't quite sure.

"I see. Well, here it's only the society children have their profiles made, and so it mought offend the parents."

"But wouldn't they be pleased to have something they can't usually afford?"

"Well, now, it's not a matter of affording. It's only a bit of paper."

"Don't they ever want to enjoy what upper society might enjoy?"

"It's not like that, either. How can I explain it to ye? It's... well, it's like the charwoman doesn't mind being looked down upon by the butler as long as she's treated better than the chimney sweep, do ye see? Everyone has their place. Naw, don't look at me that way. It gives them comfort. They know who they are and there cooms a great satisfaction with that. In truth, they get angry if someone suggests another way."

Theodosia sighed as she remembered touching the arm of Aunt Selda's personal maid and how the woman took it as an insult. "I could live here years and not understand, I'm afraid. But, for today, let's ask the children. And if they don't want one, they shan't have one."

Fiona's eyes sparkled. "I like yer thinking all too well, Miss. And though it lands me in a kink o' trouble, I'll go and get some paper for ye. Ye're dangerous close to makin' me an American."

If the children thought they shouldn't, they never expressed the opinion, because for the next hour, Theodosia cut a silhouette of every child in the room. Then for an hour more she taught them how to do it on their own. Some of the students showed a great ability for the art, and their teacher wondered at their God-given talents.

The poorest children seemed to stare at their profiles a little longer than most. Fiona told her that though the children wouldn't speak of it, they'd probably never seen their likenesses beyond reflections in a stream bed or a water bucket. The knowledge at once amazed and disgusted Theodosia. "A bit of paper to tell them who they are, while in America they could truly make something of themselves," she mumbled rather smugly. Still, as she looked about her at the happy faces of the children and listened to their kind farewells, she felt that all in all the day was a great success.

But the day could not be seen as a great success for Austin Brooks.

He too had come to Thistledown that morning but at the crack of dawn and with a step so fierce dogs and chickens scattered before him into the hedgerows and thickets to keep out of his way. His face was pale and shiny with sweat—sweat from anger as well as from the effort of the walk.

He made his way toward the center of the village to the little cottage behind the church, and after knocking with loud determination, a bleary-eyed servant boy creaked the door open and let him enter. The boy led him to a by-room where he was asked to wait for the Reverend. As he waited, he paced about the little office. He stopped only once at the mantel to thump it with his fist, and then he began to pace once more.

Finally, still tying his robe about him, the Reverend Pickett entered the room. "Good morning." He smiled. "And what brings you here so early? Care for some breakfast tea?"

Austin nodded stiffly in greeting. "No tea, thank you. I'm sorry to disturb you so early."

"Oh, it's nothing, really. As they say, I had to get up anyway..." He smiled once again. "To greet a visitor."

Austin hardly heard his jest. "Yes, well, I've come into a bit of a shock, Reverend... and there's only you to tell." He glanced at the servant boy, and with a nod from the Reverend, the servant turned, left the room, and shut the door behind him.

"Well then, sit down. Sit down, Austin. This is what I'm here for."

The Reverend took the chair at his desk while Austin sat himself across from him, on the very edge of the leather seat, as if at any moment he might wish to flee.

"What is it, son?" the Reverend asked with a kind smile.

"*Son*. Ha. Yes. That's the very word, Reverend, the very word." Austin wiped the sweat from his chin with one hand and laughed nervously. "Just yesterday morning I knew who I was." His right hand flew out from him, but then he brought it in to thump it on the arm of the chair. "But..."

"But?" asked the Reverend.

Austin tapped his fingers against the wood of the arm and then suddenly gripped it fast. "But then, you see, Reverend..." He laughed again sharply. "Just last night I found I am not the son of Alfred Lord Brooks."

FIVE

෴

Lucy Locket lost her pocket,
Kitty Fisher found it;
Nothing in it, Nothing in it,
But the binding round it.

Nursery Rhyme

෴

It had rained on and off again all morning and the ladies of Star Cottage were confined to sewing in the parlor. Theodosia could only stand the passing hours by telling herself that perhaps tomorrow would be sunny and she might walk around the grounds. Walking was her mainstay—her means of getting out—and her only form of exercise, to date. When she'd first considered spending a summer here, she had at least hoped to attend a ball or two, but her aunt had told her only this morning that she would not be attending the Ladies' Charity Ball with them because "her cards had not yet arrived from the print shop."

"Couldn't my name be written in? My father considers my hand quite good at a copperplate script."

"Vulgar!" Aunt Selda quipped. "The suggestion is completely vulgar. No, you simply shan't attend a ball or go with us on visitations until they arrive." And that was that. Never mind that Selda Bannoch had deemed it perfectly acceptable for Theodosia to visit Brooks House for tea without a calling card to announce herself.

Theodosia sighed and then fell to wondering if Fiona might consider a visit to her classroom twice in one week odd, but her aunt interrupted her thoughts.

"Theodosia, now that you have properly met the Brookses' sons, you must tell me what you think of them," said Aunt Selda with a confidential grin. It was the sort of look Theodosia's mother gave her when she had something delicious to tell, but to see it on

Aunt Selda gave Theodosia an entirely different feeling.

How can the two sisters be so different? she thought as she looked into her aunt's sparkling eyes. *The same parents, the same upbringing and all the same advantages. Uncle Robert isn't like Selda either, although he can be gruff at times.* She cast down her gaze, pondered how to answer politely, and decided on, "It seems Mr. Alfred Brooks is to be a great scientist."

"He will be, he will be," replied Selda cattily, but Theodosia was concentrating on her sewing and didn't see the look or hear the intent of the words. "But one does not need to refer to his Christian name. As the eldest, he is simply Mr. Brooks, and someday *Lord* Brooks."

Cecelia Bannoch breezed into the parlor smelling of powder and a heavy perfume. "He needs a bit of refining, but his maman will help to make something of him, I'm sure."

"Mr.... *Allan* Brooks asked me all about America." Theodosia tried to hide the irritation in her voice.

"And how did you reply, cousin?" asked Cecelia with false interest.

"Well, it's certain I did not reply to please him, but it can't be helped. I only told him the truth."

Aunt Selda snorted slightly. "Yes. There's no pretty picture to be made of America. I've heard publicists try to fill the English youth with notions of sailing off for gold and such. The Brooks men most certainly belong here in their own place."

Theodosia understood Selda to mean she thought the girl had spoken poorly of America. "Oh, no, Aunt. I gave him a fair picture. I told him about homesteaders and the like..."

"Parker," said Selda stiffly.

"Yes, Parker," said Theodosia defensively.

"Theodosia, I don't believe your parents would have you boasting of your brother's present *accomplishments* to everyone you meet."

"Whatever do you mean?"

"I only mean the obvious! *They are not pleased with him.* They want more for him than this... this hunting of muskrat. Your papa should have help in his law firm."

"Beaver."

"What? Whatever. Traipsing around the woods in a leather loincloth, I suppose. Truly ridiculous behavior for any man."

"Buckskins, Aunt. He's not an Indian." Theodosia was growing furious. To the best of her knowledge, her parents had never pressured Parker to join her father. Parker always set his own course.

But then, she thought with dismay and a growing knot in her stomach, perhaps her parents would not tell her of such things. Vaguely a memory was triggered of a whispered, angry conversation between her mother and father—something about Parker going off into the woods, his being in danger, when a legal career would be safe and secure—but she was only a child of ten then and could not remember it very well.

Her aunt was implying that her parents' expectations were something Aunt Selda was privy to while she was not. The thought only encouraged her growing insecurities.

"A true Lady wishes only the very best prospects for her son," Aunt Selda added blithely.

And so you must have wished very hard for a spoiled fop, Theodosia thought harshly, remembering Frederick Bannoch, but she bit her lip for fear of saying it out loud.

"And for a daughter?" asked Cecelia.

"Of course, for a daughter, as well. Of course," said Aunt Selda, but with considerably less enthusiasm.

Cecelia gave a bitter little snort as she gathered up the sewing things from her workbag.

Theodosia looked back and forth at the two as they sat together in strained silence. Just how many secrets did Aunt Selda hold within her and how many of those secrets had she held from her own children? She stared at Aunt Selda's bent and rigid head. This was a woman of whom Theodosia was learning to be greatly afraid. More powerful than rifle shot, Selda Bannoch's words could cut a person down in as little time and with seemingly greater force, and Theodosia realized that the great task that lay before her this long summer would be to keep out of the line of fire, but today she had failed. Her eyes grew misty as she thought of her brother and Selda's unkind words; could it be her parents kept more than this from her, too?

"Excuse me, Aunt Selda, Cecelia, I believe I've left something in my room." Theodosia stood up and gave a swift curtsy. She hurried down the hall and kept the tears from streaming down her cheeks just until she was in her room and the door was shut behind her.

"I'm glad I've a thick skin, Maman. Your words don't pierce me as they do your niece."

Her mother said nothing.

"Will you make her marry Alfred then?"

"*Mr.* Brooks, Cecelia."

Cecelia put down her sewing to look at her mother. She was glad at the moment to see Theodosia—most particularly someone beside herself—falling under the weight of her mother's power, but she was not particularly glad to see Alfred Brooks take a portion of the blow. "What has Mr. Brooks done to you, Maman, that you should wish to unite him with my rustic cousin for life?"

"It would be best if you kept such thoughts to yourself." And the mother gave the daughter her hardest glance, which momentarily quieted Cecelia.

***

Austin Brooks stood in the light English rain knocking on the Reverend's door once more. And once more he was ushered into the study, but the Reverend was already at his desk.

"Did you find your answers then?"

"The solicitor would not say two sentences about it, Reverend." Austin shook the rain from his cloak and then took off his hat and cloak. "Of course, he demanded I give him the thing, but he won't get it until I know what the devil it is. Do you think he even has a copy of the will himself, sir?"

"I should think he does, yes, but he wouldn't want you spreading the content of this one about."

"He threatened to tell my fath... Alfred Lord Brooks if I didn't give it over, but I told him that I would not tell anyone but you, and then quite suddenly he seemed to want to believe it. Rather obvious he doesn't want to speak to Brooks about it any more than I."

"He is your father, Austin. Remember what we spoke of this morning. Brooks is your father in deed if not in truth. You'll have to allow for that. He's certainly treated you as a son."

"He's not been honest with me."

"Ha. You've a harsh measure for fatherhood! Who could live up to it? Look at it from his perspective." He brushed the table top with his hands. "An adopted child is treated as hired help in other homes. He wanted better for you."

"But the will says I'm to know at twenty-one, so one year from now I would have found out anyway." His voice rose as he continued. "So, looking at it as you say from his perspective, did he only care to treat me as a son for twenty-one years? Is that all he could stand of me?"

"You're angry, Austin, and it's coloring your thinking. You've a right to be angry for a time. We'll speak again on it."

"But I don't want to speak of it. I don't want to talk to... Lord Brooks. I don't want anyone to know."

They sat in silence for a moment, Austin brooding and Reverend Pickett silently praying for him.

Suddenly a look of utter disgust passed over the young man's face. "Miss Brown. She's read it."

"How do you know?"

He gave a wry smile. "I would never have looked in the book if it weren't for the fact she had reached for it before me." He gave a disgusted grunt. "No wonder she wanted to see the library again."

"Eh?"

He shook his head. "She's seen it, I'm sure." He nodded. "Of course. Treating me like a servant from the first time she met me. She must have found it the first day. I've made an utter fool of myself."

"We'll need to speak to her. This sort of thing can become

quite ugly. If she's read it, we need to discover her intentions."

"Yes, I suppose so." He remembered Theodosia's cheerful face at that moment in the library and with a slight turning of the image in his mind he could begin to see the pretty little smile as more of an evil grimace. *"No, thank you, Austin, you may go," she had said bluntly... and more than once. She had known then. She must have known then. And who had she already told?* He could just imagine her conversation with her Aunt Selda:

"Auntie, I discovered Lord Brooks' will in the library."

"Yes?" A look of brutal greed glows in Selda Bannoch's eyes.

"It says Austin Brooks is an orphan child; the Brookses never wanted to adopt him. Can you believe it?"

"Believe it? Of course I can believe it. He's never been a Brooks. A charity case! Really, I've always known it..."

"I should bring Miss Brown here right away," said Austin tersely.

"Yes, I, uh, yes. I suppose so."

Austin rose quickly to leave, but the Reverend held up his hand.

"Before you go, may we ask the Lord's guidance and blessing? I know you're grieving, but you know who to turn to now, don't you?"

"Funny that... I can't seem to get through to God today, or perhaps He can't get through to me. You pray, Reverend, I haven't really the heart for it." And Austin walked quickly from the room.

He walked straight toward Star Cottage. The rain stopped as he walked along, but he was disappointed for it suited his mood perfectly. Yesterday he was the son of Alfred Lord Brooks, and a clerk in his father's firm of Brooks Tea. Knowledgeable in the ways of the tea business, he looked forward to his last two years at Cambridge and from there assuming more responsibilities in the firm. He had wanted to build ships of trade.

Today what he wanted meant absolutely nothing to anyone.

Today he was marked the son of unknown parents. His heritage could be that of a common laborer or worse. He'd heard such children were taken from the arms of those in debtors' prison.

That was what he had really wanted to ask the solicitor: from where did I come? Who am I then? Whose child am I? But he could only speak of the will itself, a thing that meant nothing to him.

How would he fit into Lord Brooks' world now? Did his "father" expect him to continue on when he came of age next year? Or did he plan to cast him adrift? The language of the will was so convoluted it was difficult to tell; he would need an interpreter. Did it state his true name? he wondered.

"My name... my true parents would have given me another name. I have already been cast adrift." He kicked a clod of dirt before him and sent it sailing.

"Wotch out there then!" cried a youth whose cart caught the clod of dirt in the next instant. "Oah, it's only you, Mister Austin." Henry Taylor brought his cart to a halt.

Henry Taylor was a boy of seventeen who looked all of twenty-one from the work he put in on his parents' farm. Dark-haired and tall like his father, he was stronger than any boy in school and was a fine match for Austin in a wrestle.

"Hello, Henry," said Austin quickly.

"There a fire hereabouts?" Henry chided.

"No," said Austin with a thin smile, walking quickly past Henry and thwacking the side of the boy's cart as his coattails flew behind him. "Now be off with you."

Now Henry had a question for Austin Brooks, a question that had made him search for Austin ever since that morning when it first formed in his mind, but Henry was not used to a sharpness in Austin's tone and the words cut him. As Austin walked away, Henry quipped, "Well, I can see you're an important man, then, eh? A man who can't be bothered."

The words stopped Austin dead in his tracks and made Henry gulp; he'd never spoken like that to him before, and having said it and being unable to take it back, he had no idea what Austin Brooks might do next.

Austin turned to look back at young Henry with a grim expression on his face. "Not today, Henry. Not today," he said in a defeated whisper.

Austin turned his face back to the road, and Henry stood and watched him as he walked around the corner and away. The boy could have sworn he saw tears in Mr. Brooks' eyes, but he could not believe it possible. He'd never seen a gentleman cry.

Austin moved on with determination, the anger now roiling within him. Wasn't it like a woman to get a piece of information on a man and use it as she liked? As he thought of Selda and Cecelia Bannoch, he smiled. *The apple never falls far from the tree.* But then he thought morosely, *And so from what tree am I? For all I know, I've a murderer for a father or a whore for a mother. Maybe both.* He grimaced. His hands were bloodless fists at his side. *Perhaps instead of speaking to Miss Brown, it would fall to me to kill her. How should I know? Lord, God, who am I? The Scripture says 'the sins of the father are visited on the sons....'*

Austin's melancholy was interrupted by the sounds of a carriage approaching. He heard his name called out and turned to see the balding pate of Reverend Pickett as he opened the carriage door.

"Austin! Get in. I'm glad to find you. Afraid you'd be too quick for me."

For a moment Austin thought to ignore the man and keep moving down the road. But then he caught the Reverend's pleading look, and it brought him around. Begrudgingly, he stepped up into the carriage.

"I got to thinking about you as you left my office, and I thought better of sending you out here alone. A visit from you will only cause conversation in that household, and the whole matter would create a great deal of consternation for yourself, I'll warrant, at a time when you've enough on your mind."

Austin smiled slightly and licked his lips as he settled back in his seat. "You're right about that, Reverend. I'm not certain that I'm quite in my right mind today."

"Yes, it did look as though you were carrying the very fires of damnation about your neck, and I do think Miss Brown deserves the benefit of a doubt as to her guilt in the matter. Besides, the carriage would mean she wouldn't necessarily have to speak to you at all, unless she requested it."

"Have me stay put? Wait for you?" The idea didn't please him at first, but after all, this man of God was the one who had brought him to Christian faith a few years before, and although his faith felt far from him that day he owed not a little something to the gentleman, and he also thought it likely the Reverend had dealt many times with crises similar to this. Besides, he was starting to calm himself—the Reverend's whole demeanor had a way of calming him—and so he finally nodded.

"That's it. Yes. You've a lot on your mind, Austin, and this little business is only one thin root on a whole tree, don't you think?"

"A thin root." The Reverend's reference to trees amused Austin in the light of his previous thoughts and he smiled grimly and gave the Reverend another nod.

"Good. Good. Besides, I've a good pretense for a visit—some things to ask Selda Bannoch concerning the Ladies' Charity Ball, I think." Reverend Pickett was smiling casually at the young man, but he was on his knees before God for him in his heart.

***

Theodosia had dried her tears, dressed for supper and now sat in her room half-afraid to move. Supper was not for another hour, and though she'd left her sewing workbox in the parlor she was not about to go and get it—not while they were still there. She turned to a book she'd taken from her cousin's collection and looked at the title, *Was She Engaged?* She couldn't help laughing as she remembered her conversation with Austin. Wouldn't he have enjoyed using this title to bait her? Though there was no one in the room, she felt herself blushing. There was no denying it. She liked Austin very much.

She carefully opened the book and looked over the front plate; in the drawing, a young woman tended to an aging gentleman and the line written beneath it said, "Sarah resigned herself to the benevolent duty of sharing Lucy's cares as nurse and housekeeper."

"Hmm," said Theodosia. "Leave it to Cecelia to choose a melancholy love story." Setting it back down with a disappointed sigh, she looked out the window for a moment. The sky was gray, but it was not raining any more. "The sky is always gray here. Especially here, I think. Over this house. I need some fresh air." She thought of Austin's words, that Cecelia had fallen out this very window. The sash of the window was only two feet off the ground. It would be a simple matter to cross over it. She could take a short walk, come back, and no one would know she'd been gone. Delightful.

She gathered up her skirts and made it over the window sash, tearing her hem only slightly on the shutter hinge—for her a minor triumph. She passed around the portico and found the steps into the yard. Not wishing to be seen in case her aunt and cousin had moved from their appointed seats in the parlor, Theodosia moved quickly away from the house into a small wooded area. "Oh, but I wish I knew where Aunt hid my spectacles," she moaned.

But as if to bless her decision to take an afternoon stroll, in the next few seconds the sun broke through the clouds and in a few seconds more she found a path in the woods ahead of her. "This is wonderful!" she whispered, thinking of the paths she wandered as a little girl in the forest behind her Virginia home.

It took no more than half a minute for her to disappear completely into the line of verdant trees.

***

Reverend Pickett approached the door of Star Cottage, praying that he would find an innocent young girl who knew nothing whatever of wills and artifice. He had his doubts, but he banished them as he prepared his words to her in his mind. He found it was always best to provide people with the benefit of the doubt. Such explanations of behavior as he'd heard in his lifetime had demanded from him an open mind; people did the oddest things for the oddest reasons, he had often told his wife, and she would whole-heartedly agree.

The memory of his pleasant wife brought a smile to his lips as he was ushered into the front parlor. Selda Bannoch soon greeted him. They chatted amiably for a few moments before he stated his purpose, a visit with their American visitor, if he might.

And so a servant was sent to bring Miss Brown from her room.

He chatted on and on with Mrs. Bannoch about the upcoming Ladies' Charity Ball, but all the while he was planning a means to enjoy Miss Brown's company alone. Perhaps he could suggest they take a walk; it would be unlikely Selda Bannoch would wish a walk. If that was not possible, he would suggest Theodosia come to the vicarage for a tour. The home was not very old by English standards—a manor-style edifice built around 1500—but he hoped an American might be impressed with its age.

Selda Bannoch was discussing the hanging of new drapes in the church loft when the servant reentered to state smartly that Miss Brown was not at home.

The Reverend was horrified to think she was refusing to meet him; certainly, his worst fears were being realized. He looked to the Widow Bannoch, wondering if she knew.

But Selda Bannoch's attention was focused on the servant. "Whatever do you mean? Is she unwell?" She gave a nervous sidelong glance and smile toward the Reverend and cleared her throat. "An American constitution, I'm afraid."

"No, Mistress." The servant whispered the next for fear of impropriety, "I mean she isn't in the home. She's gone out."

"You can't mean she's gone. Look again," Selda Bannoch said more sharply.

The servant curtsied and left, knowing better than to cross her mistress. She walked smartly down the hall, turned the corner and went down the stairs, as she just then decided to have a cup of tea while she "looked."

Selda Bannoch smiled uncomfortably at her guest, and the Reverend, who had prepared himself for many things but not for this, smiled uncomfortably back. ᘇ

SIX

❧

With a youth's ardent passion he met her,
Seeming holy, and gentle, and wise;
And, oh, then for both it were better
Had she gave him a frown, not a fetter,
And spared him a draught from her eyes!

By "Jonquil"
Was She Engaged?

❧

Austin Brooks sat in the Reverend's carriage barely able to keep himself still.

A movement in the distance caught his eye and he looked out the carriage window toward the woods to the far left and behind Star Cottage. Probably a deer. He looked again and saw a path over along the edge of the trees. He glanced back at the front door of the imposing home, then turned his eyes back to the woods once more and thrust open the door of the carriage. As he stepped down he told the driver, "Tell the Reverend Pickett I had to stretch my legs. I'll be back soon."

The driver nodded, and Austin Brooks took the path toward the woods. His mind ran with the same thoughts that had plagued him all day. How was it he came to be adopted? Who were his real parents? What would be his future? Why would God allow this to happen to him? *Why me and why now?* he asked over and over.

"God in Heaven, why!?" he cried aloud as he entered the woods.

* * *

"Miss Mienzes?"

"Henry! Good afternoon, Henry," she answered cheerfully.

Henry had found Miss Mienzes by the school on his way home

to supper and, upon seeing her kind face, decided she might be just the sort of person to ask, since he hadn't been able to press Austin Brooks.

"Miss Mienzes, I've got a question wonts answerin'... I mean, I have a question, if you will."

Fiona smiled. Henry was one of her students of whom she was most proud. "Ask aw'y, Henry, and I'll see if I've an answer for ye."

"Well, I've been thinking ever since Miss Brown spoke to us this morning, and it's been on me mind and I've been wond..."

"My mind."

"*My* mind... that... I was wondering if you knew how much... you'd need... to go to America, that is, the cheapest way you could go there. I mean, if you could work your way across or something of the like."

"America?" Fiona's smile was lost as she looked at him. "Henry, ye're not thinking of going to America?"

"Wull..." Henry blushed. He hadn't realized the subject would displease his schoolmistress so. "I don't ask for *me* exactly. The other boys wanted to know..."

But to look at him she knew it was a lie. Her eyes narrowed as her face grew sad. "I don't know, Henry. I don't know the price. I should think there's a way for anyone who really wants to, though. Many a relation of mine has found a way. It's the will in these things that counts for something." He nodded, thinking intently on her words, but then she surprised him with her emotions as she continued, "Aw, but Henry, ye've got so much to look forward to here if ye'd only reach for it. And here be yer family, and yer friends and yer home."

"I was only askin', Miss," he said defensively. "It was... I was only askin'." He bowed and walked backward away from her.

Fiona pulled her hands together and drew them to her mouth as she watched him leave.

Henry finally pulled his hat back on his head and from a good distance said loudly, "Thank you anyway, Miss Mienzes." Then he turned and walked quickly toward home.

"See ye tomorrow then, Henry." But he was already too far away to hear. She turned and walked toward her cottage, the day's enjoyment snatched from her in an instant. "America," she said. "What have I done! They'll all be dreamin' of it now." She shook her head, then thought of her sister so far from home and blinked back the tears that came to her as she walked along.

* * *

Theodosia was enjoying her walk tremendously. She examined each of the wild flowers, recognizing some and marveling at ones she'd never seen, plucking them up in a lush handful to her heart's content. It was not an accident that she'd left behind her bonnet, parasol and gloves. Here in the deep green woods she could lay aside all the trappings of her present existence and finally give her mind over to rest and enjoyment.

Once she had a too full hand, she sat down on a fallen log and with nimble fingers began to weave the stems of flowers into one another. She quickly made a crown, just as she and her sister had done so many times as little girls. With the flowery wreath complete, and knowing she was alone, she felt free to place it squarely on her head, all the while thinking of her family and remembering the last time her sister had plaited just such a wreath for her. It seemed forever ago.

She stood up and began to walk again. "Martha, how I wish you could be here." Martha, the strong, Martha, the valiant. *She* would know what to do with Aunt Selda's rude remarks. "While I don't even realize I've been insulted until I think out what it is she's said, and by then it's too late to make a good retort... as if I could retort," she said sadly. Her father's face came to mind, and she could not imagine away his grim expression. No, she would have to behave herself no matter what. But she was counting the days until she could take a ship back home.

The path came into a circle of deep grass. Theodosia looked around to find a natural round of trees set about her like a verdant castle turret. The edge of the woods was overgrown with frothy bushes, fairy-light flowers and pale ferns just as the path had been, but here a warm, dappled light fell freely from the opening above. And so the flowers were made brighter, and the grass, if it were possible, was even greener.

Just the place for a fairy dance.

"Come and dance, Tee. If we dance and sing here in the middle of the woods, don't you know the fairies will come and join us?"

"Martie, I don't believe you."

"Just you wait and see. Come on then, dance!" her sister had commanded. *"Sing with me, 'Hand in hand with fairy grace, Will we sing and bless this place.' Come, child, or you're no sister of mine, and I'll leave you here for the fairies to steal you away!"*

And so we danced and sang until we fell down laughing and exhausted in the woods behind our home.

"There, now, Tee, didn't I tell you?"

"But, Martie, I din't see no fairies."

Martha's eyes had grown wide as she replied, "But there was a jolly fat one just under you! Why you almost stepped upon him...twice! Lucky for the little fellow his wife was there to pull him away both times."

Theodosia grinned. She was awed to hear her older sister's words. "Oh, how she must have laughed at me then—with my eyes big as saucers!" But a familiar pain grew in her heart as she thought, *But, no, she wasn't laughing at me. She said it all to please me, I know.*

Pulling her hand up to her heart, she swept her eyes up and down the path to be certain she was alone. She took a moment to straighten the flowers on her head, and then in the circle of light in the middle of the woods, she began to dance and sing.

"Hand in hand with fairy grace, Will we sing and bless this place..."

Austin Brooks was walking the selfsame path, but he was not looking at wild flowers. He did not stop to eat the wild strawberries as Theodosia had a few moments before. He was walking hard and furtively, he did not know to where.

He was thinking how pitiful a man he had so suddenly become

when he heard a small voice singing up ahead. His first inclination was to turn and walk back. He did not want to see anyone, not even to tip his hat as they passed. But the melody was gentle on the ears, and so he stopped to listen.

He walked slowly forward and around a bend in the path, and then ahead of him through the trees was a girl in a dark brown dress twirling in a circle of light.

On any other day the view might have charmed him, but on this day it was an irritation. *How dare someone be cheerful, how dare this girl enjoy herself!* might have been his thoughts if his conscious mind could have understood his soul at that moment. But Austin's anger was a living, breathing thing with a meaning and a purpose of which his soul was unaware. So then when he recognized that it was Theodosia Brown in the woods dancing as if she were a forest sprite, the only thing that came to his dulled brain was that hers was a dance of triumph meant to goad him.

She's ruined me. I have no family; my world is gone. Selda Bannoch will use the information like a stranglehold about my neck. He pulled his hands up to his face and began to hold his head as if the grip could keep his thoughts together, his mind from shattering to pieces where he stood. Slowly he pushed his fingers through his hair, knocking his hat to the ground behind him. And then the singing ended in a cry.

He looked up. Where did she go?

A brown form lay in the grass ahead of him. Quiet and still. Theodosia Brown had tripped and fallen.

His pulse quickened. Had she fainted? Hurt herself? This was truly pitiful. "Lord in Heaven," he said in a prayer he alone could understand, and he raised his fists into the air and brought them down with a heavy grunt.

And then he walked to where she had fallen.

Her body was deathly still. Her pale cheek rested on a round of moss, her brown hair lay in a tangle about her face and her arms were outstretched on the grass. A circle of flowers lay near one foot. Then he saw that her ankle was twisted under a gnarled root. And all the anger he'd been feeling moments before died away. He stooped and pulled the ankle from under the root, then rolled her to one side. He looked about for a stream or a pool nearby with water to wake her.

As he glanced down into her face once more, though, he saw she was starting to come around.

She blinked and moved her hand to her forehead. "Where...?" she asked but stopped when she caught sight of him.

"Where indeed?"

"Mr. Brooks?" She focused her eyes on the form stooping before her.

"Yes, Mr. Austin Brooks," he answered testily. The anger had returned with surprising ease.

"Oh. I must have fallen."

"Yes, you must have." He grasped one arm and pulled upward thinking she would follow.

But she cried out, "Stop! My ankle! I can't." He pulled once more in frustration. "I said I can't, sir! I can't get up." She looked into his face; she couldn't imagine what he was thinking. "This ankle... it hurts. I must have twisted it."

Dropping her arm, he said, "All right then!" in clear irritation.

Terribly confused by his behavior, Theodosia tried hard to think what she could have done or said that caused him to be angry with her. She could not think, and the pain in her ankle began to throb. "Mr. Brooks, whatever is the matter?"

"Nothing of consequence."

"Have I done something to offend you?"

"Have you?" he asked sourly. He was growing more impatient by the second. "Don't you think you can stand?"

She rubbed her ankle and pressed down momentarily. "Perhaps. Give me a moment."

He crossed his arms and frowned down at her. He was beginning to see things for what they were: she was feigning ignorance of the will because she was truly reliant on him for help just then— a pretty turn of events. Well, he would not be her fop, of that he was certain. "I'll go back to the house and tell someone you're here," he said, turning about on the path.

"No!" she cried, reddening as she thought of Aunt Selda. She gulped and more quietly she asked, "Couldn't you simply help me back? I... I don't wish to wait..."

He took a deep breath and turned back to her. *"Oh, you don't wish to wait.* Well, we mustn't make the lady wait."

"Mr. Brooks?" She stared at him and her lower lip trembled. "I really don't understand you. I don't wish to wait here... alone. I don't know why you're here, and perhaps you've some other place to be just now, but would it be such a bother for you to assist me?" Her heart had plummeted to earth. He was not the sort of man she'd taken him for after all. He was too like his brother Allan, and the disappointment at that moment hurt more than her ankle.

She spoke her piece so innocently and with such a tremor in her voice that Austin's heart was swayed toward her for a moment, but only for a moment. *Slick as glass she is,* he thought smugly. *Well, I'll not let her get away with it.* "You've said Americans are honest? Plain speakers, they call themselves? Well, I can be plain, too, Miss Brown. Can you tell me you didn't find the Brooks will in the library?"

Her face paled. She'd forgotten all about the will. "Yes, I mean, no. Yes," she said, choking on the words.

"Then you needn't ask me why I'm irritated, eh? That bit of nonsense can end right now."

Of course she should have told someone in the family. She should have, but she'd been deathly afraid Aunt Selda would discover what she'd found. "I'm sorry, Mr. Brooks. I'm dreadfully sorry."

"Not half as sorry as I am."

"But it wasn't my fault. I was reaching for something else when the book fell."

"These things happen," he said sarcastically.

"Well, *yes*... and especially to me."

"Used to it. Of course." *She must have no fear of me if she can be so bold; it's obvious she knows exactly what I am,* he thought morosely.

"And then, well, there it lay... and with my papa being a lawyer... a solicitor."

"Convenient for you," he said snidely.

"Yes, I mean... no. It's just... it's come to be a habit for me."

"A habit?" he asked with some surprise. "You must do very well by it, then."

She looked at him curiously. "Well... I have labored for my father on occasion." She rubbed her hands together and then applied her warm palms to her ankle. But her ankle was already quite warm all on its own. She winced and pulled her hands away. The swelling had begun.

"You must make quite a team," he continued.

She blushed. Her father would hardly think so.

"And what will you do with your information, that is, if you haven't already..."

"Well, I did tell one person."

They looked at each other and together said the names, "Selda Bannoch" and "Fiona Mienzes," on top of each other so that each stopped and stared at the other.

"What did you say?"

"I said I told Fiona Mienzes... the schoolteacher." Her eyes widened as she hastened to add, "Never, *never* would I tell my aunt!" As he was left wondering what exactly she meant and further if he should or could believe her, she continued, "I... I didn't rightly know who to tell, and Fiona . . ." She looked back down to the grass. "Well, she's the only friend I have here." She looked back up into his eyes and added, "I would have told someone in your house, really I would have, but I didn't know who, Mr. Brooks. I was so terribly embarrassed at finding it that day. I thought if I could become better acquainted with all of you... or even one of you... I might know... who... to tell..."

He was looking at her so oddly that she slowed her speech to take it in. It occurred to him that she might be telling the truth, and the thought was causing his throat to go dry. He coughed, but it didn't help.

"Well, 'truth will out,' as they say, and I feel better for it," she said with a flutter of a smile.

Without guile he replied, "Yes, 'truth will out,' but some truths take longer to swallow." He turned and looked back toward the house.

She checked her ankle again. It would be better for it if she removed her boot, but she was loathe to remove it in front of a gentleman. "Do you think you could help me back, now?" she asked quietly. "I think that I may stand."

"Yes." He looked up at the trees. "Yes, I'll help you back." He held out his hands to her. She held on to them, and he gently lifted her to her feet, but immediately she winced and leaned into him. The gesture bothered him as he was still trying to decide just exactly what she was about, but it was at least obvious to his confused mind that the girl was in considerable pain.

He looked about him briefly as if unsure of how to proceed when he saw her ring of flowers. "Will you be wanting the flowers then?"

"No. Heavens, no. I couldn't explain them to my aunt. She doesn't even know I'm gone." And then she thought with growing horror how it would be easier to hide a ring of flowers than it would be to hide her tender ankle.

"Oh." He turned back to her but then saw his hat on the path and, without thinking, left her side to retrieve it. "My hat," he said, but she cried out at having to stand alone on her ankle even for a moment. He faltered, caught between his hat and her voice. He quickly grabbed his hat and placed it haphazardly on his head, then hurried back to her.

She leaned on him once more and tried to take a step. Tears sprung to her eyes as she did so, and she bit her lip with the pain.

"This is no good, Miss Brown. I'll have to go and get someone."

"Oh, no. *Please* don't. I could say I sprained my ankle falling in the guest room. It wouldn't be the least unusual for me, I'm afraid."

Here he smiled, but the smile faded as the next thought occurred. "Then I'll have to carry you."

Her cheeks turned raspberry red, but she closed her eyes and nodded and with courage answered, "So be it."

Rather awkwardly he held out his arms toward her, trying to guess how he would hold her. She opened her eyes to see his dilemma and raised her arms slightly, tentatively, and then he scooped her up.

He was strong enough, and she was light enough, and so as he began to tromp back up the path he reasoned he could carry her the entire journey.

At first, Theodosia held her arm straight out behind him for fear of touching him, but as he moved briskly along she found she was destined to fall out of his arms if she didn't hang on to his coat. She glanced at his face, now no more than a foot from her own, and she thought she still could see a trace of anger. Anger seemed to be her lot this summer. "I am much obliged to you," she said. She hesitated to ask, but when she imagined her aunt's reaction to her present state, she knew she must. "I'm sorry to put you in such an odd position, but I'm certain my Aunt Selda will never understand this, Mr. Brooks. Do you think you could carry me to my window without anyone seeing us?"

A look of irritation passed over him but he nodded once and kept his eyes on the path. It occurred to him she meant she would not wish anyone to see her being carried by a man of uncertain birth. Nevertheless, he was holding her. He and no one else. And she was light and soft and smelled of the wild flowers she'd worn in her pretty hair, and then he was feeling sorry that he had to hate her for what she knew.

His thoughts were cut short by a question from the girl's pale pink lips. "Why did you think I'd tell my aunt?"

Bless her honesty. It served her well just then.

Abruptly halting in the path, he looked into her face, the long straight nose, the soft cleft in her chin, the wide brown eyes searching his own. "Well... Well... I..." He blinked and tried hard to think of why she would ask him that, but he was tired of trying to think as a she-devil might. His mouth moved toward an explanation but he faltered every time. "I don't know. I thought you might... I don't know."

"Mm," she answered, but she was thinking to herself, *Those are the most beautiful, most charming dimples I have ever seen on a man, and I think I could sit and listen to him talk for hours just to see them come and go.* Her lips took on the slightest curve of a smile as she looked with concentration upon the young man's face. The ankle throbbed as it had a moment before, but the pain did not seem real to her now. She began to think how becoming was his halting speech, how charming he was even in anger and finally how she enjoyed the tone of his voice in general. Now the contours of his face were fascinating to her as well, and with her curiosity aroused she was not the least embarrassed to examine them at length. From the wayward yellow curl on his wide brow to the tiny veined eyelids, the pointed flush on the golden cheek to the thick line of his jawbone, his face was pleasant to behold. She searched him with her eyes and there was a silence between them as she watched.

The sun gave little effort to reach down through the thickness of the trees to their little spot of earth. Deep green lay about them, bird song echoed against the branches, and a breeze blew the leaves along the path, but all this went unnoticed by the pair.

Austin Brooks was very much aware of her concentration and her little smile and equally aware of how he held her and how her arms returned his hold. Her look was one of admiration. What about him she had found to admire he couldn't guess, yet he knew it to be true. And what behavior did she expect from him now? Knowing what he was, that he had no inheritance, no family to speak of, still she gave him this budding smile? It baffled him, but he stood utterly still on the path and allowed the search to continue.

He swallowed as he viewed the gentle curve of her lips. And then, like a rippling wave on a tide of emotion, the thought reached his mind. One thought and one alone, and the consequences were not to be considered.

"I... I want to kiss you." He spoke the words as though the matter were a revelation to himself as well as to his audience.

In shock her lips parted to reply, but before any words could escape he stole them away.

The pain in her ankle was the likes of which she'd never known, but for the very first time in her life a young man was kissing her, and Theodosia Brown felt overwhelmed. That and the fact she couldn't breathe by the way he held her to himself could mean only one thing for the girl, and so fate decreed that in the next moment she fainted.

Without a sound her head fell away from him, and for one horrifying second Austin Brooks thought somehow he'd killed her. But he realized she had only fainted. "Miss Brown?" But she could not hear him. "Miss Brown?" he continued to say a little more desperately as he began again to tread toward the house.

He came out of the woods, but now he was unsure of where to go. He could take her to the carriage, but she'd said her aunt didn't know she'd gone out. He could walk her back to the window, but for pity's sake, he would have to carry her all the way to her bed. Pressing his lips together in thought, he saw a black form descending the front stair of Star Cottage. The form turned toward Austin and stood stock still. It was the Reverend Pickett.

"Miss Brown?" Austin said with urgency, but she was deaf to his words.

The Reverend Pickett hoped that now was not the moment in his long and fairly cheerful life in which he would suffer a fatal heart failure right on the front steps of Selda Bannoch's home, but for the life of him, all he could see was young Austin Brooks, hat askew and face pale, emerging from the woods with a lifeless female form in his arms, who even at this great distance could not be mistaken for anyone but the American girl. ❧

SEVEN

❧

May all to Athens back again repair,
And think no more of this night's accidents
But as the fierce vexation of a dream.
But first I will release the fairy queen.

William Shakespeare
A Midsummer Night's Dream

❧

Reverend Pickett crossed the three hundred yards between himself and his concern with an even greater effort than he would have mustered had he been late for Sunday services.

Meanwhile, Austin laid his burden on the grass before him, unable to choose her fate due to his agitated state of mind. He looked about him, then pulled up grasses and waved them in her face, all the while speaking to her in a loud and shaking voice.

Reverend Pickett soon stood over Austin and Miss Brown's face gave him pause—she was pale, so very pale.

"Austin, what's the trouble?" The Reverend stooped beside her still form.

"She's fainted, sir. Sprained her ankle. I happened on her in the woods there and she'd just fallen." He continued to fan her but was looking so intently at the Reverend that the grasses began to brush her face and nose.

Just then Theodosia raised her hand to move the offending reeds, and both men held their breath.

"What? Oh. I... I fainted. Austin?" she said quietly and a fair pink blush stole over her.

"Austin?" the Reverend repeated.

"Yes." He cleared his throat. "Austin Brooks, of course. And the Reverend Pickett. How are you... now?"

"My ankle... it hurts terribly." She glanced at the Reverend and then back to Austin.

"Yes. It was twisted under a root."

"I *know*," she replied, looking at him oddly. Had she just imagined a conversation with Austin on the path and further imagined his kiss? She stopped short her thoughts and touched her fingers to her lips. And though she quickly pulled her hand away again, the motion made Austin clear his throat and stand upright, and so she knew it was not her imagination at all. Furthermore, Austin glanced down toward the Reverend Pickett with a guilt-stricken look, and so she understood Austin's present conduct completely.

But the Reverend Pickett understood more than either of the two. He looked back toward Star Cottage and then at Austin. "I will help Miss Brown back home. If you would, Austin, I think it best you walk on through the woods. The carriage will come for you on the other side."

Austin hesitated but thought better of it and finally nodded. Bending slightly toward Theodosia, he haltingly pronounced, "I hope... I hope you will feel better soon, Miss Brown, and I hope I've not... put you to any trouble. I hope..." Here he grew completely flustered. "Well, I'm sorry to leave you here, but I couldn't decide if I should take you to the carriage or the bedroom..." He blushed vividly.

"Austin, *go!*" said Reverend Pickett firmly, and Austin, with relief and reluctance shook up together like dice in a barrel within him, took his jangled self away.

Reverend Pickett smiled as he helped Theodosia to her feet. "There now," he said, but the words were not enough to ease the pain.

They hobbled back to Star Cottage and entered the home, both praying silently that some mercy could be found in Selda Bannoch's heart. In short, each sought a miracle.

* * *

"Doxy."

"Well, I'm certain you'd know better than anyone, Allan."

"I tell you, American girls are all like that. I heard it, but I didn't believe it until we actually met her." He laughed. "She's loose, yes indeed... oh, but completely charming, Alfie. A perfect wife for you. She'll take her satisfaction from someone else, and you can be about your business."

"Oh, shut up, Allan, and don't bother me right now. This is almost come to the boil; decoction afterward of two parts... no, it was three." And he began to mumble to himself. Then he looked up at his younger brother. "Get out, would you?!"

"Of course, brother, of course," said Allan smoothly and he rolled himself up lazily from the laboratory table and ever so slowly took himself away.

He sauntered out of the building into the cool sunlight of the morning and crossed through the garden, where he peered into the orangery and saw through the glass that his mother was taking tea.

In a twinkling he was at her side.

"There you are, Mother!"

"And here you are, Allan. Away from your desk as usual."

"Had some business to do here in the house as a matter of record."

"Then have done with it and be on your way." Lady Brooks sniffed, but Allan knew his mother all too well. He sat down at the table and carefully poured himself a cup of tea.

"And what have you been up to then, Son?"

"Assuming the role of humanitarian, Mother. I was warning my brother of the pitfalls of matrimony."

"By right of your vast experience?"

"By right of my having actually observed marriages while my brother has had his nose in a book most of his life and wouldn't know a woman from a stalk of wolfsbane."

"Oh, I don't know, Allan; I think he'd note the difference in size right away," said Allan's father as he approached the tea table.

"Father."

"Son."

Allan sat back in the chair and watched his father take his tea. As he poured, the son asked nonchalantly, "Do you really think it wise to push my older brother into the matrimonial state?"

"Your question makes me immediately curious as to your interest in the matter," Lord Brooks replied with a touch of mockery as he carried his tea to his chair.

"Matrimony is not of personal interest, no, but I don't wish to see this family made a fool of," said Allan with a grim smile.

"We will not be made fools of, Allan," Lady Brooks interjected. "We know what we're about."

"Yes, but has anyone asked little Miss Brown if she's interested in our budding scientist?"

"*How can* you even think it? He is a Brooks! There won't be any question of *interest*. Of *course* she'll have an interest. I find it in extremely poor taste that your older brother felt he had to ask the same question of me earlier. This girl will jump at the chance. Jump!"

"She's an American, Mother, don't forget. They see things differently there."

"Not in the circles from which the young lady comes. No. The Widow Bannoch was very clear on the matter."

"But what's the hurry, Mother? Afraid the little dove will fly back to America before the dovecote can be built to hold her?"

Lord Brooks fidgeted with his pipe while Lady Brooks calmly poured herself another cup of refreshment.

Allan looked back and forth at the two of them and a light dawned in his little mind. "Might this have something to do with your new venture, Father?"

"Ahem." Lord Brooks shook his head and glanced at his wife.

Allan surmised his father's meaning and quickly added, "Well, I'll just get another cup..."

"Who was it had an appointment with Sir Randall this morning?" his father asked sternly.

"I have, sir, at noon," he answered with a wry smile.

"In my office?" his father asked with a nod.

By this Allan was certain he would be meeting his father right afterward to discuss business, more than likely the new venture itself.

* * *

"Is she all right?"

"Her ankle is badly sprained, as you surmised."

"Did she say anything?"

"Now, that's an interesting question, Austin. 'Did she say anything?' Hmm. And what if she had? What might she have told me, eh?"

Austin shook his head slowly and stared at the pattern on the Reverend's rug beneath his feet. He snorted. "She might have said that yesterday afternoon she ran across a fool in the woods who insulted her by word and..."

"And?"

"Word and deed. Word and deed. There... was the matter of... a kiss."

Reverend Pickett did his best to repress the smile that wished to play upon his lips. He knew the boy was grieving over his new-found circumstances, but he also knew Austin well enough to be familiar with his gentle bursts of emotion. The results were so familiar to him, in fact, the story could almost make him forget the subject of orphans altogether, but Austin brought him back to it.

"She knows about the will, but she hasn't told anyone but Fiona Mienzes. Or at least, I believe she hasn't." He put his head in his hands and ran his fingers through his hair. "Oh, I don't know what I believe anymore."

"Well, I for one am certain she hasn't told her aunt. I know the Widow Bannoch well enough to see if she has a mouse in her claw." More thoughtfully the Reverend added, "In fact, I think the only mouse she's toying with right now is poor little Theodosia Brown."

"Mmm," said Austin, thinking of other things entirely.

"Austin? We should still speak to Miss Brown to ask exactly what it is she's read and what she knows. A young lady isn't likely to understand the machinations of a will, do you think?"

Suddenly coming back to the conversation at hand, Austin said tersely, "Oh, yes, she does. She would. Her father's a bloody solicitor. Pardon me, Reverend, pardon me. She said she understood it... out of habit, she said, whatever that meant..."

"Well *whatever it meant* is most exactly what we will have to discover. Meanwhile, it sounds as though she wishes to keep the news to herself and Miss Mienzes."

Austin turned to stare out the parlor windows in the Reverend's home. He was tired, very tired. It would almost be better, he thought, to not see this through at all. It would almost be better to be gone from here and have done with it. Make his way in the world somewhere else. But even that thought drained him of energy.

The Reverend watched Austin's face. He wondered how the boy would fare in the days to come, but then an odd but pleasant thought occurred to him. He reasoned that he himself had the chance to be more the child's father than any other man, for he could claim a spiritual paternity, and where an earthly father's role passes with his death, those who have a hand in molding a human spirit toward an understanding of their God might still be allowed fellowship with their spiritual offspring in Heaven. The thought satisfied him immensely, but it soon caused him to pray, for well he knew this selfsame son was in a greater spiritual danger than he'd ever known.

* * *

"Fiona, thank you so much for coming."

"Och, however did ye hurt yerself, Tee?"

Theodosia gave half a laugh "If you must know, I was dancing in the woods and tumbled over a root."

"Were you now? Tsk. Tsk. Haven't ye been told to keep yer dancing in the ballroom?" She smiled and laughed, adding, "The roots are planed and polished into floorboards there... or so I've heard."

"Please don't torment me. I am so angry with myself already for having been so... so..."

"Ah, I'll let it go then. I see yer hurting enough as 'tis."

"Aunt Selda has commanded me to stay in my room for an entire day, but I couldn't very well traipse across the countryside on a bad ankle anyway. She really has me now. Everything I do in this household is held against me... to threaten me. If I so much as blink incorrectly, she says, 'I will see to it your papa hears of this!' And if she tells him..." Theodosia shook her head mournfully. "It would only serve to keep me here even longer."

Fiona smiled and came to the side of the bed where Theodosia lay.

"There is one good thing to come of it, though." She gave Fiona a little smile. "Reverend Pickett helped me back into the house and Aunt Selda... though I'm sure she was trying to shame me... asked him then and there if he would watch over me for the summer... for my spiritual well-being, she said, and 'to keep me out of harm's way.' She means to curb my wildness, but when I get better, I think it means she'll let me visit him. I'd like that."

"Yes, he's a good man. A kind man."

"Yes. I wouldn't mind behaving properly for Aunt Selda if it means I can keep visiting the both of you!"

Fiona nodded happily.

Theodosia lowered her voice then. "But, Fiona, there's more."

"More?" Fiona rested herself on the bed carefully to avoid the foot propped on the fat feathered pillow beside her.

"There's Austin..."

"Austin Brooks?"

"He... he found me there in the woods. Oh, it's horrid! He knows all about my finding the will. I don't know how he knows, truly I don't, but he had the nerve to ask me all about it. Of course, I told him you knew."

"Goodness gr-r-r-racious," said she, rather dramatically.

"And he thought I'd told my aunt!"

"Well, he mustn't think too much of ye then," said Fiona but drew her hand to her mouth as soon as the words came out. "I'm sorry," she quickly added.

Theodosia laughed. "It's all right. You're absolutely correct. Here I've been rude enough to read a portion of his father's will. Of course he'd think I could tell my aunt!" She smiled at her friend. "And I think my rudeness has become a poor influence on you, Fiona. Keep speaking your mind like that, and you'll soon be considered an American."

"Don't be saying that."

Theodosia barely noticed the serious tone in the admonition, for she'd gone on with her thoughts. "Still and yet, I think you're wrong about Austin. I think he likes me well enough." Her eyes grew bright, and she blushed a fair shade of pink as she remembered. "After all, he... he kissed me," she whispered.

"He *what?*"

"He did. He carried me out of the woods because of my ankle and while he carried me he... he up and kissed me."

"And what did ye for his impertinence?" Fiona asked fiercely.

"Well, I did what any proper lady would." Theodosia bobbed her head in reply.

"Ah, did ye slap him hard then?" Fiona said with widening eyes.

"No, actually... I... I fainted."

"You... oh-h-h..." And then, despite themselves, both girls went into snickering gales of laughter.

When they had calmed themselves somewhat, Theodosia continued her story. "Oh, he had such a lost look. And it was the oddest thing for we'd just been arguing, when he suddenly said to me, 'I want to kiss you,' and then he did... just like that. Fiona," she said more seriously, "that was my very first kiss..." She stopped and thought on her feelings for a moment.

Fiona looked at her and smiled tentatively.

Theodosia repeated, "First kiss. And I don't even know him, really."

Fiona sighed. "Best not to know him, Tee. A young man like that can't be relied upon. A proper gentleman would never do sich a thing. Nay. And ye said there was an argument? Well, then I should think it obvious..." Here Fiona hesitated.

"What's obvious?"

"Well, I'm afraid it's a certainty he meant to insult ye by it. Ye said he thought you were the type could tell yer aunt? There then... " She shrugged and let Theodosia take her meaning.

But quickly Theodosia looked away. "Insult me? Insult me." She was afraid to think of it and yet tried the words on for size, seeing if they fit. She remembered the kiss. She cocked her head. No, she hadn't felt insulted at all, but perhaps that was her own fault. Perhaps she *should* have felt insulted. She suddenly pulled her neck straight and looked at her friend. "But, Fiona, if he meant to insult me, whatever shall I say to him if I see him again?"

"I... I don't rightly know." Her friend studied the rug for a time and slowly it came to her. "It seems... yes, it seems ye should be writing him. Ye can tell him ye wish no further advantages taken, and that ye'll forget the incident entirely if he'd apologize properly as a gentleman rightly should."

Theodosia blanched to think of writing him, but she knew in her heart Fiona was right. It wouldn't do to let the action go unmentioned. In fact, to let it go might indicate a willingness on her part and that would never do. "Yes, I will write a note. I will." The earnestness grew in her voice, but she ended the pronouncement with a quiet, "Please help me, Fiona."

"O' course."

Theodosia told her where the writing implements could be found, and then the two promptly set to work. In Fiona's fine hand, the words were slowly drawn out from the nib of the pen, "To Master Austin Brooks. Sir. If you consider yourself a gentleman..."

* * *

"Son, drastic times require drastic measures."

Allan nodded curtly to his father, neatly suppressing the burning curiosity that had drawn him to his father's office that afternoon.

With a great heaving sigh his father went on, "You know as well as I we've had reverses in the trade. More and more competition. And you know perhaps better than I how tenuous our clients' relationships are at the moment. And so I have looked carefully into a new style of trade." He came around from his desk at that point and walked slowly to the window that overlooked the garden. His voice grew lower and more confidential. "The new venture will require... a dedication. I will need cooperation from my sons if from no other quarter."

"I am here for you, sir."

"I will tell it you first, Allan, because your gifts will be sorely needed."

A glimmer rose in Allan's eye, for his father's words touched his vanity in a way no other could. For all his faults, he was of an old school in that the singular desire to please his father was deeper than even he realized. And so his chest grew wide at this address and his shoes rose slightly on toe. A fierce sense of pride and dedication seized him as he waited on his father's next words, and he felt for one brief and glorious moment that no task would be too great, no responsibility too difficult to accomplish.

Lord Brooks had not even hoped for such from his second child, yet he *had* chosen to tell him first. He had set Allan apart because of his son's incredible talent for destroying whatever was not his, and for his ability to put himself above every other purpose in the universe, and so the father chose to tell him the news before he told his oldest son in the small hope Allan would take the responsibility as if it were his own. Only then could Lord Brooks ensure for himself a modicum of cooperation from the boy.

"An American clipper ship."

"An American clipper?"

"Precisely. Miss Brown's father is in the trade. He will assist us, I'm sure, in the acquisition, while you can help with negotiations on this end. If word gets out, trading will go poorly for us though. No one wants us to succeed."

How well his son knew.

"And your mother... let her think we've arranged the marriage on the basis of property. Floating our assets in the way we'll need to, Allan... well, I don't need to remind you, will take stern stuff on our part. Your mother shouldn't know...."

"It would upset her."

"Exactly."

"I completely understand."

* * *

Cecelia rubbed Theodosia's ankle enough to make the girl groan. "Doctor said we must rub it to keep the blood warm, Theodosia."

"Cecelia, if you do that anymore, I will surely faint. Then you may rub it all you like for a time," said Theodosia with a catch in her voice.

"Oh, you are such a one to draw complaint, Theodosia. Anyone would think *I'd* turned your ankle and not your own clumsy self." Cecelia thrust Theodosia's foot back onto the pillow with enough force to bring water to her cousin's eyes. "Maman says it serves you right for sneaking out like that. 'God's just punishment,' she said."

"Yes, I remember." Theodosia turned away from Cecelia and stared out the window. The Bannochs' summer "guest" was sitting up at the table by her bed, her foot propped in a chair, suffering more for Cecelia's visit at that moment than she had in the last day of hobbling pain. Most unfortunately, pain was Cecelia's specialty. Almost a hobby for her, in fact, as she'd spent most of her life figuring ways to apply it to other persons.

"Theodosia," said Cecelia coyly. "You are simply going to hate yourself when I tell you what your bumbling has caused you to miss."

She will tell no matter what I reply, thought Theodosia, and so she remained silent.

Cecelia stood up and took a small turn in the middle of the room, a turn fully meant to draw Theodosia's eye from the window. Curiosity aroused, Theodosia looked briefly in her direction, and there her cousin snared her. "A masked ball!" A look of triumph passed over Cecelia's pale brow as she caught her cousin's eye.

Theodosia's brows furrowed for a moment but only for a moment. She turned placidly back to the window and though her countenance was bland, her heart was pounding. A wish since childhood crushed underneath a proud foot. A ball. She would miss yet another ball. Costumed, at that. Rotten luck.

Cecelia was not fooled. Knowing full well the particulars of Theodosia's sheltered childhood she simply continued on and spared no detail in the telling. At the Crystal Palace the year before (Cecelia wore the memory of her visit there like a badge of honor) the exhibition had excited England's vision for its future. So the Queen and her handsome husband had encouraged the country in a way that only royals could, bringing their patronage to English tradesmen, the common folk, for the making of costumes, coaches and the thousand sundries required for a masked ball, a ball which none but the most uncommon would ever see.

The citizenry responded to the Royals' enthusiasm by paying them the high compliment of mimicry, and so anyone who could afford to do so and many who could not had taken to the production of their own costume balls. The ball of which Cecelia spoke would be held June 26, the Saturday after this, in honor of the passing of "Midsummer's Eve" on the 24th. It would be held at the estate of Sir Something-or-other (Theodosia didn't recognize the lengthy name), which was but a five-mile carriage ride from Star Cottage.

Cecelia prattled on that the theme of the ball would not be from Shakespeare, but one's favorite childhood characters. Frederick and she would go as Hansel and Gretel; glorious outfits were being sewn for them even as they spoke. A dirndl style for her with a hand-embroidered blouse, and lederhosen trousers in fine leather for Frederick.

Theodosia allowed herself to daydream on what she herself might have dressed as when Cecelia informed her that her mother had even chosen a character for Theodosia, and it was simply too, too bad she couldn't go, for the idea was ever so charming. "Theodosia, you would have enjoyed it so. You were to have been..."

"ENOUGH! Enough!" said Theodosia harshly. "Cecelia, you are driving me to distraction."

Her cousin's lids lowered slowly as Theodosia spoke, and when she was done Cecelia drew her head back and cocked it upon her long neck. For one blissful moment Theodosia believed she might actually turn and go, and she pressed shut her eyes and wished that it were so.

Suddenly there came a hiss from her cousin's direction which ended with the word, "Cinderella!" followed closely by an ungracious snicker, and without a word, she turned and walked briskly from the room.

* * *

After the incident in the woods and the note to Austin that followed, Theodosia expected to receive a note of apology the very next day but none had come. The ankle's swelling had left her with a round and painful ball where leg met foot. Visitors once a day. Meals served to her alone, and although Aunt Selda couldn't know how much the decision cheered Theodosia's soul, her aunt, appalled at her behavior, had decided to withdraw from her. All this gave Theodosia time to read, reflect and pray, time to be at peace and give thanks for those things which brought her joy: Fiona's friendship, the shortening count of days remaining in the summer, and the view from her window (albeit a fuzzy one as her aunt had continued in the practice of hiding her spectacles).

Late in the evening two days after the incident, Reverend Pickett paid a call to the house. He was ushered to the patient's room, where he found Theodosia propped in her chair, her ankle raised to another seat, her needlework lying dormant in her lap.

They gave each other polite nods. He asked after her health. Aunt Selda stood in the room for a time but grew somewhat uncomfortable when the Reverend's conversation turned to theology, and soon found an excuse to retire from the room.

And then they were alone.

Theodosia examined the hands in her lap. Reverend Pickett

found a chair and worked his mind around the words he might speak. Finally, he began, "Miss Brown, I am here on a matter of grave importance."

Theodosia nodded ever so slightly. Whatever he meant to say, by the tone of his voice she reasoned it was not likely to be a comfortable discussion.

He lowered his voice. "You may trust my confidentiality entirely. My interest in this matter is foremost a concern for Austin Brooks and then, of course, for your own well-being. I understand you've..."

Theodosia tried to straighten the things in her lap, a motion which caused the contents to slide to the floor. "Oh!"

The Reverend Pickett looked down and came forward to assist. He grunted slightly as he bent to pick up her things.

"I'm terribly sorry."

"Quite all right." He held up one item for her to take and then another.

He settled back into his chair and tried again. "I understand you've had access to the Brooks' will."

Her face reddened noticeably, but she nodded once more.

"Austin said it was an accident you came across the document."

"Absolutely. Purely." She darted a look into his eyes and shifted uncomfortably in her chair, which caused the needlework to slide to the floor again. Theodosia looked down at the needlework then back up to the Reverend and said in a small voice, "I've a gift for accidents."

The Reverend pursed his lips to keep from laughing and came forward to pick the items up once more. He bent his head low to keep the smile from showing.

When he had gotten back to his chair he said with some confidence, "And so you mean him no harm in knowing the contents."

"The contents?"

"Yes. Your father being a solicitor, I could see the great temptation in it, and I... well, the Lord will bless you for your restraint."

"Restraint? Do you refer to my not telling anyone but Fiona?"

"Well, yes, *that*, but..." He gave a harumph and looked about the room. Something about Theodosia's answers made no sense and let him know he must continue the line of questioning, although to pry into the matter went against the grain. He swallowed and forged ahead once more. "Miss Brown, is it possible... How... Could it be you misunderstood what you read?"

"Oh, no, I don't think so. A will's opening paragraph is very standard. It was definitely Lord Brooks' will."

"The *opening paragraph?*" His eyes widened. "Do you mean to say that you only read the opening paragraph?"

"Why, yes. Then... my conscience stung me so badly, I put it away." She lowered her eyes. "Although I did try to read it again... the next week, but Austin interrupted."

Reverend Pickett smiled dryly. Clearly, her temptation was Austin's downfall; the Garden of Eden came easily to mind. In fact, the whole story would make a rousing sermon. Pity he could never use it. "My dear, dear girl. Now I understand."

"Yes. Austin seemed quite angry with me for not telling anyone I'd found it. I see now the will must have been misplaced. Looking back on it, I can't imagine why I kept the knowledge to myself, but I seem to always do the backward thing."

"Quite all right. Quite all right. These things work out. 'All things work together for good to those who love God.'" And he was thinking as long as Austin sought His will, it would be for the good. But he pursed his lips remembering that the information he held in himself seemed far from good. Austin Brooks had left the village for a time to give himself room to breathe and think. *And pray, Austin. Pray,* the Reverend thought to himself.

It was not unusual for Austin to head into London for a load of goods for the estate as well as to check up on the shipping office. This type of errand was well suited to his role as third son. While Alfred managed science, and Allan managed clients, Austin was most often found in the tea warehouse, measuring quality and quantity and going over the figures. Occasionally he drove in with a team to meet a ship in London's harbor, inspected tea that had arrived and supervised packing or unpacking. He loved the ships most of all and would do anything to hang about the docks, and so no one questioned his disappearance when he chose to join a team to London. Only his father noted Austin's lack of decorum; he left no word with a servant of his departure and evaded the usual good-byes to family. But his father further surmised that the boy was quite taken with Miss Brown and had simply and wisely chosen to remove himself from her attentions. In his estimation it would follow that, under the circumstances, the boy had lost his typical congeniality, and so he thought no more on it.

There was a great deal of quiet between Theodosia and the Reverend after his last words. Theodosia was attempting to gather courage enough to seek out the Reverend's advice, when the Reverend suddenly spoke. "Well, Austin will be more himself when he returns."

"Has he gone?"

"Yes. He left for London yesterday, er, on business. He'll be back soon enough, I'll warrant."

"Oh. Oh, my. Well that explains..."

The Reverend's eyebrows rose in expectation.

Courage gathered or courage scattered, she decided to speak. "Reverend Pickett, did you know that Austin had the... took the... he... kissed me in the woods?"

"Yes... as a matter of odd fact I do."

She gulped. "He told you."

"He did. He's one to appreciate honesty."

Yes, she thought as much. "Well, I've a question, you see. I don't know Mr. Brooks, and... should I... have... taken insult?"

"Should you?" he queried. He smiled broadly. "You might *choose* too, I suppose, but *did* you take insult might be a question more to the point, eh?"

Theodosia blushed violently. She knew the discussion would be delicate but had no sense of what turns it might take, and so wishing she'd never brought it up, she turned her face away.

"No, no, Miss Brown. You misunderstand me. I mean do *you* think Austin meant to insult you?"

She thought on the kiss once more and had to admit it. She hadn't felt insulted at all. She turned back to him. "No."

"Well then, I believe you've read the boy correctly. Perchance you know him better than you think."

She smiled a small, wan smile to hear it and watched his face as he further explained.

"Austin... I've known him all my life. He is... he's unusual for a boy... a man... the way he grows impassioned for a thing. His parents have tried to steel him to himself, but, well, he's fought them on it... just as he does anything he sees as... unfair." The Reverend grew quiet. Looking down, he smiled. "You have a way about you, Miss Theodosia, of drawing one's thoughts straight out of one's mind. Those great searching eyes of yours must see a great deal!" He laughed as Theodosia smiled and looked away.

"I'm sorry, I..."

"Don't apologize." He tossed his head. "Good heavens, don't apologize! God's gifts and you should enjoy them! Only..." He paused.

Theodosia sought him with a look once more.

"Only, I would hope you continue to find the strength... well, as you did when you found the will in the library... the strength to hold back when necessary, eh?"

"Yes. Yes, indeed. But I'm afraid I've written a note to Austin asking him to apologize to me. In it I was not very kind."

"Well, well." He flung out his right hand. "Write him another then."

"To London?"

"Ah, there's a truth. Never mind. Wait until he returns. One note will quash the other, I should think, and a friendship will resume," he said flatly, rising from his seat.

"A friendship. Yes, I should think." But Theodosia's thoughts grew more and more unsettled as she sat.

"If your ankle were better, I'd ask you to come on rounds with me. Wonderful people in my care, and I'm afraid you're not seeing enough of the real England."

Theodosia smiled but she thought she may have seen too much of it already.

After the Reverend left, Theodosia stared out the window. Whenever she looked out the window frame to the blurry greenness beyond, the memory of her interview with Austin returned, the gentle words he'd spoken there and the kindness in his eyes. And although she couldn't see the place where the path in the woods began, she let herself remember his kiss and the way he'd held her all too close, the fleeting dimples and the curl that fell upon his forehead. Again and again she thought on their odd conversations. And then she sighed deeply as she chose to remember every good therein.

Theodosia woke the next morning feeling more rested than she had in days. Reverend Pickett's words had been a great comfort to her; his optimism was infectious. The morning song birds even seemed to sing, "All right. All right. Everything will be all right." Theodosia laughed, for the birds' song fit her mood exactly.

But a little knock on the door and a call to enter brought Cecelia sweeping into the room, and thus the morning revery was abruptly ended.

Theodosia pulled herself up to a sitting position in her bed as her cousin sailed across the room to sit beside her on the bed. The look on Cecelia's face was unsettling to Theodosia—her very presence brought with it a foreboding. Even the birds ceased their song.

After arranging her skirts and folding her hands, Cecelia brought a great smile to her lips.

Theodosia held her breath.

"What now, Theodosia?" her cousin chirped. "What do you think, my quaint American cousin? You are to have a suitor!" ∽

EIGHT

❧

A dis, a dis, a green grass,
A dis, a dis, a dis,
Come all you pretty fair maids
And dance along with us.
She shall get a duke, my dear,
As duck do get a drake,
And she shall have a young prince,
For her own sake.

Nursery Rhyme

❧

"He will be here this afternoon."

Head pounding and hands shaking, Theodosia stared at Cecelia. "Why do you say a suitor? Are you teasing me? I can never tell if you're teasing me. Who is coming?"

"Why, who do you think, you silly chit? You must have some sense of the Brookses' ways by now."

Did things happen so quickly? Could he have decided to pursue her despite her note? Surely, this was his answer. He had come back from London quickly...and on her account. She was terrified and thrilled all at once, and her heart was thumping as if it would burst.

But Cecelia continued, "Maman says you are well enough to walk to the parlor and may visit with him there." Theodosia wondered how her *maman* could judge the fact since she hadn't been to see her in two days. She was further irritated because Aunt Selda was right just the same.

"Oh, Cecelia. Really? Don't, don't jest. I couldn't stand it if you were jesting."

"The card came from Brooks House this morning. This is no jest. Maman says you are to wear my blue velvet, since you've nothing suitable. I'll bring it to you this afternoon. He'll be here for tea at four o'clock. Very prompt, I'm sure. He always is...." She snickered.

Theodosia hardly heard her cousin's words. *Reverend Pickett was so very, very correct,* she thought with a smile. *It will work out. Lord, thank you.*

But Cecelia was not enjoying the interview half as much as she expected to, for her cousin's reaction was not at all what it should have been. She wanted her cousin to be mildly horrified to hear that Alfred was coming to woo her, and instead she was accosted with a look of pure rapture on little Theodosia's face. She slowly grew disgusted. *Theodosia had had her eye on Alfred? What could she see in him?* she wondered.

He would, of course, inherit Brooks House and its entitlements, but Theodosia had never seemed interested in position. And yes, he was intelligent, but Theodosia could never hope to keep up with his mind. If one removed his spectacles from him, he might be considered handsome too, even more handsome than Allan, although Allan had clearly garnered all of the family charm. So what did this little backwoods child see in Alfie that she hadn't? She stared and stared into the happy little face but no answer came.

"I see you are not averse to the interview," Cecelia purred.

"No. No, not at all. What did you say of dress?"

"My blue velvet."

"Ah. Beautiful. Thank you. Thank you, Cecelia."

"Well, since you're so grateful, I'll... I'll go and get it now if you like."

"Yes, please. I'll put on my other chemise. Oh, Cecelia, this is too wonderful."

"Yes, just... too..." said Cecelia demurely, slamming the door behind her as she left.

* * *

Since the family solicitor had refused to discuss the will's intent with Austin Brooks, Austin had taken himself away to London, will in pocket, to find his chum from Cambridge, late a clerk in a well-known London solicitor's office.

He didn't know exactly for whom Todd Roundtree worked, but he found his friend by waiting outside the doors around the usual supper hour on a busy street in the heart of London's legal district. When Austin spied the red mop of hair, half-hidden by a tall silk hat, he waved his friend down. In a quarter of an hour the two were seated in a pub, surrounded by a noisy crew of pub clientele, but partially obscured by the height of the booth and the lowness of the ceiling. Four glasses of bitters, a loaf of bread and half a pound of cheddar later, Austin cleared the table and laid the document before his friend. Mr. Roundtree's quick eye soon made sense of the legal language, and he began the slow process of translation to the layman.

Because he knew Roundtree's background, Austin was not afraid to present the knowledge of his own questionable ancestry. Roundtree himself was "not his father's son," as the saying goes, and at school he had made no bones about it. He could empathize with Austin's plight, for now neither knew who their father might be. It was Roundtree who took the lead by joking, "Could be we're brothers, Austin!" which brought a bitter smile from Austin.

But then Roundtree became absorbed in the task at hand, and he was given to exclaim, "My God!" at every other paragraph.

Austin, greatly confused by the language, had only gotten as far as the description of himself as an adopted child before deciding to take it elsewhere for translation, and now it took a great deal of time for his friend to explain each of the remaining segments to him. The first thing they needed to straighten out was whose will it truly was: Alfred Lord Brooks was, in fact, Alfred *Simpson* Brooks and not Alfred *Sebastian* Brooks, as was first supposed. The will was actually written by Lord Brooks' father, the original Lord Brooks, Austin's supposed grandfather.

Sitting back in his seat and shaking his head, Austin wondered at the revelation. He was only a lad of twelve when the old man had died, and he'd known him fairly well. Very well, it might be said, for a Lord's grandson. The first Lord Alfred Brooks had seemed to take an especial care over his third grandchild, and now the will explained the old man's behavior. All too well and strangely. Very strangely.

Alfred Simpson Brooks' son and his wife were staying at his country estate when his daughter-in-law suffered the miscarriage of a stillborn child at seven months. The pregnancy was a troubled one from the start, and so their two young boys were left with nannies at Brooks House in Thistledown while Lady Brooks "rested" at her father-in-law's estate.

It was considered a miracle that the mother lived through the ordeal, but her husband soon found in spirit she was more dead than alive. He loved his wife dearly then—she had not grown bitter yet—and when he feared she would actually die of grief, he decided that she must have a child. A boy had died; a boy would be found to replace him.

Austin's grandfather, Alfred Simpson Brooks, helped to arrange it, and within a week, there came to the house through the servant's door a tow-headed infant wrapped in coarse linen. Austin Simpson Brooks was christened the next day, and Lady Brooks, whether from grief or joy, decided it *was* her child and she grew strong again with the baby at her side. Alfred Sebastian Brooks then wiped away every evidence of his third child's origins, and he returned with him and his glowing wife to Thistledown.

The child was gifted from the start, the townfolk said, for the premature son was even stronger than the first two had been. If Lady Brooks was bothered by the remarks, no one—not even her husband—would have guessed it. She treated him entirely as if he were her own. Her husband, too, and so he was raised as were her other sons, given over to nannies and tutored privately at home until of age for University, and there the story would have ended.

But for an old man with scientific inclinations, Austin would never have known his origins. Lord Alfred Simpson Brooks was an eccentric of the old order. He was a dabbler in science, and with the gift of success to guide his steps over the years, he took his studies further than most men would ever dream.

He had what he considered an unusual opportunity: the point-blank observation of an "adopted" child. A child had been brought into his family—an orphan whose heritage was at the least questionable and at the most nowhere near that of his "adoptive" family—and he would be given every advantage. What would happen? Would he eventually be found weak? Would blood tell? The old man was a cynic by nature and by training, and so he observed Austin closely, noting his every move. How different was he from the others?

Early on he saw the emotional energy of the boy. Was this peasant stock showing through? The barroom brawls of his natural father? He determined to discover the origin of the boy's natural family so that he could better compare the circumstances, but he was greatly disappointed in his research. The boy's mother had died in childbirth. There were no other children, and the father was nowhere to be found.

He returned to the house of his son and made only one statement: never give the child a formal adoption. It was too grotesque to think of him as equal to a Brooks.

But the "grandfather" continued to observe Austin. He was surprised to find the boy curbing his emotions as he grew. He was further surprised to find Austin more kindhearted and by far more generous than either of his brothers. Was this a weakness or a strength? He compared the boy to Alfred and his brother Allan and the empirical evidence was all too clear: Austin was the golden boy among them. A startling conclusion.

Alfred succeeded in his schooling and Allan in social grace, but Austin prospered in both and then some. It was as the old man observed Austin at play from a great distance on a gray day in spring the year before his death that it occurred to him this child should go to a college and make something of himself. It was then that Alfred S. Brooks devised the making of a will to test a theory. He would create a scientific legacy: a cynic's gift to future generations.

Like a normal entail, Lord Alfred Simpson Brooks left the estate to his grandsons and not his son, the son receiving the house and income from the properties until the grandsons inherited. But, where the oldest grandson would normally inherit on his twenty-first birthday, this will arranged for action to be taken upon *Austin's* reaching twenty-one.

And then the will grew quite complex and in this manner: The house would go to Alfred, the Younger, upon Alfred Lord Brooks' death. The business would be a shared ownership, half to Alfred and half to Allan. Nothing was left to the third "son," Austin.

At this Roundtree stopped to allow Austin time to take it in, but Austin grew impatient. "I know that much, Todd. I've read it and I've understood that much. I'll be cut off . . ."

"Next year, is it? When you turn twenty-one."

"Yes."

"Yes. This all takes place on your twenty-first birthday."

But Austin had only read the will up to that point. The rest of it he presumed explained the first of it in detail, but Roundtree begged to differ.

"This second part is quite different from the first, Austin. Did you read it?"

"No and didn't care to." But he brought his head over the table and tried to read what Roundtree pointed toward now.

"Let me go on then."

"Please," Austin said grimly. He took a large gulp of the tepid brew from the glass before him and sat back once more to listen.

Roundtree said all that would happen upon Austin's birthday, unless the town could produce three examples like himself.

Austin sat up.

Roundtree went on to explain that a large grant of monies would be given to provide for a public school building. Roundtree looked toward his friend and Austin nodded, remembering the town's appreciation of his family's generosity ten years before. The school to which Fiona Mienzes was attached was built with those monies, the first "public education" in the area. And to encourage the education of the farmers' and bakers' children, an allowance would be given every year to any household whose children attended school—so the families would have reason to keep them there. It was one of the items that had given the Brookses the title of town's patron. One young man, the son of a weaver, had actually gone on to Oxford University.

Roundtree read the next part over twice. Slowly he described it: if three scholars worthy of University could come from certain sectors of Thistledown by Austin's twenty-first birthday, the town and not the grandsons would inherit the trust.

Austin's eyes widened and his mouth fell open. "*The town?*" he asked, incredulous.

Roundtree reread the words. "'If three scholars will come from these sectors of Thistledown'—and then these are delineated: 'those who do physical labor to make their bread and the laborer's children, orphans, those who have physical impairments.' Then it says all the money will go to the town: here a dispensary will be built and a doctor retained for public use; more housing would be built and those presently occupying old structures may be afforded the opportunity of purchasing these homes at a fee set at... et cetera, et cetera, let's see... a water system provided through town and a regrading of the highways... umm... and, here, Brooks House... Outrageous! Brooks House to be opened as a *scientific house of learning.*"

Austin snorted. "That'd suit Alfie, anyway."

Roundtree continued, "And the brothers.... may stay but as curators of the endeavor at... yes, I'd have to say a very low income. But, here, the tea house would remain under Lord and Lady Brooks' care, such as it would be without capital. Unbelievable! Austin, was he quite sane?"

"Sane as you or I," Austin said slowly, thoughtfully. "And knowing he's had his way so far, I'd say the will's not been challenged. It's as if the man still lives."

Roundtree was barely listening. "Yes, yes, I see it now. And it won't be challenged. It's an unusual way to break an estate's entail, but it's signed here by two doctors, a fellow from the Academy of Science, the heads of the law firm of Chittendon and Clendening *and* that of Holcomb, Redfern and Grackle. He was quite serious. Unbelievable." Roundtree and Austin both shook their heads.

Then Roundtree found the last page and got his friend's attention once more.

It was a document written in Lord Brooks' own hand. To the point it said, "I believe the mind to be the most worthy of human instruments. To confirm for public record this belief as fact I have devised the following: I have arranged a broad experiment to encourage those with mental ability to live above and beyond their circumstances.

"If, as I have observed through the boy, Austin, all that may be wanting in the home of an English peasant's child to bring him to an earthly success is a good education, then it follows my son and my son's sons have no inherent right to claim the prosperity they presently enjoy. Nurture should oust nature. For my test you will need to find three scholars within the specific sectors of Thistledown's population I have mentioned, to then be determined as scholars by Chittendon and Clendening on the basis of the ability to attend University. I can think of no other more satisfactory test and so I let it stand as such, hostage as I am to unworthy laboratory equipment.

"If three scholars do not appear by Austin Brooks' twenty-first birthday, however, I would determine that the theory of nature over nurture had prevailed, and the bloodline of the Brookses should continue as it has and deem itself properly positioned in this world if not outwardly worthy to receive all its entitlements. From the town of Thistledown, public monies for education will henceforth be removed.

"But in either circumstance aforementioned, it must be said that Austin, a child of unquestionably low birth, has been given advantages by virtue of an education and breeding that was more than any of his kind would usually come to know, and so, because he has truly succeeded on his own although he knew it not, I felt it best to let him continue in his own success without benefit of further inheritance. Whether he is an aberration of breeding or typical of an unjustly disadvantaged class will remain to be seen.

"Thinking his circumstances through to a logical conclusion, I predict it statistically probable that when he discovers the story of his true birth, he will not wish to continue the farce of considering himself a son. His father will, I hope, never provide him a formal adoption. And so his leaving, and I fully realise the irony in this statement, would be natural to his good breeding and consistent with the sensibilities I have observed within him. If he had the thinking of the son of a peasant he might have blessed his luck, but as it is he will prefer to leave the house."

"Gawd," said Austin with a horrified grunt. "He's right. He's right, and I'll hate him for it the rest of my cursed life."

The candle burned low as the two young men drank bitters into the night. Now and then a grunt was heard from Austin. A discussion would occasionally fall between the two, but it was always brief. Somewhere in the evening Austin laughed quite loudly, causing his friend to look sloe-eyed at him for a moment.

Then Austin said in a slightly drunken slur, "Doesn't matter to me, but I think it's rather hum-hic-humorous there's been only one scholar 'n thash all. The Brookses will win... win out in the end. Nursh... nash... whish is it then?"

"That would be..." And here Roundtree belched as politely as he could. "Nashure. Nature wins, my friend. The race to the strongest runner. To that sort of winner go the spoils."

"Nashure. Mother-blessed-nashure. An' she should, bless her. 'Course..." But Austin's head was reeling and his mind was none too steady to enable him to grasp the concept, and that was just as well. He stared into his mug and suddenly started. "But it doesn't matter anywhere, 'cause the worsh thing is I love Tee, and I can't win her if I'm... orphan."

"Tea, yes," said Roundtree. "Tea has been very good to the Brookses."

Austin chuckled, and shook his head wildly. "No, no, naw. Not tea, *Tee*. Thea... Theodosha Brown. A loverly lit'le American girl... with biggest brown eyes you ever saw. I love her... I loved her anywho."

He hiccupped.

And so the evening progressed even as Austin regressed into his liquor.

* * *

Earlier that day at teatime in Star Cottage, the Bannochs received a visitor, a suitor by the name of Alfred, and his arrival caused quite a stir.

Theodosia Brown was coiffed, perfumed and polished to her shining best and then sent down the hall to the parlor to greet her waiting guest. But somewhere along the corridor she heard the true name of her suitor, and not quite believing her ears at first, asked after it and found it had not changed. Alfred, the would-be scientist, was here to woo her.

Then it was only with the harshest of threats that her aunt and cousin succeeded in bringing her to the parlor to meet him. Watching the cowed look in the eye of her little cousin when the name was given, Cecelia was now satisfied that Alfred was not the apple of Theodosia's eye. It must be Allan that Theodosia was expecting.

Her aunt, who had had quite enough of Theodosia's strong-headedness, took the opportunity to bring forth the greatest weapon she could draw on her niece: pulling Theodosia's ear close to her own there in the hallway, she informed her that *this* was what her parents wished for her this summer. *This* was what she was sent overseas to accomplish. To be wooed and married by a wealthy Englishman. She had a letter to the same effect from her father's hand; it was time for all childish behavior to cease.

Theodosia shook her head quite violently, but her aunt never rested from the task. "Do you think, you pitiful little squint of a girl, that your papa would send you all the way here for a lesson in manners? Hmm? He sent you here because I have connections he does not...connections that will enable even *you* to marry properly and help his business in the bargain."

In fact, a lesson in manners was exactly the delusion in which Theodosia had truly believed, but her aunt's words knocked it from its perch and dashed it to the floor in one effective motion. She remembered her father's firm wasn't doing well, hadn't done well for the last few years, and what her aunt was telling her, although she said it without love, did seem possible to Theodosia. Suddenly it was all too possible.

And so if her aunt had taken a stick and beaten her then and there, the words would not have wielded stronger blows to her small frame. All the doubts about herself and the questions as to why her aunt had taken her that summer in the first place—all these conspired to steal from her the ability to reason. Theodosia was literally left cowering against the wall, the soreness of her ankle temporarily eclipsed by a heartbreak the likes of which she'd never known. Weak in the knees and trembling with fright, she found herself unable to stand for several moments. Only her aunt's continual threats, particularly that she would be sent home to her father in disgrace if she did not get hold of herself, were able to bring Theodosia to the point of standing. But she was sick, quite sick; her face was pale and her eyes seemed stuck into her forehead to no purpose. She could not see. She could not think.

This was what she was here for? It made perfect sense and yet no sense at all. Surely her parents would have told her. Wouldn't they? *Wouldn't they?* The words echoed in her agitated mind as she made her way slowly and unsteadily toward the parlor, toward Alfred Sebastian Brooks, the Younger.

She spied the black clothes and drawn face of Alfred even before she entered the parlor. Her aunt and cousin were just behind her, one upon each elbow, pressing her ever forward, and she had a sudden pang of empathy for every person who had ever walked the stairs to Madame Guillotine.

* * *

Austin groaned.

His lids fluttered open but the sun seemed oddly bright to him. Pinching them shut, he wondered where he was. He was lying down. Had he been asleep? But where? Where had he been?

Last night. Tap room. Roundtree. Roundtree.

"Roundtree?" But the word did not come as easily as it should. He forced his lids open once more, felt his mouth, and when he pulled the fingers away, he found brown blood smeared along his fingertips.

"What's this?" He tried to straighten out his form.

Shoving at a metal box before him... an empty coal hod, it turned out, he grabbed hold of a broken wheel to his left to pull himself forward. He felt as though he'd been run over by a team of eight. His coat was torn, as were his britches at the knees. Scraped. Bruised. "Lord in Heaven, I've been pummelled," he said to no one in particular, gingerly touching his hand to his stomach and then his sides.

Now he rolled and stumbled forward. "Roundtree?" he gasped and looked about. An alleyway. Spent the night in an alley. Taking an accounting of the bruises as he stood, he suddenly felt for his wallet. "Gone." But, then, so was Roundtree. ᔕ

NINE

∽

Hickety, pickety, my black hen,
She lays eggs for gentlemen.
Gentlemen come every day
To see what my black hen doth lay.

Nursery Rhyme

∽

Theodosia had many things to think over. Yet, all she could
bring herself to do was stare at the greenery out the guest
room window. At least she could see the edge of the woods clearly
now, for there was no longer any pretense to keep her from wearing her spectacles. But that was the only good to come of the session, for tea with Mr. Alfred Brooks had been a horrible disaster.
She hated all of it.

As she had gone to sit in the parlor with him, it occurred to her
perhaps she could make herself truly disgusting. Then surely he
would not pursue the courtship. This was the one thing that gave
her bright hope while she sat in the parlor, unable to partake of tea
in any way. She'd hung on to the plan for dear life and only
wished time would not creep so slowly for them there. She looked
at the floor and her eyes swept toward her aunt's workbag which
happened to be sitting at her feet.

A fleeting smile came to her as she spied the treasure. From the
side pocket she could see the glint of her spectacles. So this is
where Aunt Selda had hidden them from her!

She waited for the appropriate moment. So when Aunt Selda
said something about malt bread being Cecelia's favorite and how
Theodosia really should try some, she suddenly spoke up, "Oh,
malt bread. Oh. I didn't *see* the malt bread, Auntie, but you know
I can't see a thing without aid." She bent down then, grabbed up

the spectacles, and thrust them on her face without another word.

Her aunt choked. Cecelia sneezed a snort, and Theodosia smiled toothily at them both.

But when Theodosia turned to impress Alfred with her four-eyed face, she noted with dismay that he had chosen to smile at her. It was quick, almost imperceptible, but it was very definitely a smile. And then he said quite calmly, "They are most becoming on you, Miss Brown." At this, she pulled the spectacles back off and held them tightly in one fist.

Not soon enough for Theodosia, but at the appointed time Alfred had finally departed. Theodosia left the parlor room in stoney silence and proceeded to lock herself in her room. There could be no explaining, no begging, no reason brought to bear upon her aunt, she knew it well. Her only hope was that Alfred would take to hating her. At least she knew that the uglier she made herself, the more it might please him, and so she decided to study Cecelia's art from that day forward and play the daft coquette.

Alfred Brooks had come like clockwork to Star Cottage every afternoon since the first visit, and Theodosia grew nauseous before each meeting. Yet her aunt would threaten to write her father, and so Theodosia would relent and go and sit in the parlor for him... for them.

Her ankle felt almost completely well now, but she stayed in her room as much as possible for fear of being taken on social calls.

She did not believe Alfred liked her. In fact, she was fairly certain that he did not like her, but what troubled her was that it hardly seemed to matter. He would come to call just the same, as if he were an automaton. He would sit stiffly in the same chair, chat about the same topics and generally make himself unuseful. He had shaven the affected whiskers from around the sides of his face, and though his fine visage was made more handsome by the smooth appearance, she could barely bring herself to look at him. He was not a fool, and so why would he persist in the courtship? And where could she go from here?

The very night her aunt had initiated the ritual of Alfred's visitations, Theodosia had written a long letter to her parents, carefully and painfully explaining the circumstances to them and asking for some explanation of her present situation. She ended the missive by stating, "Surely you would not wish Aunt Selda to push upon me a man I have absolutely no concern for? I might understand your wishing me a good match, but everything you've ever taught me has me believing I would be allowed to marry for love, not for position or money. I will rest my present actions upon all that you have taught me before now and hope the present situation is merely some wishful thinking on Aunt Selda's part colored by her own desires. Father, she says you have written a letter stating the intent to have me married to a wealthy Englishman, but she refuses to show it to me. I simply cannot believe such a letter exists. Please tell me. Ever your loving daughter, Theodosia."

The message to her parents was more of a means of bringing her heart some ease, for she'd known she couldn't send it. She had no money and the cost was too dear.

But then the day after Alfred's first visit, Aunt Selda had told her more: she said her father had not yet sent any funds for a return voyage and doubted whether he ever would.

Now, Theodosia had known her father would be sending the monies later that summer, that he had to wait for certain retainers to come in before she could book passage, but she'd never imagined he would not send them at all. But from the moment Aunt Selda made the claim, Theodosia truly began to despair. If it were a lie, the monies would come and Theodosia could leave, yes, but if she were telling the truth, Theodosia was more of a prisoner than she'd ever dreamed. She would have to find a way to send the letter now, and so she did what she would never have dared before: She asked Fiona if she could borrow the sum of the mail frank, to be paid back when she could. Fiona, of course, was all too happy to lend it, and the letter was mailed that very afternoon with a postscript asking for the funds to return home.

Two months. Late August. A long time to wait.

When she walked into town to post the letter, she told the post-master that she wished to have all her correspondence hand-delivered to her. He seemed cordial enough in his reply, and Theodosia was assured she could take him at his word. Whom she had no trust for was her own Aunt Selda; it was high time to begin protecting herself from the woman's wishes. This marriage was her idea, and although Theodosia was reasonably sure there was no way on earth Aunt Selda could force her to say "I do," the daily promise of Aunt Selda's "I will make you" haunted her.

* * *

The costume ball began. The Bannochs were there for supper beforehand, and so, to Theodosia's great relief, she was left behind at Star Cottage, just she and the servants. Her ankle was almost perfectly well, but she dined alone in her room on bread and cheese. She took tea as well. Wishing for company, she found herself staring out the large guest room window, but it was quite dark. She stared into the blackness, the enveloping silent dark, and felt for all the world as though she were peering into her soul.

It was not the prospect of marriage that bothered her. She had reassured herself a hundred times and finally came to believe that Alfred could not be such a fool as to marry a poor man's daughter, an American at that, when to make matters worse she disliked him and showed her dislike in every way she could. No. What caused her heart to hurt so was the betrayal of her aunt and cousins, blood relatives. *There should be a tie that binds us,* she mused, *but Aunt seems to have the knack for making nooses out of every roping.*

Her imagination drew a fanciful picture of Selda Bannoch on the path of flowers in the woods, merrily making a noose from the pretty flowers that Theodosia had lately made into a crown.

Then grimly she thought, *She would press me on Alfred despite my wishes. Lie about my parents' wishes for me. She won't show me the letter she speaks of. There is no letter! She's doing all this to torment me. Ah, but she's hated me from the first night. But is it me she hates or maman? She... it must be she hates maman.* "But why?" she said aloud. The cool night air gave no answer.

A faint knocking brought her from her thoughts. "Yes?"

"Miss. You've a visitor."

For one heart-stopping second in time, she thought it might be Austin come back from London, but she reproved herself for such a silly thought, then composed herself and went to the door.

"Master Alfred Brooks is here, miss."

"But my aunt is not here to receive him."

"Yes, miss. He... he says he just wants a talk with you, miss, a moment of your time, he says." The servant seemed as uncomfortable as Theodosia but she would not question Alfred Brooks and so she forced Theodosia to decide.

"My goodness. Well. Well..." She smoothed her dress nervously. "Well, all right, then, I suppose. I'll be right there. Tell him... I'll be right there."

She turned back into her room, straightened the lace on her cap and jabbed at her hair for a moment. A chance to be alone. Good. She could speak plainly. She would finally tell him all she was thinking. Perhaps he was here to tell her the same... without interference. This courtship nonsense could end and all would be well. All would be well.

She prayed it would be true all the way down the long hall.

* * *

Lord Alfred Brooks had taken himself away from the masked ball fairly early in the evening and had settled himself into his favorite smoking room to enjoy his pipe and think his thoughts. But he was interrupted by a messenger with a note from the London office. They discovered that Austin had checked into the usual rooming house ten days before, but after one evening spent there they had no word of him. He'd never come to the office at all. Lord Brooks stared at the paper for quite some time, and if a gentleman were in the room who knew him well, he would have noted the reddening lower lids, the stooped shoulders and the slight trembling of the sheet in Lord Brooks' palm and determined that the note contained a blow of great magnitude. A business loss. A death perhaps. But a loss. Without question a loss.

* * *

"Good evening."

"And to you, sir. Please rest yourself."

"Of course." Alfred carefully took a chair by the door. Theodosia thought he looked as he always did. Slightly rumpled, tie not quite tied, hair darting from his head in places, and his glasses sliding to the tip of his fine nose. She nodded and tried to think what he could mean by the visit; she would not be kept waiting for an answer.

Alfred began, "I understand Americans are generally less formal than we?"

"Yes... generally."

"May I presume you would appreciate straightforward conversation then—straightforward thinking—that sort of thing?"

She cringed as he said "ap*pre*ciate," hating the way he turned the 'c' into an 's-s-s-s,' dragging the poor letter through the rest of the word as if it were a dead cat, but she nodded.

"Then it is this... thus... thusly... I would like to know exactly why you wish to become my wife."

"I??? *I* wish to become your wife?? Well! I do *not* wish it. I do not wish it at all."

His knee began to jump a little at that. "I thought as much. But you do like Brooks House, eh?"

"I like it well enough... for a house," she said guardedly.

"And so you'd like to be the Lady of the House."

"No!" Theodosia was horrified with every aspect of the conversation so far. Yet wasn't it just the opportunity she'd prayed for? She tried to calm herself. "No, I do not wish to be Lady Brooks. I wish to be Theodosia Brown of America, and I... I don't want to marry you at all!"

"AHA!" he said, with the same enthusiasm he reserved for finding what he was looking for at the conclusion of a scientific test. "Aha," he repeated, but Theodosia was absolutely mystified. "Then we can dispense with these visits altogether!" he said with eyes aglow.

"Absolutely, sir." She nodded furtively. "The sooner the better for all concerned, and I'm much relieved to hear you say it! I looked for an opportunity to speak to you on this, but as you know there was none. Really, I must thank you!"

"Not at all. And so we understand one another completely." He stood and bowed stiffly. "Ah, but..." He stopped and turned in the doorway. "Would this mean then that you wish to marry sooner? I have experiments to do on the Isle of Skye before long that will keep me there a full month." As Theodosia's mouth fell impolitely open, he looked away absentmindedly and seemed to speak to himself, "Don't presume she'd want to '*honeymoon*' there—detestable word—no. Of course not. But then if I went on to Scotland and left her at the house after the wedding it might give her time to settle in, become used to Mother. Yes, she'll take some getting used to," he said with a snide laugh.

Theodosia stared at him. Was he completely mad? "Do you still mean..." She spoke each word quite slowly as if he might not understand. "*To... marry... me?*"

He looked up. "Eh?"

All pretense was gone. Her anger carried her words up from deep within her. "Mr. Brooks, I do not... I *do* not... I *do not like you!* Positively. *Do not!* I hardly know you, but from what I've seen I have quite decided you are punctilious, officious, and mired in some semblance of scientific work that keeps you from having to deal with other life forms outside a laboratory dish!"

He smiled.

"*I do not want to marry you.* Now, do you understand this or are you completely insane?"

"I had thought for a while," he said quietly, "that I misunderstood women. I had thought for a while your species meant 'yes' when you said 'no,' but you may trust that I believe you. Every word of what you have said is completely true about myself, and I must state that I am impressed with your powers of observation, seeing how I've hardly spoken two sentences to you since we began this charade. All the better for it, I say. Mother was right. You'll suit me fine."

"But why, *why* would you still wish to marry me? I have no

property. No connections. I should be considered as nothing to the Brookses!"

"Ah, if a woman could only curb her emotions, I feel certain some form of logic could prevail within her. But you've missed the obvious answer completely due to this... this flushing in your face, the racing heart, the trembling lip. I will marry you for the same reason you will marry me, of course..."

"Which reason would that be?" she asked, atremble with an impatient loathing to hear it.

"Look here. Is this some sort of feminine, um... do you need to go on like this?"

"Mr. Brooks, I do not understand you," she cried in anguish, and two great tears fell from her cheeks even as she wiped them away.

"Well. Ahem." He cleared his throat. "The emotions have completely precluded your ability to reason. I will take my leave."

"No!" She calmed herself to a whisper and forced her body to be still. "No. I will listen quietly. Please tell me."

Now he took on the role of professor, putting on a restrained and mannered voice to explain the simple concept to his future bride. "We will marry because our mothers and fathers believe we should."

She blinked.

With irritation he added, "Lord in Heaven, I hope I shan't have to explain such simple concepts to you for the rest of my life. I shall have to hire a maid to speak to you, I think," he said sharply, and then he turned and made his way to the front door.

But before he gained the doorknob, Theodosia ran up behind him. "You! *You* have misunderstood *me* completely, Mr. Brooks. So much for your... your *scientific observation!* I not only do not wish to marry you, I *will not* marry you. I *will not!* Experiment with *that!* Use logic on *that!* I WILL NOT MARRY YOU!" she yelled.

Her words echoed in the hallway and she watched as one side of his insipid little mouth began to curl upwards.

The fury burned within her.

"Well," he said with a snicker of resignation. "I didn't think you could handle it. This outburst tells me only that your parents must regret they spoiled you so. You should try not to be such an ungrateful wife, I think." But the irritation in his voice fell away. "But then it really doesn't matter whether you are, and I don't care if I never speak to you after we're married." He smiled completely now, a thin little smile, and his spectacles slowly slid to the tip of his nose. "Once we are married, we will be free from either of our parents' expectations, eh? And by the way, Miss Brown, I believe I prefer you in spectacles." He pushed his own back up on his nose. "It becomes the wife of a scientist, I think. Gives the appearance of having some sort of *intellect*, after all."

"Then I *shan't* wear them... *ever!*" And she turned and ran back toward her room.

This was a nightmare come to life. Unbelievable. Horrible. All the way back down the hall, Theodosia kept saying to herself, "They cannot make me say 'I do.' They cannot make me say 'I do.'" But when she arrived in the guest room and shut her door, she fell across the bed and cried just as hard and just as long as if they could indeed force her to marry. ∾

TEN

❧

London Bridge is falling down,
Falling down, falling down;
London Bridge is falling down,
My fair lady.

Nursery Rhyme

❧

The revelers from the ball did not come home until 4:00 A.M., and Theodosia knew they would sleep the rest of the day away. *And that is good*, she thought as she rose that morning, *for I have a visit to make*.

She sneaked out her window and hobbled on her ankle, much better but always stiff in the morning, all the way to Thistledown to knock heartily on the door of Reverend Pickett's residence. She was relieved to find him at home and was soon ushered into the by-room that Austin had visited so often. She took a seat in the chair that Austin had sat in to converse with his good friend.

But she sat in the chair that morning distracted and distraught, worrying and wondering what would happen to her if she stayed any longer under her aunt's roof. She wished she could think like Aunt Selda for a moment in time. If she could it might be possible to see what the devil she was planning, why she pursued the idea of a marriage to Alfred Brooks. If no one could be reasoned with, how could she bear it? What if the letter were real? What if she had to stay and marry him?

Reverend Pickett had not completely entered the room before Theodosia burst into tears and laid her head on the arm of the chair.

"There now. What can be so horrible?"

"Oh, Reverend Pickett. I am miserable. I have been miserable since the day I came here but more so of late and it's… it's been *awful.*" Soon the whole story came out, and Reverend Pickett grew pensive as she spoke.

"No, they can't make you marry him, Miss Brown. If they tried to publish the banns, I would not read them. If they try to obtain a license, I would not sign my name. Without your father's permission, they cannot make you."

"I can't understand my aunt's insistence or his parents'! I don't believe my aunt... I don't believe she has a letter from Papa. But why would the Brookses want me to marry him? Why?"

"Why, indeed," pondered the good Reverend. He could come up with a few answers, but they were hardly polite and hardly able in their content to reassure the girl. What was worse, as much of the girl's relations as the Reverend had come to know took the sad form of *Bannochs,* he wondered if she hadn't painted a rosier glow on her American family than she wished to admit. Was it possible she was a wayward, spoiled child? He sighed. He'd seen a hundred cases like it; she could be, but she would be that one in one hundred that did not fit any of the molds he'd seen.

"So you've written your parents?" he soon offered. "And when could you expect a reply?"

"Two months, I suppose. Just when I'm to leave... unless Papa sends the monies earlier. But, oh, Reverend, what if my aunt has the monies already and simply won't tell me?"

"Now, before you jump to further conclusions, let us move backward for a moment. Would it seem likely your aunt loves your parents and wishes to please them by marrying their daughter well?"

Theodosia sniffed and looked at him without blinking. "No, Reverend. Nothing she has done would make me think it. On the contrary, she has led me to believe she hates my family, although I know not why."

"Yes... ahem... yes, I too would believe Selda Bannoch would, er, not go to this much trouble for... well, yes. Then that leads us to the other road—why does she pursue it?" A light began to dawn in his eyes. "Could it be that the Brookses have signified to your aunt they might 'bless her' for her efforts?"

Theodosia thought on it awhile. "But why in Heaven would they wish me only for Alfred?" The emphasis did not escape the Reverend's notice.

"Why? Well, you are charming, vivacious, young, pretty, the daughter of a well-to-do solicitor, and in general, the eldest... er, marries first. Isn't that true in America?"

"Generally, although it is not a hard and fast rule," she said thoughtfully as she straightened herself in her chair. "And I thank you for your good opinion, but my papa is well-*known*, sir, not particularly *well-to-do*." She smiled. "His friends have often complained that he is too honest to succeed at the bench. My family has no *standing*, as such. I'm really no one at all."

"Well, not no one, child... well, then, we... ah, but do the Brookses know this?" She glanced back to him. "I mean to say, suppose your Aunt Selda put it in their heads you were quite wealthy?"

She sputtered, "What proof could she give them?"

"Proof? Well, harum... hrm... well, he's sending his daughter for a lesson in manners all the way to England. Not many can afford that!"

How true that is, she thought sadly. "But my aunt offered to pay my way to come if my papa would provide for the return."

"Ah! And then there is his well-dressed, well-coiffed daughter to represent him."

"I've worn mostly Cecelia's things ever since I came. As I think on it, Aunt Selda's had me wearing all her daughter's things... recently all new... and all too small for her." Her voice rose. "And she does my hair. Ah, but I ask her to. Whenever I do it up, gravity defies my efforts."

"I'm glad for your sense of humor, Miss Brown; it is from God, you know. 'A joyful heart maketh good medicine, but a broken spirit dries up the bones.'"

"I am doing my level best to keep Aunt Selda from breaking my spirit."

"Ah, well, then, you will fail," he said simply.

Aghast, she looked at him. "What? You... you think... she'll win?"

"I didn't mean to sound quite so flippant. What I meant by it was that if you are trying in your own strength to overcome her, you will fail. You need a stronger ally, don't you think?"

At first she thought he meant himself but she soon took his true meaning. He was pointing, as was his calling, to his God.

Well, she believed in God. She called upon Him now and then, whenever she was in trouble, but certain things she thought were best handled on her own. "I see," she said gently, wishing to be polite but unwilling to concede the point.

Reverend Pickett continued to smile. "When you go home this evening, Miss Brown, remember what I said. He wants to be with you on this path of yours, uphill or down, a constant companion."

She looked about her and swallowed. Trying next to make light of the conversation's direction, she said, "Surely God would wish for a better companion than myself."

He shook his head slightly. "No. He loves you as you are. Died for you... where you stand. Created you for fellowship with Him. If you question His love, think again of His Son on the cross at Calvary."

She'd never heard God spoken of this way. "Created for fellowship? But I was taught we were created to serve Him."

"We cannot truly serve what we do not truly love."

As beautiful as the words were, her thoughts immediately veered to Alfred Brooks, and it brought a grim smile to her lips. "Just what I tried to tell Mr. Alfred Brooks, Reverend, but he doesn't wish to hear."

The Reverend's brows rose and then slowly lowered. "Seek the Lord, Miss Brown. Seek Him in this matter and in all others."

"But I know His will in this situation! I merely need to convince *them*."

But the Reverend shook his head. "If you hesitate here... well, child, only look... look for a moment to who is presently winning this contest."

She thought on it, but the thought suddenly grew to terror in her heart. Pulling her hand to her chest and with a face quite pale, she looked to the kind Reverend Pickett. "I *am* afraid of them, you know. There's no pretending I'm not. I am deathly afraid they'll find a way to make me marry him somehow." Tears welled as she continued, "Tell me... tell me I can come to you should any of this get out of hand."

"Yes, yes, of course. Without fail, child, I'll be here."

She sniffed and smiled and sniffed again. "If you were not here to speak to, I don't know how I should survive this summer. How is it, sir, that you are so... open to these discussions? You are very much like my pastor at home... and not at all what I expected in an Anglican minister."

The Reverend chuckled. "I'm glad I have some surprises left in me, Miss Brown. It is quite true I am less... *reticent* than many of my peers, but there is just cause. God granted me friendship with one brother in Christ from the church of Methodism and another from Wesley's Evangelicals, and I have taken my pastorship in a different direction, you might say, ever since."

"Ah. I've heard of the revivals here."

He smiled broadly. "God is at work, just as He is so clearly at work in you."

"And I will pray, Reverend. I will."

"Ask Him to be with you. And then ask Him... to take you in a new direction, eh?"

"I will... think on what you've said," she replied carefully, still wishing to hold the reins of her life and steer her own carriage along this dark and narrow path.

She stood and turned to leave but turned back to him to ask just one more question. "And how is Austin, Reverend?"

He stared at the buckles on his shoes. Theodosia gulped and waited. "I wouldn't know," he said plainly. "If you find the time, perhaps you could pray for him as well. I believe he's in a bit of a spot right now."

"A spot?" Her shoulders fell. "An English spot. Is that something like a puddle?"

A smile flickered momentarily upon his face. "More of a deepening pool for him, I think. Yes. It would be good to send a prayer his direction."

"I will." And then she took herself away.

It was when she was halfway back to Star Cottage that she realized it was Sunday morning. But the Reverend had never mentioned it. He was completely open to her, as if he had all the time in the world to listen. "He truly believes what he says." And she thought on his words all the way back to her room.

* * *

Throughout Austin's childhood, respect for one another among the Brookses was elicited through fear, manipulation, and the avoidance of shame. The proper description for a call to action among them was termed "duty" or "service required," but the underlying message remained—"Do this or you will be shamed; do this or we will cast you out." And in the realm of social requirement they found their hearts' desire: here they rested in obedience to social norms so they could be rewarded by the same. So it was the family had had a dark beginning in the shipping trade, but over time the Brookses believed they could find their way to the top of the social heap. In fact, they could see no other course of action, for they could sense no other way in which to define themselves.

But Austin had found a definition for himself that set him on a completely different path from that of his family. Yet this new understanding, his relationship to God, had come to him purely within the context of social privilege: of bread on the table, of clothing, of shelter.

Now with the privileges stripped away and his future left in doubt, he found himself laying aside the mental trappings of that life as well, and so, as if becoming a Christian had simply been one of the benefits of proper breeding, he put aside his God, but it was anger and not logic that forced his hand.

And in the bowels of London, he took up a new search for self, but he found nothing there on which to hang his opinion. Nothing and worse than nothing. And it was when he was in some alleyway, taking food from the back door of a poorhouse, the thought would come to him that all he had ever been was an orphan. An orphan taking scraps. And he would look into the eyes of the one who handed him the bread, and he would not thank the giver.

* * *

Quickly forgetting all of the Reverend's good advice, Theodosia thought long and hard on how she herself would dissuade Alfred from his suit. She finally settled on two means: One, she would make herself up to be quite silly with finery. If he liked plain and practical, she would be the opposite.

But the second means would be, she was sure, the more effective: He was a man of science, or, stated more correctly, a man *in* science. Whatever he was studying, she would find out and pursue it as far as she could go and then make a nuisance of herself. *God gave me a mind,* she told herself, *and I will use it until Alfred begs me not to. I will make him hate the thought of marrying me yet. Ha!*

As soon as was reasonable and her ankle felt perfectly well, she asked Aunt Selda to visit Brooks House with her to learn more of Alfred. Aunt Selda, taking it as a personal triumph, applauded her sudden good sense and straightway planned an afternoon.

The very next day, Theodosia found herself taking supper in the dining room at Brooks House, and, to everyone's surprise—most especially Alfred's—she positively fawned over him. She asked him all sorts of questions about his work and looked absolutely radiant as well.

She was exquisitely dressed and her hair was done up in the latest fashion. Lord Brooks stared boldly at her throughout the meal as if seeing her for the first time, while Alfred, the Younger, dutifully answered all her questions, all the while wondering why she cared. She amazed him still further by requesting an escort through the garden after the gentlemen had had their port.

Lady Brooks wondered at the change in her, but Selda Bannoch just smiled as if to say, *You see, I told you she had potential, and I knew exactly how to fix her to this match,* while Lord Brooks thought to himself he was beginning to understand why Austin had been so taken with the girl.

Cecelia had lent Theodosia the newest form of crinoline for use that afternoon. It was an odd contraption, this petticoat rounded with hoops, but Theodosia found to her delight that the merest movement of her hips caused her skirts to sweep seductively, and so she walked with a womanly sway while on Alfred's arm as they headed down the garden path. She had watched Cecelia's practiced motion a hundred times and enjoyed the game of it now, quite sure she'd actually seen a bloom of rose on Alfred's cheek as she brushed against him once. The plan was working just as she had hoped.

She had invaded his privacy, and now she would invade his mind.

"And, so, *Alfred,*" she said carefully, "since deciding to become your wife to please my parents, you can see I have settled in to the idea completely. To be a proper wife, though, I must know even more about you. You have yet to be specific with me regarding your experiments."

Alfred was never happier than when speaking of his experiments—even if it were only to a woman—and so casting suspicion aside he went into a lengthy and detailed description of his recent dabblings.

Theodosia noted every word, applying her mind to the concepts to trigger memories there. She had read a few of Parker's books of science a long, long time ago and determined to drive Alfred to insanity with her half-knowledge.

He was at the moment experimenting with salt water and wished to create a purifier that would draw salt so that one could have fresh water from the sea. He had tried sand and was ready to experiment with coal. When he was quite done with his explanations and the two were seated quietly under the selfsame bower Allan had used to speak with her, Theodosia began her own line of inquiry.

"Well, I'm sure all one has to do is think what salt is attracted to and there's your solution."

"Yes. That is why I have created mixtures of..."

"It seems to me salt is attracted to caves," she said while surreptitiously moving toward him on the bench.

"Excuse me?" He paled as her hand brushed his arm.

"The Austrian salt mines. They are underground, are they not?" she said with a beautiful little smile.

"Yes, but what does that have to do with…"

"Salt is obviously attracted to the lower depths, and so perhaps if you created a pipe that went underground…"

"Preposterous. Has nothing to do with it."

"Can you explain to me the salt mines then?" She moved even closer.

"Well, they are a natural deposit gathered…" He pulled his hand to his collar and coughed.

"Underground. As I said. You would do well to…"

"Miss Brown, you may not presume to tell me how to do my research," he said suddenly. "You know nothing about…"

"I know about Austrian salt mines. Everyone does. You know, Alfred, sometimes one ignores the obvious for the obscure, the latter having a certain fascination, I'm sure, but one would miss the point…"

"I have not given you leave to call me by my Christian name," he said stiffly.

She tried not to smile but to no avail.

Alfred, who had not the experience of his younger brother, was completely mystified by her behavior, at once attracted to her physically and yet repulsed by her skewed logic. It gave him an odd sense of being torn in two, and he quite suddenly got a headache which then gave him reason to take himself indoors.

Theodosia sat under the bower and smiled to herself. *Oh, Alfred,* she snickered, *you have so much to learn of Theodosia Brown.* Two days later, they had an invitation to Brooks House again, and this time Theodosia requested Alfred show her the laboratory in which he worked. He readily agreed.

He was obviously quite proud of the equipment and the various results of study, and, after walking her around the room, he once again brought the conversation around to science, but this time he did the asking.

"Here is a riddle suited to the female mind, I'm sure," he quipped. "Tell me this: If two men are dying—one has an ailment of body and the other an ailment of mind—and the doctors can only save one of the two, whom should they save?"

She cocked her head slightly. "I should think if the doctors were very clever they might take the healthy mind and attach it to the healthy body and save a little of each."

Alfred laughed. "Well, then, that raises an interesting question. Whose soul would the new man have?"

"Ah, a question of theology," she said. "I'm glad to see you think theology worthy of the female mind, Mr. Brooks."

"Well, it is certainly not worthy of science," he answered pointedly.

She gave no answer but swayed slightly with irritation. He had touched on an issue she cared about, and so the game had ended for her. In truth she answered him: "The operation would not succeed and both would die. Their souls would then enter God's purview."

"And your *reasoning?*" he said rather snidely.

"Well, it's obvious, really. God created each man as a unique product of His hand and then endowed them with souls. He would not mean for us to confuse His work, and so He would withdraw their spirits from them."

"A good answer... for a woman. But a stupid answer just the same."

"And I suppose you've the proper answer?"

"It's quite simple. The answer isn't spiritual at all, for man has no soul. And the man would live."

"And I say that's impossible. With the two men ill, you should work to save them both. They are both endowed with souls and worthy of our care."

"No, no. There the answer is physical, as well."

"You would save the mind, I know. You revere the mind above all else."

"No. No. Actually..." He smiled. "I would choose to perform whichever operation might provide the most information to the surgeons. I wouldn't necessarily choose to save the man with a brain; after all, we don't know if he's an idiot or a genius, do we?" He was quite happy with himself.

"The study of man is more important to you than all else, is it not?" she said with a distasteful look she could ill disguise.

"More than anything else."

"More than God?"

"Definitely more than God," he snorted.

Suddenly Theodosia looked about her. She pulled open one drawer and then another and Alfred soon grew irritated watching her.

"What are you doing?"

"Looking for your God, Mr. Brooks. You have him writ so small I thought perhaps you kept him in a drawer as a specimen."

Alfred's eyes grew wide, but then he laughed loudly. "I knew you weren't a fool," he said finally. Alfred had had time to think since their last interview and with some deduction had found his own conclusions. He knew she'd played a game with him on their last visit, trying to irritate and confuse him with her pseudo-science and flirtation, and so he decided to play the same game with her in turn. "Perhaps I do keep Him in a drawer," he added rudely.

Very quietly, with her eyes steady and her chin held high, she replied, "My God can hold the universe in the palm of His hand, and He is everywhere found in His creation."

"If He is everywhere, then there is no point in looking for Him."

"On the contrary, I should think it very difficult to be a *real* scientist and not come face-to-face with God daily, and so I would say that you must work *very* hard at whatever it is you do."

He smiled. "Good. Good. Excellent. Well done."

"Excuse me?"

"In future, Miss Brown, you might remember that I can find your sore spots as easily as you find mine, so let us make a bargain. I will speak no more of theology if you will speak no more of salt mines."

Theodosia blushed and lowered her eyes. She had underestimated him.

But he smiled again as he stepped forward. "You'll see I can play the game, Miss Theodosia Brown, so take care you don't fall into your own trap, eh?"

Unfortunately his words caused her to look up just in time to meet his kiss. ∾

ELEVEN

∿

When I was a little boy
My mammy kept me in,
But now I am a great boy
I'm fit to serve the king;
I can hand a musket,
And I can smoke a pipe,
And I can kiss a pretty girl
At twelve o'clock at night.

Nursery Rhyme

∿

Theodosia's reaction to Alfred's kiss was a swift and accurate slap to his left cheek, leaving herself to wonder much later and with a full head of guilt why she hadn't slapped Austin in the self-same way.

She didn't tell anyone about Alfred's kiss, not even Fiona, for she was afraid that somehow being kissed by two gentlemen so recently when she'd never kissed a man before in her life might indicate a certain predilection on her part—that somehow she had shown herself willing. She rued her decision to flirt with Alfred, but she'd only begun the ruse because he had appeared to dislike feminine affectations. Now she realized what men say and what men do can be quite different kettles of fish. After all, Austin had shown her he cared something for her and now he was nowhere to be found, but Alfred who seemed to care so little could kiss her fiercely whenever he wished. How strange men were.

The one thing that gave her rest and comfort after her meeting with Alfred were the words of Reverend Pickett. There was nothing left to do now but take his advice. She must pray. And so she found herself paging through Scriptures in the morning and taking in the words to relieve her fears and settle her heart. But she found more than just relief. After reading, she spoke to Him. And over time she began to speak with Him in a way she hadn't since a child, tentatively trusting Him with her daily life, and eventually seeing, perhaps for the first time, that to rest in Him completely was the only rest she'd ever need.

In feeling the joy and wonder in the new relationship that followed, one must forgive her for thinking her spiritual battles were over, and furthermore, that God would "fix" her troubles and all would be well. The Reverend tried to tell her, warn her, but she was not ready to hear.

In that first week of July, she began to visit Reverend Pickett in the afternoons. It became a habit of circumstance that she would ask after the Bannoch carriage to take her to the Reverend's home, and though she would be assured of its availability, by teatime Cecelia or Frederick or Selda herself would invariably have already taken the carriage on rounds. She was forced at times to go with them on their visitations, but more often than not, and especially as the summer wore on, the Bannochs were more than happy to foist her onto the Reverend's hospitality. She was surprised at first that they allowed her to walk there unescorted, but she soon realized that although her Aunt Selda was well versed in every minutia regarding matters of decorum, if the rules of etiquette did not suit her personal needs, the whole of etiquette was shoved aside.

For Reverend Pickett, it was a standing appointment. Sometimes others were present at tea, but often it was only themselves. And in those long, private conversations, asking one question on Scripture might easily catapult them into a long and cheerful discourse that would send Theodosia from the tea table more satisfied than if she had been served an eight-course meal.

At other times she went on rounds with him, visiting his parishioners, and it was then she saw, for the first time, another side to England. Kind people with a gentle quietness about them that made her feel immediately welcome in their homes. Some were shy, but if she stayed long enough, she soon saw they were generous and loving, and as Fiona had told her, close-knit in community and home. She expressed those observations to the Reverend

Pickett, and then they had a long conversation about the differences between England and America: the ancient history as opposed to the newness; the lack of land versus the mobility afforded by wide-open spaces; and the reserve of England's people in contrast to the gregarious personalities of Americans.

"I'm glad you've met a little of the rest of England, now," said Reverend Pickett after one of those talks. "I see a better picture forming in your mind."

"I'm afraid I have painted too much with black, it's true, but I still believe America is the more... the more, shall I say, righteous?"

"Righteous?!" the Reverend said with surprise. "How so?"

"Well, we are more honest and open—there is less room for guile."

"On the contrary, I consider it a virtue to reserve one's honest opinion at times and allow peace. We encourage one another to forbear."

"But of forbearance we have a great deal! We have more freedom to express our beliefs, to live as each one chooses; there is an air of tolerance."

"Yes, but that encompasses a tolerance of slavery in the east, and a tolerance of lawlessness in the west, I've heard."

Theodosia swallowed hard and looked away.

The Reverend smiled faintly. "My dear Miss Brown, I hope I have not given you offense, but I believe the trouble here is your choice of palette. There is a great temptation found in youth to paint everything in black and white, while I believe sin is the same, whether on one side of the Atlantic or another, and so I doubt there are as many differences in national virtue as you might suppose, only other avenues chosen for evil and for Truth."

Theodosia bowed her head in deference to his opinion, but she was too proud of her country to outwardly agree.

* * *

Alfred had ceased visiting Theodosia, and because his parents and Selda Bannoch were assured the match was made, neither house pressed further meetings between the two. After all, the Brookses had more important things to concern them: the disappearance of their third son.

There had been a quiet moment between Lord and Lady Brooks the morning after the costume ball. When Lord Brooks told his wife about the note, she gave no expression to her face. He went on to say he'd thought it strange Austin had chosen not to say good-bye, but the note explained the behavior well enough. He was quite sure the boy had somehow discovered his origins. The dreaded moment had come.

They sent for their solicitor who, after some amount of arm-twisting, finally informed them, yes, Austin had found a copy of the will. Where, he did not know, but he was sure the boy had destroyed the document by now. And, yes, of course the solicitor had the original.

He left Lord and Lady Brooks alone to worry over Austin's fate. "Should we send for a detective, Mr. Brooks?"

"Hmm?" He awoke from thought. "Detective? Interesting. I don't know, my dear. It's as we've always feared, isn't it? He has left us." He pulled his hands behind his back. "Wouldn't think he'd want us to find him, do you?"

Lady Brooks replied stiffly, "Quite so. He... he's in God's hands, then."

"Always has been." Lord Brooks had never encountered the thought before but suddenly wanted to believe it with all his heart. He walked to the window of the orangery and surveyed the wide yard, the park of trees, the rose garden to its side. Very quietly, too quietly, he thought, for his wife to hear him, he asked, "But will he ever forgive us?"

And though she pretended not to hear the question, she heard him and held her tongue. She had no answer. She held no hope.

* * *

Three weeks to the day on which Austin arrived in London, he came to a decision.

He had lived life as a gentleman for twenty years, but for the past twenty days he had lived like a beggar. He'd traded work for drinks and begged money for food. He'd had his coat and scarf stolen and almost had his shoes removed from his feet as he lay sleeping. He had had enough of gutter life.

So now what should he pursue? Should he go to the country and offer himself as an apprentice clerk in some small city? Should he work as a laborer at a farm? Hardly any position could be gained without some sort of recommendation. Was there anyone from whom to get a recommendation?

This last thought made him remember Reverend Pickett. In all his wanderings through the dark alleys of London, he had ceased to think of him until that moment. In truth, he felt unworthy of God's care.

He'd thought of Theodosia often, but this, too, he had decided was foolishness. She would never be his. In fact, he had decided all of his beliefs were foolishness, useful for a previous life in which he was no longer a part, and so he put those thoughts out of his mind completely.

Of a certainty, there was precious little to remind him of God in this corner of the earth. He'd seen men robbed, and women and children beaten, and he had observed himself on such a level with their kind that he raised neither voice nor hand to defend the victims.

As he rubbed his eyes now, though, and watched a wretched little man make his way down a short row of sleeping sots, poking his hands into their pockets and smiling at everything he found, Austin told himself that the difference between those that rose above and those that remained below was merely the want of opportunity.

Grasping opportunity was key.

Why should he live in the alleyways when for most of his life he had worn the great and wondrous name of Brooks? He may not deserve the name by blood, yet he could find a way to use it, couldn't he? Look at Roundtree, he reasoned. His background didn't stop him from rising up like froth in the mug. If he could go back and work for his father's office a little longer he could find another position in time, couldn't he? Somewhere far away? Perhaps ride out on one of his father's ships and leave the country entirely. Yes.

And so it was time. He would return to Brooks House and see what could be had for him there.

The thief began a tussle now with the last fellow in the row, a fellow not too drunk to understand what the little man was about.

Austin watched them with as much concern as a bull at a cock-fight, his thoughts a thousand miles from the scene. He sauntered out of the alley in which he had slept the night before, passing carefully behind the drunk who had taken to thudding the man's head into the brick wall behind him. He turned into the road then and headed toward the London docks, to the office of Brooks Tea.

* * *

"Maman, I believe I know what happened the other day when we visited at Brooks House... when Theodosia came home so flustered."

"Do you, dear?" said Selda Bannoch.

"Mr. Alfred Brooks kissed Theodosia."

Selda Bannoch put down her needle. "I'm sure I don't know what possible business that could be of yours?"

Cecelia's eyes narrowed momentarily but she soon rallied. "I just thought you'd wish to know, Maman. You seem to want the whole thing to come off. I thought you might wish to know how well you had succeeded."

"How nice of you to tell me, Cecelia. How ever could I manage without you?"

But Cecelia was so used to her mother's ways, she'd grown numb to only the most pointed of her barbs.

Cecelia had seen Theodosia running from the laboratory on their last visit; she'd stepped forward and peered in to note the redness of Alfred's cheek and his need to bring his spectacles back onto his face. That Alfred had "taken advantage" of her cousin's naive behavior was obvious, but what she might do with the information was not readily apparent to her.

In the quiet of the sewing hour several days later, she'd decided the information was worthless, except for the irritation it might cause her dear mother... and Theodosia. At the least her mother would speak to Theodosia about such common behavior and bring the girl to shame.

And so Cecelia told her.

But for some reason it irritated Cecelia more than it did Selda Bannoch when the telling was complete. Alfred's smug look as he rubbed his fine cheek returned to her memory again and again. He was turning away from the door as he pulled his spectacles back on, but she'd seen his look. She hated smugness—especially in men... especially in Alfred.

Since a child, Alfred was the Brooks boy the local children chose to torment. He was too proud to tell on them, they well knew, or too afraid of being hurt further by the bullies. Allan joined in the children's fun at his older brother's expense, while Cecelia stood back and watched Alfred's expression as the bullies tried to raise his ire. He didn't yell. He didn't quell the abuse with his fists as most boys would. He simply stood for it and then quietly walked away. She thought he was a pansy... at first.

But Alfred simply waited and then took his revenge one child at a time. And Cecelia, whose mind worked in a similar manner was not surprised when she began to hear the stories. Alfred had sneaked down to the public school and done his worst, she knew.

A report would come that oil of sulphur was placed in one boy's inkwell at school and that the entire class was let go for the day when he uncapped the stinking liquid, and Cecelia would know whose fault it was. The next day it would happen that ants took over the desk of a stout boy. Sugar was the culprit. Cecelia knew the boy was too poor to bring sugar to school. She knew who it was.

And on it went until every last child in the group who had mocked and pushed Alfred in the courtyard of the town had suffered individually; he often played to each one's own worst nightmares—like the boy who hated snakes whom Alfred... Cecelia shivered, remembering.

And so when Theodosia ran from the laboratory, Cecelia knew Alfred Brooks had exacted a revenge on Theodosia with a kiss. She resented her cousin's bumbling attempt to imitate her almost as much as she resented Alfred's disdain for the imitation. "I would have slapped him, too," she told herself, "if given the opportunity." But the opportunity was not hers, and for that she hated Theodosia all the more.

She had told her mother about the kiss, and her mother, she surmised, went to Theodosia and scolded her for her inappropriate behavior.

When the guest room door slammed shut and her mother's footsteps receded down the long hall, Cecelia felt it time to look in on her poor cousin. But as she drew up her hand to knock on the door, she heard her cousin's sobs, and then she didn't knock at all but went straight in.

"Oh, Cecelia, how could you?" Theodosia said with a voice raw from crying.

"I did it for you, Theodosia. I couldn't stand by and watch Alfred take advantage of you like that."

"But Aunt Selda thinks it's my fault."

"I never told her that. I only said that perhaps Alfred took your late improvements for encouragement. He was still a brute to do it, and you were right to slap him."

Theodosia grew bright red as she listened. "You saw it all?"

"I saw enough."

"Cecelia, I hate him. I can't possibly marry him."

"Was his kiss so awful?"

Theodosia blushed once more and wiped the tears from her eyes with her handkerchief. She trusted Cecelia little more than she trusted her aunt, and when she put her handkerchief aside, she stopped to look at her cousin carefully. Something in her eye kept her from replying. She sniffed.

"Well. Was it?" Cecelia tried to remove the interest from her tone.

But Theodosia only stared at her and slowly Cecelia became uncomfortable.

A light dawned. Short of believing Cecelia cared anything for the wooden scientist, Theodosia could believe Cecelia was jealous. Jealous that an arrangement was not being made for her. And why was there no arrangement? She was older than Theodosia and certainly more accomplished in the female arts; she was attractive if not beautiful, with a sensuality about her that drew men to her like bees to honey. Why was she not married by now? Theodosia wondered. "Cecelia... may I ask you a question?"

"About men?" She winked.

"Yes, about men. Why have you not married one by now?"

Cecelia balked for a moment. Then she drew her thin lips into a smile. "Perhaps I've not seen a man enough for my liking."

Theodosia kept herself from saying, *I find that hard to believe by your behavior,* and managed to reply, "Would anything keep you from finding the right one for yourself?"

"Your questions are much too personal."

"I see. The subjects of whom I marry and whom I am kissed by are quite open for discussion, but you... ha, you may keep such things to yourself. I see."

"Yes. Just so. It is you who are about to become engaged." Cecelia rose, for the conversation had become a discomfort to her.

"Why hasn't Aunt Selda chosen a man for you when she's so very able to do so for her niece?" Theodosia asked quickly.

"Perhaps she expects more for her daughter." Cecelia arched her neck toward Theodosia.

"More than a Brooks? Whatever in this world could be greater than marrying a Brooks? I was almost certain by this family's behavior that the sun and stars revolve around that family!"

Cecelia pushed her jaw forward and swayed her hips. "The fact is I would never lower myself to be anyone's wife, when other more profitable arrangements could be made."

Theodosia's eyes grew wide. "Whatever do you mean?"

"Humph." Cecelia tossed her head and curls away from her cousin. "You're too much a child to understand!"

Theodosia stared at her with her mouth slightly open. Suddenly she drew in her breath. "A mistress? Do you mean a mistress?"

Cecelia hadn't expected her to answer and so, without reply, fell to watching her cousin's expression. Theodosia's mouth had shut and she gulped. Cecelia smiled, but now Theodosia's eyes suddenly grew teary and her head tilted to one side. Pity. The look of pity was everywhere about her.

Cecelia could not stand to look another moment. Abruptly she turned away, muttering, "You are so very *provincial,* little cousin, I hardly expect you to understand…" She brought her hand to the doorknob.

"Oh, Cecelia, I am so sorry…" But Theodosia's words were cut short by the slamming of the door. ༄

TWELVE

❧

Oh, what's the matter wi' you, my lass,
An' where's your dashin' Jimmy?
The sowdger boys have picked him up
And sent him far, far frae me.

Nursery Rhyme

❧

O n her afternoon visits with Reverend Pickett Theodosia often
prayed with him over word from her family, but so far no
answer had come.

As time wore on and Theodosia was there for over a month,
Aunt Selda began to press her more often. Theodosia told her aunt
she expected correspondence from her family any day that would
reveal exactly where she stood. Aunt Selda would remind her of
the letter she held, but whenever Theodosia demanded to see the
missive, the discussion would end.

The truth was, Selda Bannoch did not show her niece the letter
from her father because he had written it to Theodosia and not to
herself, and she'd gotten hold of it by taking her mail. Meanwhile,
she assumed that Alfred would eventually win Theodosia's stubborn little heart. And if not her heart, her desire for position, title,
wealth, security, and a husband who could be both devilishly handsome and completely undemanding of her as a woman. What more
could one wish for? And so Selda continued to dress her Theodosia
beautifully and school her in manners and deportment while she
waited patiently for the trappings to take hold of the inner woman
as well as they had the outer.

Theodosia had indeed grown less awkward since her arrival, but
it was due more to an inner misery than any lessons her aunt may
have force fed her. Despite her good talks with the Reverend

Pickett, over time she felt herself wearing down. The intense emotions that once led her into trouble were replaced with a malaise. She felt much like a doll, dressed and primped to be shown off to advantage, with no further expectations demanded. In each of the social activities in which the Bannochs now engaged her company—including morning visits and the occasional dinner—very little interested Theodosia, and along with the lack of interest came a lack of accident. She no longer rocked on her heels, she no longer stared at a thing too long.

In short, she no longer cared a fig.

Only the meetings with Reverend Pickett and an occasional visit with Fiona could brighten her spirits. Upon returning, Austin avoided her company—avoided social occasions of any sort, in fact. Theodosia's prayers grew short again and her reading of Scripture a habit instead of a joy. Aunt Selda was steadily succeeding.

The Reverend Pickett was amazed and gratified to find that Austin had returned to Thistledown, but every attempt he made to speak to the boy ended with a polite but straightforward refusal. The Reverend was not surprised; it only led him to pray for Austin all the more.

As for Austin's parents, Austin had prepared them for his arrival by sending a note ahead of him. In it he had not made the slightest reference to his orphan status but only apologized for making some errors in judgment that led him to be derelict to duty for a time.

But a week after his return, as the Brookses took breakfast in the dining room, a solicitor was announced as a visitor. The Lord and Lady glanced at each other and then toward Austin. The red-faced glower Austin gave as his reply let all in attendance know that, henceforth, neither party should feel the need to fool the other on the subject of the will.

* * *

The ladies sat in the parlor of Star Cottage with their needlework. Theodosia was glad for the silence of the room during the past half hour.

Suddenly Cecelia brightened. "You know, I have the oddest information. Austin Brooks returned to Brooks House a week ago...."

Theodosia pricked her finger and brought it quickly to her lips.

"I know, Cecelia," said her mother tiredly.

"Ah, yes, but do you know how he spent his time in London, Maman?"

Theodosia swallowed. She didn't want to hear anything about Brooks House—and certainly nothing about Austin.

"He went drinking. Pothouse after pothouse. That's all he did for three full weeks!" said Cecelia proudly.

"Imagine. A gentleman doing such a thing." Aunt Selda clucked her tongue.

Theodosia tingled from head to toe as she considered that Austin might have gone into a drunken stupor over her. No. She quickly put that thought out of her mind. Still, she would speak to Reverend Pickett about him that very afternoon. She'd prayed for Austin all this time, and so it would be appropriate to ask after him. She'd been dying to ask about him ever since the Reverend instructed her to pray.

It *did* seem possible that finding out his relatives wished Alfred to marry her might have upset him. But then the reverses she had felt over the last few weeks gave her no confidence in fairy tales, and so after ten minutes of fanciful thought, she put the idea to rest—it was entirely too ridiculous for words.

But she thought of it again on the way to Reverend Pickett's home. As usual, Cecelia had taken the carriage out at the last moment and so Theodosia had to walk. The one good thing to come of Alfred's visits was that he'd made it known he liked her in spectacles, thus Selda allowed her to wear them once more. And so she enjoyed her walks all the more, and this day it gave her time to plan her words. She thought perhaps she could ask the Reverend about Austin without being too obvious. Surely, if anyone knew Austin's heart, it was the Reverend Pickett.

When the servant answered the door, though, Miss Brown was told that the Reverend Pickett was at the church.

"At the church?" She'd met him so often for tea at his home, the servant's words surprised her. "Of course... the church." Now she remembered. He had business there this afternoon, and she was to join him for tea in his office. "I'll go right there then."

"Very good, miss." And the servant disappeared behind the door.

The church was but a ten-minute walk up and over a green hill if one took the shortcut. Theodosia thought she'd like the shortcut, and so she strode along the road hemmed at either side by tall grass. She adjusted her spectacles, and a large dovecote standing to the left of the road caught her eye. She veered from the road then and walked through the lush field to look at the doves' home more closely. It stood a good twenty feet high, and she marveled at the architecture—it was quite fancy with the latest in cottage-style woodwork. She watched the multitude of residents on their front stoops speaking to one another in gentle if persistent tones. Some flew in. Some flew out. When she decided she'd looked long enough, she spoke loudly to their wide-eyed innocence, "Friends, when someone invites you to live in a grand residence like this and never asks you for a ha'penny's rent, it would be wise to discover what else they may want from you!" The doves looked at her blankly, answered, "Coo," and went about their business. She shrugged and moved on.

When she came to the top of the hill she let her parasol hang limp by her side and stopped to look about her. Behind her lay the outlying neighborhoods of Thistledown, the Reverend's cottage and Star Cottage among them. Low mountains lay in a long purple line far off in the distance in front of her, and the fields were plowed, rowed or left fallow, each section edged with tall trees or stone walls. The rippling patterns of the farmlands ran along the valley to the edge of that mountainous string. She looked again at the gray of the stone walls. What did it take to make them so thick and high?

Her eyes were drawn to the right and there lay the rest of Thistledown. The two churches took firm anchor on either end of town and between these two spires lay cattiwumpus the lumps and bumps of homes and businesses, mostly stone but one or two of stucco and timber, thrown together in no particular order except to keep themselves free of the street, and for some even that was a failure.

She removed her spectacles to clean the lenses. When they were clean and she could see again she looked across the rooftops once more at Reverend Pickett's church. The cross and brown shingles of the tall spire caught her eye, and she smiled slightly. And then, far up on the hill, she could see Brooks House.

It was a candy box. A long, square candy box. The yellow marbled walls and long windows were perfectly symmetrical and pleasing to the eye. The landscaping was perfect. Poplars in a row to the right and left. One small pond, one lovely bridge, the park. She could not see the rose garden behind, but she easily remembered its grandeur.

"And would I want to be Lady of that House?" A little flutter rose up in her. "Yes," it said, but it was batted down the next second. For another look at the home brought her to another conclusion entirely. "No. It is more tomb than candy box, I think, and I will not be its Lady." She smiled. "But who would have thought I might ever have the choice?" But the word "choice" gave her pause. Suddenly she prayed, "Lord, don't make me live there. Never. Your will be done, but, Lord, I pray this is not Your will. Show me the way out, Lord. Please show me the way out."

She opened her eyes and started down the path once more.

* * *

Austin decided that on that very afternoon he would take himself to Reverend Pickett's. It was time for him to tell the Reverend Pickett where he stood. He owed him that. The man had been a friend, though it was clear to Austin that his friendship in this new life was no longer required.

As he walked toward the Reverend's home, Austin's previous life seemed a thousand years distant though it was less than a month previous.

"He's at the church, sir."

"At the church," Austin grumbled. "He's not usually there this late in the afternoon."

"Yes, sir."

Austin turned and walked toward the town.

* * *

Theodosia found Reverend Pickett speaking to a family in the church foyer. He was smiling and patting hands and generally making himself useful to the group. Theodosia noticed they each held packages and when she spied a shirt-sleeve hanging from the little boy's package, it came to her what they were about.

"And have you met Miss Theodosia Brown?" Reverend Pickett drew the family around to meet her. "She is from *America*."

This last bit of information drew sighs and nods from the group, and after Reverend Pickett properly introduced them, the father spoke up. "America, is it? Oi meself have got three cousins in America."

"Oh?" said Theodosia, smiling.

"They be fishermen."

"Ah. Which port?"

"*Pill*adelphia, I think."

"I've never been. I live in Virginia."

The wife said, "Oh, Oi've got a friend what took herself to Virginia. She lives in what they call them Blue Mountains."

"Ah, yes, the Blue Ridge Mountains. Yes."

"Well, she said they was *blue*," the woman retorted.

"Yes. I've heard they look blue... at times. Quite blue." Theodosia nodded and smiled and then didn't know what else to say.

"Well, then." Reverend Pickett coughed slightly. "It's a small world... small and some of it... (cough) no doubt very blue at times. But I suppose you'll want to go home and see if these things will do for you, eh?" And the family was on its way out the door.

Reverend Pickett laughed as he brought her to his office. "And

I wonder what might be on your mind this afternoon, Miss Brown? Please yourself to have a seat."

Theodosia very carefully sat herself into an ancient piece of furniture whose disposition was difficult for her to judge.

"Yes. That chair will hold you. Not to worry. But let me see if I can round up some tea for us, eh?"

"May I help?"

"No. No. I spied Mrs. Taggert down the hall not a moment ago. I'll soon find her."

Theodosia listened to the Reverend's heavy footsteps echo down the hall. Not three minutes passed before she heard footsteps again, this time quick and furtive. She laughed and straightened her shawl, fully prepared to tell him it was quite all right if he had found no tea after all.

She turned and stood, thinking she might help him with a tray. But when she looked up, there was Austin Brooks in the doorway of Reverend Pickett's room.

And her smile froze upon her face.

He looked wild-eyed for a moment but quickly recovered. Removing his hat, he bowed to her.

"How do you do?" he spoke politely. "They said Reverend Pickett would be here."

"Yes." She curtsied slightly and looked down. "He's gone to find some tea."

"Of course. Always has to have his tea." He turned his head toward the door as if to leave.

Theodosia gulped and bent her head toward him. "You've been well, I trust?"

He gave a faint smile and waved his hat slightly. Then he looked down at her feet. "Your ankle is better."

She blushed. "Yes."

Now they both heard the Reverend's heavy footsteps, the rattling of a tea tray keeping time with the rhythm of his heel and toe. Theodosia watched Austin's face and thought she saw a sudden paleness, a tightening of the jaw muscle. She knew she must not stay.

The Reverend gave hearty greeting to Austin, but Austin only grimly returned his hail.

Suddenly Theodosia was speaking. "Reverend, I am so sorry, but I realized as you were gone that Aunt Selda wants me home by five, and I really must be going."

The Reverend came through the door, passed Theodosia, and placed the tray down next to her upon his desk.

Austin spoke up. "I didn't realize you had a guest. I'll come back another time, sir… anytime you say."

Theodosia turned to Austin. "You needn't." Then to Reverend Pickett, "I have to go, really I do."

"But you had an appointment with him!" Austin spoke too loudly.

"Why, I don't have an appointment! We simply meet for tea now and then. I will see the Reverend tomorrow."

"Well, I've only a few words to say to him, so don't feel you have to leave on my account."

"I'll leave on my own account, sir, and whenever I wish! Good day to you!" She grandly pulled her shawl about her—it was Cecelia's, of course, a glorious peach silk with foot-long fringe—but like nettles to cloth, the sweeping silken strings promptly caught a brass nail on the tray's edge.

She walked toward the door with angry steps, and the force yanked the heavy tray toward the desk's precipice. It was only by the barest luck that one of Reverend Pickett's hands still held the opposing handle so that the entire service was not pulled to the rug.

Too late for the porcelain creamer, however.

Theodosia's barest thought was that Austin had grabbed at her shawl; she whirled about to see if it were possible and was ready to clobber him with the nearest item, the Reverend's presence notwithstanding.

But when she saw that turning about had upset the creamer and that she was, in fact, held back by nothing more threatening than a copper tray, her anger was immediately quashed by a deep and burning embarrassment.

In the meanwhile Austin's visage went from anger to amusement in the few seconds it took to realize what she'd done.

Theodosia looked back and forth from Austin to the tray and then to the Reverend Pickett, who was fumbling to straighten the creamer and contain the damage. "I am so sorry, Reverend! I will clean it up for you!"

"No, no, my dear. I'll do it, and I'll see you tomorrow." Reverend Pickett pulled the silk strands from the nail to release her, hoping that between her earnestness and Austin's anger at least one of the two young people could manage to leave the room without destroying it.

"Well, I thank you!" She forced herself to lower her voice. "Thank you. I shall see you tomorrow then." She glared at Austin and swept her shawl about her once more as she passed him by.

But as she walked briskly through the open door, the second fateful sweep of the shawl caused the fringe to catch a bucket of pew-found walking sticks and umbrellas, and so even as she pressed onward and around the corner, the bucket dutifully followed her. The sticks, clattering and careening across the floor behind her, alerted her to what had occurred.

In horror she backed up just as Austin reached down to pluck the items from her shawl. Their fingers met on a walking staff which soon fell to the floor with a clatter as neither one held on. Theodosia pulled her hands to her face as Austin pulled a stray umbrella from the tangled silk without looking up at her at all.

She wanted to apologize again but she knew it would seem all too ridiculous. As Austin straightened up the stand, she gave a quiet thank you and bit her lip.

"Not at all," he said, finally looking into her eyes. "Oh, and Miss Brown. I forgot to tell you I received your billet."

Her eyes widened. "My billet?" She had completely forgotten the note demanding that he apologize.

"I would apologize for my past behavior, but perhaps it would mean very little to you now, so instead allow me to congratulate you. And all the best to you and the future Lord Brooks." He gave a smart little bow.

Theodosia looked past Austin at the Reverend Pickett even as the tears gathered for a spill and then she turned away and walked quickly from the room. ∿

THIRTEEN

❧

The lark is so full of gladness and love,
The green fields below him, the blue sky above,
That he sings and he sings and for ever sings he–
'I love my Love and my Love loves me!'

Samuel Coleridge

❧

As the Reverend Pickett sat across from Austin, he was quite sure of one thing: Austin Brooks was *almost* in love with the girl. At least two things held him back: One was Alfred's supposed "claim" on her. The other was Austin himself. The boy thought himself unworthy of the girl.

The Reverend had watched his actions with dismay, yet he believed some good could come of it—some *"good to those who love God and are the called according to His purpose."*

Meanwhile, Austin tried to gather his thoughts. He straightened his jacket, pushed his watch deep into his watchpocket and observed the Reverend, who was pulling his hand across his mouth. "My visit will be brief," Austin finally said. "I came to tell you I've renounced my faith." Reverend Pickett's hand ceased to move and he looked into Austin's eyes. Austin looked away and placed his hat back on his head. "Perhaps, if you hurry you may catch Miss Brown and have tea with her after all."

Reverend Pickett looked at the boy-man before him. He had been smiling into his hand, ready to offer the young man some tea and a little gentle advice in the ways of men and women, but now he shook his head.

Austin hesitated. "You don't believe me? I'm quite sure of myself. I've had four weeks to think on it."

"Oh, well. Four weeks. Well, as much as all that, eh? Seems to me you've had plenty of time to give it clear thought then. Time to study the world and such. And so now you've made your decision."

Austin fiddled with his watch fob and prepared to leave again. "Yes... I have studied the world rather closely of late, and I didn't see God in much of anything. I thought I owed you the truth, sir. You've been... you've been good to me in the past."

"Me, is it?" The Reverend pressed his lips together and looked up at the ceiling. "There was a time you saw the hand of God moving you." The Reverend's hand passed over the tray before him. "You felt His strength, observed His power, accepted the gift of the sacrifice of His Son, His love for you...."

Austin looked at him with a blankness of expression almost frightening in its intensity. "Yes, well, all that sort of talk... is fairly useless to me now."

"Ah, but wait... you said you owed me the truth. Well, you still owe me the truth. You didn't see God in the streets of London because you did not seek Him there. But He was there, and despite what you may tell yourself He still has His hand on you. His hand... you may not see it, you may not feel it—more than likely He has you by the collar—but as you dance this tightrope He will hold you up. He hasn't changed, Austin."

"Well, I have."

"I know you have," he said, his voice full of emotion. "I know and I just ask... and I pray that you will leave some opening for Him... and for me, for that matter."

Austin grew quiet and then without warning, the feeling came forth in a torrent. "There is nothing for me here any longer! Don't you see? A family, a place, and a faith. *Austin Brooks'* faith! It all belonged to him, not me—that fool Austin Brooks, whoever he thought he was! It's all his. Not mine! And I don't want it! I don't want it now!"

Reverend Pickett stood and moved toward him, but Austin flailed an arm to keep him away. "Leave me alone."

"I'll pray for you. Miss Brown and I have been praying every..."

"Pray for me all you like, but you'd do better to pray for the

Brookses. Mister Alfred Brooks, in particular, may need your prayers more than I." He laughed, jamming his hat onto his head.

"She is not engaged to him, you know."

"She will be. She will be. My moth... Lady Brooks always gets her way. And what difference would that make to me anyway?" he yelled. "*Blast* you, sir. I told you to leave me alone. Go take care of your poor and needy, would you? I'm telling you... I'm telling you you needn't count me in their number any longer!" Sharply he turned, pushed the door open, and without looking back took himself out.

Reverend Pickett bowed his head and went back to his chair and sat down. But in the quiet moments that followed, he heard a little sound coming from the hallway. He looked to the doorway and saw no one, but the voice came again and more persistently.

"Reverend Pickett..."

"Miss *Brown?*" He stood up, walked to the door and looked out upon an empty hall.

And then, from behind the thickness of his office door—wedged between the wall and door, in point of fact—he heard once more the little voice of Theodosia Brown. "I am so sorry to trouble you, Reverend Pickett, but I fear I have become entangled on the hinge."

* * *

Austin opened his eyes the next morning and lay still upon his bed. A slight breeze blew at the curtains. Birds sang. The world seemed at peace, but Austin was anything but peaceful. He could not force from his memory the tears in Theodosia's eyes when he'd congratulated her, or the look of sadness in the Reverend's eyes as he made his speech. To know he'd hurt them both gave him a pain in the heart he had not thought possible. Lastly, he could not forget brushing Theodosia's hand; the pain from touching her was worse than any other.

Why was this so difficult?

Why hadn't the words come more easily?

Hadn't he had that selfsame conversation with Reverend Pickett a week before in an alley behind the White Swan? And hadn't he touched Theodosia's hand in a hundred fitful dreams that came to him just before dawn and the agony of hangover? In London you could get roaring drunk and say anything you liked to anyone you pleased as long as it wasn't a constable with a truncheon.

The difference was this: in London, no one cared.

He had really wanted to apologize to Theodosia when he found her at the church, but instead he'd insulted her. And the man who meant more to him than any other? He had hurt him just as easily, perhaps more deeply. Austin could have kept his lack of faith to himself.

And resting on these thoughts as one might in a fit of morbid curiosity decide to recline upon a bed of nails (tentatively at first but willfully when one sees no hope of rising without pain), for the first time in quite a while Austin allowed himself to feel ashamed.

But then self-pity elbowed its way into his thoughts, and then anger and finally hatred for his former family gave him purpose.

Soon, he decided, he would make certain the will failed for "his brothers." *The will says three scholars must come from Thistledown,* he told himself. *The weaver's son was one. Henry Taylor could be the second.* Yes, he would see to it himself. Then he would find a third and be done with it. He decided to speak to Henry's schoolmistress right away.

And so he accomplished three things in the space of an hour: averted the pain of a pricking conscience, found justification outside himself for all his anger, and neatly and efficiently removed from himself any knowledge of the truth.

* * *

The morning after she'd seen Austin at the Reverend's office, Theodosia thought on her conversation with Reverend Pickett afterward. He reminded her to be strong and patient, and to try not to fret over her aunt's meddling, that her father's letter would come and make things right. All this advice was well and good, but none of it was what she wanted to hear.

What she wanted to hear was an explanation for the renunciation of Austin's faith, but the Reverend would not violate the sanctity of his conversations with Austin.

But she kept on asking about him, and before he knew it he had shared more about Austin than he'd ever shared concerning one of his charges, barely keeping the knowledge of his orphan status to himself. When he realized he'd gone too far, he tried to concentrate on a description of the boy as he knew him. This Theodosia was happy to absorb, and the Reverend was grateful to find a safe topic upon which to rest.

He explained to her a little of Austin's hotheadedness: a good thing when he held a righteous indignation for wrong suffering, but a bad thing when his indignation could not find itself in righteousness. "But," he said, tempering his words, "his anger never lasts. Even this... this thing he struggles with right now... you'll see. He'll come back around to his Lord. God has him by the collar."

"I see it in him. If he really meant to turn away from God, he wouldn't be so angry about it, would he?"

"Exactly, my dear. His emotions betray him... just as he wasn't angry with you at all a little while ago.... I believe, in fact, he..." Here the Reverend held himself back. The girl had a way about her. Again he was saying so much more than he should about Austin Brooks. Looking past her little spectacles into her large, brown and hopeful eyes, without thinking he had almost ignored the most basic of counselor's tenets: to avoid meddling.

But with nothing to keep her from meddling in her own affairs, she blithely said, "I think he cares for me very much... as I care for him. But, Reverend, how shall I tell him how I feel?"

The Reverend coughed. Never had he had such a plainspoken young lady in his offices, and never had such plain speaking demanded such honest answers. Clearly she was not trying to be rude, only open, a trait she had in common with Austin Brooks. And so, despite all his rules, he shook his head dolefully. "Now is not the time, I'm afraid. Now would not be the time."

She accepted the verdict, though with regret. She wanted very much to at least explain to Austin how little his older brother meant to her so that he would know she had nothing to do with this foolish courtship, but *now was not the time*, and so she would try to give it up.

How she wished it *were* the time, because Austin might help her through her present sorrows by giving her a reason to hope, whereas her aunt was a constant reminder that no hope was in sight. Selda Bannoch's cruel words were like the thudding of logs against castle doors, and too often Theodosia felt herself splinter and give in to the blows.

Then she would pray hard for strength and the regaining of the sense of peace she once had—the sense that God would make everything right for her. For she was not at all certain how long she could wait before her castle doors splintered, gave way and fell.

* * *

"Alfred, when would you like to set the date?"

"Mother, don't talk such tripe. You want me to marry, and so you may be pleased to set the date yourself."

"Alfred!"

Alfred put his book down and stared blandly at his mother.

"Do you hate the girl? I won't have you marry her if you truly hate her."

Alfred pushed his spectacles back up his fine nose and thought briefly. "No, I do not hate her. She has more sense than some. Not distasteful to look upon. No, I do not hate her."

"Good, good. I'm glad to hear it. She's coming over with her aunt this afternoon and we shall speak of dates and times."

Alfred stood up and shoved the book under his arm. "Well then, you won't need me. I believe it is Saturday."

"The wedding?"

"No. Today's date—Saturday," he said with disgust.

"Yes."

"Well, I'll be in the laboratory then."

And he was gone from her presence too quickly for her to protest.

Aunt Selda had not warned Theodosia what the meeting at Brooks House might be about. She had simply taken all that morning to lecture her niece on that most simple and beguiling of words, "duty." A daughter's duty, a woman's duty, a Christian's duty—she hit upon them all.

Aunt Selda continued the diatribe on duty in the carriage all the way to Brooks House, and Theodosia's mind simply could not listen any longer. She stared at the back of the swaying carriage, and her vision began to swim and her mind drifted into other thoughts entirely. For a moment she was transported home. *Her family was heading to church. Her mother was commenting on the beautiful roses in Mrs. Fredley's yard, and her younger sister was smiling and nodding happily. Her father was looking over his family in silent approbation, and she felt safe, secure and happy. She also felt her corset was too tight and her dress too heavy. She was never more uncomfortable than on Sundays when she dressed her best and drew her corset tight.* Theodosia straightened her back and took a deep breath. It was the tight corset and the stuffy dress that reminded her of home. She smiled, but then she turned to see the profile of Aunt Selda's pinched face, her mouth still moving over the same discourse.

Theodosia sighed.

She looked out the window and saw they were riding up the carriage path to the house. They came up on two old women dressed in dusty work clothes and bent over in the grass with baskets beside them. Weeders. The carriage rolled past, and they didn't look up or stop their backbreaking labor, even when they were swallowed by a cloud of dust from the carriage wheels. For all the world Theodosia would rather weed the great lawn of Brooks House than be considered for its future mistress.

In half a minute they arrived.

In the library Lady Bannoch came to greet them. To Theodosia's surprise, the servants brought chairs to the drum table in the center of the room, and they sat down. Theodosia's view was of the back wall; up and to the right was the volume whose red leather she thought she could see from there. Her cheeks grew pink, and she looked back to the ladies.

Theodosia was soon made aware of the gist of the meeting. A letter had been sent to Theodosia's father asking for her hand in marriage to their son, the Honorable Alfred Seton Brooks. They would have an informal engagement until a reply was received, a matter of approximately two months.

All this was said without Theodosia saying one word.

Two more months. Fall.

They asked neither for her opinion nor her comment. She was, to put it mildly, stunned. She looked back and forth at the two. Perhaps she wasn't really there at all and this was some horrid nightmare.

But she knew it was not a dream, and whatever the ladies had in mind, their plans would have to stop.

"Lady Brooks!" said Theodosia in such a way as to draw their attention immediately. "May I speak?"

Her aunt gave her a vicious look from the corner of her eye, but Theodosia stared intently into the hooded eyes of Lady Brooks. "Certainly," the Lady replied.

"I do not wish to offend this House. You have been kind to me and to my aunt, but an impression has been given that my parents will expect me to marry your son, and, alas, I must tell you it is not so."

Lady Brooks smiled politely and bowed her head. "Be careful what you say. All that you do will have consequences. Think... think quite carefully before you speak."

"You see, dear, Lady Brooks has read the letter I have from your papa," Aunt Selda added. "Nothing is kept secret here. We both know your papa will approve."

It was a nightmare.

"I don't believe you have such a letter!" Theodosia sputtered. "And you cannot publish the banns. Reverend Pickett will not read them without my father's consent!" The last was said in a vain attempt to appeal to their sense of ethics.

The ladies looked at one another, neither taking the warning seriously. Aunt Selda said blithely, "Bride's nerves, Lady Brooks. Theodosia, we will take that chance. And we would never consider publishing banns, my dear—it is considered a very vulgar form of public display."

"He won't grant you a license, either."

"Then we'll apply in London. For all your queer little ways, dear, I know in your heart you wish to please your parents." At this she reached out her hand for Theodosia's as if to calm her, but Theodosia briskly withdrew her arm to a safe distance.

Theodosia's mind raced. She knew the letter must be false, yet would Lady Brooks lie about such a thing along with her aunt? Could Selda Bannoch have forged the letter? And could Theodosia's future be contained in the writing of one letter? And if they could create out of thin air a letter from her father, couldn't they create another that approved of the union? Anything seemed possible, for the impossible was happening at every turn.

The ladies returned to their conversation and ignored her while Theodosia's mind tore through one awful thought to the next. And so she sat before them silent and dumbfounded, too numb inside herself even to faint, too beyond fear even to scream. She sat and sat and waited for the session to end, looking vaguely forward to the time she could go to her room and fall upon her bed.

They drove home in silence. Theodosia walked the hall in silence. And she fell upon her bed, but she could not even cry.

She did not sleep well that night, but when she awoke, a note from Fiona awaited her. The house had received the note the day before, but her aunt had deemed her too distraught to read mail.

She let this minor irritation pass and jumped on the note like a drowning man to driftwood. In the note Fiona asked her to come for tea—that very afternoon. A return note was dispatched, and Theodosia had at least one thing to look forward to that day.

The family attended church that morning, and Theodosia drank in the Reverend's words. Austin did not attend, she was almost relieved to see, but she was sad as well. His absence reminded her to pray for him.

She only looked to the Brookses' box once to determine

Austin's absence and was not the least interested in whether Alfred had appeared. But he was there, of course, for his mother wished it, and furthermore his mother expected him to converse with Miss Brown after the service.

But his attempt to visit with her at the door of the church was taken with an angry silence on her part, and the Brooks family took note of it with great distaste. Aunt Selda, observing Theodosia's silence, came up beside her and pinched her arm until she almost cried out. And so, with a face pale with pain, Theodosia began to nod and smile ever so slightly. Finally the Brookses relaxed and Alfred was able to bow and bid adieu.

Later that afternoon, Theodosia took herself to Fiona Mienzes' apartment, the upper room of a weaver's home, and they settled down to tea. The room was clean and whitewashed. A brightly colored rug lay before the fireplace, and a few copper pieces hung nearby. Her bed ran along one wall, and a trunk lay at its feet. A couple of pegs next to the door held her cloak and bonnet. Strong furniture with artful lines was set precisely around the room, a well-turned bed of mahogany in one corner, and plaid throws lying here and there that Theodosia assumed to be the Mienzes tartan.

The quiet of the room calmed Theodosia's heart somewhat. Soon Fiona drew out all the details of the previous week and then of Theodosia's rather sudden engagement.

When she was done, Fiona lifted her chin. "Ye mustn't give in to the Brookses. Ye've got to fight them."

Theodosia shook her head. "I can't until I know my father's will. A horrible thing is gnawing within me that says they may be right."

"Surely they've no right to push ahead with this without his approval." Theodosia nodded but lowered her head. "So if they trouble ye further, they'll have me to reckon with then."

"Oh, Fiona." Theodosia took her friend's hand. "I have you and Reverend Pickett, and I thank the Lord daily for that. I don't see how I could stand this if I didn't know there was a place to hide. Without a letter from Papa, I don't believe they'll take this any further, but... they may have lied about a letter from him already, you see, and so... I don't... I don't know quite what expect..." Here Fiona sympathetically squeezed Theodosia's ar and she cried out in pain.

"What's this?" asked Fiona with a look of fear.

"Nothing... it's nothing."

"How did ye hurt it, Tee?" Fiona pulled her chair closer to her friend's.

Theodosia looked down. "I... I hurt it... I fell."

"Dinna' lie to me. Dinna lie to a friend."

Theodosia looked up and shook her head forlornly. "Aunt... Aunt Selda pinched me at the church door until I would speak to... to..." But it was no good. She leaned into her friend's arms and lay there crying for a time.

Fiona rocked her as if she were a baby, the selfsame way she had cradled a child who'd fallen in the schoolyard just two days before. When Theodosia's sobs grew quieter, very softly Fiona said, "It must be terribly frightening for ye. I canna' imagine being made to marry a man I didn't care for. Worse than death, it'd be."

"Yes." Theodosia tried not to weep again. She shook her head. "Yes, it would be. Surely God will spare me. The Reverend says to be patient. I don't think I can stand much more."

Fiona swallowed. "And may God give me strength when the time coomes, for I'll not let them near ye!"

Theodosia could only nod and smile.

When she quieted completely and finally dried her eyes, they drank their tea and it wasn't until another pot of water was set to boil that Fiona deemed it necessary to bring up another subject. "I've heard all about Austin disappearing and cooming home ag'in, Tee."

"Yes." Theodosia took a deep breath. "He came upon me at the church when I was visiting Reverend Pickett two days ago... argued with me about who should stay with the Reverend, but I insisted I'd come another time, and then..." She smiled slightly. "He gave congratulations on my... forthcoming engagement."

Fiona gave half a smile. "May I ask ye a question?"

"Yes."

"Do you love the man?"

"Fiona, love can't come that quickly."

"Oh, no? I've a different view on that since my poor sister."

"Which? The one in America?"

"Yes, the one in America. She was at Dundee Cottage... that's our home in Aberdeen... and playing the piano of all things when she fell in love."

"No!"

"'Tis true." She smiled. "A young American... on the European Tour he was... he was wandering the countryside lookin' fer his supper, and he happened upon her playing in our parlor. He stood at the window and watched her, the bold thing."

"Did she know he was there?"

"Aye! The whole time! *Liked the look of 'im*, she told me. *From the corner of her eye*—just like that. He listened to her for hours. She played every single piece she knew." She laughed. "Full afraid he'd disappear if she quit her playin'! But he din't disappear, and when she was done my sister raised herself up and then and there she curtsies to him at the window. They were engaged within the week."

Theodosia let go of a gentle laugh as she shook her head. "I think I should like to meet your sister."

With a touch of melancholy, Fiona answered, "Aye, and likely ye'll see her before I do."

They were silent for a time. Finally Theodosia asked, "Fiona, have you never thought of going to America?"

"Noo, I've got no bold American a'tryin' to steal me aw'y. My family's here, my neighbors and my friends...."

"Were you very angry when she decided to go?"

"Indeed I was and no denying, but it did na' bring her back to us." Fiona shook her head in dismay. "I know ye dinna' understand aboot our families here. Ye've been given no fair example, what with the Bannochs and the Brookses, but our families and our neighbors, they marry near and live near, and if they dinna' love one another, they learn to, or they keep it to themselves."

"But I've heard the clans feud awfully? You've said yourself you're a fighter."

"Aye, but it's our business and we settle our business when it coomes time. I know it's different there... in America, ye've no need to settle things, as ye can get up and leave whenever ye like."

"But my family is close," she answered defensively.

"Is it now? And how close is your brother Parker then?" she quipped. "No, I'll stay in Scotland, thank ye."

"But, Fiona," said Theodosia carefully, "you're not in Scotland."

"Aye. No. No, I am not." Her chin swung slightly to the right and her eyes fell away. "No, I am not, and neither is my sister," she said, but this time the tone was more thoughtful.

"I'm sorry."

"No, I'm the sorry one, to snip at ye so."

"But I didn't run away from the argument, did I?"

Fiona gave her a lopsided grin. "No, and ye dinna' shoot me with a six-gun, either." She laughed. "And ye've been callin' yerself an American." ❧

FOURTEEN

∾

Sing reign of Fair Maid
With gold upon her toe–
Open you the West Door
And let the Old Year go.

Nursery Rhyme

∾

Miss Fiona Mienzes looked around her classroom for the last time. The benches were set in careful rows. Her desk lay bare. Earlier that morning she'd listed the things that would be required for the next year: repaint chalkboard, get new map, have another shelf built, borrow other books from Brooks House? (an idea she'd taken from Tee after seeing the beautiful tome on wildflowers).

She saw the new-built shelf and borrowed books in her mind but had no idea whether the wish could come true, nor whether she would be there to see them.

As she looked at the four walls of her little domain, she remembered all the good and bad things that had filled the last school year: the day she discovered Richard's incredible talent with art, the day she punished Philip and discovered she was wrong to do so, the week Gwendolyn changed from a quiet little mouse of a girl the children ignored to a giggling little flirt of a girl the boys wouldn't leave alone. "Quick and strong as weeds they grow," she said aloud. "Some I'd like to plant in my flower box, and some I'd like to pull up by the roots!" She laughed.

"I can imagine," came a voice from behind her, which gave her a start. Austin Brooks stood in the doorway, removing his hat.

"Mr. Brooks? H-how may I help you, sir?"

"I'm sorry. I knocked but I suppose you didn't hear me. If you please, Miss Mienzes, I was wondering where I might find Henry Taylor."

"Ah. Henry's home is just down Pease Lane. Third from the church on the west side of the road."

"Very good." He seemed to struggle with the thought of saying more, but then he placed his hat back upon his head.

"It's very kind of ye to seek out Henry, sir. He would so appreciate the extra work." She lowered her eyes, for she was thinking of America and how perhaps he wouldn't leave if his family could do a little better here.

Austin looked quickly about the room, trying to decide exactly how much to say to her. It wasn't that he couldn't trust her with his plans; it was more the entanglement she might cause as Henry's schoolmistress that kept him from speaking. She might tell him how to proceed with lessons, things of that nature, and so he held his tongue and only bowed.

Fiona watched him leave. *What a kind fellow he is,* she thought. *If only he and Theodosia had a chance in this world, I think they could be happy.* But then her eyes swept the room once more, and she thought of herself so far from home and forced to stay the rest of the summer in England. Her family could not afford to keep her in Aberdeen, and so she had had to find a way to earn her keep. All because her beau, the boy from Aberdeen she'd grown up knowing she would marry, ran off to Canada two years before without so much as a good-bye.

Fiona sighed as she walked to the door of the school. "And, Fiona Mienzes, what would ye know of happiness to be wishin' it on others?" She shook her head even as she shut the school door behind her.

* * *

Austin finally found Henry fixing a stone wall out in his family's second field a good half mile from town.

"Henry!"

"Mr. Brooks?"

Austin came to a stop at the wall a few feet from the boy. "Henry, I've a business proposition for you."

"Sir? For me?" Henry rested a stone on top of the wall and

wiped the sweat from his brow with his sun-browned arm.

Austin hadn't thought much beyond this opening line, and he looked around the boy briefly to come up with a following statement. Recovering quickly, he asked, "I don't imagine you want to lay stone forever, eh, Henry?"

Henry grinned. "It's work."

"Aye, it's work," Austin said more seriously. "And it'll break you soon enough... like... all the men hereabouts." He had no need to add *like your father*, for Henry knew exactly what he meant.

"Aye," said Henry with an even look.

"Well, then, I've a proposition for you that will keep you from this sort of labor for the rest of your life. You'll make money... enough to care for your whole family. You'll do well for yourself, smart lad as you are."

Henry's mind was racing ahead, itching to know what Mr. Brooks meant and hoping beyond hope it was what he'd been thinking on for so many weeks. "What is it, Mr. Brooks?"

"Have you ever wanted to go to University, Henry?"

"University? I've had no cause to think on it. I mean, it's been good of your family to help us with schooling, but there's only so far and then... well, you know how it is. We stay by our families."

Austin winced slightly and pressed on. "Yes, but what if you could *take* your family with you?"

Henry's eyes grew wide. "I've always wanted to go."

"That's what I thought you'd say."

"Aw, Mr. Brooks. You don't know what it would mean. I know exactly what I want to do, you know... where to settle in. They say you can just look at the corn and it'll grow for you there, and I'd like an American school, I'm sure, but from what I've 'eard, I really wouldn't need University at all."

"Corn?"

"Pennsylvania! *That's* where I want to go. I've heard the Carrolls speak of it a hoondred times. We could do well there, I know it."

"I'm afraid you've lost me."

"Eh?"

"Henry, I'm talking about giving you an education *here.*"

Henry's eyes grew cold as he appeared to take his meaning. "And why would I want to do that, sir?"

"Then you could get a clerking job... in my father's firm." Austin gulped. "You'd do well and never have to farm again. Your father could rest then, Henry."

"Beggin' your pardon. I'd be ungrateful if I didn't say thank you, but I couldn't plow that bit o' ground and make a go. You know how it is, sir. If I went to University, I woon't be treated like a gentleman by the fellows. And if I come out I'd never be treated as a clerk. I'll always be a dirt farmer, like I am." He shifted his footing and raised his voice. "But a farmer's a fine thing to be had in America. He's an upstanding citizen. A man's no better nor worse for what he does in America. There's no society there holdin' some up and holdin' some down. It's just people."

"And who told you that bit of nonsense, Henry?" Austin asked, irritated by the boy's naivete.

"Miss Theodosia Brown, sir. She said it's so herself in the school the other day, and I believe her."

* * *

The only bit of it that still nagged Aunt Selda was Theodosia's persistence; she insisted her father would never wish a marriage like this and yet Selda held the very proof of her father's intentions for the girl in his own handwriting and on his legal letterhead! *One would think he would have better prepared her,* she thought to herself. *My sister should have prepared her, certainly, but she probably didn't think of it... such a numbskull—ever a nose in her books... or perhaps she thought she'd leave the task to me. Then again, perhaps they* have *prepared her and she's lying to me while refusing their wishes.* She shook her head and set her sewing aside for a moment. *Well, it's become irritating beyond reason dealing with that child. If another letter doesn't come soon, I shall have to show her the first one, and that's all there is to it.*

Selda moved her head slightly to observe Theodosia working with concentration on a knot in her needlework. *Everything she does is gangly knots. Horrid handiwork. A waste of a girl. It's really too, too amazing that I've been able to pass her off for anything. Just shows what fools the Brookses are.*

Her gaze fell on Cecelia. One of her daughter's eyebrows was arched in seeming concentration, yet her needle moved ever so slowly. *She's planning something. Daughter, what have you in mind? I shouldn't wonder if you weren't plotting against me at this very moment. Frederick, my dear departed Frederick… would that you had lived to see your children! Ungrateful and disobedient to the core. Why was it fate decreed they inherit the sullen and selfish disposition of their father? They vex me at every turn.*

Cecelia glanced up to note her mother's disapproving glance and sighed within. Her needle picked up speed as she tried to collect her thoughts. *It's of no real benefit to me that Theodosia marry Alfred, though Maman will carry on about it as if it's the most wonderful thing in the world. I don't wonder if the Browns haven't promised her something for getting rid of Theodosia for them. Well, if Maman won't tell me, I don't feel a burning need to comply with her wishes. I'll interfere in any way I please, and I'll have fun doing it besides.* Cecelia began to smile over her stitches.

Theodosia concentrated on the knot before her, determining the path of the knotted thread and working the needle in and out but then losing the path and having to start over. *Why do they think women are born to this sort of thing?* she thought morosely. *All I can ever make are knots. This is an English plot to drive me mad, the way they insist on finishing each color with knots and snippings. The American way is so much more sensible—letter to letter. Who cares if the back of our needlework is a mass of threads as long as it's pretty right side out? I wish I could make something entirely of knots—a pillow or something. Now that would be the American way.* She smiled, shook her curls and tried again.

When the misplaced knot would not come out she put the needlework down with disgust and looked about her. *Was ever a more depressing little parlor created?* she thought.

Aunt Selda had chosen navy blue for the upholstery with heavy burgundy fringe trimming its lines, navy blue curtains with burgundy trim and a burgundy, navy and gold rug. Mahogany—dark, slick and shining—was set all about. The shutters were closed, but the slats were opened to bring a little light. Only the walls gave relief from the oppressive darkness, but even they were a dirty shade of gray Theodosia detested. *It's all so different here than what I had imagined. So different from home.* The tears wanted to come again, and she was quite tired of fighting them at every turn.

She'd spent at least an hour in her aunt and cousin's company, and so her duty could be considered done. She caught Aunt Selda's eye and yawned ever so slightly. "I think it must be time for bed."

"TheoDOsia, before you go, child..." Her aunt always said the name as if it tasted of vinegar. "I saved this information for this moment so that you may sleep upon its content."

Theodosia sat calmly and nodded. They had forced an engagement upon her; would they now try to set a date for the wedding?

"The Brookses are holding an engagement party in your honor next Saturday—a ball in their home." Theodosia was too stunned to speak. "You will be the guest of honor. Of course, you and Alfred will be the lead couple. You have a little more than a week to prepare yourself. Cecelia has a dress for you. Now you may go."

Theodosia swallowed hard, thought harder, and finally said with a measured calm, "Aunt Selda, you cannot make me marry him. However much you like to dance about the truth, the truth will come. My parents will not wish this for me and I will never say *I do.*"

"Then you are a spoiled, ungrateful waif who cares nothing for her family! Your papa will bless you for tying yourself to Alfred Brooks, and well you know it."

"And would I marry with my family thousands of miles distant?"

Selda's eyes narrowed. "We are your family, too, and your family is not likely to attend for reasons I should think obvious."

"They are not at all obvious to me!" Theodosia said indignantly.

"You see, you beg me to be confrontational! So be it. I will be blunt—your parents cannot afford to come. This marriage is important to your papa. His financial security is at stake. And don't you take such things lightly. We who live in the real world certainly do not. No, we most certainly do not."

Grasping desperately for logic and reason, Theodosia asked, "What possible benefit could the Brookses be to Papa?"

"Shipping, you little fool. *Shipping.*"

Theodosia sat up straight, answering loudly, "But Papa hasn't handled shipping in years!" Yet, even as she looked into her aunt's cold eyes, a sinking feeling that *this* was why her parents wished a match took hold of her heart and chilled her to the bone. Her father had done well by shipping years ago, very well indeed, but he'd been left out of that circle for quite some time. Of course, he would jump at the chance. It was all too horribly clear.

As Theodosia grew to trembling, Selda set her needlework upon her lap and burned a long look into her niece. "You must quit playing the wounded spirit, Theodosia. Admit you've never had more attention in your life than as my niece in Thistledown! And admit you like your style of life here! Ha! I can see that for myself. Why, you've changed in a hundred ways in the last two and a half months. You don't trip so and your dress and manner has become... almost acceptable.

"But don't deign to thank your Aunt Selda. No. I've had nothing to do with it, eh? You cross, ungrateful thing! You who should be before your God in thanks for this wondrous opportunity— instead you're sitting there looking as if you'd like to pinch me. A fine thanks! Yes! A fine thanks for what I've done. Go to your room!"

And Theodosia, for fear she'd stab the woman with her embroidery scissors if she listened to her talk for one more moment, quickly and willingly obeyed.

*   *   *

Over breakfast in the Bannoch dining room next morning, Aunt Selda told a dazed and bewildered Theodosia the ball would be attended by the Brooks family, several business acquaintances and extended relatives, and that the number would exceed one hundred when the count was done.

Theodosia rallied to inform her aunt she was planning to be ill.

Aunt Selda retaliated by warning the child she'd be locked in her room the entire week with no visitors if she toyed with a pretense of sickness. With the thought of the loss of Reverend Pickett and Fiona, Theodosia warily complied, then steeled herself for her performance at the ball the only way she knew: she planned to see the Reverend Pickett every day and Fiona every other until the day of the affair.

Her relationship with the Reverend had grown such that she admired him more than any man she'd ever known. He was both friend and father to her. He seemed to have a gift for quiet conversation over tea that could lead his guests over the rough and bumpy hills of life and guide them back to the smooth road. He had a gift for empathizing with his guests and then allowing Christ to reveal Himself in their lives. As Christ had the ability to see into men's hearts when He spoke to them, so, to a lesser degree, did the Reverend; he could cut through the chatter and come to the soul of things.

When a widow woman spoke to him once of the despondency of her cat, the Reverend drew her out until she told him she thought her cat was lonely. He sensed she spoke of herself and suggested that she and some of the other ladies might gather for prayer on a given day and that way the cat could enjoy the company of more than one lap. The lady's eyes brightened and she was soon on her way, prepared to organize the prayer meeting in her home and thinking happily how much her cat might enjoy the attention of the ladies. The prayer meeting thrived, the special bond God creates with widows and orphans was soon established, and the woman never spoke of her cat's loneliness again.

This was Reverend Pickett's way with Theodosia, too, although this particular guest was not afraid to speak her mind, and so he helped her quickly and directly throughout that morbid week, causing her to realize how much she needed Christ's anchor to hold her fast when she felt the tide pulling her downstream. "Remember He does not promise to pull you from the water, only that He'll be with you out there in the struggle. Jesus prays in the Gospel of John: 'I do not ask Thee to take them out of the world, but to keep them from the evil one,' and another in John: 'These things I have spoken to you, that in me you may have peace. In the world you have tribulation, but take courage; I have overcome the world.'" The Reverend wrote them down for her, and she bookmarked her Bible with them: John 17:15 and 16:33. He'd ended that afternoon's session by mumbling to himself, "Suppose I've been in John quite often lately. It has a lot to say on the subject of orphans...."

Theodosia smiled. "That's very appropriate to me, Reverend, for I think I know a little of what it is to be an orphan." The Reverend thought to correct her by saying others they knew might have more knowledge of the subject, but he held his tongue and then they prayed.

Their last meeting was on Friday. Her apprehension over the ball the next evening was made more acute by the possibility of Austin appearing there. She wondered what to say to him. She also feared being alone with Alfred, but she would make that possibility as unlikely as she could. The whole evening promised to be one of cats and mouse, and Theodosia dreaded the game. The final insult, of course, was that the entire evening was a celebration of a certain "engagement."

Reverend Pickett heard her fears and addressed her query about Austin: whether Austin saw it or no, God was still working mightily in him. God was seeking him out even if he couldn't see it for himself.

As he spoke, Theodosia began to pull at the handkerchief in her lap. She tore at it as if she might pull it to shreds and then suddenly she interrupted him, "Reverend, I have to know. I can't stand it anymore. *Is it I?* Is it I who have made Austin so miserable of late? Tell me. Please tell me."

Reverend Pickett raised his eyebrows. "Well, no. No, not... entirely."

"En*tirely*?" Her lower lip began to tremble at the second and third syllables.

"His troubles... are of a family nature. But his troubles are most assuredly compounded by his... feelings for you. Feelings I see in him so clearly, but he cannot see himself."

"Oh," she said uncertainly.

"I mean," he said with a sigh. "Austin has had a crisis of opinion concerning himself. It has influenced what steps he might have taken to be your... friend. He feels... how shall I put it best... *unworthy*. Unworthy. Yes. That will have to do."

Theodosia studied the lace around her hankie. "I thought he cared. And I'd like to know more of him. I... I think I could spend a lifetime learning him." She pinched her lips together and shook her head. "Oh, why is everything so miserably complicated!"

He chuckled. "A human factor the scientists have yet to explain! The Bible comes closest to it, I think, what with sin and love and the differences between men and women, men and men, women and women. An infinite number of possibilities for trouble, I suppose," he said cheerfully.

"You make it sound quite charming."

"Isn't it?" He sat back in his chair and folded his fingers over his ample stomach. "I had a wife for twenty-five years that made me look forward to each and every morning. My heart broke when God took her home. Would that I could give something on this earth to bring her back... I'd do it. I'd do it. Not a day has gone by I haven't mourned my loss. But would I choose to decry the twenty-five years to be a happier man today? A man without pain? No. No and no again. I would have taken a year with her, a month, a day."

Theodosia smiled through her tears. "Are you quite sure you are human?"

"With no doubt human, I'm afraid. A merely human vessel, cracks, lumps and all," he replied with a chuckle and a grin.

* * *

The ball was to be a lovely affair sparing no expense. The Brookses opened a central wing of the home which held a grand ballroom.

The Bannochs arrived early, and Selda Bannoch was asked if she and Miss Brown wished to see the ballroom before the evening began. Selda agreed, hoping to impress the girl with future possibilities, but her aunt had commanded she not wear her spectacles that evening, and so Theodosia wondered how she would "see" anything. Her aunt led her around the room with a sidelong glance and a nod that clearly meant, "This also will be yours. Take this into account!"

From what Theodosia could see, the walls were made up of tall, pale panels, each panel painted with a pastoral scene (they were mostly green anyway) and edged with fine woodwork heavily gilded. Anything that was not gilded or oil-painted was cream-colored. One wall faced west and held floor-to-ceiling windows that were now letting in the last warm golden rays of sunset. She could see blurry pale green hills at the bottom of which, she knew, must lie Thistledown. She looked around the room once more—up toward the center of the frescoed ceiling where, willingly defying gravity, there hung a pendulous crystal candelabra by a string of glittering beads, and then she looked down to the high beeswax polish on the parquet ballroom floor—and she thought that although the room did at first please the eye, the whole of it seemed grotesquely overdone, even without her spectacles.

She looked to her aunt. "I would prefer the sunset on its own, I think."

"The plain-speak of an American! Bravo!" Allan glided past the two and pulled aside the heavy drape beside the nearest window.

"I meant no offense to your home, sir, I assure you," Theodosia said quickly.

"None taken. Who may compete with God's handiwork, eh?"

Theodosia smiled. "Who, indeed?" Allan came to stand next to the ladies; he was dressed in evening clothes and looking his best which was saying a lot for the man. *Surely there are none more charming or handsome than Allan Brooks,* Theodosia thought, *and more's the pity.*

"I shouldn't wonder if in your Virginia home one might find a fairer room," said he.

"Theodosia is very proud of her home, as well she should be," Aunt Selda quickly answered.

Theodosia's eyes narrowed slightly, but she nodded in agreement. She was indeed proud of her home, small as it was compared to this.

So far they had not seen Alfred nor Austin as they passed through the halls; they briefly met the Lady Brooks who had sent them to preview the ballroom. Now Allan led them back to the drawing room where they would wait to be called to the dance in less than half an hour. "Miss Brown, tonight you rival the vision of a setting sun," he whispered as they waited.

She promptly blushed and bowed her head and then took to staring at the skirt of her dress. It was a gown of white satin with an overlay of golden silk faille light as tissue and embroidered with little mirrored stars, each one set a hand apart. By candlelight, the stars sparkled on the faille like diamonds in a wheat field. The décolletage of the dress was trimmed with the finest white lace, complementing the softness of her shoulders. The sleeves, formed tight along the upper arm, fell downward in tissued pleats from above the elbow, as if a feathery golden trumpet hung from each arm. The dress was perfect in proportion and magnificent in its effect. Cecelia told her a dressmaker had made the dress for her because the lady "owed Maman a favor... a very *large* favor, if you take my meaning."

Theodosia did not take her meaning at all, but now she raised her head and her face grew grim. To wear it on the most horrible evening she would ever spend made the beauty of it seem shallow and base—an outward "Yes!" hiding the scream within her that cried "NO!" with all its might.

Just then Alfred Brooks came to escort her to the ballroom where they would become the lead couple in the opening quadrille. She steeled herself and placed her arm ever so lightly upon his—touching him was a thing repugnant to her, a thing which made her flesh crawl—and in reply he clamped his right hand over her forearm like an iron fetter. A tingle of revulsion went through her and her face grew pale.

The evening had begun. ∾

FIFTEEN

'Tis not how witty nor how free,
Nor yet how beautiful she be,
But how much kind and true to me.
Freedom and wit none can confine
And beauty like the sun doth shine,
But kind and true are only mine.

Charles Townshend

Only two sons were in attendance. Austin had kept himself away on the excuse of being unwell. Theodosia smiled inwardly to hear it, glad the Brookses could not twist his arm the way her aunt could twist her own, but then she was sad. Even an argument with Austin would lighten the burden of the evening.

She couldn't know the real reason he had decided to stay away.

When Lord and Lady Brooks pressed Austin in the afternoon he had replied rather tersely, "I hardly think it appropriate that you should have me dancing with your protégés." It was not good form to introduce persons of unequal social standing to one another, and so his parents instantly understood. They might have argued the point on the grounds no one but themselves knew his true status, but the look on Austin's face as he answered them quelled the speech.

Alfred danced the first dance with Theodosia and performed his duties tolerably well. Soon she told him her head had begun to ache, and so he took her to a chair, quite happy to have done with her. Alfred then joined a group of men by the side, turned the talk to science and thought the evening might be resurrected after all.

Theodosia, on the other hand, was clearly miserable and remained so.

She'd been introduced to dozens of acquaintances without a thought of trying to remember any of them and the exercise had tired her. Looks from her aunt forced her to join in conversation now and then, but her heart was not in her words, and so the hearers often gathered as much and found a way to end the introduction. Except for Alfred's dance, she would not accept any invitation to the floor. When Aunt Selda chided her for this behavior, Theodosia replied that she did indeed have a beastly headache, and as she could hardly think, was more likely to make a fool of herself on the dance floor if she was forced out upon it than if she simply sat. Selda, knowing Theodosia's past proclivity for tripping and seeing that the evening was not a total loss in that guests had begun to pity and speak kindly of the poor girl with a headache, decided to let her remain seated. Of course, propriety demanded that either she or Cecelia sit with her, and so she promptly commanded Cecelia to go and sit as well.

The cousins sat without speaking to one another, but soon Cecelia began surreptitiously to glance at Alfred by the wall. "Theodosia, Alfred is looking well this evening," she said.

Theodosia focused her vision on the skirts of the dancing ladies. "If you say he is, he must be, Cecelia; I leave the mysteries of fashion to you."

"Do you indeed? And here I thought you had begun to enjoy making yourself into a lovely to be admired. Surely you've noticed the approving looks of the men?"

Theodosia turned her head. "Cecelia, I have a terrible headache. Would you mind ever so shortening this conversation?"

"Never one to take a compliment, are you?" Cecelia said sharply.

Theodosia searched her cousin's eyes. *Perhaps if, just once, it were given in love.* She turned her gaze back to the dance and suffered on.

An entire roomful of people had met the girl, and all assumed she was mildly happy to be engaged to Alfred Brooks. They seemed willing to ignore the fact she was American. After all, they said among themselves, she would be returning to the fold if she married, and wouldn't that prove her country meant little to her? All these tidbits passed in little conversations about her. The world can become very quiet when one concentrates on voices fifteen feet away, and Theodosia's own unique power of concentration sharpened her hearing, and so she caught bits and pieces of these ruminations and then forced herself to act as though she hadn't. Ever so slowly she counted away the hours until it would be over.

At a break in the dancing, when the gentlemen took themselves to the punch bowl and the ladies retired to their dressing room, Theodosia took the opportunity to steal down the hall.

To the library.

Ah, the library. She creaked open the heavy door and peered inside. It was completely dark.

She walked softly to the drum table, found a lucifer match and lit the oil lamp. Turning up the knob to illuminate the room, she looked about her. The carvings along the bookcases cast great shadows that flickered with the yellowed oil flame, and the brass lamps and fireplace tools glowed against the softness of the mahogany. As she looked at the far wall through the glass doors she saw the promises of roses, and she remembered the moon was whole this night.

Her right hand slid through the side of her dress, and she rummaged until she found the waist pocket hidden there. From deep within, she drew her spectacles and carefully put them on.

The room became even more grand. The carvings, the subtle gilding, the rows and rows of books. Through the wavy glass in the double doors she saw the detail of full red roses dipped in moonlight. Delightful. Enchanting. A dream.

She turned to look at the curtains in the windows. "What harm would there be in my sitting in the window well and reading? None whatsoever, thank you very much. After all, I must take care of my aching head." But the truth was the headache was fast leaving her.

She carried the oil lamp to the shelves and perused the volumes nearest her. Though the ladder was available, she dare not use it. Within her there was that night a decided lack of interest in the family will. She had had enough of Brooks House and its secrets.

"Ah, here," she whispered upon finding the book on Virginia wildflowers once more. She pulled it out and then decided to find another to take to the window seat, as well. A likely little volume called *Yorkshire Verse,* full of songs and ballads from the neighboring county, came into view and she snatched it up.

With these tucked under her arm she moved to the west window and pulled back the curtain to look in. As if made for just such an evening's revery, she found a nook shelf in one corner on which the lamp might sit and tall bushes just outside the glass to keep her safe from prying eyes.

No one would see her from the outside, but if someone came looking for her inside, would they be able to detect a light through the velvet curtain? She set the lamp in the corner and shut the curtains and looked. No. How marvelous!

She pulled back the curtain once more and crawled in as carefully as she could in the delicate gown. She then tucked herself into a little golden ball in the corner of the window well and lay the volumes quietly in her lap.

Surely this was paradise.

Before long she had read "The Bleeding Stone of Kilburn Priory," "To the Flowers," "The Bilberry Moors," and "Come Where the Wild-Rose Blows," and had been transported to another place entirely. She ached for home, but somehow she knew each in her family was well, and that God was looking after her here.

She had a peace.

The flutter of pages fell away from her fingers and an inscription caught her eye: "To Austin, With abiding affection, Daphne." It was written in a young hand. She had found a book given Austin by an admiring young girl. She smiled.

And then she heard a noise.

Someone was rattling the lock of the door from the rose garden. Her breath came in little starts, and a pang of fear shot through her, but then she shook her head. There was no need to be afraid. No one could see her hiding in the nook.

Soon the door was open and heavy steps crossed the floor.

She sighed relief when she heard the door to the hall creak open.

But then hall voices could be heard, and the door was quickly shut again. Had they gone out? It didn't seem they had time to leave. *And who would hide from voices in the hall?* she wondered. But "who" came to her in an instant: *Austin. It could be Austin.* Perhaps he'd been out and was now sneaking back in. She smiled ruefully. *Perhaps he's been to see his Daphne.*

All was quiet in the room, and she finally decided he was not there after all. She turned the knob of the lamp as low as she dared and pulled herself forward to look out between the curtains, but suddenly she heard steps again. She froze. They were heading for the table. *The lamp! They're looking for the lamp—confound my poor luck!* But then the steps ceased.

"Who's there?" sent a chill down her back worthy of a dunking in the river.

It *was* Austin.

She bit her lip. Was it possible to embarrass herself with this gentleman any further? She proceeded to turn the wick up, open the curtain and show herself.

"Cecelia?" he asked, mistaking the silhouette of finely coiffed curls and the glow of the gown from the lamp behind her.

She remained still and quiet.

He wiped the curl from his forehead. "No, it couldn't be Cecelia. She would have given me a curt reply."

"I'm capable of curt replies, as well," she said.

"You." Even though she seemed to irritate him every time they spoke, still he had a catch in his voice when he said the word.

But he was not at all in a kind mood. He'd just been with Henry. As a favor to Austin, Henry had agreed to consider standing for testing, though he was certain he wanted to go to America. Austin and Henry had gone over some of the University requirements, but then Henry began talking about America once more. He was infatuated with the idea, obsessed with it, in fact, as was his entire family by now. All this hoopla Austin attributed to some childish notions Theodosia Brown had put into the boy's head, and he was thoroughly disgusted at how she had thwarted his own plans for Henry. He assumed she'd painted a pretty picture for the children far from the truth of things just to please herself, and so he was once more angry with her.

And once more she could not know the reason why.

To add to his discomfort, she looked extraordinarily beautiful at that moment, backlit by the soft light of the lamp, the glow touching her cheek and neck and causing the edge of her gown to sparkle around her like a diadem. All he could think was that her beauty was for Alfred's benefit, and that he could never hope to tell her how he felt. And so he said the furthest thing from his mind and heart. "They have you trussed up like the Christmas goose, don't they?"

Unfortunately, one could not see the sweat on the other's brow as he spoke the unkind words, and the other could not detect the tears that rose up at hearing them.

Austin coughed.

Theodosia said nothing.

To end the strained moment, Austin finally said, "If you wouldn't mind, I'd be pleased if you didn't mention my coming in like this."

Still holding the curtain out to either side, Theodosia gulped and pulled her feet over the ledge to face him. "Of course. Your business is... your business."

"Well, I agree with you completely there." He looked at the books she'd laid beside her in the nook. "I see you've made good use of the library... again."

"Uh, yes. I've enjoyed the verses here." She looked into his face. "I see this book belongs to you."

"To me?"

"Yes." She blushed. "The cover says 'from Daphne.'"

"Ah, Daphne," he said with a laugh. "Little Daphne."

Theodosia was sure he'd just gone to see her. He wasn't drunk, and so why else would a young man sneak out in the middle of the night? He'd gone to see little Daphne or some other girl. She bowed her head.

"She was a childhood friend," he said more seriously. Theodosia looked up as he added, "now gone," and immediately knew by his tone of voice that she had died.

"I'm sorry."

He nodded. "Well... now that we've touched a melancholy note, there is something I would like to discuss with you."

"Yes?" she gulped.

"I understand you spoke to Miss Mienzes' schoolchildren about America."

"Yes. Yes, I did," she said, completely baffled by the turn in the conversation.

He looked down at his shoes briefly and then cocked his head. "Well, I've had a bit of a conversation with Henry Taylor."

"Henry? The tall boy? Black hair?"

"Yes."

"A good boy. So friendly."

"Yes, and smart, too. Smart enough for University, in fact."

"Really? Could he? Can they... can you do that in England... send a farmer's son to college?"

"What do you mean, 'Can we do that in England?' Look here, the Brookses paid the way for the boy..." But he caught himself quickly and lowered his voice. "*Yes,* we can do that in *England.* He's already matriculated and he only needs to pass the entrance examinations. But he may never get to University at all. The fact is young Henry has taken some silly notion about going to America. Seems..." He opened his palms. "Well, I'm certain it was unintentional on your part, but it seems he's taken a fancy that he'd like to go to America and make something of himself... and, well, it's obvious he thinks the place is some sort of paradise for the living... and... so you see the trouble..."

She didn't see the trouble at all. Her lips were pressed together in irritation as he finished.

"If you could just speak to Henry and tell him no one will be handing him bags of gold as he comes off the boat. You see... he could really make something of himself here...." He pulled one hand to his breast. "I really believe he could... and you well know what it would mean for everyone hereabouts... Miss Brown?" Austin said, losing the light in his eye completely as he caught the look in hers. He thought he'd put it rather well, hiding his irritation and pretending to be a gentleman, and so her look befuddled him completely.

"*Master* Brooks, where shall I begin?" She looked him up and down, then gritted her teeth and smiled. "Oh, I know. Let us begin with forthrightness... honesty... those things you English keep mentioning to me as American traits. Everything... every word... every statement I made to those children was accurate, correct, and above...."

"I'm sure they were meant to be." He held forth his hand. "But don't you think the children might have dressed up what you said? And mightn't you have allowed them to... pretend a bit?" He pulled his hand to his lapel. "Good Heavens, Henry thinks... well..." He laughed at the preposterousness of the suggestion. "He's telling me some ridiculousness about it being a free society, all one and equal and that sort of thing. Thinks he'll be treated like everyone else even though he'd like to be a farmer there, and..."

"You know nothing of America. It is exactly as Henry said... as I said."

"This cannot be true," he said harshly. "There is no society on the face of the earth which has successfully rid itself of the need for royalty, nobility, or a ruling class."

"A ruling class we may have, yes. But one may become a member of that ruling class with hard work and... no, *or* an education. We feel it a democratic right to learn parlor manners, if we so choose, and our society is open to anyone who cares to learn them. The privilege is not accorded based on blood."

Austin grew tense. "It's *always* blood."

She balked and her eyes flew open. "*Not* in America! And if you stand ready to accuse me of lying, I will not discuss this with you further!"

Austin retrieved his senses once more. "I didn't mean to insult you. We happened on a discussion that means a great deal to me, that's all, and I've let my... I'm sorry." He turned away. "I shouldn't expect a young lady to see her homeland as anything but perfect and grand."

Theodosia's heart pumped with righteous indignation as she watched him put his hat on his head and turn as if to say good night. "Insult me, apologize and leave? I've seen this before. You call yourself a gentleman? I don't know what to make of you!"

He laughed. "Make nothing of me then and you'll be pleased with the result."

Her brow furrowed. "No. You want Henry Taylor to go to University, and that's a good thing, but the way you speak of it..." She shook her head. "Answer me this... is this *your* wish for Henry or your family's?"

"You know the answer to that," he said, unhelpfully.

"You refuse to give me an honest answer?"

He pulled his face toward hers slightly and cocked his head. "And why should only one of us here be honest?"

"What do you mean by that?" She pulled her hand to her neck.

He drew his hat off again and swept it to his right. "Well, here you've spoken of America, the land of equality. Praise it to the heavens! But where are you? Where are you, Miss Brown?" He pushed his hat toward her face. "You've come over here to the island of social hierarchy and arranged marriages to fit yourself out with a rich husband with a substantial title. An example of American opportunity? A reasonable way to take yourself up in this world? I call it dishonest in the extreme."

Bitterly she answered, "You go too far!"

"Ha!" He pushed his hat high onto his forehead. "Ha!" he said again, but he wasn't at all sure what he meant by it or quite how she'd take his meaning. He was flustered, irritated and confused by her, deeply in love with her, in fact, but hadn't a clue as to what to do about it.

Meanwhile Theodosia's anger overrode every other sense within her as she came from the window well and stood before him. "You know nothing about it. Nothing! You Brookses think you know everything, don't you?! So full of yourselves."

"Don't call me a Brooks."

"Oh, but you *are* a Brooks in every way, sir, with all the coldness of your oldest brother and all the insulting manners of the next."

"I am not a Brooks and *well you know it!*"

"And YOU are preposterous!" she sputtered, fearing she'd be forced to speak her feelings in a heated discussion. "I'll have no more of this." And she began to bustle past him.

He took her by the shoulders, pulled her back to face him and held her fast. "But you *read* the *will.*"

She blinked and stared at him, her brows coming slowly together as she wondered what he meant.

"So you know I'm not blood... and you pretend to honesty." He gritted his teeth. "You *read* the *will,*" he repeated, shaking her slightly.

Slowly his meaning came to her. "No. *No!* Only the first paragraph. I read only the first paragraph. I thought you knew this. I told the Reverend Pickett."

Still holding her firmly, his face fell. "I haven't spoken to Reverend Pickett since the day we were all together, and he never told me this."

She eyed him carefully. "What did you mean... you are not a Brooks?" He let go of her shoulders and let his arms fall to his sides. He looked so thoroughly disgusted with himself that, in empathy, she drew her hand to his arm, but he pulled it away and backed up a step. Turning to take a chair, he lay his hat on the edge of the drum table and sat down. The hat dropped to the floor. Austin did not pick it up but fell to staring at it where it lay. Theodosia gazed at Austin in the pale lamplight, then looked at the door and back to him once more.

Without lifting his eyes to her, he said, "The will was my...was Lord Brooks' father's, the first Lord Brooks. In it he names me as an orphan... of unknown... and *decidedly low* parentage."

She brought her hand to her mouth. "I am so sorry. I didn't know," she whispered, trying to imagine his pain.

Both heard voices in the hallway and froze. The voices grew louder but then slowly disappeared.

"You've known this for a while then?" Theodosia whispered.

He huffed and then with deliberate slowness said, "I discovered this when I was curious to know what the American visitor wished so badly to read on our top shelf ..."

So. He'd known she was reaching for the red volume—the will. Then this discovery of his origin, in fact, was her fault.

She brought both hands to flaming cheeks as embarrassment and shame welled up in her. The sorrow for what she'd done, anger at her own stupid curiosity, and knowing that she hurt him even unintentionally—all these things caused tears to sting her eyes.

"It's all right," he mumbled. "I would have found out eventually. The will stipulates..." He stopped to give his hat half a smile.

She pulled away her hands to stare at him and realized that everything Reverend Pickett had said about him was true: His anger was quick to diminish, he felt better for the honesty between them, and she believed him when he said it was all right.

They were silent and there came to her a sense of unusual calm. She understood now why he'd gotten angry with her on the path. And then there was the knowledge of his other admission: he'd simply wanted to know what she read, had taken an interest in her—it came to that, too—and so she blushed. His kiss, then, was true, as well.

She wanted there to be truth between them. All would go better for it, she was sure, the Reverend's advice notwithstanding. She had been patient long enough.

She smiled. "When you came in to bring me to tea I almost apologized for finding the family will."

"Then you really did mistake me for a servant that day."

"Yes, I really did."

"It wasn't because you had just discovered who I was." His eyes rose up and he stared at her.

"Heavens, no."

But his face grew cold once more. "Well, henceforth you may treat me as a servant, now that you know everything about me worth knowing." He looked about him. "And have no fear of my soiling the family name by intruding on the Brookses' hospitality any more than is necessary for me to arrange for another position. I won't be your brother-in-law."

"I never hoped you would." Her answer to Austin was simple enough, intended as a gentle means of hinting her true feelings. She could see he had suffered to find himself an orphan and thought it must be painful to feel oneself separated from what was once one's family, but she didn't quite understand the shame he felt. An understanding of his loss of pride was beyond her because she could not see how a man could measure himself by his birth instead of his aptitude, by chance rather than determination. Beyond this basic American thinking on the subject, she held that the best account one could give of oneself in this life would be to state one was a child of God. The determination to be His was more important than anything in life, and this last she could hold up to the Reverend Pickett who had helped her to see it so clearly in the past few weeks.

"Well said." And he stood up. To her utter surprise he seemed to take her words as a rejection. He bent and scooped up his hat.

She stepped toward him and asked in innocence, "Why do you say it in that way?"

"And what way is that?"

"Still in anger? As if I were dismissing you?"

"I should accept it graciously? I think my feelings toward you are fairly obvious. I'm not made of stone that I can ignore the Brookses working you over to their will when I still have a will of my own, albeit that of a pauper, a beggar, a..."

"Oh, Austin, listen to me now." She gently held out her hand to him. "You're quite wrong about..."

"TheoDOsia?" came Cecelia's voice from the doorway as she swept it open. "Are you in here hiding, my... OH!" She jumped a step back as if she'd been bitten. "*O-o-o-h!*" she repeated with a coyness that made her cousin wince.

Theodosia snatched back her hand, and not wishing to receive the kindness of her touch, Austin backed away from Theodosia, but Cecelia had seen it all and thought, well, what only Cecelia Bannoch could think of such a sight.

Austin set his jaw, put on his hat and walked toward the hall door. Brushing past Cecelia, he mumbled, "Good evening, Miss Bannoch."

"It is a pleasure to see you so well, Mr. Brooks." Cecelia smiled. "*So* glad our fears for your ill health were groundless."

Austin gave no reply, and Cecelia only shrugged. But from the look on Cecelia's face, Theodosia knew she considered her fun had only begun.

And now Theodosia, so ready in the previous moment to tell Austin what she was feeling for him, let the feelings surge and die. A numb anger took over. She stood waiting for Cecelia's words.

Cecelia took gliding steps toward her. "Well, my backward little cousin, perhaps we know more about men than we pretend?"

SIXTEEN

∾

The High Skip,
The Sly Skip,
The Skip like a Feather,
The Long Skip,
The Strong Skip,
And the Skip All Together.

Nursery Rhyme

∾

Hastily Cecelia began to ply Theodosia for a confession, but Theodosia prayed for strength to remain silent, and so Cecelia was spurned in her attempts. Until, that is, she struck the one delicate nerve too sensitive to hide.

"Wouldn't it be charming, cousin, if you were to marry Alfred and I were to marry Austin?"

"Who has said it!" Theodosia cried out.

"Oh, it's just the way things might go, that's all."

Through narrowed eyes, Theodosia said, "You marry Alfred, then, for I'll not have him."

"Marry him? Marry Alfred? Why, I've never even thought of it," she lied.

"And *I* never thought you'd settle for second best, Cecelia." Theodosia looked carefully into her cousin's eyes.

"Oh, so now Austin is merely second best? Poor, dear Austin. Such a fickle heart you have."

Theodosia's eyes brimmed with tears. "I don't understand you, cousin. You're talented and intelligent and blessed with pleasant features. Why wouldn't you wish to marry, rather than… rather than…?"

"Marriage finds itself awfully puffed up in your mind, I think. It will not survive your turning it into something precious. Marriage is only a convenience, a method, a game."

"No. If you could only love yourself... even as you are loved. Then you'd be able to love others."

"You are so terribly naive, Theodosia, I'm almost drawn to pity you. It causes me to wish, if only for a moment, to be charitable to you, my dear, and so I will remind you that if you do not come back to the ballroom soon, Maman will come looking and be sure to find you here."

That thought sent a shiver through Theodosia, but still she stood by the window seat, waiting for some peace to come to her there.

Cecelia shut the door behind her.

One curtain of the window was still bundled where she'd stepped down such that the glow from the oil lamp threw a soft light onto the spot where she stood. She wished she could simply sit and read the books again and forget everything that had happened, and so she looked with envy at the volumes lying on the window seat. But, no, if she did not go back, Cecelia would tell her mother exactly where to find her. She had to return.

As she picked up the volumes to put them away, she realized with a sigh of disappointment she wouldn't even have time to look at Virginia wildflowers again. She looked to the door and back to the books in her arms.

She placed the large book on top of the other there in the window seat, and as she pulled it open the pages naturally fell to one divide under her fingertips. Some bookmark must have rested there. She laid the page full open under the lamplight.

At first she thought it an odd drawing she hadn't noticed before: a withered not quite circular ring of flowers. But the image seemed vaguely familiar to her and tentatively she touched the page to find the dried flowers were not a drawing at all but real. Familiar and quite real.

A little "Oh!" escaped her lips as it came to her that this fragile thing was her own crown of wildflowers from the forest path. She took a deep breath and shut the volume.

There was the peace she'd looked for.

She returned to the ball with a glow on her cheek that guests took for a sign of returning health, as indeed it was.

She felt healthy from then on, in fact, as she found herself thinking more and more of the affections she had wished for and how they were quite real. She could manage anything now. Austin didn't feel sorry for her. He cared for her. Truly. She could even tolerate this ridiculous engagement for a time, for all her fears were suddenly pushed aside. His anger had everything to do with her "engagement" and nothing more. As she thought on Austin, she also thought of the rest of the protective circle of love about her: Fiona, the Reverend, her parents, her family. These helped to keep the Bannochs in perspective. Now more than ever it was certain Aunt Selda had lied and forged a letter from Papa to please her own odd self. The truth would out.

With her headache gone, she began accepting invitations to dance and did her best to keep up with the steps she had only recently mastered from Cecelia's instructions. She was careful to avoid any dance with which she was unfamiliar, and so she accepted every *Waltz* and *Schottische* that came her way, but avoided the *Spanish Waltz* and *Polka*. The result was that she did very well, which frankly surprised her aunt and cousins. Frederick had in the last few weeks ceased insulting her at every turn—the changing point in his behavior marked by the day she took to dressing in his sister's likeness—and so when he saw that she was keeping step rather well he invited her to dance.

While she danced with Frederick, though, she thought on Austin, as she had in every previous dance, but now her thoughts were on his status as an orphan. She couldn't know what being an orphan might mean here in England. She knew in America they were often called "home children" and were brought into a family to ease the burden of work, but their lot could be improved when childhood was over, just as everyone's could if they worked hard enough. She doubted the same could be said here, with the rigid social system tying people to their roots. A flash of memory from the homes she and the Reverend had visited came to her. *So many sad cases—the wafer-thin widow who was glad for any work and thought it a queen's duty to sort potatoes for the Brookses. The two old men who made their hands raw setting a lath wind brake in record time for a visiting duke. That poor boy who'd sold two of his good teeth to an upper-class lady who had lost two of her own. And none had set foot ten miles from their home. When there was nothing with which they could compare their lot, it was a simple task to keep such people docile and obedient. But a proper education could change everything. Everything!*

A twinge of irritation caught her as she remembered Austin's doubts about America, but she calmed herself to think he simply didn't know; he'd also seen nothing but England. England. She remembered his words and his looks as he told her what he knew of his origins. So much of the conversation's bitterness that she'd thought due to herself she now realized might have been due to his present circumstances. *What had the Reverend Pickett said? Family troubles? And that I had complicated the matter. Yes, that was it. Oh.*

She twirled around the dance floor with Frederick and passed by Alfred standing with his peers.

They passed her Aunt Selda and Cecelia sitting like well-dressed stones in a wall against the high wooden panels. *I will ask the Reverend Pickett. Yes. That's it. He will tell me how it is.* She gave Frederick a sweet grin that actually caused him to smile back at her, a thing which came as a mild surprise to both.

* * *

Austin went to visit the Reverend because he didn't know what to do. He needed advice, and only one man was worthy of the task.

"I want to leave this place, but there's the matter of Henry Taylor."

"Henry?"

"He should go to University, and I…"

"Yes, I understand from his family you've been tutoring him." He smiled kindly.

"No. He doesn't really need a tutor. It's more of... an encouragement." Austin saw the Reverend's smile. "Nothing to do with benevolence! I have to explain the will to you. You see, it states that if three scholars come from the town of Thistledown, the town itself will benefit and that includes Henry, and right now I'd rather it all go to the town than my *brothers*, but I would have to stay to make sure of a third scholar."

"What kind of benefit to the town, if I may ask?"

"The town will inherit that which the Brooks boys would otherwise receive if three scholars are found by the time I turn twenty-one."

"Aah." The Reverend raised his bushy eyebrows to their full height upon his forehead. "And your father... Lord Brooks did this?"

"No. Lord Brooks' father, my grandfather. The one who set up the trust for the children to attend school... but, of course, left nothing for the boys to afford University, the blighter—the weaver's son attended only because he'd inherited monies from a distant great-uncle who was a baronet—and so it appears *I* was a favored experiment... and for all I know I came to the Brookses just for this." And then Austin lapsed into a short description of the contents of the will.

"That... that is phenomenal. I've never heard of such a thing. Do you think a court would uphold this will?"

"Well, Roundtree says it has the best support a legal document may have. He may have been eccentric when it came to science, but Alfred Simpson Brooks was never out of his mind. Never."

"Good heavens. What a thing that would be," Pickett said, pondering the enormous monies that would fill the town to overflowing with services and goods.

"My point exactly." Austin grinned as he looked at the awe-struck man before him.

"Well, I think you've a difficult decision before you. I'm sure Miss Brown complicates things, as well.

"What do you mean by that?"

"Uh, er, only... that..."

"Ha! She'll be rich beyond dreaming... for a little while, any-way. Unless I find another scholar," Austin said morosely. "But they'll always have the income from tea."

"Austin, have you told her... of your... esteem?"

"Yes. As a matter of record, I did."

"And... ?"

"And it's just as I said. People are not always as they appear." He added under his breath, "I was a fool to have hoped other-wise."

"Not at all." The Reverend was completely befuddled. Yet he could not cross over that bridge of confidentiality and express to Austin what he knew to be true. These two young people had to learn for themselves to be honest with one another. He rolled his eyes and lifted a prayer as he realized he'd already said too much.

"Has she... talked about me... much, then?" Austin rubbed his hands against his knees.

"Yes, she has... and prayed for you much."

"Ah, well, that she pities me is obvious."

The Reverend looked skyward. "Austin, when you cease pitying yourself, look at the girl again, would you?"

Austin looked up sharply. "Pardon me, but my powers of self-criticism are rather crippled of late. I hardly know who I am from one day to another. And it'd be a wasted effort, anyway. Soon she'll be Lady Brooks and I will be long gone."

"Don't count on it."

"I *will* be gone," Austin said heatedly.

"Let us pretend we are Americans for a moment and be frank with one another." The Reverend smiled broadly. "I meant that you should not count on her marrying Mr. Alfred Brooks." He brought his hands to his lap. "You know, my discussions with Miss Brown have been most fascinating to me. She holds nothing back and yet she neither offends nor frightens me with her candor. Our discussions have been rather... delightful."

"But what of this decision?" Austin said with agitation; he'd wasted enough sweet thoughts on Theodosia Brown.

"Well, in honor of American forthrightness, I'm telling you that if you really wished to be gone from here, my boy, you would have done it by now... and straight from London. But there is something that draws you here. And I don't mean the will. It's more than one thing, I'll warrant, though it probably does all boil down to one. Now, if you want to be honest with yourself, why don't you start realizing why you came back at all? Then I'll see that self-pity fall from your eyes... like scales it will fall, and all will be revealed."

The Reverend's first few words came to Austin while he still held before his mind the shield of indifference, and so the words were smallish, bumping things that had no weight, but when the Reverend was done, the words of honesty wrapped in love had pierced the metal and struck him through the heart. Though his eyes remained cold and his body was tense with listening, inwardly he felt the blow and had fallen to his knees. He upbraided himself for coming back. Why hadn't he left from London? Why indeed? And what had the Reverend meant that Theodosia would not marry Alfred?

"But I have to have somewhere to go," Austin breathed. "I have to know where to..."

"Letters of reference? Alfred, Lord Brooks would have given them to you the day you arrived. He would have sent them to you in London had you asked..."

"But I didn't know where to go."

"You came *home*. That's where you came. To love . . ."

The last woke Austin from his stupor. The anger surged through him, turning his hands to fists of knotted whiteness by his sides. "This... *is not*... my HOME any LONGER!"

The Reverend looked at him without expression. "You're right. God resides in you, and every place..."

"Quit! Quit talking religion to me! Can't you ever quit?" Austin rose up and lowered his voice. "I've heard enough. Thank you. I'll be leaving now."

"Austin!" the Reverend's voice rang out and stopped the youth in his tracks at the doorway. "One more thing," he said with sudden cheerfulness. "That verse I found... John 14:18, *I will not leave you as orphans; I will come to you.*"

"RRRrrgh!" came up from Austin's throat. As he left the vicarage he vowed never again to darken the Reverend's doorstep, but in this strange purgatory he'd created for himself, promises, especially ones wrapped in nothing more than anger, were proving more and more difficult to keep.

* * *

Theodosia made her way to the Reverend's home to keep her appointment for afternoon tea. She smiled at the sheep in the pasture. She smiled at the men thatching the barn roof. She smiled at the flowers that clung to the stone wall along the roadway. *Sweet vagrants with nothing better to do than please the eye. Bless them. Things are going to be all right.*

She thought this last so often as she walked along in the English sunshine she began to hum the words.

The day was crisp with no clouds in sight. A perfect day, she told herself as she came over the hill toward Thistledown. Saturday. Market day. Squinting through her spectacles she saw the tents. Coming over the next rise, she could hear them: the hawkers, a musician or two, the farmers and the merchants and the crowds that came from all about to buy and sell and have a pint or two or three before returning home. *And I'll go to the market after tea with the Reverend Pickett,* she thought happily.

She paused at the top of the hill to look around her. How she loved the view here. Rolling fields trimmed with stone and bush and brook as far as the eye could see. She rested her gloved hand on the wall beside her and took a deep breath. Toward Thistledown the fields were thick with lush grasses and a herd of sheep silently worked through their all-day repast. *Thick sweaters from thick grass,* she thought with a smile. Her eyes traced the edge of town along a line of thatched stone homes, their windows and walls bright with summer flowers. Now her eye wandered back to the road to Thistledown and she glimpsed a young man making his way up the hill toward her.

Shot through with a panic she turned back to the wall, for even at two hundred yards she could see that it was Austin.

But I can tell him now, she thought boldly. And in the next instant she panicked once more. *What if he spurns me? What will happen if the Brookses discover this? What if Aunt Selda is right and Papa wishes me to marry a Brooks, and Austin is not... and Austin is not....* All this tore at her and left her breathless with misgiving as he walked up the hill.

From the corner of her eye she could see he was staring at the rutted road as he came. And he was angry. She scattered her eyes about her for a place to hide.

No. I'm not a child. I will not hide. If he is angry, I must face him anyway. Face him with what? Just see how angry he is! Stay quiet, for pity's sake.

With forced calm she stood as still as her shaking knees allowed.

He was one hundred yards away. Now fifty.

Both hands found the wall to steady herself as she looked out into the field to a lamb moving about its mother in happy circles. She tried to concentrate upon the frolicking, four-legged bundle of wool, but her vision grew blurry with the effort.

And the effort was tearing her apart.

At twenty feet Austin looked up and stopped dead in the road.

He could turn around and go another way. After all, he was only taking a walk for the sake of walking. He had no particular place to go, but now he saw she was not looking toward him. Perhaps she hadn't seen him yet.

The road was wide; he could pass behind her without notice. And what did he care if she saw him? Rather more to the point, what did *she* care? Small beads of sweat formed along his upper lip. He took up his gait once more but slowed his pace as he came toward her.

When they were fifteen feet away from one another, she could not bear the strain, and so she turned, caught his glance and looked him straight in the eye.

He stopped short to stare at her as well.

Theodosia could not have spoken her thoughts just then even if she'd tried, and so on instinct she allowed her look to tell him what it could: that here was a man she wished to know, that she was attracted to him both by sight and manner, that all things she'd felt about him from the moment he first spoke to her were full of good promise, that all she'd thought was roundly confirmed and more than passingly encouraged by the stories Reverend Pickett had told her as well.

All about him rang true for her.

And Austin had wanted so badly to dismiss her, but every moment of his day reminded him of her. He'd never met a woman more alive and fresh, and sweet and bold, and clumsy and wonderful. Ridiculous thing, passion. Made a man an idiot, yet in this girl were things he recognized in himself and things he wanted for himself and the combination of the two had made him utterly lose his reason. Reverend Pickett had once described true love to him this way: "Out of the thousands upon thousands of women one might meet, when *she* comes you have a sense you've known her all your life. That's a mighty love, a gift of God, this... this knowledge of your other half."

Austin's other half stood across a muddied road from him, and she trembled as her eyes searched his.

With every bit of strength he possessed, he made himself walk on, but he could not look away from her and his step was slow.

Theodosia turned slowly toward him as he walked away. Everything within her wanted to run across the road and hug the man, somehow make him give up this nonsense so that they could start again. But the look in his eye held her where she stood. She remembered the Reverend's words of warning and she remained quiet. He was angry, yet he would not look away from her, and so she trembled all the more.

When he had finally quit the hill, when she was alone again with the tall grass and the field of sheep and the cold stone wall behind her, she whispered, "I do love you, Austin. *Know* that I love you. Please, Lord, tell him this, *please*."

And she turned her face and her step toward Thistledown. ❧

SEVENTEEN

If you are cold, tea will warm you–
If you are heated, it will cool you–
If you are depressed, it will cheer you–
If you are excited, it will calm you.

W.E. Gladstone

R everend Pickett was in a cheerful way as Theodosia arrived, for he'd had the pleasure of watching the tea cart rolled out before him and the board was groaning with good things: cream teas from Mrs. Taggert's own hands were to be served (his favorite on both counts), and so the Reverend smiled down on the repast like a benevolent monarch. He gave the thick mound of Devon cream a wink, breathed deeply of the tart and the sweet smell of fresh strawberry preserves, and dared peek under the dome to see a comely block of creamy white butter waiting for his deft hand. He could almost taste the darkly mellowed malt bread, but the view of the golden tops of high-layered scones with little currants dotting the flaky layers below almost caused him to lose patience with his awaited guest, and then he laughed out loud. He was perfectly silly when it came to tea, but there was something... yes, there was something about a good tea. It opened hearts and minds to him at times. "In a way," he mused as he carefully counted the jam pots, "tea is a medicine for the soul."

Theodosia arrived and the Reverend gave her a hearty greeting. But when she bowed her head, he instantly surmised that she was greatly troubled. He sat her down next to him at table and began to ply her with the tea and scones thick with strawberries and cream and it was not long until she laid her heart before him.

They spoke at length about Austin's difficulties. Again the Reverend found out how easily this young girl could wrest things from his mind that he would otherwise dare not speak, and so, with the precedent of Austin's conversation with her on the night of the ball, the Reverend told her much about the will before he half-realized he'd done so. Without specifying the conditions, he explained to her why Austin felt so distant from his former life; his rights as son were preempted, he would inherit nothing, and while his parents were willing to offer him positions wherever he liked, they hadn't done the one thing that might have healed his young heart—told him he was a son to them still and asked him to stay.

And so, it seemed to the Reverend's keen eye, Austin had allowed himself to feel unworthy of anyone's love.

She listened in amazed attention, but by the time he was done she was angry. Inwardly Theodosia wished to wreak a vengeance on the Brookses. And if given the opportunity, she knew that she would.

Reverend Pickett saw the glare in her eye and calmly suggested they have more tea.

When she calmed herself with another cup, she told the Reverend how she'd seen Austin on the hill.

The Reverend smiled. "For Austin there is great hope. You have come at just the right time, I think. It's all a part of a blessed plan."

"I'm afraid I don't see it that way at all."

"Ah, but don't you? Austin cares for you and so you draw him back up from the mire. You remind him of the love of God. Love. Love covers a multitude of sins. This is not a quaint saying from Scripture, but an iron law, I've found. Austin is slowly coming around to it. I see it though he doesn't, and we may have great hope that our prayers for him are being answered."

"But what will he do with himself now?"

"He will settle accounts. He always does. He thinks his love of honesty is a sudden thing in him. It makes me laugh when he speaks of it, because I've seen it in him since he toddled around the yard! Your honesty is, I'm certain, a part of what he likes so much in you. Love, or, er... such esteem may cause a man to recognize himself in another."

She blushed but tucked the gentle thought away.

"I'm sorry. I shouldn't speak so for the boy."

"No, no. You give me hope." She smiled.

"Don't worry. You are the one he fights the hardest to stay angry with, and when he gives that up he will have found himself again. You'll see."

"And what may I do to help him see it?"

"Pray."

"But I have been."

"Patience. Patience. Obey your aunt unless she asks you to break scriptural law. And pray."

"Yes, sir." But she did not mean it.

"Tee, just a little while longer…"

"But what if I'd gone to London when he first left? If I'd only explained myself to him then, perhaps we could have cleared things up."

"But that's not the way God saw fit to straighten things."

"But nothing's been straightened yet!" In her heart Theodosia was firmly deciding she would not wait the next time.

The Reverend Pickett cleared his throat and offered her another cup of tea.

* * *

The Reverend had said she wouldn't marry Alfred.

Austin made his way back home, more uncertain than ever of himself. Lying in his bed that night and remembering her look brought him comfort whether he wished for it or no. He'd seen the love in her eyes. If she could love him, perhaps he was worth loving. And if that were true, perhaps everything she'd said about America was true as well. *Perhaps she doesn't care where I come from, eh?* But he laughed at the absurdity.

Still the sudden possibility it might be true wiped the smile from his lips. His Adam's apple rose and fell in a deep swallow. Could she? Could she love him? He rolled over in his bed and sighed.

He looked at the table beside him where his Bible was tucked into the shelf. He took it out and rolled onto his back, resting the

Good Book upon his stomach. For a moment he thought to fling it from him and say, "Well she may, but God cannot! God cannot forgive me now!" but he didn't quite believe it and so the Bible stayed.

He remembered Theodosia's face, all the hope and longing there, and watched the Book rise and fall with his breath, and finally he thought, *Today... today, perhaps God can forgive.*

"I challenge You," he said aloud. "I challenge You to rekindle my faith or have done with me. One or the other. Which will it be?" He sat up, cast open his Bible and began to thumb through the pages, believing fully that God would speak to him on the matter one way or another.

* * *

Theodosia returned to her room with a candle in hand. As she entered into the darkness, she thought of the Scripture verse, "Thy word is a lamp unto my feet and a light unto my path." She decided to read awhile and sought her Bible from the bedside.

The afternoon at Star Cottage had moved as slowly as the well-watched hands of a schoolroom clock. Cecelia, in babbling to Theodosia on the subject of American manners, surpassed even herself in rudeness as they sat sewing in the parlor, and so Theodosia claimed to have a headache and went back to her room.

With the door closed now and the darkness around her growing familiar in the candle's light, she wished the Scripture would comfort her in a way nothing else could.

But as she stared at the Bible in her hand, her mind wandered to the church service yesterday. As unsettling as it was to see the brothers, equally unsettling was the fact of Austin's absence. "I pray the Reverend is right about him." She sat down at the table and laid the candle at its edge and closed her eyes briefly, saying, "Lord, bring Austin to a new knowledge of you. 'Behold, old things have passed away, all things are new.' 'With God, nothing is impossible.'" She smiled and opened her eyes.

Remembering Reverend Pickett's sermon, she turned to

Ecclesiastes. As she looked it over, she realized she'd never read it through and now seemed as good a time as any. "All is vanity," she repeated as she began.

When she came to chapter two, verses 18 and 19, she thought of the Brookses. "Thus I hated all the fruit of my labor for which I had labored under the sun," she read aloud, "for I must leave it to the man who will come after me. And who knows whether he will be a wise man or a fool? Yet he will have control over all the fruit of my labor for which I have labored by acting wisely under the sun. This too is..."

Ker-tink.

A bird? she wondered. *No. Smaller.* Tink-tink came the sound again at the window, like a cricket throwing himself against the glass.

She took up her candle and walked to the window.

TINK!

She jumped back and almost lost the candle's flame. *A pebble?* Theodosia set the candle down with a tremor and stepped gingerly to the half-open window. *Fiona for a late visit? A messenger?* "Hello?" she said softly. "Fiona?"

"No," came the reply.

"Austin?!" Her heart pounded with the word.

"Yes. I would very much like a word with you." He came around from the column and she saw his form.

She pulled her head back in from the window and wondered what she should do. Her cheeks were burning. Propriety suggested she shut the window in his face but one look into Austin's eyes caused her to bid propriety a quick farewell. *After all,* and she pulled her face toward the window once more, *he is a reasonable man when he isn't angry, and he doesn't seem angry at all just now. Perhaps he is bringing a message from Reverend Pickett.*

"All right," she said quietly.

She watched with shock as his hands grasped the sash and pushed upward.

"But you mayn't come in!"

"Of course," he said patiently. "I only want to speak to you without having to stoop." The irony of what he'd said caused his cheeks to redden.

She clasped her hands together and stood very still. The window was now set high enough for both to stand face-to-face and no more than two feet apart.

"It's this." He wrung his hands briefly. "I want there to be honesty between us."

"I would like that."

He looked up at her, shook his head and gave her a snippet of a smile. "You have a way about you that causes me to wish to speak my mind, and yet…"

"I'm glad for it. I've prayed for it, in fact, that we could be honest with one another."

He reddened under the openness of her gaze. "Well, then." He cleared his throat. "Here it is. On the road yesterday. Your look… the way you looked at me… made no sense to me at all. I have to know… for myself… how is it… how is it possible you are engaged to Mr. Alfred Brooks?"

Quick tears formed in Theodosia's eyes and she grabbed—but not too harshly—the curtain beside her. "I *don't* love him. I wanted to tell you on the road what I feel. I wanted to tell you the night of the ball, but…"

"Ah, so you admit… yes." He bowed his head. "You marry for position." He was still unwilling to hope for himself. "Well, I can't say I blame you…"

"Austin, stop!" she said pitifully. "*Please.* You keep walking my words to places they do not wish to go! I'm trying to say I don't want to marry him at all. Aunt Se-Selda is arranging everything and I can't… I ca-ca-can't…" But she couldn't. She couldn't go on because she was suddenly choking on her sobs. Crossing her hands over her chest to hold back her tears, she found they would not be held.

Austin looked about him, held his hat back from his brow, and began to scratch his head. He hadn't expected this, but it didn't take but another moment to know his duty. If she didn't love Alfred, well... at least, she didn't love Alfred and she didn't want to marry Alfred. That was something.

He suddenly remembered her look the day before and realized that was quite a lot.

His hat fell off behind him as he kneeled on the window sash and drew his arms about her. Her hands were pinned to her sobbing chest and his arms were warm and strong about her as she let herself be held.

If ever I've felt comfort, it is here in his arms, she thought, for he held her as if he would never let her go. She put her cheek into his shoulder, and he swayed with her slightly, rocking her, and she smiled through her tears as they stood together.

When she had begun to quiet, slowly he let go his grasp, but he still held her. And still she didn't know what to make of him.

Did he care very much for her? Or was he only being kind? Looking after her as he tried to look after Henry perhaps? What was he thinking? Reverend Pickett was so certain that he cared for her. But what was he feeling right now?

Did he simply feel sorry for her, as these Brookses tried to force a marriage on her?

"Austin." She turned her face into his lapel. "I've told myself a hundred times... they can't make me marry him, and they can't, can they?"

"No. No, they can't," he said with certainty. "Not if you've already taken a husband."

"Austin?"

He pulled away and looked into her eyes. Drawing his hands to the sides of her pale cheeks he wiped her tears away with his thumbs. She pulled her hands to his and held them there.

"Austin, what did you say?"

"I said it would bring me the greatest pleasure if you would consent to be my wife, Miss Theodosia Brown."

"But we hardly know each other."

He smiled and lowered his voice into a formal tone. "Allow me to introduce myself. For the greatest portion of my life, my name was Austin Brooks. Who I am now is of constant interest to me, but this I know... that I am whole again, or mostly so, and am in my right mind... or mostly so... as I presume to ask you this. I know my Lord... again, and I believe that I have loved you since the day that I was born, perhaps earlier, and I have known I loved you since the moment you called my name the day we met."

She laughed and another tear came which he wiped away. Then he kissed her.

When they pulled away, he said, "But I am quite serious. We could travel to Scotland—to Gretna Green—and be married in a day."

Theodosia smiled shyly. "I know who you really are. Your name is Jock O'Hazeldean."

"Who?"

"Fiona taught a ballad to the children called *Jock O'Hazeldean.* The fellow steals the girl away before they can force her to marry the chieftain's son."

"Ah," he said with a smile. "Well, then I'm Jock O'Hazeldean." He was never happier with a name in his life.

She took his smiling face into her hands and gave a little laugh. "I don't know when I came to love you... I don't know when... but I tried to tell you... to speak it on the road."

"But you didn't..."

"You looked so angry."

"But not at you."

"I know."

They were quiet for a time. Then he pulled both her hands into a ball and held them in his before him. "But, Tee, you haven't answered me," he whispered.

"Ah." She looked away. "No. No, I haven't, have I?" A smile came and left her face. "Austin, I want to spend the rest of my life learning who you are." She said the words quite carefully, but seeing his growing smile she quickly added, "and nothing would please me more, but..."

"There's a problem..." he said with a catch in his throat.

"Yes. Yes. There is a problem. I am young... and... despite what

I've said, I do wish for my parents' approval." Seeing his face pale she rushed to add, "And they will approve. Oh, Austin, they *will* approve."

"Will they? They'll approve of an orphan with no monies to speak of? Of questionable background?" He looked up briefly and brought his head back down. "I was a fool to put it to you. I've insulted you by my asking..."

"Enough!" she said. "Listen to me!" She squeezed his hands and shook them. "Everything I said about America is true, Austin. Everything. No one cares who you were born to, where you came from. How could we?" She laughed. "When you people sent so many of your prisoners to our shore? Where I come from no one wants to examine their family line too closely." She spoke quickly now, wanting him to understand, to accept what she told him; she wanted to take back the words that had hurt him, but all she could do was keep explaining... and explaining. "Papa jokes he traced the family tree back to a horse thief and stopped his looking then and there."

Austin smiled hesitantly.

Theodosia said more quietly, "Do you mean to tell me that if you hadn't discovered you were an orphan you would have watched me marry Mr. Alfred Brooks without a word?"

He smiled. "I was never one to hold back..."

"Yes, Reverend Pickett has told me quite a lot..." She giggled. "Of your strong-headedness... honesty above all else... of a temper quickly shown but quickly mended. He knew you'd seek the Lord again."

"He knows me too well."

"I could not have survived these weeks without him and his verses of comfort. *God will always provide a means of escape from temptation.* That is the very one I've clung to. I know there will be a way out of this... somehow." She looked into Austin's eyes. "And *you* should take it! Oh, take it, Austin!"

"Escape?"

"Yes! From all these horrid expectations!"

"The Brookses have no expectations for me now...."

"I'm not speaking of theirs but of *yours*... You catch yourself up in old expectations... as you did just now, thinking you had no right to ask for my hand. But you see, I come from a place where there are no such expectations, and somehow you must have believed me or you never would have asked. Besides which, God has no such expectations for us. The only thing that's important is to know who we are in Christ."

"That would be enough for your father?" he said doubtfully.

"Yes. Yes, it is! We are His children... eternally. No one else's... eternally. You see? Reverend Pickett has helped me to see it so clearly."

Austin furrowed his brow but began remembering all the things the Reverend had taught him, most especially the things he'd told him after Austin found the will, things about being a child of God above all else. *"Things it takes a lifetime for a Christian to learn, Austin, will be forced on you by this: to know God as your true Father, fellow Christians as true brothers and sisters."* If anyone else had tried to tell Austin as much, he'd have gotten a punch in the nose, but the Reverend had spoken with a true concern, and so the sting of truth was neatly and efficiently removed.

He raised his brows. "I suppose that's what I've been doing these last few weeks, trying to purge myself of my old life, trying to believe I can start over. I thought God spoke to me this morning on it... and I did believe." Then he shook his head. "Aye, but it's easier to see yourself as a child of God when you've a point of reference.... being someone's child in the first place."

"Is it?"

"Of course."

She smiled. "But God is our Father, and my papa is nothing like Him. Should Mr. Brown of Alexandria County have been used as a reference point, I may have never found my Lord."

"And you are sure your father, this same man, will accept my suit of his daughter?"

"Yes. *Yes,*" she said emphatically. "He is not the most patient man in the world, but he is fair-minded in the long run. He will be glad, I'm sure, to have me out of his hair."

Austin cleared his throat and grew serious. "I want to believe you." He looked out into the darkness. "But there's a house of aristocrats and would-be aristocrats that would like to meld your family into their own, and... and they will keep you from escaping if they can."

"They cannot make me say 'I do!'" She quickly lowered her eyes. "Lord willing, there is only one to whom I will ever speak those words."

He brought her chin up with his thumb. "Then I thank God for it." And they kissed once more.

They held each other for a while before Austin, with a great deal of reluctance, took himself away from Theodosia's window.

* * *

One more month on the calendar remained before Theodosia could expect a reply from her father. With her future "settled," she was left alone at Star Cottage more often than not, as Selda, Cecelia and Frederick made their way to several balls and social functions in the area. The upper crust had, as usual, removed themselves from the summer heat of London and made their way to their country estates, or better yet, to the estates of their friends where they would rest and play all summer long. The Bannochs were intent on being with them in their play until the day they all left for the reopening of Parliament in August.

And so Austin now came to Theodosia's window twice a week to share quiet conversations with her—with or without the aid of moonlight. One week he told her of his childhood and of Thistledown. The next, of his first two years at Christ's College, Cambridge.

She found his careful descriptions kindly coupled with a gentle regard for her own interests, and so, when he spoke of his college, he made her feel as though she stood with him. Together they admired the Fellow's Garden, side by side they wobbled into the thin little boats called "punts" which Austin then gracefully poled along the Cam River to the next little town where they sat down for tea. They sat together in the pew in the nave of King's College Chapel and listened to the choir whose music reverberated from the stone as if the very walls were alive. Together they walked the Mathematical Bridge and wondered how a bridge was built without nails or mortar, and then she sat with him for supper in the Commons and relived his conversations with his friends—even one with the lady of the kitchen: "But bleu cheese is s'pposed to be moldy, Master Brooks"—"I agree, Mistress Tibbs, but this cheese began as a cheddar...."

One evening she quite mildly presented a wish to truly walk the paths of Christ's College with him someday, and he lowered his head and admitted to her that no ladies were allowed within its walls. From this admission burst forth a discussion of America, Theodosia's land of opportunity, that kept things lively for a time.

She told Austin of Parker's peculiar calling, and he stated his amazement her father had not made him enter law. Then she told him of her older sister's marriage to a common laborer, all because she loved him, believed in him and knew he would do well for himself, as indeed he had. Her family loved him like a son. And, yes, her family entertained senators and governors now and then, as well as lowly office clerks, and often they were all together at the same table. She wanted him to see that this common courtesy to all was not peculiar to her home but to the entire country.

Plans were in the making for a system of public education. A man could greet anyone in the streets without introductions, without waiting for a first acknowledgment from a lofty Earl. Jobs were given on the basis of ability, not necessarily connections. A recommendation letter was nice to have but not required. You merely needed to prove yourself, to show your skill. In fact, it was not unusual for persons to knock on the door of the President's White House in Washington and stand in line for an interview, all this despite recent arguments between certain factions from the North and from the South.

Austin had a certain look in his eye after these conversations, and Theodosia hoped he would go with her when she left. She was smiling at the future.

But Austin continued to speak to Henry Taylor about University. Henry seemed to take the advice, saying he'd think on it, which gave Austin some bit of hope, but at other times he would let slip something about America and then Austin would grow impatient with him. Then, without thinking, Austin would go home and speak disparagingly about America to the Brookses, something he never allowed himself to do with Theodosia for fear of insulting her. When Austin would begin a tirade on the former Colonies, Lord Brooks would remember his Shakespeare and think, "Methinks thou dost protest too much." Then he would raise his brows and look with concern toward his wife. ᴖ

EIGHTEEN

∾

Bobby Shaftoe's gone to sea,
Silver buckles at his knee;
He'll come back and marry me,
Bonny Bobby Shaftoe.
Bobby Shaftoe's bright and fair,
Combing down his yellow hair,
He's my ain for evermair
Bonny Bobby Shaftoe.

Nursery Rhyme

∾

There are times in one's life when an incidental motion, a decision to travel to the right instead of the left, to look through a window rather than pass down a hall, will change the course of one's existence. In the third week of the waiting month, after a long day of arranging for certain barges from Thistledown to haul certain barrels of tea up from London, and a pleasant evening spent at Theodosia's window, Austin decided to take the west road, the deep drover's road, rather than the road through town to return to his room at Brooks House.

The road was dark and the night pitch black, but as he walked his heart was immersed in the strong sense that all would be well. It was a peace he could not comprehend other than to know that it began somewhere in being right with God and ended with Theodosia.

Taking a loping path that edged a thick wood, he walked quickly, with vigor and a strident step. He'd ceased taking the family carriage some weeks back—it reminded him of things he'd like to put behind him. And he didn't like to walk a horse in the dark. Too dangerous. No, he was on his own and could walk on the feet God gave him. And so he did.

He walked until he came to the edge of a thick stone wall that separated forest from field. He took one step past the wall and in the next moment he felt a stinging, tingling lightness in his head and then he felt nothing at all.

A thin young man holding a heavy club stepped from the wall to watch the dark mass of Austin's body fall to earth.

* * *

"Go and straighten those things about your face you so recklessly refer to as *curls*, Theodosia. They will be here at any moment. Go to your room this instant!" said Aunt Selda sharply.

Theodosia sighed but then complied.

The Brookses were coming for a breakfast.

Star Cottage was polished and shining and ready for them, and Aunt Selda was in her element. Everything must be perfect. The staff knew it must be perfect because their lady had said it one hundred times that morning as she'd flitted about, snapping wrists with her fan to make her point—one snap for the maid when she did not fold the napkins properly, two snaps for the boy who almost dropped the knife box as he came from the pantry. All the best silver and linens, the finest flowers and food must be presented to the ever-important Brookses. Selda Bannoch needn't have told Theodosia why it was important to her that the house look equal to their standing, but she troubled herself to do so all morning long.

And then they came.

Aunt Selda did her best to make sure proper conversation was had during the meal, but as the fish grew cold and the bread grew hard, an infinitesimal amount of irritation crept into her voice. A bit of impatience, some too-long pauses in her responses. Out of curiosity, Theodosia began to look about her for an explanation. Was not the table perfect? Yes, it was. Was there something she should be doing she had not done? But Aunt Selda was not looking at her. No, it was not she. Who then? Or what?

Then it came to her. The Brookses were not cooperating. They were a little less than amenable to Aunt Selda's every suggestion, her every turn of conversation. Theodosia watched closely now as Aunt Selda and the Lady Brooks began a new topic, something in relation to their children's accomplishments, and Lady Brooks became downright unsociable. What could it be?

Ah. Might the Brookses have had a row with Austin over her? Her heart rose into her throat, but she went back over the half hour since the family's arrival in her mind and sensed no evidence of irritation with her. Of course, that could be good manners on their part, but as Theodosia glanced at Lady Brooks' profile just then, she realized the woman looked completely distracted. Her husband was obviously nervous about the fact, and Aunt Selda was at a loss as to how to redeem the situation.

What could it be?

After breakfast, the group retired to the parlor, and people drew themselves into little knots of conversation: Allan, Cecelia and Frederick, Lady Brooks and Aunt Selda, and with discomfort Theodosia saw Alfred watching her. She was not pleased to see she had caught his eye, and to make matters worse he soon came to her side and requested a walk with her in the garden. She nodded stiffly and they made their way down the hall to the rear of the home.

They entered the backyard and walked along the path toward the forested park behind the house. Then Alfred made it clear why he'd wanted her attentions. He was theorizing recently, he said, and was interested in knowing her opinions on child-rearing.

This stopped Theodosia mid-step. "Mr. Brooks, despite what you may think of Americans, my manners are not so barbarous as to believe this conversation proper."

His eyebrows rose, and with his most condescending smile, he said, "Perhaps for a moment you have failed to remember I am a scientist. Ah, but of course you were thinking of our engagement. I find your interpretation highly amusing, but I assure you it was not meant personally." Theodosia blushed to a fiery red. "No, my interest is purely scientific."

Horrified at the sudden range of possibilities, she quickly asked,

"Do you mean to have your experiments include children now?"

"Ha! No." He gave half a smile and a grunt. "No, of course not. Ha! Can't stand 'em."

She gave a rueful smile, thinking to herself she might have guessed as much.

"No, I was only thinking of something I ran across in my grand-father's research that gave me pause. In his writings he was saying children should be given over to tutors at a much earlier age than is presently encouraged." Prickles raised the hair on the back of Theodosia's neck. "Their minds absorb more than we think in the first years. Of course he was speaking only of the upper classes..." And he droned on.

But for the first time since meeting this pinch-nosed, white-browed would-be scientist, he had utterly captured Theodosia's attention. She hung on his every word, wondering what his grand-father might have said about Austin in those papers.

"I think a child's mind is a very simple thing for a time, and so a woman is best suited to care for young children because, of course, she has a simple mind as well, and then tutors should manage them when they have gone beyond a woman's capabilities."

The cocksure statement jarred Theodosia momentarily from thoughts of Austin. "Why bother with women at all then, Mr. Brooks? Why not have the children raised by monkeys?"

He laughed. "Yes, if children have the mind of monkeys, why not?"

"And was your mind so simple when you were young?" she asked with blatant sarcasm.

"Quite possibly. But I remember the year I said to myself, *I now know more than Nanny. It is time to go to be taught,* and they wouldn't let me have a tutor for another year."

"How horrible for you."

"Horrible for Nanny anyway." He paused to smile. "She died right after I started school and I rather always enjoyed the thought I killed her."

Theodosia would have laughed if his tone were not so undeni-ably serious.

"But you haven't answered my question, Miss Brown, although I presume you haven't the fortitude for motherhood and so will encourage our children to the earliest education possible."

"I will not consider your last remark," she answered coldly, "for it will exist only and forever in the form of theory. No. I would like to move back to your original remarks. Why do you not educate your women so that they could teach the children more if the children were able? Think how much more you might have learned that year had your nanny been able to teach you more. Your year would not have been wasted."

He blinked and looked at her. "Surely you cannot be serious."

She shook her head slightly as she gazed past the spectacles at the end of his nose up into his steely eyes. "Have you so little experience with the fairer sex as to imply that we cannot grasp what a child might understand?"

"A boy child, yes. Although, to be fair, I can think of one or two women who might even comprehend my own research, but they are a rarity… an oddity, if you will." He smiled.

She thought to parry with him then… to ask how much education the women in question had received that they could understand the twisted machinations of his mind, but he looked so smug and satisfied with himself she knew she could not make him understand all that a woman is… and what she could be. "Pointless," she muttered.

"I agree. Quite pointless for a woman to be educated, and so my original theory stands that the training of a young boy child should be with a woman, but as soon as he shows an interest in rudiments such as mathematics and the alphabet, he should be sent to a tutor."

"You have made up your mind before speaking to me, and so I wonder why you pretend to seek my opinion at all."

"Well, *I* think it's been a useful discussion," he replied.

"Useful. Yes," said Theodosia with a sudden calm. "For one of us it has been useful, for while I have not answered your queries, I must say you've answered all of mine… though they were never asked."

"Have I?"

"Yes, indeed. Completely. And I am pleased to inform you there is not one more thing—not one iota of information—I'd like to hear from you again… ever… *on any subject,*" she told him calmly.

"Typical of a woman to dismiss pure logic with emotion."

"On the contrary, Mr. Brooks, I reject your logic and methods because they are patently unscientific and thus unworthy of the mind."

"UNscientific?" he balked.

"Within J.S. Mills' *System of Logic,* did he not put the advanced thinker above all others as a means of introducing social change?"

"What? Yes… I, uh, to put it *simply,*" he said, trying desperately to recover.

"To put it *plainly,* yes, but a scientist who approaches his studies with a solution already in mind is only able to find what he is looking for—no more, no less—and what he finds is rarely the truth… is rarely beneficial to anyone but himself. In short, a wasted effort."

She did not wait for a reply but turned and walked alone to the back door of Star Cottage. Thank goodness she'd just read from that boring book. For once within a conversation with Alfred she was able to light the cannon's fuse and blast away!

Theodosia came through the door leading to a wide mud room through which she could find the hall that led to either her bedroom or the parlor. She stood quite still, unsure to which room she should go. She was too tired from the previous conversation to speak to anyone in the parlor, but she knew her aunt would come looking for her in her bedroom if Alfred returned from the walk alone.

And so she stood and breathed deeply, closing her eyes and lifting a prayer for strength. Finally, allowing her eyes to grow accustomed to the relative darkness of the room, she looked about her.

A monstrosity of a hat rack lay to her left—a tall mirror surrounded by garishly carved ram's heads, curlicues and every manner of trim from which poked wooden hangers for Cecelia and Frederick's many hats. To her right lay a pile of muddy boots and gnarled walking sticks which those same children used with abandon in their own form of grown-up play. She looked at the door to the hall before her and thought she heard voices from the other side.

Yes. Through the oak she distinctly heard the strained and tinny voices of Lord and Lady Brooks.

"Why would he leave before he had secured one?"

"He cannot stand to see us. I know. I *know*," said Lady Brooks.

"This is neither the time nor the place to bring this to the fore!"

"We should have told him ourselves. Years ago we should have told him."

"And he would have left us all the sooner, with a scandal in his wake," he hissed in agitation. "No. What's done is done. It's clear Austin's left us for good now, and we'll simply have to adjust... adjust as we knew we'd have to one day. We did not so long ago think of ever seeing him again. He gave us a few days more, that's all, and now... now we have to accept it." But his voice was neither firm nor convincing.

"It was cruel of him to come back at all then, only to leave us without so much as a word," his wife said in a rather petulant tone. "Could it be that little chit out walking with our Alfred?"

"No, of course not. We can be sure it's not because of Miss Brown this time. But think of all our discussions at supper. He's made it all too clear he hates America, and everyth..."

In the mud room Theodosia heard no more. She had stepped back and now stumbled to her left, grabbing at the hat rack to try to steady herself, but the horn she grasped on the nearest ram's head came off in her hand with a cold snap as she fell back against the wall and then thudded to the floor.

When she turned her eyes to Heaven to ask why this had come to her, all she could see was the shadowy figure of a ram: the tongue, the awful grin, and the blank eyes staring down into her own. And so she looked down to the floor and threw the broken horn across the space with a clatter.

With a broken sob she huddled in the corner of the mud room on the cold stone floor, feeling every bit the part of a suddenly abandoned child.

* * *

Something was oddly familiar to the young man about the position in which he found himself: Hunched down and groaning on the road. The blood on his fingertips that came from his nose. The pain. But his head, ah, his head was aching, ringing like an anvil under hot iron.

He forced his hand up along his head and gingerly touched his scalp where he found a bloody lump. He pulled his hand away with a cry—someone or something had struck him and struck him hard. And his nose, had it bled from that blow? Or from another blow? He didn't know. It didn't matter; his whole body was on fire with pain.

Pushing himself up slightly from the ground, he was suddenly nauseated and caused himself to stay still. He looked about him slowly and wiped his bloody nose with his sleeve.

He didn't know how long he'd lain there, his clothes torn and his body cold from the moist ground, but after he focused his mind on his predicament there was something that came to bother him more than loss of time, even more than the pain that kept him pinned to earth and slightly incoherent; he couldn't quite remember who he was.

And he should know, he thought.

He should know who he was but nothing would come.

Trying again to push himself up from the rocks and mud, he let out another groan. Finally, he held on to a rock from the wall beside him and stood up and looked about. Morning by a rock wall. A grassy hill. A road.

To where? From where? Where was he going?

Papers. Certainly, he carried something that would bring a memory. He searched his pockets but found only a note that read, "Five kegs of China Black, Barge Kildere. London. Second Monday." Some numbers were squiggled beside it. He didn't even know if it was written in his own hand.

But he could read the note, could understand the language. Barge, China Black: he knew their meaning. Why then could he not understand who he was?

He looked down at his clothing. Muddied and torn as they

were, these were the clothes of the upper middle class. He knew that too, somehow. But was he wearing them before he was struck? And who struck him? He could remember nothing. Nothing. A cold sweat took hold of him; he shivered and pulled his coat about him. His next thought was even more odd. He wished to pray. He wished to pray, yet something held him back. No. The sense was gone from him. He would pray.

When he had finished voicing his concerns, all in the name of Christ Jesus, God's Son, Amen, a strange smile came to his lips. He knew God and yet did not know his own name, and so he wondered if the latter should really matter to him at all. *Perhaps,* he thought to himself with a mild laugh, *it was always thus.*

With great pain he proceeded to check himself for broken bones. Grateful to find none, he wondered where he should go from there. And where was he? He looked before him and saw no markers. Behind him was a field and hill. It seemed he had an equal choice of paths and so he went in the direction in which he'd faced when he stood up, thinking to ask someone along the way where he might find the docks.

The docks.

Why was it he knew the barge was at a dock on a canal? *Barges are always on canals, aren't they?* he wondered. No. Some were in cities. The city. London.

He stepped and stumbled and stepped and stumbled again and slowly he began to make his way.

* * *

The Brookses had left and so Cecelia retired to her bedroom. She sat down before the glass of her vanity and thought, *When Theodosia marries him, things will become only more interesting. Will I hold an open flirtation with Alfred to humiliate my dear little cousin? Or will I have a more clandestine affair? Which would be the more challenging?*

Alfred coming to me in the rose garden by the light of a full moon. No. No. He is no romantic. He would not care for such...

Suddenly another image came to her. *Alfred telling me with eyes grown cold that he's had enough of me.* A chill passed through her. *Would he tire of me? No, never,* she told herself with a sudden bitterness. *I will tire of him first! And then poor Theodosia will be stuck with him for life.* But the bitter irony she wished to inject into her sentiment was lost. "Stuck with Alfred" was a thing incongruous to her, she suddenly realized, for "stuck with Alfred" was exactly what she'd like to be.

She yanked her hand mirror to her face.

As she softened her angry look, she saw that the image before her was not ugly, that a certain sensuality within her had always managed to make the most of her sharp features. Above all else, the image was fashionable.

What had Theodosia said? "I never thought you'd settle for second best, Cecelia."

Her eyes filled with tears. Theodosia had also said she was talented, intelligent and blessed with pleasant features. *Love yourself... as you are loved.* Her head rose up. She *was* worthy of Alfred. By Heaven, she *was!*

But her shoulders fell. She was not. There was no dowry for her and never would be. The Bannochs only appeared to be rich. *Love yourself as you are loved? No one loves me truly, and love won't get me what I want.*

Quietly and with a catch in her voice she said to herself, "Cecelia Bannoch, you are a pathetic creature to fall for this sort of thing. He will not stay in love with you, and you *cannot* marry him. Marriage is not your cup of tea. Marriage *is not...*" But she ended the short-lived speech as the tears began to flow.

With a cry of fury she hurled the mirror to the wall. It left a lovely dent in the plaster as it shattered and fell to pieces on the floor. As she realized what she'd done Cecelia threw back her head and began to laugh. Bad luck. She was making her own bad luck. Wasn't it too funny?

It was simply too funny for words.

* * *

Selda heard the crash in Cecelia's room and meant to give her pouting daughter a piece of her mind, but as she reached the hall, her maid came up with a letter for her.

It was from her brother-in-law in America, and Selda Bannoch quickly walked to her room to read it. She smiled in triumph—she would soon make an announcement of the marriage of her niece, Theodosia Rose Brown, to Mr. Alfred Brooks of Brooks House, and all would be well. Perhaps another party at Brooks House....

She took the letter to her desk, arranged the papers around it and lay the envelope before her. Then she slowly broke the seal. Unfolding it, she began to read, but almost immediately she saw the message was not good news. Not good at all.

With growing horror, she saw that this letter, in stark contrast to the one preceding, carried not one gentle thought toward her person. It began by flatly stating there would be no marriage for his daughter to Alfred Brooks. Unless, of course, Theodosia wished it, but he happened to know for a fact that she did not. He then informed her if there *were* a marriage between the two, the family would come and personally put the lot of the Bannoch family out on the street. He did not know what she hoped to gain by such an arrangement, but whatever anyone had promised her it could not match the litigation that would follow should his daughter find herself married against her will. In any case, Theodosia was not to be manipulated further. Monies were issued to a bank in London in Theodosia's name for a return voyage and she was to come home at once. *At once.* And in postscript in an angry, agitated hand he'd written, *"If one hair upon my daughter's head is harmed, if she has suffered in any way, your relationship to my wife notwithstanding, I will take it upon myself personally to escort you to the gates of Hades."*

***

At noon, Theodosia and Fiona found themselves at Reverend Pickett's door and were ushered into his study.

Theodosia looked about her and smiled as she entered the cozy space. She would not see this room again for a long, long while, if ever, and she drank in its mottled appearance for the last time. The clutter, the homeliness, the books, the deep chair, and, of course, the tea table. But then with a pang she knew it was not the room she would miss at all but the man that made the room.

When Reverend Pickett found the ladies waiting for him, immediately he asked after Theodosia, for he'd heard of Austin's disappearance from a servant in Brooks House. He patted her hand and squeezed it gently. "Our prayers haven't been wasted, Miss Brown. There is an explanation for all our trials... though truth be said we may never know the reason."

"Yes. I'm afraid I overheard his parents when they took the news. He left without a word. I thought everything was... I thought we were... we had an understanding, but now... I don't know what to think or feel."

"Three months ago I would have said it was impossible," he replied. "Completely unlike him. But he's been through so much of late, I hardly know what to make of him."

Theodosia faintly smiled. "He told me once to make nothing of him and I should be happy with the result."

"Yes. That's the sort of self-pity could cause him to run away once more. But he'd come back from that, hadn't he? This is certainly beyond our understanding."

"You don't believe we should go and look for him then?" asked Theodosia.

The Reverend's bushy brows rose.

"No. No, of course not," said Theodosia with pained resignation. She'd remembered what Lord Brooks had said: *He hates America. He lied to me, but he seemed so honest and sincere, but then he left.* Fiona leaned into her and placed an arm gently about her shoulders.

"We can pray. We will pray," the Reverend said thoughtfully.

And so they bowed their heads.

When the young ladies left the Reverend's home, they were quiet, their steps measured and slow.

"I have to look for him, Fiona. I can't rest until I really know why he left again."

"But, Tee! Ye can't traipse about the countryside—a lady!"

"But I can't go back. I can't go back to waiting and waiting. That house is like one long, black tunnel with no light in it, no air." She twined her fingers into the fringe of her shawl and twisted them up tight. "No. I can't go back. I decided before I left for the Reverend's home."

They walked along in silence. The sun had come up a few hours before, and they were growing hungry.

"We'll go to m' home and talk about it over a cup," said Fiona firmly.

"No. I've done with talk, Fiona." Theodosia tried unsuccessfully to untangle the button of her glove from the fringe.

"What are ye going to do alone? Ye've no money. Ye've no clothes. What skills have ye to make a trade?"

"I have a fine hand to write with." But her fine hand was at that moment hopelessly entangled.

"Ye'll not be hired!"

"Fiona, I have to go!" Theodosia finally yanked her gloved hand free from her shawl.

"But ye don't even know *where* to look!"

"London. I know he's in London."

"London! Gutters and the rats, ye mean."

"I'll find him. I will, and I'm not afraid of rats or gutters."

Fiona looked hard into the eyes of her friend.

Theodosia stared back, resolute, unshakeable. And so it was with something akin to a nod of recognition that Fiona took Theodosia by both hands, looked her in the eye and said, "Then I'm cooming with ye."

Theodosia shook her head, but Fiona squeezed her hands. "Listen to me. I've been thinking on it. I was only waitin' for a summer position, and nothing was cooming up. I had meself as a Lady's companion, but the Lady died. An' I can't go back home. I promised I'd bring... I'd bring somethin'..."

"Then you can't afford to go with me."

"If I stay in town one more day I'll owe another month's rent, which I've only half of as it is, but it's enough to get us settled in London at least, and it'll be easy for me to find a place there. I have a trade, ye know, letters of reference as a tutor and a teacher. So we'll go together. Ah, don't be lookin' at me like that. It's what I would have done eventually. I would have taken meself to London." And she was only stretching the truth by fifty miles or so to say it.

"Are you certain?"

"Well, I'm certain I want to be going with ye, now."

"I… I'll have to go back to the Bannochs one more time to get my things."

"I'll meet you at the west crossroads in two hours then, for I'll go home and pack, as well, and we'll walk from there to the docks."

"The docks?"

"Cheaper than a carriage ride and almost as quick. I'm bound to make our monies last."

Theodosia smiled and brushed away a grateful tear. "They say the Scottish are thrifty."

"Do they now? And do they ever say whether we've a choice in the matter?"

Theodosia, despite the heaviness of their circumstances, could not help herself and laughed as Fiona's chiding look turned into a smile. ⌒〰

NINETEEN

∾

There was a little girl who had a little curl
Right in the middle of her forehead,
When she was good, she was very, very good,
But when she was bad, she was horrid.

Nursery Rhyme

∾

Cecelia knew her mother had received a letter and that she had removed herself to her room to read it and therefore the letter must be very important. The letter, she was reasonably assured, must be from her uncle concerning Theodosia. She looked forward to observing the expression on her mother's face when she returned to the parlor, the look that would tell her everything she needed to know about the letter's contents.

She waited.

And she waited.

But her mother did not return for quite some time. This was an answer too, she realized. The news was bad. Either Theodosia was correct and the Browns were stupid enough to refuse the Brookses' offer, or they had termed the marriage acceptable but her mother would not gain from the alliance what she had wished.

Then it came to her the only way to know would be to read the letter herself.

When her mother finally returned to the parlor, she, of course, kept her own counsel. She took herself to her writing desk, and in silence began to pen a note. Cecelia passed behind her mother's chair to judge that it was being written to the Brookses.

She smiled knowingly and excused herself from the room fairly certain her mother would be lost in her task for a time. She went directly to her mother's bedroom, opened the secret drawer in the wardrobe and found more than one letter lying there.

How delightful.

She read from the one which was still warm from her mother's hand. *So the fools didn't wish their daughter to marry Alfred! Amazing.* She hadn't realized just how wonderful that news might be to her. She actually had to refrain from dancing about the room in delight.

* * *

Theodosia quickly gathered her things from the Bannoch guest room. As she tossed her embroidery work into her portmanteau, the little scissors from her chatelaine fell out and stuck upright in the floor. "Someone is to visit!" She smiled wanly to remember the old saying. She bent and plucked the scissors from the wood. "And I will not be here when they arrive."

The carpetbag was full. She turned to the window, pulled up the sash and began to step over the sill when she heard a small but persistent knock upon her door.

She looked back with irritation and then with fear. The scissors were right after all. She looked to the window. It was now or never.

"Theodosia, open this door," a thin voice said. "I have delightful news for you!"

Recognizing Cecelia's voice, Theodosia bit her lip and began to pull herself out the window, but she forgot to watch her footing. She cried out as she felt her legs give way and then she stumbled forward onto the stone portico, her bag promptly falling open and scattering its contents along the stone.

Theodosia gathered her things in a mad rush, but Cecelia came from around the corner of the house and descended upon her crouching form.

"Cousin! You are leaving us?" she said mockingly.

Theodosia continued to gather her things and did not look up at her. "Yes, I am. I am going to London, and if you try to stop me, Cecelia Bannoch, I swear I'll knock you down!"

"Theodosia, you have painted me all wrong." She crouched,

picked up a stray stocking and held it out for Theodosia. "I have brought you *wonderful* news."

Theodosia hesitated. She took the stocking slowly from her hand, all the while observing Cecelia's face.

She smiled coyly. "Yes, I have what could be the most important information you will ever hear!"

Theodosia half rose and came upon Cecelia so violently the two went thudding backwards into the boxwood that lined the portico. "WHERE IS HE?" cried Theodosia. "You tell me or I'll..." She had Cecelia pinned, but her cousin just laughed in her face.

"Ho! Ho! Where is who, Theodosia?"

"You know!" she said coldly.

"I can only presume you mean fair Austin. Has he run away again, poor thing?" She straightened herself and then attempted to set her hair comb back in place.

Theodosia sat back, stunned by the coldness in her words.

"Oh, Theodosia, your life is like your pitiful needlework: there are so many strings left unclipped, you are fairly tangled up in them. Aside from Austin, there is the matter of Alfred. He is the first knot to untie, isn't he?"

Theodosia's eyes grew wary.

"Well, he shall be knotted no more. This letter arrived an hour ago and it is from your papa." She pulled the papers from her apron pocket and held them out.

"PAPA!" said Theodosia with unbridled joy. She snatched the papers from her cousin's hand. Hungrily she read his words and laughed and cried. "I knew it! I KNEW it! Ooh, your dear maman has much to answer for. And there is money for me in London! Oh, thank you, Lord! Oh, Austin will be so pleased to know that I was right!" Her smile faltered. "Austin..."

Theodosia blinked and looked out over the park behind the home. The sun shone through the dark green leaves of the forest, and a cool mist cast a pale green hue on the grounds below. The thick trees at the edge of the wood were soft with lichen. Her eyes glimpsed the opening in the woods, the place where the trail began, and for a fleeting moment she wished with all her might she could run to the grassy circle of light and find him waiting.

But she knew he was not there.

"That wasn't the only thing I found in Mother's drawer." Cecelia added. "There was another letter, too... under that one... and this one was addressed to *you*."

Theodosia looked puzzled as she took the other letter. "To me?"

"Yes, I must say, your papa does not seem quite right in the head to have such a difference of opin..."

"QUIET... please! This doesn't make sense. Let me read..."

It *looked* like a letter from her father, but it wasn't quite right. His letterhead. His signature. Was this the forgery? She glanced up at the greeting once more—"Dear Tee-mouse"—and suddenly she understood. "Parker."

"It didn't say anything about Parker...."

She waved the letter toward Cecelia. "This is a letter written by Parker."

"Oh. Oh." She snorted. "Maman took it for the real thing...."

"He loves a good jest... what did you say? What?" With growing amazement Theodosia carefully read the contents of the letter and looked down at the signature. The whole thing was a jest written as if it were from her father. She shook her head in disbelief, dropped the letter into her lap and looked out again toward the woods. She had forgotten how angry Parker was to hear that his little sister was being sent to England for lessons in manners. He didn't see the need. He'd ranted on and on about it when he visited a month before she left. Upset the household terribly. She had forgotten.

Evidently Parker had played a practical joke on his little sister as he so often loved to do. This letter, written as if from her father, made wild references to her marrying an Englishman and the like. Parker's writing was quite similar to his father's, and but for the "Dear Tee-mouse," her brother's name for her, and the outrageous comments within, it could easily pass for her father's hand. It passed so well, in fact, her Aunt Selda had taken it for her father's.

"This completely explains Maman's behavior," said Cecelia with a bitter laugh. "It's really very badly done, and your brother should be quite proud of himself to have pulled the whole thing off."

"But then why... *why* did Aunt Selda believe it?"

"I suppose because she wanted to... did you read the part that mentions Maman?"

Theodosia looked over the letter once more. "Here? *We both know, dearest, that property is ever more important than money and money more important than love. For my part I promise to shower the Bannochs with a proper importance if only they can find you a nice Earl or perhaps a moderate Duke. I suppose a Lord will do, if one is pressed, but let a Baron go, for they aren't worth the trouble. I might bribe your Aunt Selda into action, I think, if she might suppose to inherit little Star Cottage by the bargain.*"

Cecelia threw back her head and laughed, but Theodosia shook her head. "What did he mean by this... about Star Cottage?"

"Don't tell me you don't know? Auch! You work in your father's office for years and you don't know his holdings?"

"Holdings?"

"Your papa owns our house... Star Cottage."

"He does?"

"Why else do you think we took his poor daughter in for training? Maman couldn't refuse him. We're living off your father's charity and a small stipend from my father's pension."

Theodosia reddened. "But I... I thought Aunt Selda invited me..."

"Out of the goodness of her heart?" cried Cecelia. "Pshh! You're pitiful!"

"Yes, well I can see how foolish I was to think it." Theodosia understood now why she was there. All in all, she was relieved to finally understand. Her eyes fell on the letters once more. "Well, this is completely Parker and utterly the opposite of my father's form of speech, of course, not to mention the coarseness..." She let out half a laugh. "Oh, Parker. How could you?" She looked up, gave a sigh and caught her cousin's glance. "I can't say as I blame him. You know, your maman really knows nothing of our family or she would never have taken this seriously."

"My maman," said Cecelia thoughtfully, "knows nothing of family."

"Why ever did you show me these? Why now?"

Cecelia jutted her jaw forward and then looked away. "To be rid of you, of course."

"That's all there is to it?"

"What else is there?" She sniffed. "Unless it could be that I'd like to wear my own dresses again... or that I won't have to spend my every waking moment teaching you how to parade about like a fool just so you can enchant Alfred."

Now it was Theodosia's turn to understand. "I can see why you like him."

"Whomever do you mean?"

Theodosia smiled. "Alfred told me the other night there were only one or two women in the world who understood his science. He called them rare. I don't think there are two of you, Cecelia. I think he meant you."

"And you, I suppose."

She shook her head. "I may understand him, but I don't... you admire him. Yes you do." Timidly she added, "And I hope... I hope that it might work out for you both."

"Don't be a simpering idiot, Theodosia. I'll not make a fool of myself for any man."

"Oh, do Cecelia. *Do* make a fool of yourself." She grabbed her cousin's hand and squeezed. "Give in to it. It's wonderful."

"You are impossible!" She drew her hand away. "As out of your element as a Bishop at the gaming table and much less fun to watch. I will leave you to your work. I wish you the best of luck in finding your precious Austin." She smiled widely, rose and brushed herself off. "But as the more experienced woman here," she said with a batting of her eyes, "I think I should point out that when a man runs away from a woman it might be reasonable to assume he doesn't wish to be found by her."

She swallowed hard. "You may be right, Cecelia. You may be

perfectly correct, but if I do not dare to look for him I'll never know."

"Then you're a complete fool."

"Maybe. But since you have freely stated your opinion, I will give you mine as well. Mr. Alfred Brooks makes a fool of himself by deciding what he is looking for before he has found a thing, but you are the more foolish, I think, for having never looked at all."

"As if you knew anything about purest love, you little hypocrite... sneaking Austin to your window at night."

"We talked, Cecelia. We always talked, and he stayed at the window."

Cecelia balked at the answer. "You *talked?*" She swayed slightly and sniffed before rushing headlong into her next thought. "Well you *would*. Anyway, I told you I don't want to marry. Marriage is meant for spoonies like yourself—a fool for love—and I don't care to be a party to it."

"Your maman doesn't wish it, you mean."

"Maman has nothing to do with it!" she cried, momentarily losing her composure.

"Oh, but she has *everything* to do with it."

"You're wrong. We want the same things, she and I. I shall have Alfred on the side like a dish of fruit, and when I grow tired of him, I shall take yet another dessert for myself, and I will be free, and I will be very, very... satisfied." She punctuated the message with a short laugh.

"Like your dear maman, I know, free of love and satisfied with nothing."

"You banter on and on about love and intelligence and beauty, as if these belonged together, but you've forgotten money. Oh, I know, you're too simple to concern yourself with such trifles. Don't you realize that even if I wanted Alfred, *which I don't,*" she added hastily, "I have no dowry to attract him?"

Theodosia gulped. "I'm sorry. I didn't think..."

"No, you didn't. And that is the most basic reason why, my dear little cousin, Cecelia Bannoch doesn't consider marriage for herself, for the only man she could afford to attract would be far beneath her. My maman made the mistake of overeducating me, you see, and now..."

"Cecelia, have you ever spoken with Alfred about... this?"

"Spoken!" Her brow furrowed in a pitiful look. "Oh, Theodosia, not everything can be solved with a little conversation. You spoke with Austin quite a lot, didn't you, but he didn't stay, did he? No. Perhaps if you'd done more than simply talk, you could have kept him a while longer." She slowly raised one brow as she eyed her cousin.

"You're wrong," Theodosia whispered.

She smiled cattily. "Am I?"

Looking into those cold, knowing eyes, quite suddenly Theodosia did not wish to stay in Thistledown a moment longer. If she did, she might begin to believe her.

* * *

"Allan, I want you to look over our assets once more and find a way to juggle the numbers."

"I've done all I can, Father."

Lord Brooks looked sternly toward the child. "Are you refusing?"

"I'm telling you it's useless. It's a pipe dream, and you know it." Allan thought of how he'd spent the last week gambling and neatly missed all of his business appointments. He needed a quick excuse, and his father's failing business was a good, albeit dangerous, choice.

Lord Brooks' face grew red with anger. "How dare you, boy! I made this company. I know my business."

"I've tried to get around our creditors, Father, but they haunt me at every turn. We would do well to go back to our former form of trade. We're no good at honest business."

"*Austin* is good at it," he growled. "He would make sense of it, where you give up and head for the gaming table."

"Then get your precious Austin to look over the numbers." Allan had heard too much of Austin lately.

"Austin isn't here."

"Ah! Don't I know it! You've skulked about ever since he left, you and Mother. If I had a son that left home as often as he does, whenever the mood strikes, I'd make him pay for it in spades."

"He is more of a son to me than either of you!" he said through gritted teeth.

"And Brooks House is an embarrassment to me, sir," Allan sneered. "I receive no respect in business, because everyone knows where we came from. If I lose myself in gambling, it's because it's the only pursuit worthy of my efforts."

Lord Brooks clenched the edge of the table and leaned toward Allan. "I will find Austin," he hissed. "And when I find him, I will get on my knees and beg him to take the business for himself, for there are none more worthy in this house. Now get out!"

* * *

When Austin found the road sign, it gave him a small thrill to recognize the name carved there: *Thistledown*. It was most definitely familiar. This led him to reason someone there might know him, but with this thought came a sudden fear of being recognized.

He wasn't at all sure he could manage it. What good would it do to be told his name when he had no memory of it, or to be brought to a home he did not recognize? And what if he were married? What if he had children? He couldn't face it... or them. Not yet. God willing, there would be a time. Meanwhile, he felt a purpose drawing him onward. A barge. A dock. He was hungry. He would find work at the docks and food, of that much he felt certain.

And so, with determined step, he made his way around the town toward the docks knowing, yet not knowing, exactly where he was bound. When he came upon the men, ragged like himself, working the docks for a living, he remembered the note about a barge in his pocket. Could he be a barge man? He addressed the man who had leisurely looked him up and down all this time, "Have you... any work?"

"Lookin' for work, are ye?" He turned his head to his men and winked. They snickered. The barge man would never have believed it. The young man's dress was cut of fancy cloth, but it was clear he'd come into some hard luck... or, he chuckled to himself, maybe a late night at the pub. Well, it might be amusing to see a gentleman do some work for a change. Yes, by George, he could certainly make him work if he wanted it so bad. He'd like nothing more than to give a gentleman some pain. He'd even pay for the pleasure.

"Yer' in luck then!" he yelled and the men behind him laughed. He stepped up and slapped Austin on the back. "Think ye can haul barrels? Right, then. Two shillings a day for loadin' an' come aboard."

* * *

"I took a barge from Aberdeen to London," said Fiona. "It's not the worst sort of travel."

Theodosia shook her head. "No, the worst must be a train."

"Ye've been on a train!"

"Yes, but I cannot recommend it." Despite the afternoon's heat, Theodosia's hands were cold as ice. She was by no means certain of what they were doing. Her conversation with Cecelia had destroyed a vast portion of her hope, and she was left feeling nervous and depressed as she and Fiona made their way to the docks of Thistledown.

Young Henry had seen Miss Mienzes as she headed out of town with her heavy-looking portmanteau and had run to her to wonder why she was leaving. When she told him, he immediately offered to carry both the ladies' baggage to the docks. And so he had, and they were grateful.

"What's the trouble with it then?" Henry asked.

They waited, but Theodosia didn't answer.

"Tee? What about the train?" asked Fiona.

Theodosia tried to focus on the questions. "The train? Oh, the train. Well, it's just that you go for a little ways, and then you stop.

You go and stop and go and stop, and between the swaying and the noise and the dirt when you're going, and the mystery of how long you'll wait when you're stopped, you wish you'd... stayed at home." She bowed her head.

"I've heard the boilers burst sometimes," Henry said.

Theodosia looked up and smiled faintly. "I caught a burning coal in my apron once. I was sitting by the window because I wanted to watch everything. My maman grabbed up the bucket of water the company provides and doused me with the whole of it before I knew what was happening."

Fiona laughed. "No wonder ye've no care for trains!"

"Fiona, are we doing the right thing?" Theodosia stopped in the road suddenly. "Isn't London too dangerous? Am I asking too much of you?" Tears welled in Theodosia's eyes and her little nose turned pink.

Fiona looked at her friend and then nodded her head toward town. "Ye've burned yer bridges back there, Tee Brown, as have I, and there's no fire bucket large enough for the both of us."

"Will we be safe?"

Fiona shook her head. "We wouldn't want to be too near the docks, but it so happens I've a place in mind. The Crooked Tree Inn. The man who runs it was a good friend of my father."

"The Crooked Tree Inn." Theodosia sniffed, wiped her cheek and then gave a halfhearted laugh. "There's a name that's easy to remember."

Fiona smiled, but she thought to herself, *I daren't yet to tell her about the note I left for the Reverend Pickett.*

And so the three walked on.

* * *

Austin began loading barrels to the front of the barge, piling them into small pyramids and lashing them together. While he worked, the other boatmen, five in all including their taskmaster, took no small pleasure in watching the young man grunt and groan over the oaks. Once, Austin almost rolled one of the precious cargo overboard and the head barge man stopped working to curse him through and through. When he'd said what he could of Austin's lack of brains, he cursed his puny arms, then fell to disparaging the fellow's family and questioning his heritage altogether, and so he finally asked him loudly, "What's yer name, lad, so's I can curse yer father good and proper?"

Austin took the man's abuse, thinking all the while that he was very hungry and if he didn't finish what he had started he'd be thrown off the barge without pay, but when the barge man asked his name it stunned him.

He looked down at the dark barrel before him and brought his brows together. What was his name? Quickly he looked around him and something caught his eye. Something familiar.

"Yer name, boy, yer name," the barge man yelled. "Are ye deaf?"

But Austin was watching a brown-haired young woman at the door of a dock house sweeping oyster shells out over the threshold. His eyebrows rose in a hazy recognition as he turned his face to the man. "Broom!"

"Broom?" the man asked doubtfully.

Austin nodded. It sounded right to him... or mostly right. More right than wrong, in any case, and it pleased him immensely to have remembered.

"Broom." The man grunted. "No wonder ye work like yer made of brush, then." He turned to the other men. "I've probably had no rights to curse a man with such a name." They laughed. "Right then. Get back to work, *Broom*." And the old man laughed with the others as they laid into the hauling of barrels once more.

When the loading was done, Austin sat on the edge of the boat, working his sore arms up and down and wondering where he should go from there. He had thought he might be a barge man. He had thought it all the way up until the split second in which he tried to heft that first barrel and right away his body told him he'd never done this sort of work in his life.

Now his neck and back were so stiff he could not even turn to look at the barge man standing beside him prepared to give him his pay. Austin simply held out his hand.

"There now. Be off with ye."

"Sir?"

"I said ye can go now. Ye've done your work. Ye done it poor and ye done it slobberly, but ye done it—so there."

"May I ask where your barge is headed?"

"London, o' course."

"May I go with you?"

"With?" The man gave a great harumph. He allowed another harumph to escape before he bent over and held out his palm for the return of his shillings.

"I'm hungry."

"Then get off my boat," the man replied.

Austin craned his neck toward the fellow as best he could. "You have bread. Give me bread and I'll pay you."

"Get off or I'll send you off," the man repeated.

"I'll work better for you with food in my stomach," Austin said with all the humility he could muster.

The barge man spat overboard but then he nodded, went to his duffle bag and pulled out a small loaf. When he returned, he held the bread in front of him. "The shillings, squirt." Austin had no time to be disgusted with his loss, for his mouth had already begun to water. Quickly he gave the money back and then set upon the small dry thing like a hungry wolf.

And the barge pushed off for London.

* * *

Hot and hungry, the young ladies and Henry arrived at the docks around teatime.

"Henry, I've put aside some meat pies and a jug of water in my bag."

Henry watched a particularly burly-looking horse pull a barge along the canal as he laid the bag down.

Fiona observed him and asked, "Henry, will you be standing for Cambridge soon?"

"No, I'll not be going to University," he replied. "My family's booked passage for Philadelphia."

Theodosia understood his meaning right away, and she stepped to him quickly, tripping slightly over her bag as she came. "But, Henry, it's what you've been working for!"

"Working for?" asked Fiona.

"Austin was preparing Henry for Cambridge," Theodosia told her.

"I think I should have been told!" Fiona said indignantly.

"Beg your pardon, Miss Mienzes," Henry said. "But I was never so certain I would take the tests. I'd no reason to speak to you on it, really."

Theodosia placed her hand on Henry's shoulder. "There's only one reason I could give you for still taking those exams, Henry, besides the fact it will have meant an awful waste of your and Austin's time if you don't. Wouldn't you want to know when you come to America's shore that you could attend a University? If you can gain entrance to Cambridge, it's a certainty you could test to enter any college in the United States."

"That so?"

"Yes, you see, if you stand for Cambridge you'd have the papers to prove it, too."

Henry's brows came together. "Then I could go to school in America."

"America would consider herself lucky to have you, Henry," said Fiona.

"We have good schools there." Theodosia reached down and took out the bread and jug. "There's Harvard... although it is for seminarians, mostly. There is a college in Virginia that was chartered by King William and Queen Mary, the College of William and Mary."

"And you think they'd take me?"

"My, yes... if you had the papers for entry to Cambridge, they certainly would."

"I could do that." He decided rather quickly and then gave the ladies his first broad smile of the morning.

* * *

After he finished the meager bread, Austin leaned back upon his palms and listened to the barge men as they served themselves bread and cheese and drank their good warm beer. He was thirsty but they offered him nothing, and with no money for barter he asked for nothing from them. He would not beg... yet.

Soon the barge man had him restack an inner group of barrels for no purpose, Austin saw, other than to see if he would comply.

As time wore on and the beer kept coming, the head man grew loud and began complaining to his men about the way of the canals. Austin listened halfheartedly as the fellow brought the conversation to a head: he told them all quite flatly their way of life was doomed.

The men balked at his prediction and began arguing the point each in their own way. Canals were cheaper, faster and more sure than locomotives, one said. They didn't go everywhere, but they were there for the main routes, said another. No train could outdo 'em, said one who'd had too much to drink.

Austin watched as the head man stood and, pulling himself together as if in Parliament with a speech to give, brushed aside their arguments with one large, off-balance wave of his hand. He had decided, he said loudly, to tell them the truth. A railway man had bought this and seven other barges. And then he burped as if to underscore his message.

One fellow cursed. "Ye can't run a blasted boat on a blasted railway, can ye?"

The head man laughed. "Now yer catchin' on, Sikes. Them's that bought us'll leave us to rot."

"What d'yer mean, Cap'n?"

"I mean... that I'd've told ye before only they'd not let me 'til we were on our way. This is the last ride, boys."

The fellows grew sullen and looked down among their boots. The silence that fell between them was thick as each man figured on his fate.

Austin had squatted to work the last knot of rope, but when he heard this he turned on his heels away from them, wishing to leave them their privacy.

But soon he felt a watchful eye upon his back and he turned to see the head barge man staring down at him.

"Ye're a gentleman ain't ye?"

"I... I don't know."

The men snorted at the lame answer.

"Ye *don't know*? Ye're dressed well enough. Ye talk fine. So is ye or ain't ye?"

"I really don't know." He rubbed his hands together nervously. "Truth is, I can't seem to remember."

"But ye remembered as was yer name?"

"Broom?"

"Broom. Broom." He looked back at his men. "S' funny, but I thought the man what here bought this tug was named Broom." His eyes were clammy with alcohol and his voice grew fierce as he stared at Austin once more. "Woun't it be rare if this were his son, boys? Woun't it be rare?"

The men behind him understood at once and rose up unsteadily to come toward Austin at the head of the barge.

"Maybe the man sent 'im here to spy us out. To see the last of us. Make sure we don't stir up trouble. Fact is he's been listening to us with his back turned and here I've been telling the God's truth about his Pater. So, Broom... *can yer swim?*"

Austin scrambled up from his seat and held his hands out as if they could protect him from the mob. "I don't know. And I don't even know if that's my name."

Another round of laughter. The head man said, "Means he's not sure of his name since we come round to 'em, eh?"

"Let's sweep the blighter overboard," another behind him said loudly. "See if he's made o' cork."

"That's a clinch, Red."

"Sweep 'im!" And the men rushed toward him.

There was nowhere to run. He looked behind him for a split second and in that instant felt himself pushed hard and saw the waters rise up as his body twisted and fell.

The shot of cold waters took him in.

In the first fleeting moment, he was grateful. He wanted to

leave them. He'd had food and the water drenched his sweating body and instantly brought a cool relief.

But as he adjusted to his circumstance and his arms began to ply the quiet canal, his eyes grew wide with terror.

He realized he did *not* know how to swim.

The canal was but fifteen feet wide, yet it may as well have been fifteen hundred, for he was set in the middle and he could not reach the grass. The barge passed five feet from him but none reached out a pole to help him. In fact, the men on board and the fellow that gripped the barge horse were as callous to Austin's fate as the horse that plied the trail along the water's edge, and so the boat was pulled farther and farther from Austin. And the men walked the edge of the boat and watched his struggle.

"Can't swim!" Austin yelled, and they laughed happily and slapped each other on the back to hear it.

One called out, "Well, there's 'ar answer! Y'ain't a gentleman after all." And they laughed and laughed.

Austin tried to touch the bottom with his feet, but there was no bottom and he could not hold himself up.

As they saw him begin to slide under, they let out a whoop, but the sounds were swallowed by the waters as Austin went down.

The water was sluggish and cold and he did not want to die there.

When he came back up, choking and sputtering, the men were silent and the boat was ten feet away from him. They were lined along the back edge, but not a one of them moved.

"For God's sake, help me!" But there was no reply. "God help me," he whispered as he went down a second time. Flailing his arms desperately he could think only of getting to the edge of the canal now. As he thrashed about under the sluggish waters, an anger and a passion to live tore through him, a fierce need to survive took hold, and the raw energy gave him strength.

And then he felt the toe of his left foot catch a rock.

With great effort he wrenched himself around to bring his body over it, his feet square upon it, and then he pushed upward.

Up. Up. His head broke through barely above the water. But he was alive! He was on a rock. The rock would not move and he was alive.

Never had he felt so alive.

The barge was well away from him now. The men yelled and pointed and cursed his good fortune. But he just smiled at the sky. And he laughed. He gurgled water as he laughed, but he spit it out and laughed again.

He laughed as loudly as he could to make certain every last one of them could hear him. ◆

TWENTY

Little Tom Tucker,
Sings for his supper;
What shall he eat?
White bread and butter;
How will he cut it without a knife?
How will he be married without a wife?

Nursery Rhyme

Fiona haggled with every barge that came into the quay to unload and finally settled on a family-owned vegetable barge bound for London within the hour. The ladies were asked to sit under the tentlike structure in the center of the barge area, usually considered the "family room" to the thin woman whose husband steered the boat. Five children scrambled on the deck—three sons in their youth that helped to load, unload and set the roping, and two younger daughters, one of whom helped her mother with the cooking. The very youngest, who toddled about the deck barefoot, was apparently put upon the earth to give her family a central focus for all their worries.

Fiona and Theodosia insisted that the woman and the girls continue as before with their activities, and so the two sat under the tent as the family milled about them. Theodosia watched the river pass, admired the view and listened to the bird's song, and Fiona kept her eyes riveted upon the toddler.

About halfway to the city, the mother helped the oldest daughter light the fire under their tiny stove. The stove was set toward the front of the barge—well away from the tent for fear of fire—and the mother told the toddler, whose name was Peaches, to stay close but not too close. Peaches proceeded to blithely do exactly as she pleased, which was to walk to the edge of the barge, lean over it and talk to the friendly face she saw wiggling along the water's surface.

Fiona's eyes were focused on Peaches, and she tried to stay still in her seat as the girl took uncertain steps closer and closer to the edge. Something flew around Peaches head now, and Peaches tried to shoo it away. Her shooing caused her steps to grow even more erratic and ill-placed. Fiona looked to the mother and back to the daughter and back to the mother and then stood up just as Peaches bent down and sat on the deck.

Fiona's motion caught Theodosia's attention and she wondered what was the matter, but Fiona had already strode over to the girl.

"What is it, Peaches?" asked Fiona.

"It's a buzzin'," said Peaches as she hit her ear.

The mother rushed over and caught her daughter up in her arms. "Peaches! Wot's buzzin'?"

"There 'tis a'gin!" she squealed and hot tears came to her eyes.

Fiona looked at the child's ear, and saw a spot of blood in the lobe.

"A bug it is!" cried the mother. "Oh, what'll I do!"

"Get me a lucifer," said Fiona.

"You'll not burn it out!"

Fiona shook her head. "No, no. I only mean to hold it to her ear. Take her down below. The bug'll come to the light... or the warmth. But it'll come."

"Listen to her, Ma'am, she's a teacher," Theodosia said.

The group managed to bring Peaches down the slight stair and huddle with her in a corner of the barge. Fiona lit the long match and held it beside the child's ear. At twenty seconds, the mother's eyes had grown to slits and the child was whimpering.

Fiona told the child to be still.

At twenty-five seconds, the child cried out again, and the mother began to tell Fiona exactly what she thought of her.

At thirty-five seconds, the woman told her daughter to go up and put a cup of oil on the stove, because her own mother had sworn by hot oil for "such as this."

At forty seconds, Fiona told her flatly, "I'm sorry to be the one to tell ye, but yer mother was an idiot."

It was pure providence that, at forty-five seconds, the bug crawled out, for the mother had determined that in five seconds more she would strike another lucifer match and put it to Fiona Mienzes' head.

When things calmed down, Fiona and Theodosia were once more ensconced under the canvas canopy, and Peaches, who had calmly decided that Fiona Mienzes was worthy of her worship, had crawled into her lap and would not be moved.

Fiona chatted with her lightly, and Theodosia watched with admiration. Then she looked back over the water and a memory came to mind that caused her to laugh out loud.

Fiona looked at her, green eyes stars of light, black lashes batting expectantly.

"I was just thinking of Parker." In fact at that exact moment Theodosia was thinking how much Parker would enjoy meeting pretty Fiona, but she went on. "When I was Peaches' age, I used to follow my poor brother around. One day when he wanted to go off alone, he told me to go catch a bee. He meant it in jest, you know, to shoo me away, but because I knew he knew everything there was to know about nature, I went straightway to my favorite clover patch to find myself a bee. Watching the furry yellow backs of those warm-looking bumble bees, I wondered to myself why I had never thought to catch one before that day. So I stooped down and caught one up. You know the rest."

Fiona laughed and shook her head. "Yer brother's a wicked man, to be sure. I hope yer father tanned his hide."

"Oh, he wanted to." Theodosia laughed. "He wanted to, but Parker explained it all away. He told my father he thought I had better sense than to accept the challenge." Theodosia coughed back the laugh. "It was the beginning, I'm afraid, of my papa's thinking I had no sense at all."

"And the beginning of yer curiosity nigh onto killing ye."

"That is certainly another way to look at it."

***

Austin counted himself fortunate when he was plucked from the waters by the next barge floating down the canal. They fed him, gave him a blanket to lie under and told him to find a spot in the hold, and although his clothes were still wet, he soon fell asleep. When he awoke the barge had arrived at the London docks, and his clothes were dry. Austin thanked the crew by helping them unload their goods. The sleep had done his muscles good, and though he was sore, he was able.

When the work was done, they asked him along as they headed for the pub, but Austin felt the need to look around. The docks felt familiar and he was in a mood to try and understand why.

He walked up and down the wharfs hoping for some bit of recognition to come to him. One boat in particular caught his interest. The name was *Argyle* and it appeared to be unloading boxes of tea, but then he thought, without knowing quite why, that it was too early for tea to be in port. He observed the workers for the longest time, but he slowly grew afraid to ask someone about the boat.

* * *

Theodosia and Fiona arrived in London and steadily made their way to the bank. Fiona gave three pennies to Peaches' oldest brother to take their bags to The Crooked Tree Inn while Theodosia looked about her in amazement at the city. She took a quick sniff. Dirty air and the smell of dead fish. It was all she could do not to gag as she retrieved her handkerchief from her little reticule and pulled it to her nose. And the noise! All about them were workers on the docks and for as far as the eye could see, there stretched a row of warehouses, some of which, she thought, must be tea, and one of them must belong to the Brookses.

As they walked toward the bank, Theodosia watched ragged looking children run freely about the muddy graveled streets, hawkers cry their wares, and carriages and horses lumber past. The metal pattens strapped to the bottoms of the ladies' shoes to protect them from the road added a loud clacking noise to the general chaos. Trash, refuse and human waste lined the avenues; the streets were so filthy that a street sweeper could be found at almost every corner to whom you could pay a penny to sweep the filth as you walked behind him. But as the ladies gained the heart of the city, magnificent architecture could be seen. Well-dressed lords and ladies walked the avenues, the windows were dressed to tempt buyers, lovely wrought-iron fencing lined the walks, and occasionally a mounted soldier in magnificent uniform moved among the various carriages and wagons. So much to see and learn. London was indeed a wondrous place.

They found the bank, and as they entered through the doors, Theodosia felt the hope rising up in her that all would be well. They would have funds to stay in town awhile as they looked for Austin, and surely they would find him.

Yes, the bank was open, but her hopes were soon crushed, for the letter from Theodosia's father was not enough to open the account.

Fiona and Theodosia pleaded with the clerk, showing him the letter clearly stating funds had been sent to the bank in London, but without clear letters of reference or a suitable person to stand on the girl's behalf, the clerk informed them that the monies would stay right where they were.

"Such a barbarism!" cried Theodosia, and she and Fiona left the bank. "Are these medieval times that a woman cannot even secure funds that are placed in her own name?!"

"Be glad they don't know of yer 'engagement' to Mr. Alfred Brooks."

"Why?"

"Because then *he'd* be the one ye'd have to call on to take yer moonies out."

"Auh! But it's only an engagement!"

"Well, it's only a bank, Tee, and if they've any reason whatsoever to hold on to yer money, they'll do it. Look here, though, we could send for the Reverend Pickett."

"No!" A blush rose to Theodosia's cheeks.

"I don't see as we've a choice, Tee."

"No, please, no. Let's... let's just think on it awhile," parried Theodosia.

Fiona gnawed lightly on her upper lip, well knowing the Reverend would be on his way already. "Are you afraid the Reverend will send you back to your aunt? I really don't think he would, now."

Theodosia looked at her friend steadily.

"Well, then..." Fiona shrugged. "I suppose I've enough to last us a few more days, anyway."

From there they went looking for The Crooked Tree Inn, and Theodosia fell into deep thought as they walked.

Fiona knew her friend was thinking hard on something, because she bumped into people as she went along and twice she stepped on her own hem. On the second stumble Fiona smiled, took Theodosia by the arm with a strong and steadying grip and led on.

* * *

Austin walked from the *Argyle* around to another wharf where he saw a great clipper ship that took his breath away. Beautiful in her sleekness and the set of her sails, her name was *Hurricane*. From the look of the cargo, it appeared the boat was carrying mostly cloth. This was not as familiar to Austin as tea seemed, but it was still of interest and so he made his way toward the loaders and asked the ship's business and whether they needed hands.

"Y'ain't union then?" the fellow asked.

"No," said Austin. "Do I need to be?"

The fellow smiled. "Not on this tug. We're fer America. But tell me why should Cap'n hire ye if ye've never worked the boats?"

"But I have. I know how to load these tight and dry." And then he explained the snug loading of cargo into the lower decks and the man's face went from irritation to an expression as much akin to rapture as a toothless old sea dog could manage. Austin had taken himself by surprise as well, and by the end of the conversation he was almost giddy with his newfound knowledge. By George, he really *did* know shipping!

He didn't know *how* he knew, but still, he seemed a useful person after all. The old man happened to agree, and after a short interview with the captain, Austin had himself a job. They would be taking on goods for a week's time before setting sail.

"Do you need another man to cross?"

"Got all we need for crossin'. It's unloadin' on t'other side that'll be a chore, eh?"

Austin nodded. America sounded good to him. Very good. He would find a way to go. It seemed a good place to start things over. Somehow he'd manage to cross.

He settled into the first day's routine of working sunup to sundown, taking his meals in a dockside pub, and sleeping in a sailors' flophouse. And for the first time since waking in the middle of the path near Thistledown, Austin felt comfortable in his surroundings.

* * *

"I've thought on it, and I'm certain he must be clerking in one of the tea stores." The young ladies had settled into the inn, a smallish building set ten blocks from the docks, and were making the most of regular accommodations. They counted themselves lucky to have a wide window that overlooked a large avenue, a dividend gladly provided by the proprietor in honor of his old friend Angus Mienzes, Fiona's father.

Fiona frowned as she sat on her bed and began to repin her hair at the back of her head. "The docks aren't safe."

"But what if we didn't go as ourselves? What if we were an old lady and her nurse? Wouldn't that be 'safe'? Come on now, Fiona, we have to do *something*. The money will run out if we don't."

Fiona's hands fell away from her head, and she stared for a long while at her friend. "Who's to be the nag and who's to be the nurse then, I want to know?"

"You choose."

"The nurse, then. I'd feel more comfortable with you in a wheel-about. Did you see what you did to that poor man's apple cart?"

"He said it was his fault."

"O-o-o-h, it was. *Clearly* he put himself in harm's way gettin' near to ye." She went back to fixing her hair.

"I can't seem to help it," said Theodosia. She stood at the window staring out over a myriad of rooftops and smoking chimneys.

"Yer just too determined. It's like your mind can only go top speed in one direction at a time, and your poor body must try to keep up."

Theodosia turned to smile at her friend. "I know what I want, and then it's all I can think of."

"But have you ever stopped yourself?"

"Yes. I did this summer. I did when the Reverend Pickett told me it was the Lord's will to be patient. That I should stay at my aunt's and obey."

"And was he wrong, then?"

Theodosia turned quickly to the window. Her jaw came forward slightly and her head tilted upward as she pulled back the curtain and stared out over the rooftops once more. "We're here now, so it's pointless to answer. Besides, it won't take long to find Austin, and when I do, we'll have it out and be done... come what may, and if I don't find him, I'll... then I'll call on the Reverend Pickett to stand for me so I can get my monies, and I'll take a boat for home." She turned back to her friend. "And you'll look for a teaching position here."

"Oh, my, yes," said Fiona in a happy voice, but she darted her eyes away and closed them—the dark lashes hanging on her pale cheek for a breath of a moment—only to open them and smile brightly at her friend; the whole of her meaning was all too clear.

And although at that very moment both women knew they were lying to each other, neither had the courage to admit it.

* * *

"Should we keep this up?" asked Fiona.

"I'm sorry you have to be the one to wheel the bathchair, Fiona, but please do keep this up. I have to find him." Fiona was rolling Theodosia along in a rickety chair they'd purchased from a used-items shop near the inn. They had put on their best black dresses, took the bedcover from one of their beds to wrap around the "invalid," and then upon Theodosia's head they had placed the most important portion of her costume: an ugly.

The unusual bonnet commonly called an "ugly" was thus named because it was, in fact, a hideous-looking contraption whose panels and boning resembled the back of a large armadillo. It was pulled low around and over the face by means of draw-strings. Uglies were created to protect a lady's face from sunlight, and this one served to hide Theodosia's countenance completely.

But despite the excellence of their costumes and their success at gaining the sympathy of nearly every tea house employee they encountered, they found no one to match the description of the old woman's "long-lost grandson."

Theodosia asked Fiona to stop for a moment when she found herself drawn to a gaudy-looking poster plastered on the side of a building. Fiona just chided her and pushed her chair away, and soon they had worked their way to the step at "Chatham's Tea Exchange."

Two clerks came out and offered to assist in carrying the wheeled chair into the waiting room. And Fiona provided Austin's description to the employees once again.

* * *

As Austin made his way past the Chatham's Tea Exchange, he thought to give assistance to the two fellows carrying an old woman in a bathchair into the establishment, but the men succeeded at the task just as he approached, and so he fell to watching the dirty gravelled road pass beneath his feet once more.

The captain had sent him on an errand into town, and he hardly knew where he was going, but he was glad to breathe a different sort of air.

The putrid scents that hung about the docks only made Austin long all the more to be out on a ship where the only smell to assail the senses on deck might be sea breezes whipping through the sails, the only sight the meeting of sea and air. He was not long by these thoughts before he was of a mind that by hook or by crook he would leave for America on this or another ship in a week's time.

* * *

Theodosia stood up, threw back the ugly from her head and forcibly made her way past the two shocked clerks who'd helped to bring an invalid into the store.

"Tee! What're ye doin'!" cried Fiona furiously.

"He's out there!" Theodosia rushed headlong to the front door of the tea house and settled into a fight with the old brass door handle. A commotion and a shouting rose from the clerks as she pulled.

"Ye're talkin' like a mad woman!" Fiona yelled.

"No. He's out there, and I've got to get out of here." The handle gave way and Theodosia opened the door with a whoosh of air that caused the rolls of paper lying on a nearby clerk's desk to roll off the wide expanse and onto the floor in a chaotic heap. The clerk fell to his knees and cursed loudly as he gathered them up.

The fellow who'd spoken to the nurse and her charge was incensed at the sudden mobility and obvious youth of the "dear old woman" and immediately threatened to call a constable on them for the outrage.

Fiona turned back to him and grabbed at the wheelchair. "I ha' been forced to represent the girl as an old woman, because no one'll let an insane young woman, sich' as herself, through their doors, and furthermore, ye should count yerself lucky the girl decided to leave the building while her fits was on! Now moove out o' me w'y."

"How dare you!"

She yelled over her shoulder as she passed, "But she'd be all right if she finds him, don't ye know." Fiona wielded the chair like a weapon through the unsteady group of clerks that had filled the aisles to stare and laugh, and she soon found herself outside.

Theodosia was by then standing on the street and looking desperately to the right and left and back again. Hundreds to her right. Hundreds to her left. None of them were he.

Tears soon blurred her vision.

When she felt Fiona's hand upon her shoulder, she let the tears give way and sobbed into Fiona's shoulder like a child.

After her tears, Theodosia, still sniffling, insisted she be the one to roll the chair back to the hotel. "After the trouble I've caused," she added. Fiona, whose arms had truly suffered that morning from thumping the chair along the thick streets, accepted the offer with hardly a murmur.

And so Theodosia rolled the chair and they walked along. Narrowly missing a vegetable cart, Theodosia said thoughtfully, "Chatham's was the third place to ask if we'd contacted a solicitor to search for him."

"Oh, but they think we're looking for a lost grandson with an inheritance."

"Aren't we?" asked Theodosia in a hush. "I'm just thinking that going to the Brookses' lawyer... *solicitor*, would be a very good step indeed. Surely Austin would have contacted them in some way... for Henry's sake, if not his own."

"There's some sense in that," Fiona conceded. She flung out her hand to warn off an approaching group of elderly women for Theodosia was staring blankly ahead.

"Do you know who the Brookses' solicitor might be?" asked Theodosia, unaware of how the chair wheel caught just enough of the last woman's basket to force her to turn about only to be caught and steadied by her friends.

Fiona looked back with wide eyes, but when she saw the old woman had survived, she turned back to Theodosia and rubbed her sore arms once more. "Oh, that's easy enough, and *watch where yer goin', please.* No one in Thistledown ever called for legal counsel but the Brooks. Aye. I know their solicitor, but if I know them as I think I do, they'll be even less help to ye than the Brookses themselves."

"But don't forget, the law is *my* trade, Fiona," she said to her friend in happy concentration, thus failing to notice the hawker's tray until it was too late. The wide bread tray the fellow carried was snagged by the arm of the chair and pulled along with them for a moment. The motion jarred the contents such that a loaf of round bread fell into the wicker seat. Theodosia, seeing the hawker but not the snag, stopped the chair, looked down and picked it up.

Just as the fellow managed to pull the straps of the tray loose from the wicker seat, Theodosia calmly returned the loaf to him. "No, thank you, sir. Not today."

And the fellow, who had been calling out his wares non-stop since sunrise, was left entirely speechless as they strolled away.

* * *

Roundtree thought to himself it was ironic, really, that Austin Brooks was causing this much trouble. Here, the will lay dormant for years and everyone had forgotten the thing until Austin Brooks came 'round with a copy. Holcomb had no idea what a jewel it was until he'd shown him. Of course, the town would never win, but it would take years to find it out. Meanwhile, there was a regular income to draw from the estate, by heavens! He knew his employer, Holcomb, meant to base his retirement on the case.

To Holcomb he said,"I've found him on the ship *Hurricane*, sir, but he doesn't know who he is."

"Well, of course he doesn't know who he is, Roundtree."

"I mean to say that he was mugged, and…"

"Of course he was mugged! If you're wanting my undying gratitude for that little bit of quick thinking, you've another thing coming, you blithering fool. I could have found another way to get the copy of the will away from him."

"But, sir, I'm not speaking of the night he was with me. No. I mean more *recently*. Again! He doesn't know his own name!"

Holcomb gave him a severe look.

"I swear it," Roundtree said firmly. "He's told everyone on board the same story. He thinks his name is Broom!"

"Well, what if he starts remembering, eh? What if he starts dabbling in this business again, trying to drum up sympathy for the town, getting up scholars and the like? Lord Brooks won't stand for it."

Roundtree didn't take long to think upon his meaning but only smiled grimly. "That much money, eh, Mr. Holcomb?" he said softly.

"A fortune," said Holcomb. "Odd's truth—a fortune. Now go and make yourself useful—buy him off, whatever, but take your rampant stupidity elsewhere, would you?"

* * *

"My name is Miss Theodosia Brown, recently affianced to Albert Seton Brooks, the Younger, and I've come to discuss with a member of the firm the disposition of Lord Brookses' will." Theodosia pressed her spectacles carefully upward as she stared down her nose at the young clerk behind the desk of Holcomb, Redfern, and Grackle.

"A member of the firm will be with you shortly, miss."

"It had better be the solicitor in care of the will in question, young man, or I shall remember who was responsible for misrepresenting me."

The fellow seemed only slightly impressed as he left the desk, but Theodosia was pleased, if not calmed, by the fact that within a minute, he had returned. "Miss Brown? You may see Mr. Holcomb now."

Theodosia's lower lip began to tremble as she stood up, and so, to avoid this small display of fear, she lowered her head and through sheer strength of will she followed him.

An angry looking young man, tall with red hair, was fiercely jamming his hat over his head as she passed through the hall. He rudely stared back at her as she glanced his way, and so she averted her eyes.

Theodosia was ushered into a large and grandiose chamber. Her eyes searched the room quickly, but they rested on one wall: It was filled with one magnificent sideboard, a combination of glassed bookshelves above and cabinets below, but it was what was behind the glass that intrigued her. She could not take her eyes from the rows and rows of books.

"Miss Brown?"

She turned to see a small, thin man with a simpering grin. He was watching her with some amusement, it seemed. His look caused her to straighten her back and clear her throat. *I can do this!* she told herself. *I can!* "Mr. Holcomb, I have come here today to speak to you on a delicate matter to which your ears and your ears only shall be privy."

"You have my promise on that, Miss Brown."

"That is kind of you, sir, but after telling you what I've come about, I shall not need *your* promise, you will need mine, for I have come to offer my services to you."

"Go on, please."

Oh, she shouldn't have, but... she did. "I believe you are aware that I have read the Brooks will."

"Mmm." He pushed himself deeply into his leather chair.

"And you are aware, also, that the boy, Austin, found the will after my discovering it and has had the family in chaos ever since." Holcomb made no response. "You may also be aware of my engagement to Lord Brooks' oldest son, Alfred."

"Yes." He drew his fingertips together and began to rock his chair ever so slightly.

"To come to the point, then, I must tell you I intend to be the future Lady of Brooks House *soon*... and for a very, very long time thereafter—this was my goal ever since stepping foot on your shores—and there is but one small detail that may keep me from my goal and you know it well."

"Do I?" he replied, still rocking.

"Yes, sir. Thistledown and Austin Brooks *must not win*. Brooks House must remain mine... Albert's, and I will do anything to make it so. Anything."

Holcomb cocked his head and looked at her for a long while. It was like speaking to the devil himself. She tried to keep the shiver from her spine and the tremble from her lips. She was not positive she had accomplished either. Afraid she was losing ground, she continued, "I am fairly certain Austin Brooks is in this city." She noticed Holcomb's eyes widen ever so slightly. Almost imperceptibly, but she had noticed. "I am afraid he means to harm the estate; I have a *relationship* with Austin that would cause him to trust me. I could... *encourage* him to go to America if I could only find him."

Holcomb's eyes bore through her. "I don't know Austin Brooks' whereabouts." His Adam's apple rose and fell in a swallow, and she knew that he was lying.

"It would serve both our interests if you *could* find him, sir. A lady cannot go about the city unattended looking for young men. You have the resources to find him, and when you do, you may find me at The Crooked Tree Inn. In whatever way you may need assistance—*whatever way*—I will promise to assist you. When you think to doubt my sincerity, please remember this: I *have* read the will, and if I had wanted to cause mischief for the Brooks family, I would have done so before now. Thank you and good day."

"Wait."

"Sir?"

"Have a seat once more, Miss Brown. I see your point, and I think you should know that things are already well in hand."

"Well in hand?"

"Yes. We do happen to know Austin's whereabouts. Roundtree is on it. He's going to encourage him to, uh, leave the area."

"Is he? How... how very interesting. Tell me..." She swallowed. "Where is he?"

"Oh, don't trouble yourself."

Her heart sank to her boots, but another thought occurred. "Do... do you have a copy of the will?"

"Ah-ah-ah," he taunted, his index finger outstretched. "Of course, we have the original, as well as the copy Austin had."

"Oh... and how did you manage to get it from him?"

"Roundtree. Roundtree has his ways... a little heavy-handed perhaps, but effective, nonetheless. I believe he used a coal hod, if I'm not mistaken...."

She hoped he had not observed that her face had grown quite pale. "So... I've nothing... to worry about, it seems."

"It does seem that you may put yourself en*tirely* in our hands." Holcomb stood up, came around to her chair, and took one of her hands in his. "My dear, you're trembling."

"I... always tremble... when I hear good news."

He gave her a thin smile. "Then I always hope to be giving you good news, Miss Brown, for I find your... *passion* for this matter of great interest."

"You have positively stopped my heart from beating, sir, but I must go. I have a note to write to Alfred... explaining my whereabouts. He mustn't... be suspicious of me, you know. So, really, I must go right away."

"By all means. But, my dearest Miss Brown, I know where I may find you?" He raised her hand to his mouth, and, with a skeletal grip, held it there and then pointedly pressed his lips to her glove. Her stomach lurched within her.

"I must go now, sir." Theodosia tried to keep the tears from her eyes. She left the room in a rush.

Holcomb stared after her and then tapped his empty pipe against the desk. "Dimmed flattering. Haven't had such an effect on a woman in years. You've still got it, Holcomb. By George, you've still got it."

Theodosia practically ran out of the law offices, for to be sick right there in the reception area in the offices of Holcomb, Redfern and Grackle would not have served her purposes at all just then.

* * *

It was the way in which Austin walked that first caught the Reverend's notice. As the Reverend went around the docks asking if two comely young ladies had passed this way—one with brown hair, brown eyes, spectacles, traveling with a black-haired, green-eyed Scottish woman, both youngish, might be trying to book passage to America—a certain movement caught his eye and he stopped dead in his tracks right there on the docks and began to stare. Already sunburned from the two days' work preceding, Austin had allowed a stubble beard to begin on his lower face, and he looked now like many of the men he worked alongside. His shirt and vest and pants were dirty. Others who knew him may not have recognized him, but the Reverend Pickett recognized him at once. "Thank God in Heaven," said Reverend Pickett under his breath, "it's he!"

He looked about him with a smile of unbelief as if to tell someone the good news but realized with chagrin he was alone. He turned back toward the young man and wondered if it were his imagination. No. Out of the teeming millions, he had found Austin Brooks. He smiled again, knowing full well there were no such coincidences in this life.

He walked toward the boat and wondered what he might say. Working ships? Austin might be working to pay passage. That would be typical of him, not wishing to use his parents' money to enable him to leave. But a dock worker? It seemed all the more certain now the boy didn't wish to be found. And he had changed his appearance drastically. How should he approach him?

Catching the captain's eye, Reverend Pickett walked up and gave a short bow of deference. "Sir."

"May I be of assistance, sir?"

"Yes. I'd like to inquire as to the name of one of your laborers? The fellow there... carrying those three boxes up that plank. He looks quite familiar. Do... do you think I might speak with him for a moment?"

The captain looked over the pile left to load, and then nodded.

Reverend Pickett stepped carefully forward and waited for the young man to return from the hold.

But when Austin came back up he headed straight down to the boxes again and did not see the Reverend at all.

The Reverend did not know whether or not this was intentional, but now he was forced to approach him again. He stepped back to the pile as Austin lifted boxes one onto the other. "Son, may I have a word with you?" he asked.

Austin looked around with surprise. "Me, sir?"

Reverend Pickett was momentarily halted by his answer. "Do you not know me?" he finally sputtered.

Austin briefly pinched his lips together but finally licked them and answered, "No, sir, I do not know you."

The Reverend's eyes narrowed with concern. "You... you do not lay claim to the name Austin Brooks?"

Austin stared at the man and his eyes widened at the sound of the name. "Did I know you, sir? Do you know me?" he asked.

The Reverend was taken aback. The boy was putting on a very good act. He quickly reasoned this would be a way for Austin to ignore all that had gone before—a way, yes, but not a good one. "Are you saying you don't know *me* then?" he asked.

Austin looked blank for a moment, then looked around him. "You seem... well, if I did, sir, I don't remember now. I don't wish to be rude..."

If he hadn't said the words so gently, the Reverend might have taken it for a reproof, a swearing off, but something in his tone caught him short. "Are you saying you *don't* remember or you don't *wish* to remember?"

"I don't honestly know, sir." Austin felt himself pulled on as many sides as he might have. "You... you are familiar, sir, and obviously a man of the cloth, but I don't... I can't recall your name."

"Reverend Pickett of Thistledown."

"THISTLEdown! I caught a *barge* from Thistledown!"

With agitation the Reverend said, "My boy, you *grew up in Thistledown!*"

Austin dropped open his jaw and stared hard at the fellow. He tried to speak but couldn't.

"You... have you lost your memory?"

Austin remembered the day this odd journey began. "Two days ago I woke up in a path. I was... I'd been hit on the head... here . . ." He pointed indelicately to a still blackish lump on his skull. He gulped and looked the fellow in the eyes again. "By what name did you call me?"

"Austin Brooks. Your name is Austin Simpson Brooks."

"Brooks. Brooks. Broom. Yes. I almost had it then."

Reverend Pickett was at a loss to know how to proceed.

He knew the worst was yet to come for what could he say of Theodosia? Obviously Austin had forgotten her as well. Not by choice, but still.... And Austin's parents should know he's alive... all of them should know he didn't run away from them. Not intentionally. He drew his hand to his chin and rubbed it momentarily. "You didn't run away then," he said absentmindedly.

Austin looked around him once more then back to the boxes. "Sir?"

"You were traumatized by a blow to the head. Of course. Your family and friends have worried over you, myself included. They... they thought you might have run away."

"Oh. I don't think... I don't think I'm ready to see anyone... just yet. You see how it is..." He fell to staring at the boxes as Reverend Pickett cast about his mind wondering what next to say. Finally Austin asked in a quiet voice, "Was I in shipping before?"

The Reverend watched the profile of the boy. "Yes. Yes, your family is in shipping. Tea."

"Tea." He nodded slowly. "That is quite familiar. Yes. I like tea, do I?"

Reverend Pickett's voice grew gravelly. "Yes, well, hrrum... you were clerking for your father."

"Clerking?" His head shot up to look at the Reverend. He barked a laugh. "*Clerking!* I should have known! I know how to pack the da... the things, pardon me, but I've no back and arms to haul them!"

The Reverend smiled and let out a chortle. "Well, now you know why." He was heady with the strangeness of the circumstance, almost enjoying the oddity. Here was a completely new man, but with all the humor and gentleness of the youth he knew. Strange the paths God chooses for us now and then. But would God ever choose for the boy to remember?

Before he could say any more, Austin spoke, "I'm a Christian, aren't I?"

Reverend Pickett's mouth fell open. But he quickly rallied. "Yes, you are. You remember that much, eh?"

"Yes. I remembered... to pray... when I awoke. I was quite lightheaded for a time... and it just occurred to me to . . ."

"Fascinating. Thanks be..." The captain moved toward the two in what was an obvious reminder to Austin to get back to his task. The Reverend cleared his throat. "I'll leave you to it then. We'll speak again?"

Austin looked at him carefully and finally nodded. "If you wish."

"Your ship... not leaving for a while?"

"No."

"Good," said Reverend Pickett. "Good." He backed away as he spoke, not quite believing what had just happened and half afraid that if he turned away, the boy would disappear once more. But this was not a dream. Austin's disappearance had had a cause, and the trauma he suffered explained the circumstance—he was not likely to disappear again. Of this the Reverend Pickett was fairly certain, if certain at that moment of nothing else.

He walked slowly back to The Crooked Tree Inn, forming in his mind a hundred different ways to present the news to the young women. He had discovered from Henry for what hotel the ladies were bound, and so had hastily arranged for a pastor to replace him on Sunday and made his way to London.

Has Miss Brown found him already? He shook his head. *And what could she have said to him if she had? The truth of this would break her heart. The truth. That boy loved the truth. What an awesome thing it is. Picked clean and yet the boy knew he was a Christian.* "Oh, that I had such a faith," he mumbled. "May we all come to know who we are as easily as this lad knows himself. Yet I would never have wished this on him, never." He shook his head sadly as he pushed open the door to The Crooked Tree Inn. ∾

TWENTY-ONE

~

One, two, three, four, five,
I caught the fish alive.
Why did you let it go?
Because it bit my finger so.

Nursery Rhyme

~

Theodosia was at first so incredibly happy to hear that Austin was alive and well she barely understood the Reverend's concern.

"But he's all right! It's a miracle you found him. And he's all right. Thank you, Lord. He's all right!"

"Yes, yes, but you're not hearing me. He's not quite himself."

"What do you mean he's not quite himself? You said Austin is working on the docks! We were warned away from the ships, you know. We would have found him eventually, I'm sure, and now all will be well! I'll see him before I have to go! I'll convince him everything will be all right for us. Everything will work out. It's good...it's really good he's taken himself from Brooks House. Oh, Fiona, isn't it tremendous!" She grabbed her friend by both arms and drew her into a twirl right there in the dining room of the inn.

"Theodosia, *listen to me,*" he said sternly and the dance abruptly ended. The Reverend had never called her by her Christian name before, and that he would invoke it now sobered her immediately.

"What's wrong?"

"He... he can't remember."

Theodosia's heart rose up in her throat and she pulled her hand to her cheek. "Whatever do you mean he can't remember?"

He shook his head sadly. "Doesn't even know his own name. The boy can't remember any of his former life. He was struck on the head, as I said, rather severely. He told me I seemed familiar, but that was all. And he remembers that he's a Christian."

"Again? He was struck on the head again?"

"I don't know what you mean exactly."

Fiona piped up, "She visited Holcomb's offices. Turns out his assistant, Roundtree, Austin's supposed *friend*, knocked him on the head to steal the will when he first came to London."

"Good heavens."

But Theodosia was not thinking of that now. She swallowed and said carefully, "Surely... surely *I* will be familiar to him."

"My dear, I know nothing of this sort of thing, but the man didn't even know his own name. Didn't know his family was alive let alone looking for him."

"Well, they're not looking for him! I am! Not them!"

"They would if they thought he'd respond. They would wish to understand his present condition. I'll need to write to them right away," he said almost to himself.

"Write. By all means, write to them," said Theodosia angrily. "But *I* am going to the docks to see Austin."

The Reverend grabbed her hand and held it. "Theodosia, you may get a horrible shock. He doesn't even look himself." He shook his head mournfully. "And you *cannot* go to the docks without escort. Miss Mienzes, please tell her."

Fiona nodded in agreement. "Ye know it's dangerous, Tee."

"Write your note then, Reverend, but straight afterwards take me there... *please.*" She grew teary and squeezed the Reverend's hand as she grabbed hold of Fiona's as well. "Oh, oh, I know where he is. I'll be all right now. Everything will be all right. You'll see. You'll see. I know God means for everything to work out... He must... He will...."

The Reverend looked as sadly at her as ever he had. "But my dear, dear child, what will you do if he doesn't know you?"

Tears stung her eyes and rolled down her cheeks at the impossible thought. "I don't know." She looked into his eyes. "It's in God's hands."

"That it is," he agreed.

* * *

Earlier in the day, Lord and Lady Brooks sat in their solicitor's office to see what could be done to find Austin.

Lady Brooks' gloved hand rested on the edge of Holcomb's desk. "Holcomb, how good are these people?"

"They've never let me down."

"They must do everything they can to find him," she said.

"Are you certain they should?" Mr. Holcomb turned his gaze to the man staring out the window.

Lord Brooks was watching the street, as he had every day since Austin left them. He thought he saw the boy a hundred times, and London only made these feelings more acute.

"Pardon me, sir," Holcomb said.

"Hmm?"

"I say, do you really wish us to find the boy? After all the trouble he's been…"

"The boy's been no trouble at all, Holcomb. No trouble at all. I agree with my wife wholeheartedly. Find him at all cost."

"At all cost," Holcomb repeated the mandate he loved more than any other to hear, especially coming as it did from the lips of a rich client. "Of course."

"I heard him speak of America," said Lord Brooks. "Have any ships left in the last week?"

"None. There are two due to sail next week, however. We'll look them over."

"Fine." Lord Brooks continued to gaze out the window. Taking a deep breath, he turned back around and cleared his throat. "Let's make our way back to the rooms, my dear." He looked at Holcomb. "The Hyde."

"Of course."

"If your Ladyship wouldn't mind waiting in the foyer, might I have a word with his Lordship?"

She gave a curt nod and left and Holcomb turned to the business of explaining to his Lordship that his credit was at a crisis point, that creating a bill of sale on his personal property to use as collateral on a loan for a foreign-made clipper ship was straining the patience of the bank as well as those to whom he already owed monies. Lastly, he pointed out that it was illegal to imply the house and properties could be used as a guarantee, since the house and its grounds were tied up in his father's entail.

"Who has said we have tried to use the house as a guarantee?" Lord Brooks sputtered, dropping the monocle from his eye.

"It is not a rumor, sir. *Your son*, Allan, apparently has boasted that your home is not entailed. Granted, it was said after a long night of cards and brandy."

Lord Brooks grumbled to himself.

Holcomb added, "Perhaps now would be the time to settle the dowry for Miss Brown, eh?"

"Brown! That's no longer a possibility."

"Excuse me?"

"Miss Brown's father will not permit the marriage."

"Really?" Holcomb's fingers moved together involuntarily, touching the tips once, twice, before he took a breath and pulled his hands to his back.

"How much longer will they grant us, Holcomb?"

He frowned and shrugged. "A week, perhaps?"

Brooks shook his head but then looked up suddenly. "Holcomb, why didn't you tell me before now?"

Holcomb's eyebrows rose. Even before Brooks finished asking he had his answer. Holcomb was simply protecting his interest in the Brooks estate and had no particular wish to jeopardize the dwindling funds by pouring them into a clipper ship.

Quietly, Lord Brooks said, "Holcomb, anyone would think those monies were yours."

"If it weren't for me, sir, you and your sons would have destroyed the estate. Would you hate me for protecting the entail?"

Brooks slammed his fist on the table before him. "What's ours is ours to destroy! And how dare you cast a judgment!"

"How, indeed?" said Holcomb evenly.

* * *

When Theodosia came almost to the edge of the wharf, she stopped and a quiet terror seized her heart. She wanted to know Austin was all right, but she did not want to find that he didn't know her.

Suddenly grabbing hold of the Reverend and Fiona's arm to either side of her, she whispered, "Perhaps I can just see him from a distance. I need... time. I don't think I can speak to him... just yet."

"Yes." Reverend Pickett patted her arm. "That's wise. He's been through a lot. He said he didn't wish to see his parents because it would be too hard on him. He might feel the same way about you, my dear."

But as he spoke Theodosia was thinking that she was more afraid Austin would not feel anything at all.

They were fifty feet from the boat now and watched the men working on the deck. Austin was nowhere to be seen.

The Reverend scanned the deck carefully. "Remember what I told you of his appearance. Don't be frightened of the change. He doesn't even have a decent set of clothes to lay upon his back."

"I don't care," said Theodosia plainly. "I will know him."

And just as she said it, Austin raised his head. He was winding rope at the starboard and now he rose, holding on to the railing as he came up.

"There he is!" cried Theodosia.

The three stood in silence watching him.

Finally, Fiona whispered, "For a sartainty he looks every bit the sea dog."

"Yes, indeed." The Reverend smiled as he remembered Austin's words. "He was shocked to find out he'd been a clerk."

Theodosia smiled too, despite the oddness of the circumstance. "I... I think I want to speak to him after all." Almost absentmindedly, she opened her parasol and slid it up over her head, all the while watching Austin work and saying to the Reverend, "You said he knew he was a Christian. Surely a man's soul remains the same. If he truly loved me once, he will know me now...."

"Ah, but human love is a dangerous thing," replied the Reverend quickly. "There are no guarantees...."

Theodosia tipped her parasol to gaze at the Reverend with a questioning look.

"No," said the Reverend quickly. "You're right, of course. Love shouldn't change. But, please, you'd do well to consider the physical trauma. Why don't you speak with him tomorrow?"

She nodded quickly but then more slowly shook her head and pulled away from them. "Please," she said, "I need to go... alone."

The Reverend held his breath as he watched her walk forward and prayed she was right about love and that his instincts were quite wrong.

She had to dodge a few of the packers as she came closer to the boat, but the parasol of a lady on the quay caught the eye of both the captain and Austin as they spoke together up on the deck.

When they looked her way, she stopped and peered carefully at Austin from beneath the parasol's multicolored fringe. But he only glanced at her and had then quite leisurely turned back to speaking with the captain. She gulped and looked away. A tingle crawled up her spine and despite the noise around her she could hear the pounding of her heart within her ears. Though the Reverend had given her kind warning, somehow in her heart she believed Austin would see her on the deck, yell, "Theodosia!" and run down the plank and into her arms.

That he didn't run to her made her wonder... wonder if this were all a game of his. Their love was so young and so fragile, she could half-believe it and so the tears welled in her eyes.

She wiped them away. Should she speak to him? She would have to before she left for America. But maybe tomorrow would be a wiser choice after all? The pounding in her ears grew to a roar and finally she glanced back up again.

The captain was coming down the plank and Austin was gone. "May I help you, miss?"

She was so stunned, she had no ready reply.

The captain looked amused with her. "Might you wish to ask

after the ship or perhaps the cargo?"

She nodded uncertainly, then stole a look back up the plank to where Austin had stood.

But no one was there.

"Well, this beauty is the *Hurricane*. She's made of iron and driven by a screw-propeller. She ships cloth to America and brings the raw cotton back. We're due to sail in three days' time, and, I'm proud to say, we're the fastest clipper in this harbor."

"America?" she asked with surprise.

"Yes, indeed. May I presume you are an American?"

"Yes. Yes, I am, and I am looking for a passage back." She relished the excuse to scan the deck with her eyes. Suddenly she looked back to the captain. "But I understood there were no ships due to leave for America until next week."

"That would be English passenger ships. Yes. But we leave in three days' time and we do, in fact, have two very fine cabins for guests. Just check with the shipping office behind you there. Benton and Sons. That'd be us."

"Fine. Well, that's fine. Thank you very much, Captain." And she curtsied.

"My pleasure, miss." He tipped his hat, then turning toward the ship he yelled up the plank, "BROOM!" This startled Theodosia so greatly she stepped backward into a pyramid of small empty barrels, knocking several from their perch.

The captain looked back toward her while Austin started down the plank.

Red with embarrassment, Theodosia struggled to maintain her stance and then began to pull the edge of her cloak from the splinters of a fallen barrel. When she looked up and in bold-faced horror saw Austin approaching to assist her, she dropped open her mouth and with a mighty pull yanked the corded tassels free.

The ripping sound caused Austin to pull up short three feet from her. He stared at her cloak. "I suppose I'm too late, miss."

She couldn't speak but stood there, her parasol hanging from one hand and the cord of little tassels from the other. She blinked and blinked again.

He finally looked up into her troubled face and his own turned slightly pale.

This was someone he was sure he should know.

The noise and bustle of the dock fell away and all he could think was, *If I've never known her, I should like to.* For behind the delicate little spectacles she had the deepest, brownest eyes he'd ever seen, and the pinkest lips set now to quivering, and the sweetest little cleft in her chin which made him...

He looked away. Whoever he once was, he was now a dock-worker and she was obviously a lady. The noise and the crowds came back in a rush as he said loudly, "I'll be glad to pay for any damage, miss."

The captain came up behind him. "May I assist?" he asked in a commanding tone.

Still, she couldn't speak and her eyes filled with tears again; all that the Reverend had tried to warn her about Austin was true.

Austin looked back into her face again and was horrified to see that she was preparing to cry. "Really, I'll pay. I'm good for it. Isn't that right, Captain?" he said quickly.

"Yes. By all means, we'll pay."

Theodosia wiped at her tears furiously and then took to straightening her lenses. "No. No need. This was entirely my fault. And I'm quite sorry. My fault."

An American! Austin thought as she spoke. Bells rang in his head but they were maddening for he couldn't know why. "You're an American, then!" he sputtered.

"Yes," she said defensively.

"An American!" he repeated dumbly.

"Don't mind him, miss," said the captain with a sharp look to Austin.

"Yes, I'm an American," said Theodosia quietly, "and you, sir... you are *not*." And she gathered her skirts, her parasol and tassels and practically ran from the spot.

Austin turned his face to the ship and struck his forehead with some force, causing the bump at the top of his head to begin to ache. "Idiot!" He should never have presumed to speak with her.

The captain had taken to staring at Austin ever since the girl had made her odd pronouncement. "Yes, you're an idiot! You should have let me handle it. You and your talk of America. *An American. An American.* Repeating the thing like a lunatic. You frightened the poor child half to death, and she was interested in a passage, blast it all. Keep it up and I'll not be lettin' you come with us to America, do you hear?"

It was the first time Austin had hope the captain meant to take him when they left for Philadelphia in three days.

Austin smiled broadly in thanks but the captain only spat, "Clean this area, would you?" And as he walked away, he continued to mutter, *"An American, an American,"* in a whining voice.

"Yes, sir. Right away, sir." And Austin went to work.

* * *

"Roundtree, why would a Miss Theodosia Brown be looking for Austin Brooks?"

"Miss Brown... Miss Brown... seems he said something about her. Yes. When he was quite drunk Austin confessed his love for her, as I recall... an American, I think."

"She's read the will, you know. That's how Austin came across it."

"Ah. He never told me how he came across it."

"Yes, well, she was here, asking about Austin... claimed she was affianced to Alfred Brooks, but Brooks said it fell through. What do you make of that?" He failed to tell Roundtree the "confession" he had made to her about Roundtree's heavy-handed methods and the way in which they'd gotten Austin's copy back. He'd let Roundtree figure that out for himself when the time came.

"I make of it a very dangerous situation."

"Exactly. So I want you to do something about the problem... both of them. She's at The Crooked Tree Inn. Alone, she said. Waiting for my word. She offered to 'help' us by convincing Austin to go to America, told me she wanted to make certain Alfred gets the money."

"I can use that information."

"No. Keep my name out of it. I want it as quiet as Chatham's death."

"Yes, sir. I can do that."

"I know that you can, Roundtree, because you completely understand how very important it is that you succeed."

***

The Reverend, Fiona and Theodosia returned to their rooms at the hotel where Fiona tried to comfort her.

But Theodosia would not be consoled. She'd been tossed and turned by love all summer long, one moment filled with hope and dreams and the next filled with despair and foreboding. But this... there was no happiness to be found in this. None. Ever. It was as if he were dead. And so, in turn, was she.

She cried until supper time. She couldn't eat. When she finally quieted, she sat on the chaise in the room she and Fiona shared and felt as though someone had emptied her of life. One month. Less than one month, really. Austin and she had had three weeks together in which to dream of where they might live and what they might do, and now there was nothing.

If he were her husband today, she could take him in her arms and comfort him in their loss and then, with the bonds of marriage tying them to one another, they could start anew. But, wishing her parents' blessing on the union, she had gently refused him when he asked for her hand. Yet, that was a good decision at the time, wasn't it? Surely all this was God's doing. Only why?

But this was the way of it. She had seen love and now she would see it leave. She would accept it, but she would not accept it graciously.

The worst of it was knowing she would take him just as he was if he gave her half a chance. A hundred times she'd wondered at her sister's decision, marrying a laborer and hoping for the best. She'd wondered if when the time came she could make the same decision for love. Would it matter to her that he be a gentleman of sorts?

And now she knew for a certainty that none of it mattered. His soul was the same, and his soul was what she loved—would love— as a woman would devote herself to a husband suddenly bound by a physical ailment. It would not matter. You would be glad for the time you had. Your love would help you to care for him and you would put all other thoughts aside.

The true trouble and pain was in seeing that he really didn't know her and thus didn't seem to need her love. She'd hoped for the merest sign of recognition, but he had merely treated her as a dockworker might a lady. No more and no less. His English sensibilities were clearly intact while his soul was suddenly found a far distant thing.

And it was killing her.

"Fiona, I want to go to the docks... tonight," she said through gritted teeth.

"We can't! It's half past eight and dark as pitch."

"I'm going to find him... to speak to him."

"But it's just now raining."

"Doesn't matter."

"But ye don't even know as he's on board!"

"Ships have to be watched, don't they? Someone on board will know. Someone will know." The certainty in her voice came from a strong feeling deep within her. She would find him. There were thousands upon thousands of people in the pubs and alleys and boarding houses, and yet she knew she would find him.

Fiona's cheeks burned with energy to see her friend in such pain. "But, m'dear, m'dear, what would ye say..."

"It'll come to me, Fiona. It will. It has to."

Fiona thought surely her friend had lost her mind but, like the afternoon in which they'd decided to travel to London, it was obvious Theodosia wouldn't be talked out of her plan.

"We'll ask the Reverend then," Fiona finally said.

"No, he'll simply try to talk us out of it."

"And perhaps it'd be best if he did, then!"

Theodosia set her jaw. "You may stay and chat with the Reverend, Fiona, but I'm going to the docks. I *know* I can find him. And it's come to me what I have to ask him, too. The Reverend has told me over and over to be patient, and all summer long I was patient—through Alfred's insulting visits, through an engagement party, through my aunt's outrageous behavior—and now I've done with patience."

"But the Reverend says to wait on the Lord. If it's God's will..."

"Why isn't *my* will good enough! I'm the one who loves Austin. I love him, and I have to ask him something, and I can't go back home without knowing the answer, and I have to know *now* because I think I shall go absolutely mad if I don't!"

The same independent spirit that caused Theodosia to walk the woods alone was playing about her eyes, and so Fiona was kept from trying to dissuade her further. Soon, the two were headed to the docks once more, Fiona praying as they walked.

More than once the ladies were insulted by comments from passing strangers. "What'll it be, then, for the two o' you?" and other suchlike pleasantries caused Theodosia's face to pale and Fiona's to redden with anger. The two hurried on. When they found the boat, they saw a watchman, but no one else on board that they could see.

Theodosia whispered to Fiona in the darkness that they should wait near the ship and watch for Austin.

Fiona began to argue that neither Austin nor anyone else was going to be coming aboard at night, that this idea was insane from its beginning, and that they were likely to be found belly-up in the Thames by morning.

But as the Scottish teacher made her best arguments, Theodosia began to wander down the road away from her. "I'll bet he's gone down this way," said Theodosia, walking with determined steps toward a row of noisy pubs.

"The pothouses aren't fit for ladies' company. Are ye out of your mind! That way's death, Tee Brown!" Fiona tried to grab Theodosia's arm.

But Theodosia pressed on.

"At least move toward the doorways so we're not so out in the blessed open!" And Fiona finally succeeded in laying hold of Theodosia's wrist.

Just then a fellow swaggered toward a door to the nearest pub a few feet away. The raucous noise grew loud as the door opened, and when the door slammed shut behind him the street grew quieter once more. But something about the gentleman and the violent noises from the sailor's pub got through to Theodosia. Her face grew pale as they stood in the road. The danger in their situation became clear with the passing of every drunken sailor, and Fiona did not have to struggle to pull Theodosia aside and under the eaves of a dark doorway.

Down the causeway from them, Austin saw a shipmate get into fisticuffs outside a nearby pub and went to help the fellow out. It didn't take much to subdue the two as they'd both had enough drink to make themselves loose and limp. Austin set the one gently down against a lamppost, then proceeded to bring the arm of his shipmate, Pondsy, around his neck and pull him up and away from there.

Pondsy was too drunk to state his present address at dockside, and so Austin decided to lay him on the deck of the *Hurricane* and let the morning light or the captain wake him. Which of them would be the more gentle on the fellow was hard to tell.

They made their way along the docks and Austin soon groaned under the weight of him. Four days' labor had made Austin's hands raw and his arms tingle with pain at times, but when a man finally expects to have nothing more to lift than a pint for the evening, and finds instead he's got a man to pull that weighs twenty stone, his arms and legs are likely to give way. And so Austin struggled with his burden as if he'd had as much to drink as his waltzing partner. He began to whistle a tune he'd learned the day before and then sang to keep his mind from the weight of his burden. "What will ye do with a drunken sailor, what will ye do with a drunken sailor, what will ye do with a drunken sailor, earl-i in the mornin'…"

Theodosia saw him—to be precise, heard him—before Fiona did. She had begun to ask Fiona's forgiveness for coming out like this when she heard Austin's voice and stopped to stare.

When Fiona turned to look, she grasped her friend's wrist even more tightly. Theodosia protested and Fiona said, "He's drunk, he and his friend! No! Let me! Let me call him over. You know he can't remember his name. Ye want him to at least remember ye've had a conversation, don't ye?"

Theodosia looked out toward the two and then back at her friend. "I suppose that's reasonable."

In her sing-song voice, Fiona called cheerfully, "There now. I'll be right back," and proceeded out into the dark causeway. "Hullo there," Fiona said fearlessly as she walked toward the men.

Austin's song ceased as he turned slightly to look at her. "Not now, miss," he said gruffly, still making his way.

"Are ye both drunk, sir?"

Austin laughed. The doxies didn't often take no for an answer. "No, miss, but I'd say one of us is drunk enough for the both of us."

"Oh. Well then..." She began to scratch her ear nervously beneath her bonnet. "Can... can ye set yer friend down then?"

Austin rolled his eyes and pulled the man up beside him as best he could. His friend gave a mighty burp as his head fell back. "Listen, miss. I don't mean to offend you, but I'm not in the least interested," said Austin.

As it dawned on her just what he meant by the remark, Fiona became so embarrassed she almost turned around and walked away, but she bent her head forward and pushed through the dreadful feeling. "I've a friend wishing to speak to ye, sir, if ye wouldn't mind."

"Do you?" said Austin.

From the darkened doorway Theodosia pulled her hands to her mouth and tried hard to hold back the tears.

"And does your friend want to help me carry this man back aboard ship?" he asked with all due sarcasm.

"Och, no. We canna' help you there." Fiona looked helplessly back at Theodosia standing in the darkness of the doorway.

Austin squinted to try to see where Fiona was looking and he didn't like the situation at all. He didn't know a lot about these dock whores, but he knew they weren't to be trusted and the bump on his head throbbing from the weight of his burden reminded him not to court danger. A face-to-face fight he could deal with, but no more dark alleys. More quickly now he began again to shuffle toward the boat.

Fiona bowed her head in failure, but then she felt something brush past her and looked up to see Theodosia come around to the other side of the drunken man and pull his other arm up around her shoulder.

Austin was stunned to see the girl come and assist him. He'd only been trying to put the other girl off, joking as he had.

But she shows some spirit, he thought with mild surprise. Then he furrowed his brow. *Unless, of course, she's unburdening Pondsy's pockets just now.*

He spoke up, "See here, you don't have to do that." But she didn't answer. He couldn't quite make her out in the dark there; she was a little thing in a poke bonnet. The bonnet looked familiar. Oh, but he was tired of things that looked familiar. He turned his head and concentrated on the ship looming up in the darkness as they stumbled along. *Well, it only serves the fellow right if he loses his money to her,* he thought.

They worked themselves over the stone of the quay, up the plank, and the watchman, who'd seen the same story replayed a hundred times before, said not one word but only observed them carefully as they came.

Pondsy gave the smallest grunt upon being released from their care. Austin struggled to put a sack under the fellow's head and then scrounged around for a canvas tarpaulin and pulled it up and across the prostrate form. He rested his hands upon his knees as he leaned over and laughed. "May the angels watch over you, eh, Pondsy?"

He had forgotten all about Theodosia and was surprised to see her still standing beside him when he was done. He was even more surprised when she fell into his chest, wrapped her little arms about him and held him close.

She was trembling.

He held his arms out from his side, not knowing quite what to do. "See here, miss," he said quietly. "I've no money..."

The watchman interrupted, "Drunk is one thing, but none of

that. None of that! Get her off. Bad luck, a woman, 'specially one as that." He spat overboard to form a proper ending to the statement.

"Come on, now," said Austin gently, but she held him all the more tightly and then he laughed. This was truly awful.

The watchman came up behind them. "Get her off, Broom, or I'll throw her off personal, d'ye hear?"

"Yes, sir. We're off." Austin suddenly thought to scoop the little creature up in his arms. This she did not fight.

They walked down the plank and just as they reached the quay she pulled away from his chest to look into his face.

It was a good thing he'd reached level ground because he lost all semblance of control and stumbled more than slightly when he saw who she was. "It's you!" But he did not release her.

"Do you know me?" she asked in a frightened voice.

"The American!"

Her eyes filled with tears once more. "Yes. But *do you know me*?"

He looked into each of her eyes, the cleft of her chin, the curve of her lips and, just as he had that morning, regardless of the odd circumstances, all he really wanted to do was kiss the girl. He shook himself free from the thought. "See here, miss, I am deathly tired of being asked that question..." Still he stared into her eyes by the light of the moon.

"Then... do you *wish* to know me?" She waited.

They stood for the longest time before he could answer. How could he presume to take advantage of the girl? And what would she want with a dockworker? Whatever the reason, it was quite obvious she wanted him to say yes to her question. "Yes, but I..." The look of joy that crossed her face caused him to stop midsentence.

"Yes?" she asked, her voice full of hope.

But he asked himself again what a lady could want with a dockworker? No, a clerk? Had she known him from before?

Suddenly he was quite certain of it. His forehead grew smooth, and his arms relaxed their hold. Suddenly he knew that he had always known her, and now everything about her made sense. But even though he'd solved the mystery, still he could not keep his voice from cracking as he asked, "Are you... are you my wife?" ∽

TWENTY-TWO

❧

Tom, Tom, the piper's son,
Stole a pig and away did run!
The pig was eat, and Tom was beat,
Till he ran crying down the street.

Nursery Rhyme

❧

Cursing his luck as he stood in the shadows of the dockside building, Todd Roundtree watched Austin Brooks as he held his precious Theodosia Brown.

Roundtree had succeeded in quietly following Theodosia and the other woman ever since they'd left the relative safety of The Crooked Tree Inn. He was at first irritated to find Theodosia was *not* alone, but he fancied himself not surprised that Holcomb was incorrect about her.

Holcomb knows nothing, said Roundtree to himself, *while Austin and Theodosia know too much.*

He had remained in the shadows until the women neared the docks, and then the fog had taken away the need for shadows and he'd come quite close to them once or twice. *Fools to be out on a night like this*, he told himself. *They deserve what they get.* But they'd always turned their heads toward one another at the wrong time and caused him to drop his step once more.

Now grinding his teeth ever so slightly, Roundtree thought it was too bad he hadn't been able to kill her. He was so close. Not five minutes before, when Theodosia's friend had pulled her into the darkened doorway, he'd felt that sweet quiver of anticipation: the moment had arrived. If he moved to strangle Miss Brown, the other would run screaming for help. Help was hard to find by the docks on a foggy night, and by the time she could return, he'd be gone and Miss Brown would be quite dead.

But then Austin had come along.

Austin Brooks. Unbelievable!

As Roundtree was forced to watch the situation growing between the two foolish females, the dockworkers, and then the ship watchman, it became painfully obvious that his duties surrounding the inquisitive Miss Brown and the confused Master Brooks would have to wait.

But even as Roundtree skulked back into the fog and the shadows to begin his wait once more, he felt quite certain his chance would come.

* * *

With things in such a delicate balance, Theodosia had to rely on the tone of Austin's voice to know what to make of his question. It took her half a minute to understand that when he'd asked if she were his wife it was because he seemed to hope she was.

Finally, she replied in a whisper charged with emotion, "In spirit, sir, I believe I am your wife."

Again his voice broke. "What?"

"I mean to say, God willing, one day I will be yours... and I will be patient."

"Ah." But his brows furrowed even as he smiled.

"We loved each other once, and... I do... yet."

So, this woman had loved him, thought Austin. And whoever he was now, she seemed to love him still. It was a miracle, pure and simple. Blushing he quickly said, "I suppose I should set you down."

"I suppose," she answered without enthusiasm.

He set her lightly down, never more sorry to be relieved of a burden, but as soon as she touched earth he grew uncomfortable and found it difficult to look her in the eye.

She lowered her eyes to see his discomfort. "I'm sorry... for approaching you the way I did. I think..." The tears welled full and she continued to look down. "... I believed that if I could draw near to you, somehow... you would remember..."

"Miss…"

"Theodosia," she said almost reproachfully and sniffed.

"Theodosia…" he mumbled. In a stronger tone but with obvious regret he added, "Dear lady, I have no memory of you…" He looked at her and caught her eye. "I'm certain I want to remember… if that's any comfort."

"Oh, but I don't need comfort. All I need is for you to know me… us."

He pursed his lips before blurting out, "Well, that I can't!" His eyes searched hers. "I can't." He shook his head. "It's quite impossible. I really don't know… much about anything just now, you see?" It grieved him to say it, but it was the plain and simple truth.

Theodosia grew so hurt by the words she turned away and it was then that Fiona came slowly forward.

"This is Miss Fiona Mienzes," Theodosia whispered.

"I am a schoolteacher in Thistledown. Your parents hired me to teach the town's children."

"My parents. I don't know them."

Theodosia and Fiona glanced at each other, and Fiona cleared her throat. "It's time we go and find the Reverend Pickett, Tee."

"Yes. The Reverend Pickett. He introduced himself to me today."

"He is at the inn."

"And fast asleep, but we will wake him up, won't we, Tee."

"She calls you tea?"

"My friends call me Tee."

At the repeated sound of the girl's nickname, a flicker of recognition came and went. It irritated him. "*Tea*, did you say?"

"Tee, yes!" said Theodosia, with sudden enthusiasm. "Do you remember?"

"The Brooks… deal in tea, yes."

Theodosia's enthusiasm died with his pronouncement. She closed her eyes slowly, lowered her head and allowed the pain to pierce her through.

Fiona looked to Austin and motioned with her head toward the inn. "Would you care to come with us, then? The Reverend could talk... explain things to ye, if ye like."

But Austin was studying Theodosia as Fiona asked the question. He'd seen the closing eyes, the bowing of her head, and he knew in his heart he had hurt this girl—this Theodosia... Tea, but it couldn't be helped. How could he explain? Does one take a stranger into one's arms and speak of love? Even if the thought is pleasant, the task is nigh on impossible, for it would be a lie. So two things were becoming clear: she could speak of love to him, and he could break her heart unless he could somehow remember.

It came to him how little he cared to hear about his own past. The thought tired him completely. But then his eyes came to rest on Theodosia's tiny gloved hands clasped before her, and he saw how they trembled. He wanted to tell her there was nothing to be afraid of ...

Don't take afternoon tea so seriously.

His head shot up. Irritating beyond belief to be unable to direct your mind to where you wanted it to go. Incongruous thoughts crowded into his mind as if they belonged there. As if they were there before. *Are these memories?* he wondered.

Well, he at least owed it to the girl if not to himself to find out more about his past and so he turned his head and nodded grimly to Fiona. And so they went.

* * *

After getting over the shock of seeing the young ladies at his door, and receiving the news that Austin was in the pub of the inn, the Reverend came downstairs and they all soon found a comfortable if noisy spot in the room. The Reverend began telling Austin about himself, and their conversation continued into the wee hours of the morning.

At times Austin would suddenly hold up his hand as if he could take no more. Then he would take to staring into the worn table or his pint glass and everyone would fall quiet for a time. Other times he ran his fingers through his hair distractedly, a mannerism Theodosia had seen him do a hundred times if once, but every time he did it now, she wanted to cry.

Eventually Austin would ask another question and the discussion would continue. The past was gone over fairly well, the present thoroughly explained, but the future was left out of the conversation entirely. This was done inadvertently by the Reverend but Theodosia was glad for it. Ever since they'd sat at table, Austin and she could hardly meet each other's gaze, and Theodosia had grown a headache during the long talk.

Theodosia recognized much in the Reverend's reminiscences, and so she would nod heartily to his recall. Then Austin would cock his head and ask if she'd been there and she'd blush and shake her head no. Austin finally understood that she had been told all about him by the Reverend, at which point she grew so embarrassed she ceased to speak or react to the stories in any way. The Reverend had very carefully woven his way through the outline of Theodosia's relationship to Austin, but this was the final aggravation to her senses, and her headache grew quite severe.

At a certain point in the discussion, the Reverend asked if the ladies would mind sitting in the booth across the aisle. They complied, and Theodosia rightly presumed the Reverend Pickett was telling Austin about the contents of the will and all he knew of Austin's true identity. She heard Austin exclaim "Roundtree!" once and realized the Reverend had told him about the mugging.

Finally Austin held up both hands. "Enough! I cannot take it in. No more."

And the evening's end had come. Theodosia stole one glance at Austin and wished she could think of some words of comfort, something to assure him all would be well. But then she realized it was *she* who needed comforting—*she* who needed someone to tell her all was well. Austin, in truth, did not need her at all, she thought as she watched Austin leave the inn's tavern without even looking back.

As Theodosia walked up the stairs with Fiona toward their room the dull throb in her head became a piercing pain. Waves of nausea began to pass through her, such that she could not think. What she truly wished for was to stand very still in a dark room. If that didn't work, she thought, perhaps dying might do the trick.

Once in the room, she arrived at the washing stand in the nick of time, and when she was done with her business there, her head felt much better. Fiona doused the lights and Theodosia lay as still as she could in her bed, but she found no peace in resting. She could not sleep for thinking on all that had passed that evening even though she knew it would cause her head to ache once more.

Watching Austin attempt to digest his past in one torturous sitting had made Theodosia's heart sick as well as her head, and the most painful part of all? What Austin might wish for himself now that the slate was rubbed clean. With little time in which to make such heavy decisions, she wondered if she should yet leave the country. Would it be better for him, giving him time to decide his fate and theirs? The ease with which Austin had left them that evening hurt more each time she remembered it. He had not looked back. Quite suddenly she realized it might be that Austin's family would wish a reconciliation and that he would choose to live his life with them. *They would use him. They would not love him as I could.*

This last thought chilled her to the core. She balled her feather pillow into a hard knot beneath her cheek. *They will not win,* she thought. *They will not! I will find a way to make him remember. I will find a way to make him well. I must. I will.* She let go of a long sigh and commanded herself, *I shall rest.*

But rather than ease itself into slumber her turbulent mind merely adjusted itself to think on another portion of the conversation with Austin, and so it was that the minutes and then the hours slipped away.

* * *

Unable to sleep, Austin made his way to the ship early. He stepped over the body of his friend, Pondsy, lying on deck, and went to work on the other side. As he worked and waited for the sun to rise, he wondered just where the day would take him.

Luckily for Pondsy, Austin happened to be topside when the captain found him. Austin quickly walked over and explained to the captain that it was Pondsy's own fault he was lying there, but joked that if he hadn't placed him on board the fellow was likely to have found himself on another ship entirely this morning. Austin was pleased that his words seemed to have appeased the captain, while in fact the captain's sudden quiet was due to having noted the gentleman that strode the quay below. Without further remark, the captain dismissed Austin to his work.

Later that morning, Austin himself noticed a black-suited fellow who seemed to disappear among the boxes whenever Austin came down the plank. He began to feel unnerved by it and finally the time came he decided to do something about it, gentleman or no.

And so it was as he carried a particularly tall stack of boxes to the quay, he decided to put a quick end to the game. He took the boxes to the farthest point of the dock and when he saw the black coattail disappear around a stack of barrels, he turned and walked as if to pass around the other side but then doubled back and reached around the barrel to grab a collar or whatever he could.

The man was tall and Austin had in fact laid hold of his vest. He pulled the spy gruffly forward to look him in the eye.

"What are you doin'!" he hissed.

Roundtree pushed back his hat with his free hand. "See here, let go of my vest, would you? I only want a word."

Austin let go of him.

Roundtree cocked his head slightly and narrowed his eyes.

"I've work to do." And Austin turned to go.

"I can make this conversation worth your while."

"Not interested," he said still walking away.

"It's about America."

Austin stopped and turned.

"I thought that might interest you. I can give you passage to America… if you'll do a job for us that…"

"There's many a sailor who'll take you up on it… Roundtree, but not this one." The name surfaced unbidden from his mind. He remembered it whole, and as he did he also remembered the exact last time he'd heard it mentioned.

Roundtree's eyes flew open and Austin smiled. "Yes, now I

know who you are, but you're at a distinct disadvantage for you don't know me anymore." And Austin turned back to make his way up the plank.

"Wait there. Wait. Passage to America, I…" Roundtree followed.

"I'm not interested in anything you have to offer, old *friend.*"

Roundtree caught up and pulled on the back of his shirt. "Listen, you fool. It's for your own he—e-a-al-thhh… ai-ye-ahh-hh!" Roundtree yelled as he went forward, pushed carefully between two stacks of boxes by the seat of his pants.

And then over he went and down—fifteen feet into the murky waters of the Thames.

"GACK! GAm… Ya… Get me out!" he cried, struggling among the drifting objects whose slimy surfaces he vainly tried to grasp.

Austin laughed under his breath as he looked over the edge, and his fellow sailors came around to laugh at the fellow as well. Only the captain was not amused.

In a few moments it became obvious that Roundtree did not know how to swim, and though the sailors thought it a good joke to see him struggle, it was all too close to recent events for Austin, who suddenly sniffed back his laughter and looked around. He ran up the plank, uncoiled a rope and let it down to the fellow, all the while chuckling mildly to see the man so thoroughly denuded of his pride.

The fellow grasped the rope and sputtered and pulled and cursed as he made his way up the side of the boat, all of which made the fellows laugh the more loudly. The slime made the going a slippery mess, but eventually he found his footing.

When he came topside he struggled to stand and then immediately lunged for Austin. The crew was faster. Two dockworkers easily grabbed hold of him as he passed and shoved him sideways toward the plank. He grabbed hold of the plank rope and steadied himself, then looked them over and decided flight was the most expedient choice. But as he went he looked at Austin once more and gave him a message as clearly as if he'd spoken.

What Roundtree thought with perfect clarity just then was that as soon as he could find a dry pistol to replace the one in his vest pocket, he would return, and Austin would not find himself so lucky in the next contest of wills.

* * *

And Lord Brooks had seen it all. He'd grown tired of waiting for the solicitors to find the boy and began to pace the docks himself when he recognized Austin just as the lanky, red-headed fellow began to speak with him. He didn't interrupt the conversation, as Austin seemed to have things well in hand. The fellow offered him passage to America, and his boy refused. Excellent. Soon the persistent youth wound up in the drink, and everyone had a good laugh over it, Lord Brooks included.

He laughed up until the moment the young, wet gentleman passed him on the docks muttering under his breath. His laughter fell short when he recognized him: it was the red-headed assistant from Holcomb, Redfern and Grackle.

The solicitors were supposed to be finding Austin. When they did they should be contacting his father, not offering him fare to America. It was fairly obvious what Holcomb was trying to pull, and it angered Lord Brooks. Yes, the whole of it angered him mightily. ᔕ

TWENTY-THREE

❧

Twinkle, twinkle, little star,
How I wonder what you are!
Up above the world so high,
Like a diamond in the sky.

Nursery Rhyme

❧

Theodosia rose from her bed in the early hours to pace the room in tired thought.

But nothing came clear to her.

She went to the casement window and pushed one side open to lean out into the cool night air to try to think. The fog had settled somewhat, and so she looked up above the jumble of rooftops into a dusky but star-filled heaven. She took in the beauty and then fell to staring at the glow of Venus. "Sun, moon and stars: three things we and the English see alike. I wish my love could know himself as clearly as I know Venus tonight."

She had felt Austin's hesitance and understood it. Why shouldn't he wonder about them? She had her own doubts, too. Does one love a person's soul or his manners or his talents or his looks or some combination of them all? Did she truly love Austin now or the memory of who he was? From the moment they spoke to each other the first day she'd come for tea in Brooks House of Thistledown, she'd felt at ease with him—as if she'd known him all her life. And when she watched him help his friend board ship the night before she thought she saw again the man she loved, and a fierce longing rose up in her then and there which caused her to fling aside all sense of decorum and hug him properly with all her might.

And then it was as if she were trying to hold him together: the man she knew with the man he was. But she was unable to do so.

Now another thought found its way to her mind in the middle of this long night—one more in keeping with her natural curiosity for life. She very much wanted to understand what had happened to him, to his mind, from the force of the blow. Surely there was a doctor somewhere in this great city of London who might have seen this sort of thing before? Austin should understand what happened to him. Perhaps it would help him. And if he could only remember, all their troubles would vanish. She should speak to him about it. No. She had to speak to him about it. *Now.*

She looked at Fiona sleeping and knew she ought to wake her, but she wanted time with Austin alone.

Ah, a note. That would do.

She dressed hurriedly, dashed off a note and then made her way to the docks. The roadways were dark, the coal gas lamps having been out for several hours, and so she concentrated on the road before her.

The sunlight crept through the streets and the fog was still thick, hanging yellow in the air. She was halfway to the docks before she realized she didn't know where Austin was staying. This made her stop in the road, which in turn caused Roundtree, who had taken to following her ever since she'd left the inn, to stop and turn about to keep her from seeing him. His sudden turnabout made it possible for the vegetable cart, that otherwise might have passed behind him safely, to roll indelicately over his right foot. At this, Roundtree cried out in pain and began hopping about on the remaining foot.

When Theodosia heard the cursing cry of pain not too far behind her, her heart quickened and she surged forward, tripling her previous pace. She immediately decided to go on to the docks anyway, assured that if she stood near his boat she could speak to Austin as he came on board, whenever that might be.

To her disappointment, she found Austin already aboard and working.

This gave her time to think on things, and think she did. She sat down on a portion of a cargo box and laid it out in her mind. She had heard about head injuries, that a second strike on the head would sometimes bring the memory back—just as the first strike had knocked it out of the mind in the first place. But she didn't know if this were rumor or true. Casting her eyes along the riggings, she thought it wouldn't take much for a man to get hurt on board ship. She watched with fascination as a man climbed up the rigging of the mainmast and set to work on some ropes there, and she wondered if Austin ever climbed up there, and whether he might fall and hit his head and be cured.

Folly. She shook her head. *A simple blow to the head is not enough.*

Coincidentally, Todd Roundtree was thinking the very same thing, only of her, as he stood not two hundred yards away in the shadow of a building. He put the stick back on the ground, and pulled a rope from his pocket.

Theodosia was watching Austin as she thought things through, and now she realized something was terribly wrong. His work was slow. Very slow. Austin looked down from the deck just then and noticed her.

She waved to hail him.

He nodded uncertainly.

She beckoned to him to come down, even as she whispered to herself, "Please come down. I only want a word with you."

Austin looked irritated by her request, yet he turned and walked to his captain and soon he was making his way down the plank. But he was moving oddly.

She shook her head slowly as he moved down the plank. Her mind said, *No. There is something wrong here. Everything stop and start again...* And then it happened.

Austin was ten feet from her when something in him snapped. She saw it strike him like a blow, and she caught the scream in her throat just as he began to go down. He stumbled once and then fell forward to the stone along the quay.

His body jumped and he turned onto his back and began to writhe in pain as if someone were stabbing him.

Theodosia rushed to his side and fell on her knees to hold him. Men on deck were shouting and then crowding around them, but no one seemed to be helping. But then an older gentleman was at his head, trying to hold it still as the convulsions continued while a woman took Austin's other arm. *Good!* thought Theodosia. *They know what this is. They are here to help us. Thank you, God.*

And so it was with surprise her mind slowly focused and she saw that it was Reverend Pickett kneeling at Austin's head and Fiona Mienzes at Austin's other side.

Theodosia began to pray aloud, but she could not shut her eyes—she could not keep from staring at Austin as she prayed. She was afraid he was leaving her.

Austin's eyes were open but rolled up into his head and his mouth was gaping. Spasms racked his arms and legs, and she prayed that the horrible shaking would cease. Three minutes that seemed three hundred passed before the snapping movements began to decrease. And then he grew quiet. He shut his eyes, but he did not or could not speak.

And this new unknown was worse than the other to Theodosia.

Above the heads in the crowd, the Reverend waved to the captain.

"I know a doctor, Captain," said the Reverend, "and I'd like to take him there straightaway. He had a head injury about a week ago that has disturbed his mind... his memory, that is. This must be related, but perhaps this doctor will know, eh?"

"Yes. Shall I call a carriage?"

"Thank you."

Theodosia listened in wonder. The fact that the Reverend knew of a doctor and that they would be on their way to him at any moment was the closest thing to a miracle Theodosia Brown had ever known. It was an answer to prayer, but then it occurred to her she hadn't prayed for this at all. She was too busy trying to fix things on her own.

But, then again, it had all worked out. Yes, everything would soon be all right.

The sailors loaded a listless Austin into a carriage and bundled him into the seat. His eyes were still shut and his mouth was closed as well. Theodosia asked if she might sit next to Austin, and the

Reverend nodded. The carriage started up and when Austin made no movement at all, she gingerly took his hand in hers. Still there was no response. And then it was her worry increased as worry does when the future looks as black as it did to Theodosia Brown just then.

She tried hard to keep from wondering if this was all he would ever be. Instead she made herself pray hard, begging God not to end his life and hers this way.

The carriage rolled along at a leisurely pace, for although they wished to be at the doctor's as soon as possible, no one knew what sort of trauma had caused the spasms and none wished to initiate them again.

Theodosia was praying with eyes pinched shut when Austin's hand suddenly grabbed her fingers tight. With a wince she looked up to see him staring at her with lids half open, his face pale and drawn.

"You are Miss Theodosia Brown," he said slowly.

"Yes, yes! You remember!?"

"Yes... I met you... a few days ago."

Her heart sank. "Yes," she gulped. "You've had some sort of convulsion. We're taking you to a doctor who specializes in head injuries."

His eyes came alive. "No doctors!"

"Just an examination, son, nothing more," said Reverend Pickett earnestly.

"Well I don't want... I don't care... I don't..." But it was an effort for him to frame his words.

"But the convulsions... you don't want them repeated, do you?" asked Reverend Pickett.

"Convulsions..." Austin looked blankly at the Reverend, but then his eyes grew wide with recognition. His head fell back against the rocking carriage seat, and the color drained from his face once more. "No. Not that. No."

Theodosia shivered and they rode along in silence for a while.

At one point, Austin loosened his hold on her hand, but Theodosia resisted his motion. Then he pulled his hand away, but his eyes searched her face with a look that made her blush. She spoke up if only to keep him from scrutinizing her. "I know you can't take all of this in at one time. It's too much for anyone to ask. If you like, the doctor could tell me the news..." But she realized her boldness and so she stammered, "...Or, or the Re-reverend Pickett. Then he-he could tell you as much as you want to know... whenever you like..."

He looked at her carefully, then turned to Reverend Pickett. "That... would be good of you, sir."

In thirty minutes the effects of the convulsions had for the most part left him, and so, to everyone's relief, when they arrived at the doctor's office he was able to leave the carriage on his own.

The doctor's office was a neat affair, the second story of a brick row house. The place was clean and seemed well-organized. All this helped Austin's friends to feel they'd found the proper place to tell his story.

A Dr. Porter greeted the group and, after quitting the ladies in the side parlor, he led the Reverend and Austin to his comfortable study. Austin was asked to sit in a chair centered in the room, a thing which made him instantly uncomfortable, but the doctor's fine chatter soon eased him into the surroundings.

Theodosia paced the parlor rug as Fiona stood by the windows. Both women prayed as they waited.

The first palpable sign of relief from Austin came when the doctor said, "Excellent!" upon hearing he'd just suffered convulsions. He busied himself taking Austin's pulse and checking his reflexes. "Excellent, really. Perfectly normal. Your mind is trying to heal itself. Sometimes it gets a little tangled up, as it were, but believe me this is all for the good."

"But will I have another convulsion?" Austin asked.

"Could be. Could. Wouldn't be a problem. They'll lessen. Lessen and lessen. You may never have another before your memory returns."

"What? What?!"

"Oh, your memory will completely return. But I've only one question: are you *quite* sure your injury was physical?"

"Eh?"

"No emotional trauma that might have caused your mind to draw a blank, as it were?" The doctor went on to answer himself as he found the still black and blue mark on Austin's head. "Ah, no. Here it is. Well, then. Just give yourself time, young man. Good spot for an injury. Couldn't have picked a better. Two weeks ago, you say? To the side and you might have died. To the back and your skull might have cracked. And one more good knock in the same place could leave you permanently senseless. Fascinating, isn't it?"

"How long will it take my memory to come back, then?"

"Hard to say. Could be two weeks. Could be two years. I had one case a while back where it took five, but his wife was such an unpleasant thing I could never determine the truth in the matter."

The Reverend laughed.

Austin tried to smile, but his mind was racing to the next question. "Will it come back of a sudden then?"

"Sometimes. More often in fits and starts, fits and starts, as it were… and count on two years, son, not two weeks. Patience will be required in enormous amounts, I'm afraid. But I could almost put it in writing that your memory will return. The brain's a wonder at healing, as it were."

"As the Lord made it to be," said Reverend Pickett happily. "But we'll be praying the healing comes sooner than later. This lad's already been through enough." He refrained from adding, *as it were*, for fear the doctor mightn't appreciate the humor.

"Quite so. What you've had, my boy, is a laceration to the brain. This is besides the hematoma at the top of your head. You've probably had headaches. Disorientation. Dizziness, as it were."

"Yes."

"Good thing you're young. Were you able to speak just after the uh, the uh… blow?" He explored the bruise again as he spoke.

"To think, anyway."

"Good. If you were to hemorrhage… well. You haven't and so you're not likely to."

"How will I know if I hemorrhage?"

The doctor gave a little laugh and a hearty snort. "Well, first of all... *you'll be dead.*" And he laughed again.

And here the Reverend laughed with him and cried out, "As it were!" before he could stop himself.

But Austin had paled. "I see," he said, trying hard to put it all in perspective. He wiped the sweat from his upper lip with a free hand. "Well, is there any way to avoid convulsions, sir? I had an awful headache and was rather confused and angry when this thing came on."

The doctor was frowning at the Reverend but now turned back to Austin. "There's no consistency to it. One fellow was sure his choice of beer could start him up," he said, apparently quite serious. "But to be honest, no, there's nothing you can do to keep it from occurring again. However, since this occurred at your place of employ?" Austin nodded. "I would suggest you try to keep yourself from work today. You're a laborer, are you not?"

"That's right. A dockworker. And my captain won't be too impressed by my excuse."

"Well, I can't keep you from working, but it only makes sense that you should try not to reproduce the exact circumstances that caused the first convulsion."

Austin nodded. "I don't think I could."

"Fine."

The doctor proceeded to help Austin up from the chair. "There's a lad. Thank you for coming by. And you should be grateful to have found me, boy. There's many a fellow out there who'd have bled you for your trouble, as it..." But he glanced at the Reverend and suddenly clipped the phrase short. "Hmph... *Then* you'd have a headache, by George. You know, these idiots don't look at the research at all but go about with their..." And he began to bend the Reverend Pickett's ear on the lack of qualified doctors.

Austin stepped out of the office and Theodosia stopped mid-worried-stride to stare at him. She pulled at the handkerchief between her hands, the mantel clock tick-tock-tick-tocked, and from outside came the sound of horses' hooves clopping. Large carriage wheels clattered past. It was not possible for her eyes to open more widely or for her shoulders to more visibly shake under the strain.

"Ladies," Austin said, "the doctor assures me my memory will return."

An audible breath escaped Theodosia, but then she grew rigid once more, wanting to ask the question, *When?* but not daring.

As if reading her mind he continued, "He said it might be soon but also it might take as long as two years."

"*Two years,*" Theodosia whispered.

"He doesn't know."

"But it will return?"

"Yes, yes, it will return." He brought his hat to his head.

To her dread she noticed he could no longer look her in the eye.

Reverend Pickett and the doctor stood now in the hallway and the doctor was continuing the conversation as the Reverend made for the front door.

Theodosia looked to Fiona and Fiona came and took her hand. Looking back to Austin, Theodosia said, "That's good then. That's very good news, isn't it?"

"Yes." He stared at his boots and wished he could give her more hope, but he knew they would find no easy solutions to their trouble.

As the little group moved to the door, Theodosia saw that the Reverend had stayed behind momentarily and was now reaching into his vest. She came up to him quickly and brought up her purse.

"No, no, my dear. My responsibility, please."

"But I have the extra monies from my passage..." she whispered.

"No, no. You mustn't. You may need it for your return voyage."

"All right, then. Thank you." She turned to go but almost collided with Austin as she did.

Austin had come forward with an offer to pay for the doctor's services himself, but he'd stopped short as he overheard Theodosia's remark. "You're leaving for America," he said flatly.

"I... I don't know," she said.

"I believe I overheard you say you are leaving."

"I don't know," she said again but with a catch in her throat.

He gave half a laugh. "You're beginning to sound like me, Miss Brown." He turned and walked back to the door, not wishing her to see the anger in his face—an emotion he could hardly explain to himself, let alone to her.

My Lord, what should I do? she prayed desperately.

And then she followed him.

He started down the steps, but sensing her behind him, he stopped. He began to go up the stairs to pass her. She watched him as he walked up and past her, all the while her heart thumping wildly.

But instead of reentering the building when he gained the top step, he turned and seemed to wait for her. Theodosia herself turned, walked back up the stairs and stood beside him to look into his face. Austin looked back at her in amazement.

"Are you going down or not, miss?" he asked.

"I was going down. Why did you come back up?"

"I don't know" He reddened with the words. "Rule of etiquette, I suppose... I remembered."

"You remembered a *rule?*"

"Yes," he said, more irritated than not. "A gentleman is to follow a lady down the steps."

Theodosia gave him a look that brought an embarrassed flush to his fair skin. "Yes, you're right. It is a rather stupid rule at that." He shut his mouth, jammed his hat forcefully upon his head and stomped down the stairs. Halfway down he yelled out for a hackney cab.

Theodosia came down the steps as quickly as she could. "Austin, wait, please... please stop!"

A cab pulled up and Austin made large strides toward its side door.

She cleared the last step and was grateful for it, but in the midst of this false sense of success she failed to notice the bootjack firmly planted in the stone to the side of the last stair.

Meanwhile Austin paused after yanking open the carriage door.

She cried out and Austin turned around in time to see her falling, but he was not in time to catch her. Holding out her hands, she caught herself fairly well, but her foot was still stuck in the bootjack. He came to her side and tried to help her up but became frustrated that she did not seem able to stand.

"Stop! My ankle!" she cried as he yanked on her arm. "My ankle's caught." Awkwardly she tried to gain balance on the one foot so that she could free the other. She was almost standing now.

"*Mustn't let the lady wait,*" he grumbled.

"What did you say?" Her eyes flew open and Austin looked at her sharply.

But then he blushed. "Nothing."

"Nothing? What have I done this time?" she said, her voice trembling.

"Good heavens, miss, I wouldn't know." Theodosia was upright now, but he still held her arm.

"Why are you angry with me then?" But she was glad to be asking. She smiled as she waited to hear his answer.

He raised his voice. "I'm not angry! And is your ankle going to be quite all right, then?" he asked, his voice still high.

"My ankle is fine. It's wonderful. I don't care a whit if I've hurt myself, again, because I said I was going to America, and you're angry that I was going to America, and that's absolutely wonderful!" she cried out happily.

He sputtered, "Well, I'm sure that as long as you are able, you may go wherever you like, miss, *as will I.*" He dropped his arm and stepped toward the door of the carriage once more. Pausing, he almost turned his head to her, but then he decided better of it and only looked at the side of the carriage as he said, "Thank the Reverend Pickett for me, would you? And tell him I'll pay him back. I'm good for it..." But under his breath he muttered, *"I'm fairly certain."* Then he pushed forward his chin, stepped up and fell back into the carriage seat.

Theodosia came to the door awkwardly. Her ankle stopped her from following him inside as she wished, and so as the driver snapped the reins to go, she could only say one thing. "Austin Simpson Brooks..." she whispered, "you are my other half!"

His mouth fell open as the carriage pulled away, and yet she held the naive hope her words were enough to force him to remember. ᪥

TWENTY-FOUR

Dickery, dickery, dare,
The pig flew up in the air,
The man in brown soon brought him down,
Dickery, dickery, dare.

Nursery Rhyme

Lord Brooks took the time to sit in a pub around the block from the offices of Holcomb, Redfern and Grackle to ponder what he would do.

He watched the young clerks standing to eat their lunches at the bar, seemingly confident and happy with their lot (at the very least they were a well-fed group) and he felt a profound sorrow to think of Austin at the docks. *He should be here,* he thought grimly. *It is all my fault. Eleanor was right. We should have told him long ago.* He downed the last of his bitters and rattled the glass on the table. "Enough of this self-pity. Holcomb is the one should be suffering now," he whispered. He laid his money down and pulled himself up and away from his seat. He knew exactly what he must do.

He climbed the stairs of Holcomb, Redfern and Grackle, made his entrance and proceeded to announce himself to the receptionist. Then he sat down in a stiff chair and waited.

Soon the red-headed young man, polished and tall, walked steadily toward him. None of the rascal's behavior at the quay was present now. All about the youth was calmness and congeniality. *Amazing what a dry set of pants will do for a boy,* thought Lord Brooks with a subdued snicker as he stood to his feet and held out his hand.

"Mr. Roundtree?"

"At your service, sir."

"You received my note?"

"Yes, sir."

"Then you are in a position to assist?"

"I believe I am," said Roundtree quickly, eyeing the hall from which he'd come. "Please, right this way," he whispered. Lord Brooks nodded curtly and began to follow him but with a little smile beneath his moustache.

The two settled in a side office and Lord Brooks began, "You see, son, I was ready to go to the court, but the process could take years and would ruin reputations needlessly. Austin has gone his way. This has nothing to do with him now. I simply need to make certain the family entail is properly prepared, and, as I've said, Holcomb's and my goals seem to have shifted into, er—how shall I put it—*shifted away* from one another... and into opposing camps."

"I see."

"Whereas," Lord Brooks said steadily, "I do not consider the firm itself to blame—only Holcomb. I believe you understand me. I'd rather spare the expense of starting in a new firm, spare the firm a needless embarrassment in the process... an embarrassment, I might add, that begins with you, eh?"

Lord Brooks paused and Roundtree shuffled the papers on his desk with shaking hands.

"You seem a resourceful boy," Lord Brooks went on, "able to find what you're looking for, able to go after what you've found. Yes, I saw you at the docks, heard every word, but, as I told you, I don't hold you responsible. You were acting in Holcomb's interest, I know."

Roundtree gulped and stared. Lord Brooks had caught his solicitors with their hands in the proverbial biscuit jar, but being a man of uncommon sense it seemed he wished to rearrange the office to his liking rather than send them all to jail on charges of conspiracy. It was, of course, the gentleman's way of dealing with things.

"So... may I count on you to displace Holcomb?"

"Yes, sir. Only... how is it I'm to... to, uh... displace Mr. Holcomb exactly?"

"Oh, come now, Roundtree. There are so many secrets to be had in an office such as this. You must know secrets after lo these many years... well, in your tenure. A bright boy such as yourself?"

Roundtree smiled nervously. Yes, he could think of one or two things, but then again, Holcomb had an equal number of nasty surprises for Roundtree if it were to come to that.

"Ah, my boy, I know what you're thinking." This was the point in the conversation in which Lord Brooks knew he would have to bluff and bluff hard. He took a deep breath. "But the difference is I'd be behind you, you see. The Brooks name... The Brooks fortune. Holcomb can't stand up to it." He leaned forward on the desk and looked steadily into Roundtree's frightened orbs. "No one can."

He stood up and eyed the boy. Roundtree's reaction would reveal if the boy really knew his business, for most of London was aware of Brooks' shaky financial status.

But Roundtree was remembering Holcomb's words from the day before and so he smiled despite the tenuous circumstances.

"But then, I need hardly point out you have little choice in the matter," Lord Brooks lied further.

Roundtree looked up quickly. Lord Brooks' manner had quite suddenly changed to that of a large and rather dangerous animal. Roundtree gave a dry swallow.

"Come on, then. What could you get us on the old boy?" Lord Brooks pressed with fire in his eyes.

"Em-embezzlement."

"My boy, embezzlement is hardly so unusual as to warrant the dismissal of a well-placed solicitor. In fact, the thing's practically required of a man in his position."

"But what if it led to murder?" Roundtree said more firmly.

"Mmm."

"But I... I needn't tell you all the circumstances... need I?"

"Oh, but you do. Indeed, yes. I insist upon knowing every detail. You see, if I'm going to risk my reputation in a court of law, I have to know everything. No surprises." Lord Brooks briefly looked around him and began to tap his foot. "And it must be a very large sum... very large. Come on then. I haven't all day."

"All right." Roundtree gulped once more and clasped his hands together tightly. "It was the Chatham case last year..."

"Earl Chatham?"

"Yes."

"I knew Stuart well. Go on...."

And so he did. In fact, once the dam had burst in the boy, he couldn't stop himself from remembering every blessed detail of the events leading up to the Earl's unfortunate "suicide." And so Lord Brooks fell to smiling as the young man continued. Happy with himself and his world, he was as delighted with life as the time a lion charged across the sand toward him only to fall into a pit prepared especially for him. He remembered the look of utter surprise on the lion's face as the ground gave way beneath him. As he listened to the young man, Lord Brooks anticipated an even greater pleasure in the sight of Holcomb's fall from the heights.

"Lastly, sir," Roundtree added, "there was the business of Austin."

"Yes. I shouldn't like Austin to go to America, Roundtree. I should like to offer him a comfortable existence in Thistledown."

"But if he stays, he may try to destroy the inheritance. He was training a boy named Henry for the tests."

"Well. Doesn't matter. There won't be three scholars. It's a simple matter. There won't be three scholars, and so we won't be litigating my father's will ad infinitum, and I promise you a tidy sum if you keep it as simple as that. You will, of course, help me make certain there are, indeed, no more scholars."

"It will be my pleasure, sir."

"Thank you."

"And what of Miss Brown?"

"Miss Brown? What about her?"

"She may complicate the matter of the will."

"What does she have to do with the will?"

"Austin told me she's the one who discovered it in the library. That's why he found it."

"Really! Bah. Only a woman. She couldn't possibly understand the legal ramifications of a..."

"She's the daughter of a solicitor, sir."

"The prying little chit."

"Would you have me buy her off?"

"Wait. Find out how much she knows. No point in wasting family funds, now is there?"

"Yes, sir."

"Good. Then we have an understanding."

"We do indeed, sir. Austin comfortable. No scholars found. Find out what Miss Brown knows, and bribe her as needs be."

"Right. And a handshake between gentlemen to seal our new relationship, Roundtree. Yes. You're going to go quite far in this business, I can see that."

***

Later that afternoon Fiona, the Reverend, and Theodosia took a walk along the Strand. Fiona noted Theodosia's mood and brightly suggested they take themselves to the nearest bookstore. The thought cheered Theodosia considerably, and the three were soon winding their way in and out of bookstores all along a twisting little side road called Charteriss Court.

Finally they came to a huge bookstore with a wonderful selection of old and new titles, and best of all, it was filled with delightful little reading nooks at every turn. As Theodosia browsed through the gardener's section she thought on all she had learned of Austin this afternoon. She was happy to know he would remember. Granted, it might take two years, but she could wait. The trouble was where she should wait. Here in England? She doubted her parents would allow it. With Fiona? Perhaps. But Fiona had enough trouble eking out a living for herself. She knew for a certainty she could not stay with her aunt.

And then the books took her interest once more, and the words and pictures of one sweet-looking tome and then another filled her mind and eased her heart.

As they browsed the bookstore, Reverend Pickett glanced over to Theodosia. *She is naive about her America, and too quick to judge England,* he thought and sighed. *But that is youth, for pity's sake.*

The young filter all they see through a set of rose-tinted spectacles and never doubt their visions as I am left to doubt mine. I know the world and the world knows me. Yet Christ remains victorious.

Fiona feigned interest in a gothic novel as she looked toward Theodosia and thought, *She was willin' to come lookin' for him in London, and she's takin' it bravely to find he doesn't want her. I wonder, does America make brave women or do brave women make America? Her brother traps beaver, but her father's a barrister. What a strange country my sister chose to make her home. I wonder where I'd fit into such a place?*

Theodosia looked up to see both the Reverend and Fiona staring at her. They looked abashed and lowered their eyes, but Theodosia shook her head and grew uncomfortable. "I'm fine, and I don't need to be looked after by you two as if I were a babe in arms. Here. I've found a book I want to read for a while at the table over there. Would you both mind coming back for me in an hour?"

Fiona looked at the Reverend and the Reverend nodded. "All right, then," said Fiona. "One hour. Then we'll go to the inn for afternoon tea."

"Perfect." But when they did not move, Theodosia brought her chin out slightly, parted her lips and raised her brows, telling them without words, *Go on with you.*

And so they parted.

***

"Holcomb, I want you to gather my files."

"Excuse me?"

Lord Brooks took a deep breath. "Gather my files. Especially the original of my father's will. I'm taking them elsewhere."

"Do you realize what you ask, old boy?"

Lord Brooks laughed and leaned his palms along the edge of the ornate desk. "Do it, Holcomb. Do it now."

Holcomb looked over at Lord Brooks. He snorted, pulled his pipe to his lips and inhaled deeply. He blew the smoke in a thin stream and walked leisurely to the window. "Are you upset that we haven't found your boy?" He turned back to Lord Brooks and smiled. "We've looked over the docks. We've been through the pubs. I've a man checking the brothels as we speak."

"Holcomb, you haven't heard me. You will gather my files, and I will leave with them."

"And why the sudden change?"

"Because I have you," said Lord Brooks.

"Do you?" He laughed.

"Two words: Earl Chatham."

The smile was lost. "Has my assistant somehow compromised the firm's confidence? Been telling secrets?" he hissed.

Lord Brooks nodded solemnly.

"Well," Holcomb said blithely, suddenly riding up on his toes. "Hell, fire and damnation." He stopped and tapped his pipe in the bowl before him. "Yet I'll wager my tale isn't half as interesting as your own."

Lord Brooks continued to stare at Holcomb. "Holcomb, I'm taking my business to Chittendon. Any other papers you find should be sent there."

"Sloppy job, Earl Chatham," he said as if he hadn't heard him. "I'd grown too used to having my own way, I think. Yes. Good choice Roundtree made. Nice choice."

"Holcomb..."

Holcomb lit his pipe. "Quite all right. By all means, I'll get your files." *Brooks wasn't the most solid case, anyway,* he thought. *I could make more out of the Grants. I'll do it. Start on it next week.*

He brought the files back to the desk, and Lord Brooks began to thumb through them.

"They're all there, Brooks. Surely you know I am capable of keeping papers in order."

"Are you? If that's so, sir, why cannot I find the copy Roundtree stole from Austin?"

Holcomb stared at him and shifted his pipe from one side of his mouth to the other.

Lord Brooks gave a derisive snort. "Of course. Roundtree still has it. Decent of you not to tell him my story, Holcomb."

Holcomb laughed and refilled his pipe. "Hmph. Mayhaps I'm losing my taste for blood."

Brooks looked up. "You? Ha."

"Or maybe... maybe I feel there's still something to be made of an old acquaintance, eh, Brooks?"

Now Lord Brooks lowered his chin and raised a brow.

"Any more money to be had in opium, old friend?" Holcomb asked. "Or is the tea trade pure as snow now?"

Lord Brooks looked back at him and flashed a smile beneath his ponderously large moustache.

"You know," Holcomb continued, "I was rather counting on the litigation around your father's will to see me through retirement, and now I'm forced to look around for something else. *Downright* inconvenient, if you ask me. If you gave to me the names of your connections in *trade*, I should think it's the least you could do. And if you do, I think I'd be of a mind to recommend you to Lord Andrew Fulton's bank, that is if you're still longing to procure an American clipper ship."

Brooks smiled, gathered a pen from the desk and proceeded to write something on a slip. He folded the paper and handed it to Holcomb, announcing, "Here. It's *the very least I can do*. But I'd be careful you don't get your throat cut. Opium is not as safe a trade as it once was."

"Somehow I believe I'll manage," said Holcomb, looking the names over carefully.

Lord Brooks studied his face and grunted. "I believe you will." And he tucked the files under his arm. "Good day to you, Holcomb."

"And to you, *Lord* Brooks."

***

Theodosia took herself to the corner where a table and four high-backed Windsor chairs sat undisturbed. She sat down, adjusted the oil lamp and opened the book.

Eglantine Roses, she whispered and fingered the leather volume. It was in worse shape than the one owned by the Brookses, but the gilding on the leather was still there. The cover was still quite pretty, still warm to the touch. She opened the volume and read the preface.

What she read surprised her and then made her wonder. *"A gift of Eglantine roses to a friend or lover has come to mean 'I wound to heal,'"* the preface read. "I wound to heal," she said softly.

"May I take that as an introduction?" spoke a voice nearby.

Theodosia jumped in her seat as if she'd been bitten. With her heart in her throat she looked up to see the young red-headed man from Holcomb's office pulling his hat from his head with one hand and sweeping open his cloak with the other as he gave her a low bow.

"Sir?" she said as a small terror seized her.

"Todd Roundtree at your service, miss. Have no fear. I am not here on Mr. Holcomb's account. I am here on behalf of Austin Brooks."

"Austin Brooks... Austin Brooks whom you once mugged, sir?" she whispered.

"Miss Brown, please allow me to be frank. Austin Brooks is an old and dear friend of mine. We went to University together. I was forced to do what I had to in order to wrest from him what did not belong to him."

"The will belonged to Lord Brooks!"

"Exactly."

She swallowed and looked about. "This is hardly... why are you here for Austin?"

"I know this is unusual. Please observe." He pulled a sheaf of papers from his coat and lay them on the table. "Lord Brooks' will."

"Oh, my."

"Yes. Please, you must trust me. I took the liberty of freeing this document from Mr. Holcomb's file, because Holcomb did not intend for Austin to ever see it again. I want to help my old friend. You know... he has recently lost his memory."

"Yes, I know. I know it all too well." She tried hard to hold back the emotion in her voice.

"I want to help him, and I thought that you might be of a great service in that regard."

"How so?"

"Austin told me how you found the will."

"Yes…" She paused with expectation as her mouth grew dry.

"Yes," he said grimly. "And there are things in it, you may remember…" He cleared his throat. "In the will . . ."

She bowed her head and felt her cheeks grow hot.

He continued, "… things that will be decided on quite soon. Do you know… what I mean, Miss Brown?"

She nodded and stuttered, "His twenty—twenty-first birthday, yes."

Roundtree nodded and smiled. "Yes. Without Austin's awareness of the true situation, you see, things could go against him."

"I don't think things could go more against him if they tried."

"Exactly. I'm… in a position to enable you to do something very brave to help him."

"What? Anything."

"Return to America and wait for him." Sensing her immediate reticence, he held out his hand. "Wait, now. Austin is very confused, and that's why he's made this simple request. He thinks it's best you return home to wait for him. He wants to stay and help the town, and having you with him will, he feels, do more to confuse the situation for him. He has things… to do…"

"You mean, like Henry Taylor?"

"Exactly like Henry. I'm sorry, but only for a dear friend would I have come on such an errand. I fully realize the enormity of Austin's request, but is it possible you could consider it?"

"Oh, sir." She held back her tears and felt her heart slowly break. "I will go if that's what's best. If that's what he really wants. I have the monies now, and I can book passage within the week." Her eyes scanned the table and fell upon the papers lying there. She gulped. "But before I do go, would you please… I know it is presumptuous of me, but I cannot help but ask it. Will you allow me to read the will... *again?* I feel certain that if I read it... *again*... I'll be better able to understand how I'm helping him by my leaving, you see. To know it helps... Thistledown... and Austin."

He sighed. "I've very little time."

"Please."

He nodded. He'd known he would say yes all along. She knew he'd mugged Austin. She would have to die, and it seemed so appropriate—almost humorous—that a bookstore should be the place in which she breathed her last.

Theodosia placed her little hand upon the folds of the will. She had every reason in the world to read it. This was an act of love, wasn't it? She felt sure she *could* help, that something could be found to untangle the legal knot.

And so Theodosia Brown began to read the will, and Round-tree began to pace behind her chair. People came through the aisles. People went away. People came through once more.

"Ah!" she said.

"Eh?"

"This! Have you seen this?"

He looked over her shoulder. "The paragraph on the evaluation of who's to be considered a scholar? Yes."

"There's already been one, you know, the son of a weaver, I was told. And there is Henry Taylor, of course, and I believe he will at least stand for Cambridge this year, although he's going to America soon after. But you see that's all right, because it doesn't require anyone to actually *attend* University. And you see that's two, then. So Austin will only have to find one."

"Excellent," said Roundtree uncomfortably.

But Theodosia was reading at a feverish pace now, totally absorbed. The floor grew quiet. No one was about. Roundtree approached.

Theodosia held up her hand. "This! You see this! Ah! This is tremendous. It's done!"

"What's done?"

"There *are* three scholars!

"Whatever could you mean?"

"Austin Brooks. Austin is the third. I realized it and I looked back, and indeed it does say *orphan,* and there is no reference to the type of schooling required, so it doesn't matter that he was tutored. He is from Thistledown, you see, and the Reverend Pickett has mentioned to me more than once that Austin's father never formally adopted him. Therefore he qualifies as the third scholar! It's done! Thistledown has won! Isn't it wonderful?!"

"Wonderful." He drew his hand across his sweaty brow. "Just too almighty wonderful for words." Now he could think of two good reasons to kill her.

***

"Austin?"

Austin Brooks turned to see a tall white-haired gentleman. He wanted to get to the hotel where he presumed the Reverend was having afternoon tea with the ladies. He needed to speak to Theodosia and had no time for strangers.

"It is Austin?" The man stopped near to him but was looking wary.

"Yes. Yes, my name is Austin Brooks."

"Well, of course it is! Austin Simpson Brooks."

"Do I know you, sir?"

For this odd question Lord Brooks had no ready answer.

"Yes, well, I'm in a bit of a hurry, if you wouldn't mind, sir." Austin turned to leave.

"Young man," he sputtered, "*I named you!*"

A chill ran up the young man's spine as he looked at the fellow again. "You are... Lord Alfred Brooks," he said without emotion.

"Are you well?" He stepped closer.

Austin gave a halfhearted laugh. "As well as can be expected, sir, for having lost my memory."

"Who's... What's this? Lost your *mem'ry?*"

"Yes, sir. Apparently I was mugged." He brought down his chin as he swept away his hat. "Struck on the head." He looked up at

Lord Brooks. "Some sort of trauma occurred."

"You lost your… you're saying you don't recognize me, then?"

Austin looked about him, then pursed his lips. "I'm sorry, sir, but it's quite true, and… furthermore…" He cast his hat back on his head. "I don't really care to discuss it with you."

"You… *you don't care to discuss it.* Just what the devil does that mean?"

Austin brought his chin forward. "It means, sir, that from what I've heard of my family and my poor beginnings, it's just as well I've forgotten. I appreciate your concern, but as you can easily see I am otherwise fine. Now if you'll excuse me." And Austin rudely walked away from the awestruck gentleman.

Lord Brooks was so stunned he let him go.

Later, when Lord Brooks informed his wife that he had found Austin, she was silent for a time. Plucking at the handkerchief in her lap, she finally murmured, "And how did you find him?"

"Well, he… he was going from the docks."

"Waiting for a ship, is he?"

"No. He's working there, my dear."

"Took a clerking job with someone else without a letter of introduction. What scoundrel took him on?"

"No, my dear. He's working there… as a loader."

"A *dock*worker?"

Lord Brooks nodded gravely. "But I'm sure if he knew himself he wouldn't stay there a minute more."

"Whatever do you mean by *if he knew himself?*"

"I believe… he's suffered a sort of trauma and he's lost his memory."

"Lost his memory? *Lost* his memory? What chicanery is this? Then we must tell him who he is and who he is not. He is not a dockworker; he's a Brooks, for heaven's sake! He can't pull this sort of ruse…"

"It's not a ruse, my dear."

She blinked. "A Brooks is not a dockworker!"

"If you'll remember, my *sweet,* my father kindly wrote him out of the will. And now someone has kindly informed him of his orphan state, and so upon what basis am I to appeal to him that he *is* a Brooks?"

"Well, you could *kindly* write him back in, couldn't you? And get him out of this situation?"

Suddenly a light came into his eyes. "Yes. Yes, I believe now I could, my dear. Now I could. It's an excellent suggestion."

"Go and tell him, Mr. Brooks."

"Yes, my dear. Care to join me?"

"No. No!" She shuddered. "I'll not go to see a boy working the docks!"

"Yes, love. I understand." And he took himself away.

But as he left, the Lady Brooks began to mutter to herself, "*Lost* his memory. Trauma? Pssh. Very convenient, I say. He's taken a job on the docks to humiliate us, waiting for us to come round and reinstate him into our good graces. What an ungrateful cad to pretend this loss."

But the bitter insights were lost to the stale air of a now empty room. ᘓ

TWENTY-FIVE

∽

"Beauty is truth, truth beauty–
   that is all
Ye know on earth, and all ye
   need to know.

"Ode on a Grecian Urn"
John Keats

∽

Theodosia finally reached the portion of the will in which Austin's grandfather had written the letter. It was the cruelest piece of work she'd ever seen, and she had to stop reading at the end of it to wipe away the tears. As she pulled off her spectacles and laid them aside, she mumbled, "What a work he's done. I see his intent. He says in this letter the scholars must attend University, but I note the legal document itself has left it out as a requirement. So it's still true... there are three scholars." Holding her hands to her cheeks, she pressed shut her eyes and rested in her thoughts. Roundtree had made no comment from behind her, and so her mind wandered again to Austin. She prayed for his soul—that he would not grow bitter again in this recent rediscovery of his origins, that he would know he was loved: loved by God as well as by herself... that he would walk closely with His Lord. And that he would make a wise decision concerning Thistledown. But this last thought caused her to remember why this fellow had come. Austin wanted her to return to America; Austin would make these decisions without her.

Slowly she raised her head and willed her tears to hold themselves back. She reached for her spectacles, and as if in a dream, she thought she saw the form of Austin Brooks walking toward her from afar.

With the embarrassing realization Austin would find her perusing the will, she stood up forcefully, and as she did so the high back of her chair rammed into Roundtree's chest. As his head snapped forward from the blow, his chin met the top of Theodosia's head which caused her to cry out. But that was nothing compared to the pain Roundtree suffered, for, unluckily for him, Fiona Mienzes had done Theodosia's hair up that morning. The high bun was elegantly decorated with a tortoise shell comb firmly placed—the comb, a simple design consisting of delicately carved, but surprisingly sturdy, raised spikes.

As Roundtree realized he was wounded, Theodosia realized she had hurt him, and so she shoved her chair back even further to turn around and see, which caused him to reel backward. He was howling in pain by then as he grabbed at his bleeding chin.

"Oh, my—your chin—I am so sorry!" she cried in a fluster even as she pulled on her spectacles.

She was horrified to see him thump against a heavy bookcase, but then her eyes focused on something dangling from his other hand.

A rope.

For once in her life, Theodosia Rose Brown did not have to concentrate a second longer to understand that she was in mortal danger. Why this fellow would try to kill her she didn't care to stop and ask. She bolted around the table and dashed toward the door of the bookstore, even as Roundtree was righting himself, cursing all the while. And as she reached the door, she heard him call out, "Oh, yes, you'll be sorry, Miss Brown. Completely sorry!"

It seemed to take forever for the door latch to open, but she made it to the street. She cried out for a constable even as she ran toward The Crooked Tree Inn.

***

On his way along the darkening streets, with the discomfort of remembering his rudeness to Lord Brooks prominent in his mind, Austin also took to remembering the Reverend Pickett's words, reminding him of how he'd wrestled with his demons that summer. He was forced to realize that the only measure of a man was his relationship to God. All else, the work of kitchen maids and sailors, and the pride that rises and falls within humans as easily as the tide of the ocean, or the beating of a heart, will fade to lesser importance when one is confronted by one's God—the God of truth and light. This he held to as he walked. He need not be on the defensive as he was with Lord Brooks, for he had the Great Defender by his side and in his heart.

These thoughts were pleasant to him but doubly enjoyed for a thing not counted on beforehand: now and again thinking on the Reverend Pickett's words struck chords of recognition bound to other conversations he'd had with him long ago. All this was just as the doctor had predicted and it gave him confidence to know he might soon resume his whole self. And with the Reverend's kind persistence, it was obvious his spirit would be restored much sooner than his memory.

And it had all begun when Theodosia Brown said to him at the carriage window, "Austin Simpson Brooks. You are my other half." The words had caused him suddenly to remember—not all of it, but just enough.

A girl on a hill. His other half.

He smiled to think of it as he walked toward The Crooked Tree Inn.

***

"He would have succeeded. I was a hairsbreadth from letting him kill me, and all because I wanted to read that *stupid, stupid* will," she sobbed.

Fiona was comforting Theodosia in her way. She patted her friend's shoulders, but she was so angry with her for endangering herself, she was practically striking her with the force. And then she was hugging her tight once more and smoothing her hair and crying with her.

"What was I thinking?" Theodosia had tried to explain what happened to her to Fiona and the Reverend Pickett as they sat in a booth of The Crooked Tree Inn having late afternoon tea. "I just thought I could do something for Austin."

"Your motive was a good one, my dear," the Reverend Pickett gently told her, "but do you see now you can't work alone?"

"Yes." She wiped her face. "Yes, I do. I see that everything I've done has served to ruin him. If it weren't for me, he wouldn't have found the will. Then he wouldn't have gone to London, and he would never have been there for Roundtree to strike him. Everything is my fault."

"Oh, come now. It's arrogance to assume that everything that happened to Austin Brooks stemmed from your occasionally overzealous curiosity, and self-pity will not lead you to the truth, either. No. The boy took himself to London. He contacted Roundtree. And if he'd been more sure of who he was in Christ, as sure as he is now, he would never have had to go to London in the first place. I don't see where any of his sin is your fault, my dear. At least limit yourself to your own unique sins, eh?"

"Yes." She sniffed. "Taking things into my own hands... and dangerous hands they are. It's just as Papa said. I'm a hazard to everyone I meet. Please excuse me." And with that she left the table and ran upstairs to her room.

***

Austin was disappointed to find Theodosia had already left the table. "This must be a difficult time for her," he said.

"Not by half," said the Reverend sadly. "She just wanted to help you and was almost killed doing it.

"What?"

"Roundtree. Apparently Miss Brown made a visit to Holcomb, Redfern and Grackle when she was trying to find you, and I believe that somehow, for whatever reason, Holcomb ordered Roundtree to try to kill her. He tried this very afternoon."

"I've got to speak with her. Is she all right, then?"

"There was a time this summer," the Reverend said, "I had to give her the selfsame advice I'm about to give you now—and that is to give her time."

"But I haven't any time. I've decided to sail for America."

"But you'll both be heading for America then."

Austin laughed. "Do you have any idea how large an animal this America stands, sir?"

"Yes, but surely her village is nothing but a hair on the creature?"

"I don't know. I haven't any idea, really."

"Well, I've been counsel to hundreds of young people over the years, and I've seen those with heart and no mind, and seen those with mind and no heart, but I've never seen a couple blessed with both who couldn't eventually find one another out. Give her a little time to clear her head, once more, and I'm sure you two will figure out a solution. Meanwhile, we'll keep a close watch out for her. I've alerted the authorities to look for Roundtree, but if I were you I'd watch your back until they catch him."

Austin smiled and cocked his head. "Was I always this much trouble to you, sir?"

"This and more! This and more!" the Reverend said good-naturedly. Soon a rumbling sort of laugh took hold of him. "But, to be quite honest, I don't remember you taking my advice as easily as you do now."

★★★

"Tee?"

"Yes, Fiona."

"I've something to tell ye and something to ask ye."

"Yes?"

"I've been proud to be your friend up until this evening, for up until this evening, ye weren't the self-pitying wretch I see in ye tonight."

"Oh, thank you ever so."

"Now hear me out. Ye've made yer mistakes. Ye should live with them. Ye almost died, but ye're not dead, although here ye're actin' as though Roundtree did his work, after all. Ye've simply got to ask forgiveness and go on."

"But I do. I ask and ask, but I keep right on making the same willful mistakes over and over. It's no use."

"Who told ye bein' a Christian was easy? It's hard as nails to give everything over to Him. Ye have to give in to Him again and again and then again! Ask me, I'm a Scot! I'm more stubborn than ye could ever hope! That's right! But it's lettin' Satan have the day to believe God's done with ye. God gives ye the strength to hand yer will over to Him, so stand up and let Him fight for you, woman. Don't give in, or I'm done with you. I'll not have a friend who gives up so easily."

"I could say the same for you, Fiona Mienzes," Theodosia spat back. "If you love your bonny Scotland so much, why aren't you there?"

Fiona pinched her lips together momentarily, but then she took a deep breath and let it go. "Well, na', since ye brought it up, ye're right." She crossed her arms. "I've been avoiding tellin' ye, but that's the other thing I've coom about. I want to ask ye a favor. I've made a decision I'm going to America, and I was wondering if yer boat had room for me. I've got the money for the ship. I took a bill of sale on my furniture in Thistledown. I don't know as ye cared to notice, but it was considered finely crafted, my father bein' a carpenter."

"They were quite beautiful."

"Oh, I know. It broke my heart to sell 'em. I'd had a fella' make an offer for 'em before, and so I took it as we left."

"I'm sorry you had to do that. Thank you. I'd be pleased to travel with you, Fiona."

"Once I'm in America, I'll stay with my sister until I find work."

"Oh, Fiona, yes. I'm sorry. Yes, of course. Oh, that's wonderful. I mean to say, I know that's a horrible decision for you. How will you feel to leave your family, though?"

"As ye put it so plainly, I'm not at home now, am I? No. And they can't afford me there either. Lord knows when they find I've sold off Father's pieces, they'll banish me anyway. But if I grow rich in America, I can coom back and buy a little land for them, can't I? Then they'll forgive me." She brushed away a stray tear.

"Yes. Yes, you could, and I'm sure they'll forgive you."

"They say it's possible there... to make a little money," she said, sounding uncertain.

"It is."

Fiona's voice grew low. "Ye know, I'm counting on ye to be right about this America, Tee Brown, and if ye've been stretching the truth to match a fisherman's tale, I promise I'll bring the Mienzes clan down on ye like a rain of fire."

Theodosia laughed and stood and hugged her friend, and Fiona finally gave way to laughter and tears, as well, and then they hugged again.

***

The next morning and one day before Austin was to leave for America, Lord Brooks waited by Austin's lodgings thinking he might have a word alone with the boy on his way to the ship. And so as Austin came forth in the early hours Lord Brooks came to walk behind him, slowly increasing his stride to catch up to the youth.

For Austin, thoughts of America, Theodosia, the Reverend Pickett, and the few scattered memories that had returned to him just last night—all these and more clamored for attention in his mind as he walked the last half mile in the morning fog toward the ship's quay. And so he was surprised by the vicious yank upon his arm and he felt his body spin about.

Roundtree had already cocked the trigger as Austin spun to face him, and if Lord Brooks had not been eight steps behind the two, Austin surely would have died then and there.

Many years had passed since Brooks had been in battle, but the shock of energy that surges through a man in the moment of the charge came to him instantly. Without decision or thought he rushed forward and swung his cane down with a heavy crack on the barrel of the pistol, sending it skittering to the stones.

A half-mad Roundtree, previously intent on the pleasure of see-ing a bloody hole blown into the chest of Austin Brooks, was com-pletely confused at having his pistol suddenly knocked from his hand. His senses immediately told him Austin could not have done it—indeed, the pale-faced youth still looked as shocked as he had the moment before. But before Roundtree could even look about him to find the cause, Brooks' cane swung around and found the back of Roundtree's skull, and so Todd Roundtree thought no more upon this or any other problem.

Austin blinked while Lord Brooks stood staring at his prey, holding his ornate cane, bloodied by the blow, over the body as if Roundtree might rise again in the near future. As Austin's thoughts cleared, his eyes finally came to rest on the gentleman who had apparently saved his life. A great vein on Brooks' brow was throbbing, his face was ruddy with the effort, and his breath-ing was ragged. While staring at that pulsing vein, Austin slowly recognized the form of the man—the man who claimed to be his father.

Lord Brooks straightened himself then and took a careful look at his cane.

Austin stammered, "I th-thank you, sir."

"It would please me greatly if you would call me Father."

Austin found he couldn't answer.

A crowd was gathering now. "May I walk you to your ship?" Lord Brooks calmly asked.

Austin nodded slowly.

The two began to make their way toward the *Hurricane,* but Austin noted that his legs felt weak beneath him. Never in his short memory had he come so close to death. He looked back at the scene behind them, and then he turned to this man who wished to be called his father and said again, "Thank you."

"It was my duty, son."

In silence they made their way to the ship, and Austin felt the burden of the quiet between them. His walk grew stronger as they neared the ship, but now it was his heart that failed him. He didn't know what to say to the man.

"A word with you before you go topside," Lord Brooks said.

"A word," Austin repeated.

"I am curious as to how much you do remember?"

Austin looked blankly at the fellow's face. "With no offense intended, sir, nothing of you, nor of my... Lady Brooks and your... sons, nothing of Thistledown but the dock I came upon several days ago. I have some smattering of memory of the Reverend Pickett and of a young lady, Miss Theodosia Brown. It was the Reverend Pickett who told me everything he could about my origins." Austin lowered his head.

"Reverend Pickett!" Lord Brooks said with surprise. "The audacity of the man..."

"He made it quite clear, sir," Austin said with rising indignation, "that what he was telling me was what, in fact, I had told him at the beginning of the summer, about my finding the will, how I left the home and... came... to you again." He reddened. "Doesn't matter now," he mumbled. "I'll be off soon. But I want to thank you for all you've done for me. Not just... no, not just that... for everything. I know and understand that it's a rare thing a boy like me had a chance to be raised in the way I was raised."

Lord Brooks looked at the young man and felt a pain that defied description. How he wished just one of his children could feel what this boy did. "Where will you go?"

"America."

"I thought you hated America," he said.

"Apparently not."

Lord Brooks' voice grew strained. "But I've changed solicitors and there's no reason my father's will should continue to bind us. With a slight change here and there, I could make you a legitimate heir now!"

Austin colored at the description. With a deep breath he looked Lord Brooks in the eye. "I thank you for the offer. And I know what the offer means to you and to me, sir. Believe me, I do. You do me honor...."

"Honor is only half what I could do...."

Austin shook his head. "I will not be able to accept your generosity. *Not...* not that it isn't a temptation, but I'd simply like a clean start. I'll be leaving on this ship to settle in America. There's work for me there. I know. And it's... where I belong."

"For pity's sake, take your inheritance and make even more of yourself then! You don't have to stay here. Just take the monies."

"No, sir. You're too kind."

"Nonsense! It's the least I can do, son."

"But I am not your..."

"No. In every way which is important to me, you are my son. If ever I have done anything good in my life, it was to pluck you from the ignominy of a peasant's life and raise you under my roof."

"But did my mother have any say in the matter?" he said, holding in his anger.

"Lady Brooks?"

"No," he clipped. "My mother."

Lord Brooks cleared his throat and let his arms fall to his sides. "No, she didn't have a choice." Austin's face hardened. "I was told she was a stranger recently come into the town. Unmarried and origin unknown. She died in childbirth the day I found you. The neighbors had taken you in and didn't know quite what to do with you."

Austin took a quick breath but setting his jaw he nodded once and then twice. "I thank you for telling me the truth."

"I have vowed honesty between us from now on. And along those lines I mean to ask you if you have indeed forgotten everything, how is it you come to be working on a ship?"

"I like ships. I'd like to own one someday."

Lord Brooks' brows rose high as he studied Austin's face. "Would you? I wonder, then, if you wouldn't mind a different sort of offer from my hand."

"Sir?"

"I aim to own an American clipper ship; if you will not take an inheritance, would you care to manage the purchase and run the ship yourself... from America?"

"I hardly think I'm prepared..."

"I'll help you through it. The truth is, since you were old

enough to read the record books you've shown a proclivity for the industry that neither of my *other* sons possess."

"It would be a... a grand thing."

"It isn't charity, you understand. You'd be working... and hard."

Austin searched his face, and Lord Brooks waited quietly for an answer. Now Austin glanced behind Lord Brooks, to either side, down at his shoes, and finally raised his head to meet his gaze once more. And then he said with deliberate slowness, "I believe I cannot think of one blessed reason to decline your offer... Father."

***

Meanwhile Theodosia arranged passage for herself and Fiona Mienzes on a large passenger ship leaving for America the following week. The Reverend Pickett came to the *Hurricane* later that morning to tell Austin about Theodosia's leaving. This forced Austin to have to decide whether to go on to America without a resolution between them or to stay in England another week and keep trying to convince her—of what he was not exactly sure— with the latter decision providing him no guarantee of passage at all. He decided he must try to speak to her again.

And so, late in the afternoon of the day before the *Hurricane* was to leave, Austin came to the hotel while the three were having cream teas. But when Theodosia spied Austin coming through the dining room doors, she stood up and left the table to retire to her room.

Sitting at the little desk in her room, she tried to calm herself by reading the Bible. She cleared her throat and opened the book to read whatever comfort she could find. She read in Hebrews, "I will never leave thee nor forsake thee," and it only made her think of Austin. *God's love,* she thought morosely, *is most perfect. Mine is not. Mine is more of a death knell.*

It was now August 28. Three months had passed since she'd come to England, and she was amazed to find herself so changed in so little time. And she had lost so much as well. Strange to feel the deep loss of a thing she'd had no knowledge of at all four months before. Strange she would have these memories to remind her of her loss, while it was merely the loss of such memories that would keep her and Austin from each other now.

And how odd it was to be suddenly removed from the very innermost thoughts of another, the plans and hope and joys once shared—all snatched away—and reduced to a long description at a table in a noisy pub.

The pub. Austin was downstairs even now with that lost look upon his face. He came around for Reverend Pickett, not for her, and she couldn't bear to know it.

Now she sighed, her self-pity complete and the feeling of it overwhelming. She rose and went to the window to pull the curtains shut, to make the room as dark as her mood, but she paused to look out onto the clutter of rooftops, the smoke and the noise of London, and she thought with a pang in her heart that soon she would be home.

But—her home should be with Austin.

She pulled the curtains shut with force. "Oh, Theodosia," she moaned, "you've muddled everything." She sat down at the table, laid her head upon her arm and slowly began to rock her head. Everything was wrong and the whole of it could not be corrected. "Lord, help me," she said aloud. "Lord, help me, Lord, help me, no, I cannot do this on my own."

She heard a sound at the window and with a frightened shock she looked over to see an intruder. ༄

TWENTY-SIX

Once I saw a little bird
Come hop, hop, hop;
So I cried, "Little bird,
Will you stop, stop, stop?"
And was going to the window
To say, "How do you do?"
But he shook his little tail
And far away he flew.

Nursery Rhyme

"Austin?!" she said, bolting up from her seat and fiercely wiping a tear from each cheek.

He stood before her gulping, red above his collar, with one foot over the sill, the curtains still in his way, and his hand raised to his hat. He was clearly unsure of what he'd done by coming up the outside stair and entering her window.

"Ge-get out of here!" she finally thought to say, grabbing hold of the back of the chair as if it were a ready weapon.

For a moment he seemed ready to do just that, looking down and pulling his head back out the window. But then, with sudden force came a "No!" as his head returned, followed quickly by the rest of him, and then he stood before her in the darkened room. "Not until I've said what I've come to say, please." He swept his hat so forcefully from his head that it flew out from his fingers like a bird in flight. Quickly motioning to try and grab it, he came forward but awkwardly, and as he tried to catch himself, he stumbled forward and then stepped back.

And his hat fell at Theodosia's feet.

And so Austin was lost in staring at the girl. The situation had suddenly become most embarrassing.

Theodosia pressed her lips together. For the first time in her life she had observed someone acting as she acted when she so frequently lost control of an object; it pained her not to laugh out loud. But because of the overwhelming fear she held within her at that moment, she didn't laugh and instead made herself look away.

He took a step forward to retrieve the wayward hat, at which point she released the chair and moved toward the door. "Then I will leave," she said.

"Stop!" he cried, the hat forgotten. "Just wait, please. *Wait. I* am the one who's leaving. I am leaving tomorrow... *Tee,* and that is just why I've come, and that is why I beg of you to hear me out."

The sound of her name stopped her movement, but still she did not turn to face him. She wondered how he dared call her "Tee," then she wondered why he had chosen to call her "Tee" just then, and then she wondered what he meant by calling her "Tee" in such a soft, sweet way. She looked toward her shoulder but did not dare turn about.

He faltered. "And who knows if we'll... we may never..."

His gentle tone tore at her resolve until she whirled about and quickly said, "All right!"

"All right? All right." In a flutter, he looked around him. Slowly she came back to stand at the chair once more. "I know my coming in like this is improper, and all I can think to excuse my behavior is that I'm... well, I don't know what I am anymore."

"A child of God," she whispered.

"A child of God, yes." He looked at her and more boldly said, "Yes, and, as such, I have a right to know His will for me." But on the last his voice cracked and he bowed his head.

If he could have seen her face by daylight he may not have felt so all alone just then, but the lamplight hid the tremble that shook Theodosia's small frame.

"I... I didn't intend... but I saw you in the window as I passed..." He held his arm up in the air but brought it down again with a whump. "I was going back to the ship. I was going back to the ship, determined to sail tomorrow without a resolution between us, but something in me told me to look up and... there you were, and by the lamplight I could see such an... an incredibly sad expression on your face. I know I was arrogant to presume I was the cause of your sorrow, but from that I determined that if I was I should at least come up and try... and try to... undo..." He seemed to search for the words.

"The damage... if you could?" she finished for him, awed that he could so easily repeat the very words he'd spoken to her months before without seeming to remember he'd ever said them. He nodded solemnly, and she crossed her arms and held them tight.

But then he stopped and looked into her face. "I've said that to you before, haven't I?"

She bowed her head to try to keep herself from weeping right there.

But he saw the movement and pressed his lips together and looked back to the window. With a grim smile he shook his head in self-disgust. "Even if that's so, I've only insulted you once more." He pulled a hand to one brow and scratched it. Then the hand dropped. "It's no use, this." He laughed and prepared to take himself back out the window to the fire escape.

"Wait, please, Austin. There *is* more to be said."

He stopped and pulled his hands from the window's frame to stare back at her. For the longest time they stood there watching each other's eyes, and she grew so uncomfortable in the silence that she stooped to retrieve his hat for him. She took a tentative step forward to hand it to him.

He slowly took the hat from her. "If you're... if all you're going to tell me now is that I should be pleased to not forget my hat on leaving, I'm bound to tell you... I'd just as soon be pleased to throw myself off this balcony as take those stairs."

She bit her lip to keep it from trembling as she smiled and shook her head.

He smiled back with sudden ease. "There is hope, isn't there? Yes. And there's been all too much left unsaid between us." He pulled himself back from the window. "Things I've said before... and things..."

Tears gathered again in the corners of her eyes as she stared at him. "It's all right. I thank you for... trying. I bless you for trying, really... but it's all been too much, and you needn't apologize."

"Hush, please, and let me finish."

She nodded and wiped the tears from her eyes.

"I've... begun to remember."

Her eyes flew open and she fumbled with her hands, then laid hold of the chair again.

"It's a rather new experience, remembering events... quite whole... most frustrating to suddenly have the memories there at my disposal... as if I could have remembered them all along if only I'd tried. Most strange, though." He paused and looked at the ceiling. "Most strange is the thought that although I seem to know less than half of myself at present, I should already know... my other half." He pulled his eyes to hers and rested them there. "Is it possible you understand me?"

In the small light of the table lamp Theodosia's smile could be clearly seen. She studied Austin's face: his eyes, clear and steady; his mouth, set as it was with a smile of firm resolution; his blond-brown beard, grown thick enough that his dimples no longer showed. A pleasant chill passed through her to realize she would never have to leave him. Never, ever, ever.

"Yes, and I thank God for it," she said quietly, but her brows furrowed. "Are you quite sure?"

He smiled and then began to twirl his hat and then he sniffed and twirled his hat and smiled again. "Quite," he said half-laughing now. "Though I still haven't understood how you might... care for me in my... present condition."

She blushed and bowed her head and raised it to smile at him once more. "Don't you? But it's just as you say. You... you are my other half."

"Yes. This is most amazing to me."

"Someday," she said quietly. "Someday we will look back on this and perhaps we'll understand... why God allowed it."

"I look forward to that." He laughed. They laughed together, and then, "May I... kiss you?"

She continued to smile but looked about her and shyly nodded. He stepped forward with eagerness.

But the chair still stood between them, an unwanted guardian. She pulled at it slightly to bring it behind her at the same time that he grasped it to pull it toward him and away, and so they only succeeded in wedging it neatly between them once more.

With an impatience bordering on madness, Austin suddenly yanked the chair forward, but it was just as Theodosia, completely irritated with her own clumsiness and fearful of it ruining the beauty of the moment, pushed as hard as she could. And so the chair came toward Austin with a force that sent him sprawling.

His back and then his head hit the floor with a resounding ka-thunk, and a groan escaped his lips.

"Oh, Austin! I am so sorry! It is all my fault!" She rushed to his prone form in the darkness.

"Argh, I'll have myself another lump now."

But Theodosia was thinking desperately, *Is this the answer to our prayers?*

Austin sat up, rested his back against the wall and rubbed his head. He pinched shut his eyes and opened them again to see Theodosia close beside him.

Quickly she began. "I've heard that if you've amnesia, you can be hit on the head again and it will all come back. Can it be you remember everything now?"

Austin groaned again. "*Two years,* Theodosia Brown. It's going to take two years before it all comes back, and you will have to have a bit of patience. I'm telling you that *right now,* because I'm afraid you'll take it upon yourself to crack me over the head now and then in hopes of a miracle."

"Oh," said Theodosia pitifully. "It doesn't work then."

Austin's eyes grew wide, and, ever so slowly, Theodosia realized what she'd said. But love, being a forgiving creature, soon had them both laughing into tears.

"Dear Austin." She wiped the tears of laughter from her eyes as they pulled themselves from the muddle and stood up. "I'm afraid this sort of thing happens to me all the time. I'm... considered a dangerous woman, truly."

He pulled the chair upright and placed it firmly against the wall, giving it a look that dared it to move on its own. And then he looked back at her and his mouth eased into a smile. "Well, from now on," he said, stepping carefully to her, "I give promise—whatever happens shall happen to us both." And then he took from her the kiss he'd been wanting, and it seemed to him at that moment he'd been wanting it forever.

* * *

Reverend Pickett raised a brow to see the change in Theodosia, for she returned to the tea table smiling and buoyant.

Fiona, similarly surprised, exchanged a glance with the Reverend and then straightway asked Theodosia what had caused such a dramatic change in her spirit. But Austin entered the inn's door at that moment and headed toward their table, and, rather than answer her friend, Theodosia simply watched in rapt attention as he came up and calmly sat himself at table.

A moment or two of awkward silence passed before Austin detected the Reverend's and Fiona's shocked expressions, and a moment or two more before he fully realized that, in his enthusiasm to join her company, he'd given Tee no time in which to explain his presence.

But with so recent a happy reunion between them neither were prepared to pretend they hadn't spoken to each other, and so Austin looked at Theodosia and Theodosia looked at Austin and they began to smile at one another.

And as the Reverend watched the blooming blush that crept across their young faces, he slowly began to chuckle and in no time it had welled into a chortle. He laughed and laughed and coughed and then laughed so hard he had to pull his napkin to his mouth to muffle the sound, and when he saw the look of shocked amazement on Fiona Mienzes' face, it only made him laugh the more.

Epilogue

Theodosia Rose Brown married Austin Brooks in June of 1853 in the rose garden of her family home in Alexandria County, Virginia. Her sisters and brother were in attendance, as well as her friend, Fiona Mienzes, who had by then become a schoolteacher in the city of Alexandria, Virginia.

Theodosia's brother, Parker, when told what sort of trouble he had caused by his prank, reasoned to the family that it was Aunt Selda's fault and not his own. Besides which his sister obviously had things well in hand, and so after her marriage he went back to the north woods, with little or no guilt felt in the matter. He was an inveterate prankster until the day he died.

Under the guidance of Lord Brooks, Austin purchased an American clipper ship and soon set up a shipping business from the harbor of Alexandria. From that beginning he worked at building ships for English trade, and this he continued to do until the Civil War. He then signed up for duty in the Union Corps of Engineers, as he and Theodosia already had four children. They lived a happy life in the strength that God provides, and for all the challenges life threw at them, nothing ever quite compared to the peculiar challenges wrought that summer in the village of Thistledown.

Austin had turned twenty-one in the fall of '53, and so the will went into effect even though an ocean lay between himself and the document. Theodosia's legal interpretation of the will was found by the English Courts to be accurate and correct, to wit: three scholars had indeed been found.

Lord Brooks suffered a heart attack three months after the will had begun in probate and died soon after. But he left the American clipper ship and the business at Alexandria to one Austin Simpson Brooks.

A six-month contest in the courts determined Thistledown the "natural" heir to the Brooks estate, and it fell to Lady Brooks and her sons to contest their decision. If Lady Brooks had had her husband to help her, she might have rallied strength and fought the solicitors, but by then too much had been taken from her. If Alfred Brooks had wanted anything more than to be head of the scientific institution the Brooks Estate was to become, he might have fought it. And if Allan Brooks had had the least interest in his half of that scientific institution, he might have stayed around to fight, but circumstances had drawn each of them away.

So Lady Brooks kept the tea company and did modestly well, choosing to live in London rather than personally watch her former residence transformed into a laboratory. Albert, however, was perfectly happy to manage the new library of science, and he surprised everyone two years after its beginning by announcing his engagement to Cecelia Bannoch. Cecelia had no dowry to provide, but the penniless son of a Lord, as Albert had most certainly become, did not have to satisfy anyone's expectations, and so Cecelia and he married with no difficulty at all. As for Allan Brooks, his "discussion" with his father concerning his lack of responsibility affected him profoundly, and the family discovered too late Allan had a solemn talent for holding a grudge. He never forgave his father for the harsh words, even after his father's death, and he struck out for California gold soon after the discussion. No one ever heard from him again.

The town of Thistledown was much improved over the years with the addition of a true hospital, sturdy roads, fine public schools and—most important to the residents—private ownership of lands and homes. All this was provided by virtue of the inheritance Lady Brooks' sons should have received, but never once did Lady Brooks allow herself to feel the monies were being better spent. And to her dying day she never did regret her decision to avoid the docks of London to bid good-bye to the youth she had once considered a son.

As for the Bannochs, when Theodosia came home and described her summer at Star Cottage, her father threatened to throw the Bannochs out on their pampered noses, but mercy prevailed as Theodosia described to her father how much the home meant to Aunt Selda. "And her things, Papa, are all she really has.

She can't know what it means to have a family like ours." And so mercy tempered justice, as true justice should allow, and Mr. Brown finally gave Star Cottage to Selda Bannoch, lock, stock and barrel.

And how fared the life of Selda Bannoch after receiving Star Cottage? Her son, Frederick, married a rich widow and lived out his life on the woman's Thistledown estate, publicly performing his duty to his mother but letting it be known privately how little her opinion meant to him. Albert and Cecelia made their way around Selda by ignoring her completely. And so Selda Bannoch was destined to live alone in Star Cottage, surrounded only by her velvet chairs and finely polished tables—objects whose heart and soul were nothing more than horsehair and shellac. These she loved with all her heart, and how they loved her in return was her reward.

Grace Chapel Library
Havertown, Penna.